THE YELLOW WALL-PAPER
AND OTHER WRITINGS

2021 Modern Library Trade Paperback Edition

Introduction copyright © 2021 by Halle Butler

Published in the United States by Modern Library, an imprint
of Random House, a division of Penguin Random House LLC,
New York.

MODERN LIBRARY and the TORCHBEARER colophon are
registered trademarks of Penguin Random House LLC, in 2000.

LIBRARY OF CONGRESS CATALOGING-IN-PUBLICATION DATA
Gilman, Charlotte Perkins, 1860–1935.
The yellow wall-paper and other writings / Charlotte Perkins
Gilman.
p. cm.
ISBN 978-0-593-23125-8
Ebook ISBN 978-0-593-23034-3
1. Women—Literary collections. I. Title.
PS1744.G57 A6 2001
818'.409—dc21 00-058743

Printed in the United States of America on acid-free paper

modernlibrary.com
randomhousebooks.com

2 4 6 8 9 7 5 3 1

THE YELLOW WALL-PAPER AND OTHER WRITINGS

CHARLOTTE PERKINS GILMAN

Introduction by Halle Butler

MODERN LIBRARY

NEW YORK

CONTENTS

INTRODUCTION

HALLE BUTLER

When I first read "The Yellow Wall-paper" years ago, before I knew anything about its author, Charlotte Perkins Gilman, I loved it. I loved the unnerving, sarcastic tone, the creepy ending, the clarity of its critique of the popular nineteenth-century "rest cure"—essentially an extended time-out for depressed women. The story had irony, urgency, anger. On the last day of the treatment, the narrator is completely mad. She thinks she's a creature who has emerged from the wallpaper.

The rest cure caused the illness it claimed to eliminate. Beautifully clear.

The unnamed first-person narrator goes through a mental dance I knew well—the circularity and claustrophobia of an increasing depression, the sinking feeling that something wasn't being told straight. Reading "The Yellow Wall-paper" felt like a mix of voyeurism and recognition, morphing into horror. It was genuinely chilling. It felt haunted.

The story is based on Gilman's experiences with Dr. Silas Weir Mitchell, late-nineteenth-century physician to the stars. Mitchell administered this cure of extended bed rest and isolation to intellectual, active white women of a high social standing. Virginia Woolf, Edith Wharton, and Jane Addams all took the cure, which could last for weeks, sometimes months. Gilman was clearly disgusted with her experience, and her disgust is palpable.

"The Yellow Wall-paper" was not iconic during its own time, and was initially rejected, in 1892, by *Atlantic Monthly* editor Horace Scudder, with this note: "I could not forgive myself if I made others as miserable as I have made myself [by reading this]." During her lifetime, Gilman was instead known for her politics, and gained popularity with a series of satirical poems featuring animals. The well-loved "Similar Cases" describes prehistoric animals bragging about what animals they will evolve into, while their friends mock them for their hubris. Another, "A Conservative," describes Gilman as a kind of cracked Darwinian in her garden, screaming at a confused, crying baby butterfly. "Similar Cases" was considered to be among "the best satirical verses of modern times" (American author Floyd Dell). It sounds like this:

There was once a little animal,
No bigger than a fox,
And on five toes he scampered
Over Tertiary rocks.

And so on.

Gilman is best known for "The Yellow Wall-paper" now, due to Elaine Ryan Hedges, scholar and founding member of the National Women's Studies Association, who resurrected Gilman from obscurity. In 1973, the Feminist Press released a chapbook of "The Yellow Wall-paper," with an afterword by Hedges, who called it "a small literary masterpiece" and Gilman "one of the most commanding feminists of her time" though Gilman never saw herself as a feminist (in fact, from her letters: "I abominate being called a feminist"). Nor did she consider her work literature. In the introduction to the copy I received, Gilman was quoted as saying she wrote to "preach . . . If it is literature, that just happened." She considered her writing a tool for promoting her politics, and herself a one-woman propaganda machine. Hedges notes in her afterword that Gilman wrote "twenty-one thousand words per month" while working on her self-published political magazine *The Forerunner*.

———

Rereading "The Yellow Wall-paper" in the spring of 2020, when I was asked to write this introduction, I was still impressed by its urgency and humor and its eerie quality. It felt deeper and more symbolic than I'd remembered, as if it were about more than it seemed. I hadn't remembered that the yellow room was a former nursery with bars on the windows.

I was intrigued to find that Gilman had written a collection of essays called *Concerning Children* (1902, dedicated to her daughter Katharine "who has taught me much of what is written here"). The first essay in *Concerning Children*—which is not included in this collection—is disorienting: the torture and dismemberment of guinea pigs, the printing press, "nerve-energy," foreclosures, the *hypothetical market value of babies*, are all examples summoned and threaded through with this ideology:

> [T]here are degrees of humanness... If you were buying babies, investing in young human stock as you would in colts or calves, for the value of the beast, a sturdy English baby would be worth more than an equally vigorous young Fuegian. With the same training and care, you could develop higher faculties in the English specimen than in the Fuegian specimen, because it was better bred. The savage baby would excel in some points, but the qualities of the modern baby are those dominant to-day.

The "if" is a chilling, willful blind spot, considering the history of the United States, and that Gilman, as the niece of the novelist Harriet Beecher Stowe, almost certainly believed herself to be of this better "stock." I also think it's clear that by dominant "modern baby," Gilman means white baby. This should put all of Gilman's quests for modernization into very stark light. Looking again, the "if" seems not blind, so much as shockingly coy.

——

The majority of Gilman's short fiction centers around the economic liberation of white women. The main path to security for Gilman's women was finding, and keeping, a good husband—no matter the sacrifice. Her characters have inherited debts from their husbands, sacrificed their artistic ambitions for their children, been nearly forced out of their homes in widowhood, are in peril of disgrace. Society, as it stands in these fables, offers no good solutions to these problems. Live with your ungrateful children, leave your home, turn your husband's mistress to the streets to save your social standing, forget the piano, etcetera. It's a suffocating world, and Gilman describes its effects with compassion. But unlike, say, Edith Wharton (or even "The Yellow Wall-paper"), Gilman attempts to offer solutions. Her protagonists work together, forming daycares, opening their homes to women's clubs, taking on boarders, empathizing with each other, unprivatizing their homes and lives, making and saving their own money, and working together in harmony. The stories show a smooth, almost comically conflict-free path to solving social problems.

An interesting example of Gilman's "problem-solved" format is "If I Were a Man." Mollie (the ideal wife) wishes to become a man at the start of the story, and has her wish granted immediately. À la *Being John Malkovich*, she is absorbed into the consciousness of her husband on his commute to work. As she becomes more and more male, she sees the world differently.

While she's rhapsodizing over how amazing men's shoes, pockets, and pants are, Mollie, as a man, sees a woman for the first time and is shocked by the absurdity of women's hats. "Never in all her life had she imagined that this idolized millinery could look...like the decorations of an insane monkey."

And then in the next moment, when Mollie, as her husband, gets tickled by the feather on a cute woman's hat ("he felt a sense of sudden pleasure at the intimate tickling touch"), she realizes that all hats are made by men for men's titillation. A great misdeed, a great unfairness, has been done to her when men scold her for wanting hats that they themselves have designed and told her to want.

By the end of the story, Mollie and her husband exist in a balance of shared temperaments, each learning from the other, and as a result, growing more virtuous.

I like this story well enough (who among us has not, I guess, marveled at men's pockets), but it's tough to swallow. The ease of the solutions in much of her political fiction feels off. The men don't mind the new order, once they consult their reason. The women are happy to join in, always have been. These are Gilman's fantasies of the world, as it could be for her and others like her. Describing these clean solutions seems to be her obsession, and she does it over and over.

In her collection of essays *Women and Economics: A Study of the Economic Relation Between Men and Women as a Factor in Social Evolution*, Gilman again lays out her ideas for liberating women. The key step is recognizing marriage as a sexuo-economic bargain, and ridding the culture of the myth of marriage as necessarily natural and born of love. As Gilman sees it, selfishness and stupidity are inherent to the existing household model. The man goes out to make money to bring back to the wife, who is taught to want stupid baubles with no conception of the labor that went into their making, and has no productive or creative outlet of her own. This degrades the mother. The children inherit her degradation both genetically and by observation, and the perpetuation of this cycle is what is keeping "the race" back. The goal is to financially liberate women so they can exercise their breeding power. Concerningly, Gilman's proposed liberation goes hand in hand with eugenics. Her fixation on breeding and genetics runs through her fiction as well.

Herland, Gilman's sci-fi novel about a land free of men, is an example of this. The inhabitants of Herland have no crime, no hunger, no conflict (also, notably, no sex, no art). They exist together in dreamlike harmony. Held one way, Herland is a gentle, maternal paradise, and the novel itself is a plea for allowing these feminine qualities to take part in the societal structure. Held another, we see how firmly their equality is based in their homogeneity. The novel's twist is that the inhabitants of Herland are considering whether or not it would benefit them to reintroduce male qualities into their society, by way of sexual reproduction. *Herland* is a tale of the fully realized potential of eugenics, and for Gilman, it's a utopia.

All of this is especially troubling when you consider that Gilman was a staunch and self-described nativist, rather than a self-described feminist, as the texts surrounding her rediscovery imply. Nativists believed in protecting the interests of native-born (or "established") inhabitants above the interests of immigrants, and that mental capacities are innate, rather than teachable. Put bluntly, she was a Victorian White Nationalist. When Gilman is described as a social reformer and activist, part of this was advocating for compulsory, militaristic labor camps for Black Americans ("A Suggestion on the Negro Problem," 1908). Part of this is pleading for racial purity and stricter border policies, as in the sequel to *Herland,* or for sterilization and even death for the genetically inferior, as in her other serialized *Forerunner* novel, *Moving the Mountain.*

These ideas of Gilman's are hard to reconcile with our current conception of her as a brave advocate against systems of oppression—a political hero with a few, forgivable flaws.

———

I lie here on this great immovable bed—it is nailed down, I believe—and follow that pattern about by the hour. It is as good as gymnastics, I assure you. I start, we'll say, at the bottom, down in the corner over there where it has not been touched, and I determine for the thousandth time that I *will* follow that pointless pattern to some sort of a conclusion.

This is the narrator of "The Yellow Wall-paper." She's looking for her blind spots, searching for a conclusion, as her eyes trace the pattern of the wallpaper over and over, on a nailed-down bed in a derelict mansion. What does it mean? Does it simply condemn the patriarchy? If the story is deeply symbolic, and a meditation on hidden patterns, what are they? We know this story as a condemnation of the barbaric practice of the rest cure, but when we scan it, what else?

An attempt: The bed is nailed to the floor—the narrator has no control over her role in reproduction. The ancestral home, as a symbol for genetic inheritance (a theme Gilman uses in both her essays and fiction), is in disrepair, because of it. The narrator is lost because her husband won't listen to her—without collaboration between men and women, the mother is lost, and the cycle of disrepair (she *becomes* the shredded wallpaper) continues. And as for the yellow wallpaper itself? She wants it whitewashed.

It's common to separate out "The Yellow Wall-paper" from the rest of Gilman's work, to place distance between it and her racism and passion for eugenics: it was just the time she lived in. Yes, the time she lived in was squeamish to publish a short story critical of patriarchy, and eager to embrace a cute poem about eugenics. But what about now? What makes us squeamish is an important study.

"The Yellow Wall-paper" is a story about hypocrisy, oppression, and legacy. It's a story about patterns hidden beneath patterns. The wallpaper oppresses the narrator until she starts to see herself in it, to identify with it. She becomes the woman in the wallpaper, becomes the wallpaper itself, and then she escapes, barely—and deeply tainted. If we can learn from the story's enduring literary idea (the idea that, according to Gilman, "just happened"), it's that a half-truth is not an answer. What's hidden is dangerous. Motives are important.

For anyone who has thought of Gilman as a hero of early feminism, I would urge another look. You will find patterns of humanity here, but it won't be as simple as it seemed.

—

HALLE BUTLER is a writer from the Midwest. Her first novel, *Jillian*, is a brief account of a medical secretary's drunken social blunders and callous treatment of her coworker. Her second novel, *The New Me*, is a brief account of a depressed temp worker. She is a Granta Best Young American Novelist and a National Book Foundation "5 Under 35" Honoree.

STORIES

THE YELLOW WALL-PAPER

It is very seldom that mere ordinary people like John and myself secure ancestral halls for the summer.

A colonial mansion, a hereditary estate, I would say a haunted house, and reach the height of romantic felicity—but that would be asking too much of fate!

Still I will proudly declare that there is something queer about it.

Else, why should it be let so cheaply? And why have stood so long untenanted?

John laughs at me, of course, but one expects that in marriage.

John is practical in the extreme. He has no patience with faith, an intense horror of superstition, and he scoffs openly at any talk of things not to be felt and seen and put down in figures.

John is a physician, and *perhaps*—(I would not say it to a living soul, of course, but this is dead paper and a great relief to my mind—) *perhaps* that is one reason I do not get well faster.

You see he does not believe I am sick!

And what can one do?

If a physician of high standing, and one's own husband, assures friends and relatives that there is really nothing the matter with one but temporary nervous depression—a slight hysterical tendency— what is one to do?

My brother is also a physician, and also of high standing, and he says the same thing.

So I take phosphates or phosphites—whichever it is, and tonics, and journeys, and air, and exercise, and am absolutely forbidden to "work" until I am well again.

Personally, I disagree with their ideas.

Personally, I believe that congenial work, with excitement and change, would do me good.

But what is one to do?

I did write for a while in spite of them; but it *does* exhaust me a good deal—having to be so sly about it, or else meet with heavy opposition.

I sometimes fancy that in my condition if I had less opposition and more society and stimulus—but John says the very worst thing I can do is to think about my condition, and I confess it always makes me feel bad.

So I will let it alone and talk about the house.

The most beautiful place! It is quite alone, standing well back from the road, quite three miles from the village. It makes me think of English places that you read about, for there are hedges and walls and gates that lock, and lots of separate little houses for the gardeners and people.

There is a *delicious* garden! I never saw such a garden—large and shady, full of box-bordered paths, and lined with long grape-covered arbors with seats under them.

There were greenhouses, too, but they are all broken now.

There was some legal trouble, I believe, something about the heirs and co-heirs; anyhow, the place has been empty for years.

That spoils my ghostliness, I am afraid, but I don't care—there is something strange about the house—I can feel it.

I even said so to John one moonlight evening, but he said what I felt was a *draught,* and shut the window.

I get unreasonably angry with John sometimes. I'm sure I never used to be so sensitive. I think it is due to this nervous condition.

But John says if I feel so, I shall neglect proper self-control; so I take pains to control myself—before him, at least, and that makes me very tired.

I don't like our room a bit. I wanted one downstairs that opened on the piazza and had roses all over the window, and such pretty old-fashioned chintz hangings! but John would not hear of it.

He said there was only one window and not room for two beds, and no near room for him if he took another.

He is very careful and loving, and hardly lets me stir without special direction.

I have a schedule prescription for each hour in the day; he takes all care from me, and so I feel basely ungrateful not to value it more.

He said we came here solely on my account, that I was to have perfect rest and all the air I could get. "Your exercise depends on your strength, my dear," said he, "and your food somewhat on your appetite; but air you can absorb all the time." So we took the nursery at the top of the house.

It is a big, airy room, the whole floor nearly, with windows that look all ways, and air and sunshine galore. It was nursery first and then playroom and gymnasium, I should judge; for the windows are barred for little children, and there are rings and things in the walls.

The paint and paper look as if a boys' school had used it. It is stripped off—the paper—in great patches all around the head of my bed, about as far as I can reach, and in a great place on the other side of the room low down. I never saw a worse paper in my life.

One of those sprawling flamboyant patterns committing every artistic sin.

It is dull enough to confuse the eye in following, pronounced enough to constantly irritate and provoke study, and when you follow the lame uncertain curves for a little distance they suddenly commit suicide—plunge off at outrageous angles, destroy themselves in unheard of contradictions.

The color is repellant, almost revolting; a smouldering unclean yellow, strangely faded by the slow-turning sunlight.

It is a dull yet lurid orange in some places, a sickly sulphur tint in others.

No wonder the children hated it! I should hate it myself if I had to live in this room long.

There comes John, and I must put this away,—he hates to have me write a word.

—

We have been here two weeks, and I haven't felt like writing before, since that first day.

I am sitting by the window now, up in this atrocious nursery, and there is nothing to hinder my writing as much as I please, save lack of strength.

John is away all day, and even some nights when his cases are serious.

I am glad my case is not serious!

But these nervous troubles are dreadfully depressing.

John does not know how much I really suffer. He knows there is no *reason* to suffer, and that satisfies him.

Of course it is only nervousness. It does weigh on me so not to do my duty in any way!

I meant to be such a help to John, such a real rest and comfort, and here I am a comparative burden already!

Nobody would believe what an effort it is to do what little I am able,—to dress and entertain, and order things.

It is fortunate Mary is so good with the baby. Such a dear baby!

And yet I *cannot* be with him, it makes me so nervous.

I suppose John never was nervous in his life. He laughs at me so about this wall-paper!

At first he meant to repaper the room, but afterwards he said that I was letting it get the better of me, and that nothing was worse for a nervous patient than to give way to such fancies.

He said that after the wall-paper was changed it would be the heavy bedstead, and then the barred windows, and then that gate at the head of the stairs, and so on.

"You know the place is doing you good," he said, "and really, dear, I don't care to renovate the house just for a three months' rental."

"Then do let us go downstairs," I said, "there are such pretty rooms there."

Then he took me in his arms and called me a blessed little goose, and said he would go down cellar, if I wished, and have it white-washed into the bargain.

But he is right enough about the beds and windows and things.

It is an airy and comfortable room as any one need wish, and, of course, I would not be so silly as to make him uncomfortable just for a whim.

I'm really getting quite fond of the big room, all but that horrid paper.

Out of one window I can see the garden, those mysterious deep-shaded arbors, the riotous old-fashioned flowers, and bushes and gnarly trees.

Out of another I get a lovely view of the bay and a little private wharf belonging to the estate. There is a beautiful shaded lane that runs down there from the house. I always fancy I see people walking in these numerous paths and arbors, but John has cautioned me not to give way to fancy in the least. He says that with my imaginative power and habit of story-making, a nervous weakness like mine is sure to lead to all manner of excited fancies, and that I ought to use my will and good sense to check the tendency. So I try.

I think sometimes that if I were only well enough to write a little it would relieve the press of ideas and rest me.

But I find I get pretty tired when I try.

It is so discouraging not to have any advice and companionship about my work. When I get really well, John says we will ask Cousin Henry and Julia down for a long visit; but he says he would as soon put fireworks in my pillow-case as to let me have those stimulating people about now.

I wish I could get well faster.

But I must not think about that. This paper looks to me as if it *knew* what a vicious influence it had!

There is a recurrent spot where the pattern lolls like a broken neck and two bulbous eyes stare at you upside down.

I get positively angry with the impertinence of it and the ever-lastingness. Up and down and sideways they crawl, and those absurd, unblinking eyes are everywhere. There is one place where two breadths didn't match, and the eyes go all up and down the line, one a little higher than the other.

I never saw so much expression in an inanimate thing before, and we all know how much expression they have! I used to lie awake as a child and get more entertainment and terror out of blank walls and plain furniture than most children could find in a toy-store.

I remember what a kindly wink the knobs of our big, old bureau used to have, and there was one chair that always seemed like a strong friend.

I used to feel that if any of the other things looked too fierce I could always hop into that chair and be safe.

The furniture in this room is no worse than inharmonious, however, for we had to bring it all from downstairs. I suppose when this was used as a playroom they had to take the nursery things out, and no wonder! I never saw such ravages as the children have made here.

The wall-paper, as I said before, is torn off in spots, and it sticketh closer than a brother—they must have had perseverance as well as hatred.

Then the floor is scratched and gouged and splintered, the plaster itself is dug out here and there, and this great heavy bed which is all we found in the room, looks as if it had been through the wars.

But I don't mind it a bit—only the paper.

There comes John's sister. Such a dear girl as she is, and so careful of me! I must not let her find me writing.

She is a perfect and enthusiastic housekeeper, and hopes for no better profession. I verily believe she thinks it is the writing which made me sick!

But I can write when she is out, and see her a long way off from these windows.

There is one that commands the road, a lovely shaded winding road, and one that just looks off over the country. A lovely country, too, full of great elms and velvet meadows.

This wall-paper has a kind of subpattern in a different shade, a particularly irritating one, for you can only see it in certain lights, and not clearly then.

But in the places where it isn't faded and where the sun is just so—I can see a strange, provoking, formless sort of figure, that seems to skulk about behind that silly and conspicuous front design.

There's sister on the stairs!

—

Well, the Fourth of July is over! The people are all gone and I am tired out. John thought it might do me good to see a little company, so we just had mother and Nellie and the children down for a week.

Of course I didn't do a thing. Jennie sees to everything now.

But it tired me all the same.

John says if I don't pick up faster he shall send me to Weir Mitchell in the fall.

But I don't want to go there at all. I had a friend who was in his hands once, and she says he is just like John and my brother, only more so!

Besides, it is such an undertaking to go so far.

I don't feel as if it was worthwhile to turn my hand over for anything, and I'm getting dreadfully fretful and querulous.

I cry at nothing, and cry most of the time.

Of course I don't when John is here, or anybody else, but when I am alone.

And I am alone a good deal just now. John is kept in town very often by serious cases, and Jennie is good and lets me alone when I want her to.

So I walk a little in the garden or down that lovely lane, sit on the porch under the roses, and lie down up here a good deal.

I'm getting really fond of the room in spite of the wall-paper. Perhaps *because* of the wall-paper.

It dwells in my mind so!

I lie here on this great immovable bed—it is nailed down, I believe—and follow that pattern about by the hour. It is as good as gymnastics, I assure you. I start, we'll say, at the bottom, down in the corner over there where it has not been touched, and I determine for the thousandth time that I *will* follow that pointless pattern to some sort of a conclusion.

I know a little of the principle of design, and I know this thing was not arranged on any laws of radiation, or alternation, or repetition, or symmetry, or anything else that I ever heard of.

It is repeated, of course, by the breadths, but not otherwise.

Looked at in one way each breadth stands alone, the bloated curves and flourishes—a kind of "debased Romanesque" with *delirium tremens*—go waddling up and down in isolated columns of fatuity.

But, on the other hand, they connect diagonally, and the sprawling outlines run off in great slanting waves of optic horror, like a lot of wallowing seaweeds in full chase.

The whole thing goes horizontally, too, at least it seems so, and I exhaust myself in trying to distinguish the order of its going in that direction.

They have used a horizontal breadth for a frieze, and that adds wonderfully to the confusion.

There is one end of the room where it is almost intact, and there, when the crosslights fade and the low sun shines directly upon it, I can almost fancy radiation after all,—the interminable grotesques seem to form around a common centre and rush off in headlong plunges of equal distraction.

It makes me tired to follow it. I will take a nap I guess.

———

I don't know why I should write this.

I don't want to.

I don't feel able.

And I know John would think it absurd. But I *must* say what I feel and think in some way—it is such a relief!

But the effort is getting to be greater than the relief.

Half the time now I am awfully lazy, and lie down ever so much.

John says I mustn't lose my strength, and has me take cod liver oil and lots of tonics and things, to say nothing of ale and wine and rare meat.

Dear John! He loves me very dearly, and hates to have me sick. I tried to have a real earnest reasonable talk with him the other day, and tell him how I wish he would let me go and make a visit to Cousin Henry and Julia.

But he said I wasn't able to go, nor able to stand it after I got there; and I did not make out a very good case for myself, for I was crying before I had finished.

It is getting to be a great effort for me to think straight. Just this nervous weakness I suppose.

And dear John gathered me up in his arms, and just carried me upstairs and laid me on the bed, and sat by me and read to me till it tired my head.

He said I was his darling and his comfort and all he had, and that I must take care of myself for his sake, and keep well.

He says no one but myself can help me out of it, that I must use my will and self-control and not let any silly fancies run away with me.

There's one comfort, the baby is well and happy, and does not have to occupy this nursery with the horrid wall-paper.

If we had not used it, that blessed child would have! What a fortunate escape! Why, I wouldn't have a child of mine, an impressionable little thing, live in such a room for worlds.

I never thought of it before, but it is lucky that John kept me here after all, I can stand it so much easier than a baby, you see.

Of course I never mention it to them any more—I am too wise,—but I keep watch of it all the same.

There are things in that paper that nobody knows but me, or ever will.

Behind that outside pattern the dim shapes get clearer every day.

It is always the same shape, only very numerous.

And it is like a woman stooping down and creeping about behind that pattern. I don't like it a bit. I wonder—I begin to think—I wish John would take me away from here!

———

It is so hard to talk with John about my case, because he is so wise, and because he loves me so.

But I tried it last night.

It was moonlight. The moon shines in all around just as the sun does.

I hate to see it sometimes, it creeps so slowly, and always comes in by one window or another.

John was asleep and I hated to waken him, so I kept still and watched the moonlight on that undulating wall-paper till I felt creepy.

The faint figure behind seemed to shake the pattern, just as if she wanted to get out.

I got up softly and went to feel and see if the paper *did* move, and when I came back John was awake.

"What is it, little girl?" he said. "Don't go walking about like that—you'll get cold."

I thought it was a good time to talk, so I told him that I really was not gaining here, and that I wished he would take me away.

"Why, darling!" said he, "our lease will be up in three weeks, and I can't see how to leave before.

"The repairs are not done at home, and I cannot possibly leave town just now. Of course if you were in any danger, I could and would, but you really are better, dear, whether you can see it or not. I am a doctor, dear, and I know. You are gaining flesh and color, your appetite is better, I feel really much easier about you."

"I don't weigh a bit more," said I, "nor as much; and my appetite may be better in the evening when you are here, but it is worse in the morning when you are away!"

"Bless her little heart!" said he with a big hug, "she shall be as sick as she pleases! But now let's improve the shining hours by going to sleep, and talk about it in the morning!"

"And you won't go away?" I asked gloomily.

"Why, how can I, dear? It is only three weeks more and then we will take a nice little trip of a few days while Jennie is getting the house ready. Really dear you are better!"

"Better in body perhaps—" I began, and stopped short, for he sat up straight and looked at me with such a stern, reproachful look that I could not say another word.

"My darling," said he, "I beg of you, for my sake and for our child's sake, as well as for your own, that you will never for one instant let that idea enter your mind! There is nothing so dangerous, so fascinating, to a temperament like yours. It is a false and foolish fancy. Can you not trust me as a physician when I tell you so?"

So of course I said no more on that score, and we went to sleep before long. He thought I was asleep first, but I wasn't, and lay there for hours trying to decide whether that front pattern and the back pattern really did move together or separately.

———

On a pattern like this, by daylight, there is a lack of sequence, a defiance of law, that is a constant irritant to a normal mind.

The color is hideous enough, and unreliable enough, and infuriating enough, but the pattern is torturing.

You think you have mastered it, but just as you get well underway in following, it turns a back-somersault and there you are. It slaps you in the face, knocks you down, and tramples upon you. It is like a bad dream.

The outside pattern is a florid arabesque, reminding one of a fungus. If you can imagine a toadstool in joints, an interminable string of toadstools, budding and sprouting in endless convolutions—why, that is something like it.

That is, sometimes!

There is one marked peculiarity about this paper, a thing nobody seems to notice but myself, and that is that it changes as the light changes.

When the sun shoots in through the east window—I always watch for that first long, straight ray—it changes so quickly that I never can quite believe it.

That is why I watch it always.

By moonlight—the moon shines in all night when there is a moon—I wouldn't know it was the same paper.

At night in any kind of light, in twilight, candlelight, lamplight, and worst of all by moonlight, it becomes bars! The outside pattern I mean, and the woman behind it is as plain as can be.

I didn't realize for a long time what the thing was that showed behind, that dim sub-pattern, but now I am quite sure it is a woman.

By daylight she is subdued, quiet. I fancy it is the pattern that keeps her so still. It is so puzzling. It keeps me quiet by the hour.

I lie down ever so much now. John says it is good for me, and to sleep all I can.

Indeed he started the habit by making me lie down for an hour after each meal.

It is a very bad habit I am convinced, for you see I don't sleep.

And that cultivates deceit, for I don't tell them I'm awake—O no!

The fact is I am getting a little afraid of John.

He seems very queer sometimes, and even Jennie has an inexplicable look.

It strikes me occasionally, just as a scientific hypothesis,—that perhaps it is the paper!

I have watched John when he did not know I was looking, and come into the room suddenly on the most innocent excuses, and I've caught him several times *looking at the paper!* And Jennie too. I caught Jennie with her hand on it once.

She didn't know I was in the room, and when I asked her in a quiet, a very quiet voice, with the most restrained manner possible, what she was doing with the paper—she turned around as if she had been caught stealing, and looked quite angry—asked me why I should frighten her so!

Then she said that the paper stained everything it touched, that she had found yellow smooches on all my clothes and John's, and she wished we would be more careful!

Did not that sound innocent? But I know she was studying that pattern, and I am determined that nobody shall find it out but myself!

———

Life is very much more exciting now than it used to be. You see I have something more to expect, to look forward to, to watch. I really do eat better, and am more quiet than I was.

John is so pleased to see me improve! He laughed a little the other day, and said I seemed to be flourishing in spite of my wall-paper.

I turned it off with a laugh. I had no intention of telling him it was *because* of the wall-paper—he would make fun of me. He might even want to take me away.

I don't want to leave now until I have found it out. There is a week more, and I think that will be enough.

———

I'm feeling ever so much better! I don't sleep much at night, for it is so interesting to watch developments; but I sleep a good deal in the daytime.

In the daytime it is tiresome and perplexing.

There are always new shoots on the fungus, and new shades of yellow all over it. I cannot keep count of them, though I have tried conscientiously.

It is the strangest yellow, that wall-paper! It makes me think of all the yellow things I ever saw—not beautiful ones like buttercups, but old foul, bad yellow things.

But there is something else about that paper—the smell! I no-ticed it the moment we came into the room, but with so much air and sun it was not bad. Now we have had a week of fog and rain, and whether the windows are open or not, the smell is here.

It creeps all over the house.

I find it hovering in the dining-room, skulking in the parlor, hid-ing in the hall, lying in wait for me on the stairs.

It gets into my hair.

Even when I go to ride, if I turn my head suddenly and surprise it—there is that smell!

Such a peculiar odor, too! I have spent hours in trying to analyze it, to find what it smelled like.

It is not bad—at first, and very gentle, but quite the subtlest, most enduring odor I ever met.

In this damp weather it is awful, I wake up in the night and find it hanging over me.

It used to disturb me at first. I thought seriously of burning the house—to reach the smell.

But now I am used to it. The only thing I can think of that it is like is the *color* of the paper! A yellow smell.

There is a very funny mark on this wall, low down, near the mop-board. A streak that runs round the room. It goes behind every piece of furniture, except the bed, a long, straight, even *smooch,* as if it had been rubbed over and over.

I wonder how it was done and who did it, and what they did it for. Round and round and round—round and round and round—it makes me dizzy!

———

I really have discovered something at last.

Through watching so much at night, when it changes so, I have finally found out.

The front pattern *does* move—and no wonder! The woman behind shakes it!

Sometimes I think there are a great many women behind, and sometimes only one, and she crawls around fast, and her crawling shakes it all over.

Then in the very bright spots she keeps still, and in the very shady spots she just takes hold of the bars and shakes them hard.

And she is all the time trying to climb through. But nobody could climb through that pattern—it strangles so; I think that is why it has so many heads.

They get through, and then the pattern strangles them off and turns them upside down, and makes their eyes white!

If those heads were covered or taken off it would not be half so bad.

———

I think that woman gets out in the daytime!

And I'll tell you why—privately—I've seen her!

I can see her out of every one of my windows!

It is the same woman, I know, for she is always creeping, and most women do not creep by daylight.

I see her in that long shaded lane, creeping up and down. I see her in those dark grape arbors, creeping all around the garden.

I see her on that long road under the trees, creeping along, and when a carriage comes she hides under the blackberry vines.

I don't blame her a bit. It must be very humiliating to be caught creeping by daylight!

I always lock the door when I creep by daylight. I can't do it at night, for I know John would suspect something at once.

And John is so queer now, that I don't want to irritate him. I wish he would take another room! Besides, I don't want anybody to get that woman out at night but myself.

I often wonder if I could see her out of all the windows at once.

But, turn as fast as I can, I can only see out of one at one time.

And though I always see her, she *may* be able to creep faster than I can turn!

I have watched her sometimes away off in the open country, creeping as fast as a cloud shadow in a high wind.

—

If only that top pattern could be gotten off from the under one! I mean to try it, little by little.

I have found out another funny thing, but I shan't tell it this time! It does not do to trust people too much.

There are only two more days to get this paper off, and I believe John is beginning to notice. I don't like the look in his eyes.

And I heard him ask Jennie a lot of professional questions about me. She had a very good report to give.

She said I slept a good deal in the daytime.

John knows I don't sleep very well at night, for all I'm so quiet!

He asked me all sorts of questions, too, and pretended to be very loving and kind.

As if I couldn't see through him!

Still, I don't wonder he acts so, sleeping under this paper for three months.

It only interests me, but I feel sure John and Jennie are secretly affected by it.

———

Hurrah! This is the last day, but it is enough. John is to stay in town overnight, and won't be out until this evening.

Jennie wanted to sleep with me—the sly thing! but I told her I should undoubtedly rest better for a night all alone.

That was clever, for really I wasn't alone a bit! As soon as it was moonlight and that poor thing began to crawl and shake the pattern, I got up and ran to help her.

I pulled and she shook, I shook and she pulled, and before morning we had peeled off yards of that paper.

A strip about as high as my head and half around the room.

And then when the sun came and that awful pattern began to laugh at me, I declared I would finish it to-day!

We go away to-morrow, and they are moving all my furniture down again to leave things as they were before.

Jennie looked at the wall in amazement, but I told her merrily that I did it out of pure spite at the vicious thing.

She laughed and said she wouldn't mind doing it herself, but I must not get tired.

How she betrayed herself that time!

But I am here, and no person touches this paper but me,—not *alive!*

She tried to get me out of the room—it was too patent! But I said it was so quiet and empty and clean now that I believed I would lie down again and sleep all I could; and not to wake me even for dinner—I would call when I woke.

So now she is gone, and the servants are gone, and the things are gone, and there is nothing left but that great bedstead nailed down, with the canvas mattress we found on it.

We shall sleep downstairs to-night, and take the boat home to-morrow.

I quite enjoy the room, now it is bare again.

How those children did tear about here!

This bedstead is fairly gnawed!

But I must get to work.

I have locked the door and thrown the key down into the front path.

I don't want to go out, and I don't want to have anybody come in, till John comes.

I want to astonish him.

I've got a rope up here that even Jennie did not find. If that woman does get out, and tries to get away, I can tie her!

But I forgot I could not reach far without anything to stand on!

This bed will *not* move!

I tried to lift and push it until I was lame, and then I got so angry I bit off a little piece of one corner—but it hurt my teeth.

Then I peeled off all the paper I could reach standing on the floor. It sticks horribly and the pattern just enjoys it! All those strangled heads and bulbous eyes and waddling fungus growths just shriek with derision!

I am getting angry enough to do something desperate. To jump out of the window would be admirable exercise, but the bars are too strong even to try.

Besides I wouldn't do it. Of course not. I know well enough that a step like that is improper and might be misconstrued.

I don't like to *look* out of the windows even—there are so many of those creeping women, and they creep so fast.

I wonder if they all come out of that wall-paper as I did?

But I am securely fastened now by my well-hidden rope—you don't get *me* out in the road there!

I suppose I shall have to get back behind the pattern when it comes night, and that is hard!

It is so pleasant to be out in this great room and creep around as I please!

I don't want to go outside. I won't, even if Jennie asks me to.

For outside you have to creep on the ground, and everything is green instead of yellow.

But here I can creep smoothly on the floor, and my shoulder just fits in that long smooch around the wall, so I cannot lose my way.

Why there's John at the door!

It is no use, young man, you can't open it!

How he does call and pound!

Now he's crying for an axe.

It would be a shame to break down that beautiful door!

"John dear!" said I in the gentlest voice, "the key is down by the front steps, under a plantain leaf!"

That silenced him for a few moments.

Then he said—very quietly indeed, "Open the door, my darling!"

"I can't," said I. "The key is down by the front door under a plantain leaf!"

And then I said it again, several times, very gently and slowly, and said it so often that he had to go and see, and he got it of course, and came in. He stopped short by the door.

"What is the matter?" he cried. "For God's sake, what are you doing?"

I kept on creeping just the same, but I looked at him over my shoulder.

"I've got out at last," said I, "in spite of you and Jane. And I've pulled off most of the paper, so you can't put me back!"

Now why should that man have fainted? But he did, and right across my path by the wall, so that I had to creep over him every time!

THE GIANT WISTARIA

"Meddle not with my new vine, child! See! Thou hast already broken the tender shoot! Never needle or distaff for thee, and yet thou wilt not be quiet!"

The nervous fingers wavered, clutched at a small carnelian cross that hung from her neck, then fell despairingly.

"Give me my child, mother, and then I will be quiet!"

"Hush! hush! thou fool—some one might be near! See—there is thy father coming, even now! Get in quickly!"

She raised her eyes to her mother's face, weary eyes that yet had a flickering, uncertain blaze in their shaded depths.

"Art thou a mother and hast no pity on me, a mother? Give me my child!"

Her voice rose in a strange, low cry, broken by her father's hand upon her mouth.

"Shameless!" said he, with set teeth. "Get to thy chamber, and be not seen again to-night, or I will have thee bound!"

She went at that, and a hard-faced serving woman followed, and presently returned, bringing a key to her mistress.

"Is all well with her,—and the child also?"

"She is quiet, Mistress Dwining, well for the night, be sure. The child fretteth endlessly, but save for that it thriveth with me."

The parents were left alone together on the high square porch with its great pillars, and the rising moon began to make faint shadows of the young vine leaves that shot up luxuriantly around them;

moving shadows, like little stretching fingers, on the broad and heavy planks of the oaken floor.

"It groweth well, this vine thou broughtest me in the ship, my husband."

"Aye," he broke in bitterly, "and so doth the shame I brought thee! Had I known of it I would sooner have had the ship founder beneath us, and have seen our child cleanly drowned, than live to this end!"

"Thou art very hard, Samuel, art thou not afeared for her life? She grieveth sore for the child, aye, and for the green fields to walk in!"

"Nay," said he grimly, "I fear not. She hath lost already what is more than life; and she shall have air enough soon. To-morrow the ship is ready, and we return to England. None knoweth of our stain here, not one, and if the town hath a child unaccounted for to rear in decent ways—why, it is not the first, even here. It will be well enough cared for! And truly we have matter for thankfulness, that her cousin is yet willing to marry her."

"Hast thou told him?"

"Aye! Thinkest thou I would cast shame into another man's house, unknowing it? He hath always desired her, but she would none of him, the stubborn! She hath small choice now!"

"Will he be kind, Samuel? Can he—"

"Kind? What call'st thou it to take such as she to wife? Kind! How many men would take her, an' she had double the fortune? And being of the family already, he is glad to hide the blot forever."

"An' if she would not? He is but a coarse fellow, and she ever shunned him."

"Art thou mad, woman? She weddeth him ere we sail to-morrow, or she stayeth ever in that chamber. The girl is not so sheer a fool! He maketh an honest woman of her, and saveth our house from open shame. What other hope for her than a new life to cover the old? Let her have an honest child, an' she so longeth for one!"

He strode heavily across the porch, till the loose planks creaked again, strode back and forth, with his arms folded and his brows fiercely knit above his iron mouth.

Overhead the shadows flickered mockingly across a white face among the leaves, with eyes of wasted fire.

———

"O, George, what a house! What a lovely house! I am sure it's haunted! Let us get that house to live in this summer! We will have Kate and Jack and Susy and Jim of course, and a splendid time of it!"

Young husbands are indulgent, but still they have to recognize facts.

"My dear, the house may not be to rent; and it may also not be habitable."

"There is surely somebody in it. I am going to inquire!"

The great central gate was rusted off its hinges, and the long drive had trees in it, but a little footpath showed signs of steady usage, and up that Mrs. Jenny went, followed by her obedient George. The front windows of the old mansion were blank, but in a wing at the back they found white curtains and open doors. Outside, in the clear May sunshine, a woman was washing. She was polite and friendly, and evidently glad of visitors in that lonely place. She "guessed it could be rented—didn't know." The heirs were in Europe, but "there was a lawyer in New York had the lettin' of it." There had been folks there years ago, but not in her time. She and her husband had the rent of their part for taking care of the place. "Not that they took much care on't either, but keepin' robbers out." It was furnished throughout, old-fashioned enough, but good; and if they took it she could do the work for 'em herself, she guessed—"if *he* was willin'!"

Never was a crazy scheme more easily arranged. George knew that lawyer in New York; the rent was not alarming; and the nearness to a rising sea-shore resort made it a still pleasanter place to spend the summer.

Kate and Jack and Susy and Jim cheerfully accepted, and the June moon found them all sitting on the high front porch.

They had explored the house from top to bottom, from the great room in the garret, with nothing in it but a rickety cradle, to the well in the cellar without a curb and with a rusty chain going down to unknown blackness below. They had explored the grounds, once beautiful with rare trees and shrubs, but now a gloomy wilderness of tangled shade.

The old lilacs and laburnums, the spirea and syringa, nodded against the second-story windows. What garden plants survived were great ragged bushes or great shapeless beds. A huge wistaria vine covered the whole front of the house. The trunk, it was too large to call a stem, rose at the corner of the porch by the high steps, and had once climbed its pillars; but now the pillars were wrenched from their places and held rigid and helpless by the tightly wound and knotted arms.

It fenced in all the upper story of the porch with a knitted wall of stem and leaf; it ran along the eaves, holding up the gutter that had once supported it; it shaded every window with heavy green; and the drooping, fragrant blossoms made a waving sheet of purple from roof to ground.

"Did you ever see such a wistaria!" cried ecstatic Mrs. Jenny. "It is worth the rent just to sit under such a vine,—a fig tree beside it would be sheer superfluity and wicked extravagance!"

"Jenny makes much of her wistaria," said George, "because she's so disappointed about the ghosts. She made up her mind at first sight to have ghosts in the house, and she can't find even a ghost story!"

"No," Jenny assented mournfully; "I pumped poor Mrs. Pepperill for three days, but could get nothing out of her. But I'm convinced there is a story, if we could only find it. You need not tell me that a house like this, with a garden like this, and a cellar like this, isn't haunted!"

"I agree with you," said Jack. Jack was a reporter on a New York daily, and engaged to Mrs. Jenny's pretty sister. "And if we don't find a real ghost, you may be very sure I shall make one. It's too good an opportunity to lose!"

The pretty sister, who sat next him, resented. "You shan't do anything of the sort, Jack! This is a *real* ghostly place, and I won't have you make fun of it! Look at that group of trees out there in the long grass—it looks for all the world like a crouching, hunted figure!"

"It looks to me like a woman picking huckleberries," said Jim, who was married to George's pretty sister.

"Be still, Jim!" said that fair young woman. "I believe in Jenny's ghost as much as she does. Such a place! Just look at this great wistaria trunk crawling up by the steps here! It looks for all the world like a writhing body—cringing—beseeching!"

"Yes," answered the subdued Jim, "it does, Susy. See its waist,—about two yards of it, and twisted at that! A waste of good material!"

"Don't be so horrid, boys! Go off and smoke somewhere if you can't be congenial!"

"We can! We will! We'll be as ghostly as you please." And forthwith they began to see bloodstains and crouching figures so plentifully that the most delightful shivers multiplied, and the fair enthusiasts started for bed, declaring they should never sleep a wink.

"We shall all surely dream," cried Mrs. Jenny, "and we must all tell our dreams in the morning!"

"There's another thing certain," said George, catching Susy as she tripped over a loose plank; "and that is that you frisky creatures must use the side door till I get this Eiffel tower of a portico fixed, or we shall have some fresh ghosts on our hands! We found a plank here that yawns like a trap-door—big enough to swallow you,—and I believe the bottom of the thing is in China!"

The next morning found them all alive, and eating a substantial New England breakfast, to the accompaniment of saws and hammers on the porch, where carpenters of quite miraculous promptness were tearing things to pieces generally.

"It's got to come down mostly," they had said. "These timbers are clean rotted through, what ain't pulled out o' line by this great creeper. That's about all that holds the thing up."

There was clear reason in what they said, and with a caution from anxious Mrs. Jenny not to hurt the wistaria, they were left to demolish and repair at leisure.

"How about ghosts?" asked Jack after a fourth griddle cake. "I had one, and it's taken away my appetite!"

Mrs. Jenny gave a little shriek and dropped her knife and fork.

"Oh, so had I! I had the most awful—well, not dream exactly, but feeling. I had forgotten all about it!"

"Must have been awful," said Jack, taking another cake. "Do tell us about the feeling. My ghost will wait."

"It makes me creep to think of it even now," she said. "I woke up, all at once, with that dreadful feeling as if something were going to happen, you know! I was wide awake, and hearing every little sound for miles around, it seemed to me. There are so many strange little noises in the country for all it is so still. Millions of crickets and things outside, and all kinds of rustles in the trees! There wasn't much wind, and the moonlight came through in my three great windows in three white squares on the black old floor, and those fingery wistaria leaves we were talking of last night just seemed to crawl all over them. And—O, girls, you know that dreadful well in the cellar?"

A most gratifying impression was made by this, and Jenny proceeded cheerfully:

"Well, while it was so horridly still, and I lay there trying not to wake George, I heard as plainly as if it were right in the room, that old chain down there rattle and creak over the stones!"

"Bravo!" cried Jack. "That's fine! I'll put it in the Sunday edition!"

"Be still!" said Kate. "What was it, Jenny? Did you really see anything?"

"No, I didn't, I'm sorry to say. But just then I didn't want to. I woke George, and made such a fuss that he gave me bromide, and said he'd go and look, and that's the last I thought of it till Jack reminded me,—the bromide worked so well."

"Now, Jack, give us yours," said Jim. "Maybe, it will dovetail in somehow. Thirsty ghost, I imagine; maybe they had prohibition here even then!"

Jack folded his napkin, and leaned back in his most impressive manner.

"It was striking twelve by the great hall clock—" he began.

"There isn't any hall clock!"

THE GIANT WISTARIA · 27

"O hush, Jim, you spoil the current! It was just one o'clock then, by my old-fashioned repeater."

"Waterbury! Never mind what time it was!"

"Well, honestly, I woke up sharp, like our beloved hostess, and tried to go to sleep again, but couldn't. I experienced all those moonlight and grasshopper sensations, just like Jenny, and was wondering what could have been the matter with the supper, when in came my ghost, and I knew it was all a dream! It was a female ghost, and I imagine she was young and handsome, but all those crouching, hunted figures of last evening ran riot in my brain, and this poor creature looked just like them. She was all wrapped up in a shawl, and had a big bundle under her arm,—dear me, I am spoiling the story! With the air and gait of one in frantic haste and terror, the muffled figure glided to a dark old bureau, and seemed taking things from the drawers. As she turned, the moonlight shone full on a little red cross that hung from her neck by a thin gold chain—I saw it glitter as she crept noiselessly from the room! That's all."

"O Jack, don't be so horrid! Did you really? Is that all! What do you think it was?"

"I am not horrid by nature, only professionally. I really did. That was all. And I am fully convinced it was the genuine, legitimate ghost of an eloping chambermaid with kleptomania!"

"You are too bad, Jack!" cried Jenny. "You take all the horror out of it. There isn't a 'creep' left among us."

"It's no time for creeps at nine-thirty A.M., with sunlight and carpenters outside! However, if you can't wait till twilight for your creeps, I think I can furnish one or two," said George. "I went down cellar after Jenny's ghost!"

There was a delighted chorus of female voices, and Jenny cast upon her lord a glance of genuine gratitude.

"It's all very well to lie in bed and see ghosts, or hear them," he went on. "But the young householder suspecteth burglars, even though as a medical man he knoweth nerves, and after Jenny dropped off I started on a voyage of discovery. I never will again, I promise you!"

"Why, what *was* it?"

"Oh, George!"

"I got a candle—"

"Good mark for the burglars," murmured Jack.

"And went all over the house, gradually working down to the cellar and the well."

"Well?" said Jack.

"Now you can laugh; but that cellar is no joke by daylight, and a candle there at night is about as inspiring as a lightning-bug in the Mammoth Cave. I went along with the light, trying not to fall into the well prematurely; got to it all at once; held the light down and *then* I saw, right under my feet—(I nearly fell over her, or walked through her, perhaps),—a woman, hunched up under a shawl! She had hold of the chain, and the candle shone on her hands—white, thin hands,—on a little red cross that hung from her neck—*vide* Jack! I'm no believer in ghosts, and I firmly object to unknown parties in the house at night; so I spoke to her rather fiercely. She didn't seem to notice that, and I reached down to take hold of her,—then I came upstairs!"

"What for?"

"What happened?"

"What was the matter?"

"Well, nothing happened. Only she wasn't there! May have been indigestion, of course, but as a physician I don't advise any one to court indigestion alone at midnight in a cellar!"

"This is the most interesting and peripatetic and evasive ghost I ever heard of!" said Jack. "It's my belief she has no end of silver tankards, and jewels galore, at the bottom of that well, and I move we go and see!"

"To the bottom of the well, Jack?"

"To the bottom of the mystery. Come on!"

There was unanimous assent, and the fresh cambrics and pretty boots were gallantly escorted below by gentlemen whose jokes were so frequent that many of them were a little forced.

The deep old cellar was so dark that they had to bring lights, and the well so gloomy in its blackness that the ladies recoiled.

"That well is enough to scare even a ghost. It's my opinion you'd better let well enough alone?" quoth Jim.

"Truth lies hid in a well, and we must get her out," said George. "Bear a hand with the chain?"

Jim pulled away on the chain, George turned the creaking windlass, and Jack was chorus.

"A wet sheet for this ghost, if not a flowing sea," said he. "Seems to be hard work raising spirits! I suppose he kicked the bucket when he went down!"

As the chain lightened and shortened there grew a strained silence among them; and when at length the bucket appeared, rising slowly through the dark water, there was an eager, half reluctant peering, and a natural drawing back. They poked the gloomy contents. "Only water."

"Nothing but mud."

"Something—"

They emptied the bucket up on the dark earth, and then the girls all went out into the air, into the bright warm sunshine in front of the house, where was the sound of saw and hammer, and the smell of new wood. There was nothing said until the men joined them, and then Jenny timidly asked:

"How old should you think it was, George?"

"All of a century," he answered. "That water is a preservative,— lime in it. Oh!—you mean?—Not more than a month; a very little baby!"

There was another silence at this, broken by a cry from the workmen. They had removed the floor and the side walls of the old porch, so that the sunshine poured down to the dark stones of the cellar bottom. And there, in the strangling grasp of the roots of the great wistaria, lay the bones of a woman, from whose neck still hung a tiny scarlet cross on a thin chain of gold.

THREE THANKSGIVINGS

————————

Andrew's letter and Jean's letter were in Mrs. Morrison's lap. She had read them both, and sat looking at them with a varying sort of smile, now motherly and now unmotherly.

"You belong with me," Andrew wrote. "It is not right that Jean's husband should support my mother. I can do it easily now. You shall have a good room and every comfort. The old house will let for enough to give you quite a little income of your own, or it can be sold and I will invest the money where you'll get a deal more out of it. It is not right that you should live alone there. Sally is old and liable to accident. I am anxious about you. Come on for Thanksgiving—and come to stay. Here is the money to come with. You know I want you. Annie joins me in sending love.   ANDREW."

Mrs. Morrison read it all through again, and laid it down with her quiet, twinkling smile. Then she read Jean's.

"Now, mother, you've got to come to us for Thanksgiving this year. Just think! You haven't seen baby since he was three months old! And have never seen the twins. You won't know him—he's such a splendid big boy now. Joe says for you to come, of course. And, mother, why won't you come and live with us? Joe wants you, too. There's the little room upstairs; it's not very big, but we can put in a Franklin stove for you and make you pretty comfortable. Joe says he should think you ought to sell that white elephant of a place. He says he could put the money into his store and pay you good interest. I wish you would, mother. We'd just love to have you here. You'd be such a comfort to me, and such a help with the babies. And Joe

just loves you. Do come now, and stay with us. Here is the money
for the trip.—

Your affectionate daughter, JEANNIE."

Mrs. Morrison laid this beside the other, folded both, and placed
them in their respective envelopes, then in their several well-filled
pigeon-holes in her big, old-fashioned desk. She turned and paced
slowly up and down the long parlor, a tall woman, commanding of
aspect, yet of a winningly attractive manner, erect and light-footed,
still imposingly handsome.

It was now November, the last lingering boarder was long since
gone, and a quiet winter lay before her. She was alone, but for Sally;
and she smiled at Andrew's cautious expression, "liable to accident." He could not say "feeble" or "ailing," Sally being a colored
lady of changeless aspect and incessant activity.

Mrs. Morrison was alone, and while living in the Welcome
House she was never unhappy. Her father had built it, she was born
there, she grew up playing on the broad green lawns in front, and in
the acre of garden behind. It was the finest house in the village, and
she then thought it the finest in the world.

Even after living with her father at Washington and abroad, after
visiting hall, castle and palace, she still found the Welcome House
beautiful and impressive.

If she kept on taking boarders she could live the year through,
and pay interest, but not principal, on her little mortgage. This had
been the one possible and necessary thing while the children were
there, though it was a business she hated.

But her youthful experience in diplomatic circles, and the years
of practical management in church affairs, enabled her to bear it
with patience and success. The boarders often confided to one another, as they chatted and tatted on the long piazza, that Mrs. Morrison was "certainly very refined."

Now Sally whisked in cheerfully, announcing supper, and Mrs.
Morrison went out to her great silver tea-tray at the lit end of the
long, dark mahogany table, with as much dignity as if twenty titled
guests were before her.

Afterward Mr. Butts called. He came early in the evening, with his usual air of determination and a somewhat unusual spruceness. Mr. Peter Butts was a florid, blonde person, a little stout, a little pompous, sturdy and immovable in the attitude of a self-made man. He had been a poor boy when she was a rich girl; and it gratified him much to realize—and to call upon her to realize—that their positions had changed. He meant no unkindness, his pride was honest and unveiled. Tact he had none.

She had refused Mr. Butts, almost with laughter, when he proposed to her in her gay girlhood. She had refused him, more gently, when he proposed to her in her early widowhood. He had always been her friend, and her husband's friend, a solid member of the church, and had taken the small mortgage on the house. She refused to allow him at first, but he was convincingly frank about it.

"This has nothing to do with my wanting you, Delia Morrison," he said. "I've always wanted you—and I've always wanted this house, too. You won't sell, but you've got to mortgage. By and by you can't pay up, and I'll get it—see? Then maybe you'll take me—to keep the house. Don't be a fool, Delia. It's a perfectly good investment."

She had taken the loan. She had paid the interest. She would pay the interest if she had to take boarders all her life. And she would not, at any price, marry Peter Butts.

He broached the subject again that evening, cheerful and undismayed. "You might as well come to it, Delia," he said. "Then we could live right here just the same. You aren't so young as you were, to be sure; I'm not, either. But you are as good a housekeeper as ever—better—you've had more experience."

"You are extremely kind, Mr. Butts," said the lady, "but I do not wish to marry you."

"I know you don't," he said. "You've made that clear. You don't, but I do. You've had your way and married the minister. He was a good man, but he's dead. Now you might as well marry me."

"I do not wish to marry again, Mr. Butts; neither you nor anyone."

"Very proper, very proper, Delia," he replied. "It wouldn't look well if you did—at any rate, if you showed it. But why shouldn't you? The children are gone now—you can't hold them up against me any more."

"Yes, the children are both settled now, and doing nicely," she admitted.

"You don't want to go and live with them—either one of them—do you?" he asked.

"I should prefer to stay here," she answered.

"Exactly! And you can't! You'd rather live here and be a grandee—but you can't do it. Keepin' house for boarders isn't any better than keepin' house for me, as I see. You'd much better marry me."

"I should prefer to keep the house without you, Mr. Butts."

"I know you would. But you can't, I tell you. I'd like to know what a woman of your age can do with a house like this—and no money? You can't live eternally on hens' eggs and garden truck. That won't pay the mortgage."

Mrs. Morrison looked at him with her cordial smile, calm and noncommittal. "Perhaps I can manage it," she said.

"That mortgage falls due two years from Thanksgiving, you know."

"Yes—I have not forgotten."

"Well, then, you might just as well marry me now, and save two years of interest. It'll be my house, either way—but you'll be keepin' it just the same."

"It is very kind of you, Mr. Butts. I must decline the offer none the less. I can pay the interest, I am sure. And perhaps—in two years' time—I can pay the principal. It's not a large sum."

"That depends on how you look at it," said he. "Two thousand dollars is considerable money for a single woman to raise in two years—*and* interest."

He went away, as cheerful and determined as ever; and Mrs. Morrison saw him go with a keen light in her fine eyes, a more definite line to that steady, pleasant smile.

Then she went to spend Thanksgiving with Andrew. He was glad to see her. Annie was glad to see her. They proudly installed her in "her room," and said she must call it "home" now.

This affectionately offered home was twelve by fifteen, and eight feet high. It had two windows, one looking at some pale gray clapboards within reach of a broom, the other giving a view of several small fenced yards occupied by cats, clothes and children. There was an ailanthus tree under the window, a lady ailanthus tree. Annie told her how profusely it bloomed. Mrs. Morrison particularly disliked the smell of ailanthus flowers. "It doesn't bloom in November," said she to herself. "I can be thankful for that!"

Andrew's church was very like the church of his father, and Mrs. Andrew was doing her best to fill the position of minister's wife—doing it well, too—there was no vacancy for a minister's mother.

Besides, the work she had done so cheerfully to help her husband was not what she most cared for, after all. She liked the people, she liked to manage, but she was not strong on doctrine. Even her husband had never known how far her views differed from his. Mrs. Morrison had never mentioned what they were.

Andrew's people were very polite to her. She was invited out with them, waited upon and watched over and set down among the old ladies and gentlemen—she had never realized so keenly that she was no longer young. Here nothing recalled her youth, every careful provision anticipated age. Annie brought her a hot-water bag at night, tucking it in at the foot of the bed with affectionate care. Mrs. Morrison thanked her, and subsequently took it out—airing the bed a little before she got into it. The house seemed very hot to her, after the big, windy halls at home.

The little dining-room, the little round table with the little round fern-dish in the middle, the little turkey and the little carving-set—game-set she would have called it—all made her feel as if she was looking through the wrong end of an opera-glass.

In Annie's precise efficiency she saw no room for her assistance; no room in the church, no room in the small, busy town, prosperous and progressive, and no room in the house. "Not enough to turn round in!" she said to herself. Annie, who had grown up in a city flat, thought their little parsonage palatial. Mrs. Morrison grew up in the Welcome House.

She stayed a week, pleasant and polite, conversational, interested in all that went on.

"I think your mother is just lovely," said Annie to Andrew.

"Charming woman, your mother," said the leading church member.

"What a delightful old lady your mother is!" said the pretty soprano.

And Andrew was deeply hurt and disappointed when she announced her determination to stay on for the present in her old home. "Dear boy," she said, "you mustn't take it to heart. I love to be with you, of course, but I love my home, and want to keep it as long as I can. It is a great pleasure to see you and Annie so well settled, and so happy together. I am most truly thankful for you."

"My home is open to you whenever you wish to come, mother," said Andrew. But he was a little angry.

Mrs. Morrison came home as eager as a girl, and opened her own door with her own key, in spite of Sally's haste.

Two years were before her in which she must find some way to keep herself and Sally, and to pay two thousand dollars and the interest to Peter Butts. She considered her assets. Here was the house—the white elephant. It *was* big—very big. It was profusely furnished. Her father had entertained lavishly like the Southern-born, hospitable gentleman he was; and the bedrooms ran in suites—somewhat deteriorated by the use of boarders, but still numerous and habitable. Boarders—she abhorred them. They were people from afar, strangers and interlopers. She went over the place from garret to cellar, from front gate to backyard fence.

The garden had great possibilities. She was fond of gardening, and understood it well. She measured and estimated.

"This garden," she finally decided, "with the hens, will feed us two women and sell enough to pay Sally. If we make plenty of jelly, it may cover the coal bill, too. As to clothes—I don't need any. They last admirably. I can manage. I can *live*—but two thousand dollars—*and* interest!"

In the great attic was more furniture, discarded sets put there when her extravagant young mother had ordered new ones. And chairs—uncounted chairs. Senator Welcome used to invite numbers to meet his political friends—and they had delivered glowing orations in the wide, double parlors, the impassioned speakers standing on a temporary dais, now in the cellar; and the enthusiastic listeners disposed more or less comfortably on these serried rows of "folding chairs," which folded sometimes, and let down the visitor in scarlet confusion to the floor.

She sighed as she remembered those vivid days and glittering nights. She used to steal downstairs in her little pink wrapper and listen to the eloquence. It delighted her young soul to see her father rising on his toes, coming down sharply on his heels, hammering one hand upon the other; and then to hear the fusillade of applause.

Here were the chairs, often borrowed for weddings, funerals, and church affairs, somewhat worn and depleted, but still numerous. She mused upon them. Chairs—hundreds of chairs. They would sell for very little.

She went through her linen room. A splendid stock in the old days; always carefully washed by Sally; surviving even the boarders. Plenty of bedding, plenty of towels, plenty of napkins and tablecloths. "It would make a good hotel—but I *can't* have it so—I *can't!* Besides, there's no need of another hotel here. The poor little Haskins House is never full."

The stock in the china closet was more damaged than some other things, naturally; but she inventoried it with care. The countless cups of crowded church receptions were especially prominent. Later additions these, not very costly cups, but numerous, appallingly.

When she had her long list of assets all in order, she sat and studied it with a clear and daring mind. Hotel—boarding-house—she could think of nothing else. School! A girls' school! A boarding school! There was money to be made at that, and fine work done. It was a brilliant thought at first, and she gave several hours, and much paper and ink, to its full consideration. But she would need some capital for advertising; she must engage teachers—adding to her definite obligation; and to establish it, well, it would require time.

Mr. Butts, obstinate, pertinacious, oppressively affectionate, would give her no time. He meant to force her to marry him for her own good—and his. She shrugged her fine shoulders with a little shiver. Marry Peter Butts! Never! Mrs. Morrison still loved her husband. Some day she meant to see him again—God willing—and she did not wish to have to tell him that at fifty she had been driven into marrying Peter Butts.

Better live with Andrew. Yet when she thought of living with Andrew, she shivered again. Pushing back her sheets of figures and lists of personal property, she rose to her full graceful height and began to walk the floor. There was plenty of floor to walk. She considered, with a set deep thoughtfulness, the town and the townspeople, the surrounding country, the hundreds upon hundreds of women whom she knew—and liked, and who liked her.

It used to be said of Senator Welcome that he had no enemies; and some people, strangers, maliciously disposed, thought it no credit to his character. His daughter had no enemies, but no one had ever blamed her for her unlimited friendliness. In her father's wholesale entertainments the whole town knew and admired his daughter; in her husband's popular church she had come to know the women of the countryside about them. Her mind strayed off to these women, farmers' wives, comfortably off in a plain way, but starving for companionship, for occasional stimulus and pleasure. It was one of her joys in her husband's time to bring together these women—to teach and entertain them.

Suddenly she stopped short in the middle of the great high-ceiled room, and drew her head up proudly like a victorious queen. One wide, triumphant, sweeping glance she cast at the well-loved walls—and went back to her desk, working swiftly, excitedly, well into the hours of the night.

—

Presently the little town began to buzz, and the murmur ran far out into the surrounding country. Sunbonnets wagged over fences; butcher carts and pedlar's wagon carried the news farther; and ladies visiting found one topic in a thousand houses.

Mrs. Morrison was going to entertain. Mrs. Morrison had invited the whole feminine population, it would appear, to meet Mrs. Isabelle Carter Blake, of Chicago. Even Haddleton had heard of Mrs. Isabelle Carter Blake. And even Haddleton had nothing but admiration for her.

She was known the world over for her splendid work for children—for the school children and the working children of the country. Yet she was known also to have lovingly and wisely reared six children of her own—and made her husband happy in his home. On top of that she had lately written a novel, a popular novel, of which everyone was talking; and on top of that she was an intimate friend of a certain conspicuous Countess—an Italian.

It was even rumored, by some who knew Mrs. Morrison better than others—or thought they did—that the Countess was coming, too! No one had known before that Delia Welcome was a schoolmate of Isabelle Carter, and a life-long friend; and that was ground for talk in itself.

The day arrived, and the guests arrived. They came in hundreds upon hundreds, and found ample room in the great white house.

The highest dream of the guests was realized—the Countess had come, too. With excited joy they met her, receiving impressions that would last them for all their lives, for those large widening waves of reminiscence which delight us the more as years pass. It was an incredible glory—Mrs. Isabelle Carter Blake, *and* a Countess!

Some were moved to note that Mrs. Morrison looked the easy peer of these eminent ladies, and treated the foreign nobility precisely as she did her other friends.

She spoke, her clear quiet voice reaching across the murmuring din, and silencing it.

"Shall we go into the east room? If you will all take chairs in the east room, Mrs. Blake is going to be so kind as to address us. Also perhaps her friend—"

They crowded in, sitting somewhat timorously on the unfolded chairs.

Then the great Mrs. Blake made them an address of memorable power and beauty, which received vivid sanction from that imposing presence in Parisian garments on the platform by her side. Mrs. Blake spoke to them of the work she was interested in, and how it was aided everywhere by the women's clubs. She gave them the number of these clubs, and described with contagious enthusiasm the inspiration of their great meetings. She spoke of the women's club houses, going up in city after city, where many associations meet and help one another. She was winning and convincing and most entertaining—an extremely attractive speaker.

Had they a women's club there? They had not.

Not *yet*, she suggested, adding that it took no time at all to make one.

They were delighted and impressed with Mrs. Blake's speech, but its effect was greatly intensified by the address of the Countess.

"I, too, am American," she told them; "born here, reared in England, married in Italy." And she stirred their hearts with a vivid account of the women's clubs and associations all over Europe, and what they were accomplishing. She was going back soon, she said, the wiser and happier for this visit to her native land, and she should remember particularly this beautiful, quiet town, trusting that if she came to it again it would have joined the great sisterhood of women, "whose hands were touching around the world for the common good."

It was a great occasion.

The Countess left next day, but Mrs. Blake remained, and spoke in some of the church meetings, to an ever widening circle of admirers. Her suggestions were practical.

"What you need here is a 'Rest and Improvement Club,'" she said. "Here are all you women coming in from the country to do your shopping—and no place to go to. No place to lie down if you're tired, to meet a friend, to eat your lunch in peace, to do your hair. All you have to do is organize, pay some small regular due, and provide yourselves with what you want."

There was a volume of questions and suggestions, a little opposition, much random activity.

Who was to do it? Where was there a suitable place? They would have to hire someone to take charge of it. It would only be used once a week. It would cost too much.

Mrs. Blake, still practical, made another suggestion. "Why not combine business with pleasure, and make use of the best place in town, if you can get it? I *think* Mrs. Morrison could be persuaded to let you use part of her house; it's quite too big for one woman."

Then Mrs. Morrison, simple and cordial as ever, greeted with warm enthusiasm her wide circle of friends.

"I have been thinking this over," she said. "Mrs. Blake has been discussing it with me. My house is certainly big enough for all of you, and there am I, with nothing to do but entertain you. Suppose you formed such a club as you speak of—for Rest and Improvement. My parlors are big enough for all manner of meetings; there are bedrooms in plenty for resting. If you form such a club I shall be glad to help with my great, cumbersome house, shall be delighted to see so many friends there so often; and I think I could furnish accommodations more cheaply than you could manage in any other way."

Then Mrs. Blake gave them facts and figures, showing how much club-houses cost—and how little this arrangement would cost. "Most women have very little money, I know," she said, "and they hate to spend it on themselves when they have; but even a little money from each goes a long way when it is put together. I fancy there are none of us so poor we could not squeeze out, say ten cents a week. For a hundred women that would be ten dollars. Could you feed a hundred tired women for ten dollars, Mrs. Morrison?"

Mrs. Morrison smiled cordially. "Not on chicken pie," she said. "But I could give them tea and coffee, crackers and cheese for that,

I think. And a quiet place to rest, and a reading room, and a place to hold meetings."

Then Mrs. Blake quite swept them off their feet by her wit and eloquence. She gave them to understand that if a share in the palatial accommodation of the Welcome House, and as good tea and coffee as old Sally made, with a place to meet, a place to rest, a place to talk, a place to lie down, could be had for ten cents a week each, she advised them to clinch the arrangement at once before Mrs. Morrison's natural good sense had overcome her enthusiasm.

Before Mrs. Isabelle Carter Blake had left, Haddleton had a large and eager women's club, whose entire expenses, outside of stationery and postage, consisted of ten cents a week *per capita*, paid to Mrs. Morrison. Everybody belonged. It was open at once for charter members, and all pressed forward to claim that privileged place.

They joined by hundreds, and from each member came this tiny sum to Mrs. Morrison each week. It was very little money, taken separately. But it added up with silent speed. Tea and coffee, purchased in bulk, crackers by the barrel, and whole cheeses—these are not expensive luxuries. The town was full of Mrs. Morrison's ex-Sunday-school boys, who furnished her with the best they had—at cost. There was a good deal of work, a good deal of care, and room for the whole supply of Mrs. Morrison's diplomatic talent and experience. Saturdays found the Welcome House as full as it could hold, and Sundays found Mrs. Morrison in bed. But she liked it.

A busy, hopeful year flew by, and then she went to Jean's for Thanksgiving.

The room Jean gave her was about the same size as her haven in Andrew's home, but one flight higher up, and with a sloping ceiling. Mrs. Morrison whitened her dark hair upon it, and rubbed her head confusedly. Then she shook it with renewed determination.

The house was full of babies. There was little Joe, able to get about, and into everything. There were the twins, and there was the new baby. There was one servant, over-worked and cross. There was a small, cheap, totally inadequate nursemaid. There was Jean, happy but tired, full of joy, anxiety and affection, proud of her children, proud of her husband, and delighted to unfold her heart to her mother.

By the hour she babbled of their cares and hopes, while Mrs. Morrison, tall and elegant, in her well-kept old black silk, sat holding the baby or trying to hold the twins. The old silk was pretty well finished by the week's end. Joseph talked to her also, telling her how well he was getting on, and how much he needed capital, urging her to come and stay with them; it was such a help to Jeannie; asking questions about the house.

There was no going visiting here. Jeannie could not leave the babies. And few visitors; all the little suburb being full of similarly over-burdened mothers. Such as called found Mrs. Morrison charming. What she found them, she did not say. She bade her daughter an affectionate good-bye when the week was up, smiling at their mutual contentment.

"Good-bye, my dear children," she said. "I am so glad for all your happiness. I am thankful for both of you."

But she was more thankful to get home.

Mr. Butts did not have to call for his interest this time, but he called none the less.

"How on earth'd you get it, Delia?" he demanded. "Screwed it out o' these club-women?"

"Your interest is so moderate, Mr. Butts, that it is easier to meet than you imagine," was her answer. "Do you know the average interest they charge in Colorado? The women vote there, you know."

He went away with no more personal information than that; and no nearer approach to the twin goals of his desire than the passing of the year.

"One more year, Delia," he said; "then you'll have to give in."

"One more year!" she said to herself, and took up her chosen task with renewed energy.

The financial basis of the undertaking was very simple, but it would never have worked so well under less skilful management. Five dollars a year these country women could not have faced, but ten cents a week was possible to the poorest. There was no difficulty in collecting, for they brought it themselves; no unpleasantness in receiving, for old Sally stood at the receipt of custom and presented the covered cash-box when they came for their tea.

On the crowded Saturdays the great urns were set going, the mighty array of cups arranged in easy reach, the ladies filed by, each taking her refection and leaving her dime. Where the effort came was in enlarging the membership and keeping up the attendance; and this effort was precisely in the line of Mrs. Morrison's splendid talents.

Serene, cheerful, inconspicuously active, planning like the born statesman she was, executing like a practical politician, Mrs. Morrison gave her mind to the work, and thrived upon it. Circle within circle, and group within group, she set small classes and departments at work, having a boys' club by and by in the big room over the woodshed, girls' clubs, reading clubs, study clubs, little meetings of every sort that were not held in churches, and some that were—previously.

For each and all there was, if wanted, tea and coffee, crackers and cheese; simple fare, of unvarying excellence, and from each and all, into the little cash-box, ten cents for these refreshments. From the club members this came weekly; and the club members, kept up by a constant variety of interests, came every week. As to numbers, before the first six months was over The Haddleton Rest and Improvement Club numbered five hundred women.

Now, five hundred times ten cents a week is twenty-six hundred dollars a year. Twenty-six hundred dollars a year would not be very much to build or rent a large house, to furnish five hundred people with chairs, lounges, books and magazines, dishes and service; and with food and drink even of the simplest. But if you are miraculously supplied with a club-house, furnished, with a manager and servant on the spot, then that amount of money goes a long way.

On Saturdays Mrs. Morrison hired two helpers for half a day, for half a dollar each. She stocked the library with many magazines for fifty dollars a year. She covered fuel, light and small miscellanies with another hundred. And she fed her multitude with the plain viands agreed upon, at about four cents apiece.

For her collateral entertainments, her many visits, the various new expenses entailed, she paid as well; and yet at the end of the first year she had not only her interest, but a solid thousand dollars of clear profit. With a calm smile she surveyed it, heaped in neat stacks of bills in the small safe in the wall behind her bed. Even Sally did not know it was there.

The second season was better than the first. There were difficulties, excitements, even some opposition, but she rounded out the year triumphantly. "After that," she said to herself, "they may have the deluge if they like."

She made all expenses, made her interest, made a little extra cash, clearly her own, all over and above the second thousand dollars.

Then did she write to son and daughter, inviting them and their families to come home to Thanksgiving, and closing each letter with joyous pride: "Here is the money to come with."

They all came, with all the children and two nurses. There was plenty of room in the Welcome House, and plenty of food on the long mahogany table. Sally was as brisk as a bee, brilliant in scarlet and purple; Mrs. Morrison carved her big turkey with queenly grace.

"I don't see that you're over-run with club-women, mother," said Jeannie.

"It's Thanksgiving, you know; they're all at home. I hope they are all as happy, as thankful for their homes as I am for mine," said Mrs. Morrison.

Afterward Mr. Butts called. With dignity and calm unruffled, Mrs. Morrison handed him his interest—and principal.

Mr. Butts was almost loath to receive it, though his hand automatically grasped the crisp blue check.

"I didn't know you had a bank account," he protested, somewhat dubiously.

"Oh, yes; you'll find the check will be honored, Mr. Butts."

"I'd like to know how you got this money. You *can't* 'a' skinned it out o' that club of yours."

"I appreciate your friendly interest, Mr. Butts; you have been most kind."

"I believe some of these great friends of yours have lent it to you. You won't be any better off, I can tell you."

"Come, come, Mr. Butts! Don't quarrel with good money. Let us part friends."

And they parted.

THE COTTAGETTE

"Why not?" said Mr. Mathews. "It is far too small for a house, too pretty for a hut, too—unusual—for a cottage."

"Cottagette, by all means," said Lois, seating herself on a porch chair. "But it is larger than it looks, Mr. Mathews. How do you like it, Malda?"

I was delighted with it. More than delighted. Here this tiny shell of fresh unpainted wood peeped out from under the trees, the only house in sight except the distant white specks on far-off farms, and the little wandering village in the river-threaded valley. It sat right on the turf,—no road, no path even, and the dark woods shadowed the back windows.

"How about meals?" asked Lois.

"Not two minutes' walk," he assured her, and showed us a little furtive path between the trees to the place where meals were furnished.

We discussed and examined and exclaimed, Lois holding her pongee skirts close about her—she needn't have been so careful, there wasn't a speck of dust,—and presently decided to take it.

Never did I know the real joy and peace of living, before that blessed summer at "High Court." It was a mountain place, easy enough to get to, but strangely big and still and far away when you were there.

The working basis of the establishment was an eccentric woman named Caswell, a sort of musical enthusiast, who had a summer school of music and the "higher thought." Malicious persons, not able to obtain accommodations there, called the place "High C."

I liked the music very well, and kept my thoughts to myself, both high and low, but "The Cottagette" I loved unreservedly. It was so little and new and clean, smelling only of its fresh-planed boards—they hadn't even stained it.

There was one big room and two little ones in the tiny thing, though from the outside you wouldn't have believed it, it looked so small; but small as it was it harbored a miracle—a real bathroom with water piped from mountain springs. Our windows opened into the green shadiness, the soft brownness, the bird-inhabited quiet flower-starred woods. But in front we looked across whole counties—over a far-off river—into another state. Off and down and away—it was like sitting on the roof of something—something very big.

The grass swept up to the door-step, to the walls—only it wasn't just grass of course, but such a procession of flowers as I had never imagined could grow in one place.

You had to go quite a way through the meadow, wearing your own narrow faintly marked streak in the grass, to reach the town-connecting road below. But in the woods was a little path, clear and wide, by which we went to meals.

For we ate with the highly thoughtful musicians, and highly musical thinkers, in their central boarding-house nearby. They didn't call it a boarding-house, which is neither high nor musical; they called it "The Calceolaria." There was plenty of that growing about, and I didn't mind what they called it so long as the food was good—which it was, and the prices reasonable—which they were.

The people were extremely interesting—some of them at least; and all of them were better than the average of summer boarders.

But if there hadn't been any interesting ones it didn't matter while Ford Mathews was there. He was a newspaper man, or rather an ex-newspaper man, then becoming a writer for magazines, with books ahead.

He had friends at High Court—he liked music—he liked the

place—and he liked us. Lois liked him too, as was quite natural. I'm sure I did.

He used to come up evenings and sit on the porch and talk.

He came daytimes and went on long walks with us. He established his workshop in a most attractive little cave not far beyond us,—the country there is full of rocky ledges and hollows,—and sometimes asked us over to an afternoon tea, made on a gipsy fire.

Lois was a good deal older than I, but not really old at all, and she didn't look her thirty-five by ten years. I never blamed her for not mentioning it, and I wouldn't have done so, myself, on any account. But I felt that together we made a safe and reasonable household. She played beautifully, and there was a piano in our big room. There were pianos in several other little cottages about— but too far off for any jar of sound. When the wind was right we caught little wafts of music now and then; but mostly it was still— blessedly still, about us. And yet that Calceolaria was only two minutes off—and with raincoats and rubbers we never minded going to it.

We saw a good deal of Ford and I got interested in him, I couldn't help it. He was big. Not extra big in pounds and inches, but a man with big view and a grip—with purpose and real power. He was going to do things. I thought he was doing them now, but he didn't— this was all like cutting steps in the ice-wall, he said. It had to be done, but the road was long ahead. And he took an interest in my work too, which is unusual for a literary man.

Mine wasn't much. I did embroidery and made designs.

It is such pretty work! I like to draw from flowers and leaves and things about me; conventionalize them sometimes, and sometimes paint them just as they are,—in soft silk stitches.

All about up here were the lovely small things I needed; and not only these, but the lovely big things that make one feel so strong and able to do beautiful work.

Here was the friend I lived so happily with, and all this fairy land of sun and shadow, the free immensity of our view, and the dainty comfort of the Cottagette. We never had to think of ordinary things till the soft musical thrill of the Japanese gong stole through the trees, and we trotted off to the Calceolaria.

I think Lois knew before I did.

We were old friends and trusted each other, and she had had experience too.

"Malda," she said, "let us face this thing and be rational." It was a strange thing that Lois should be so rational and yet so musical—but she was, and that was one reason I liked her so much.

"You are beginning to love Ford Mathews—do you know it?"

I said yes, I thought I was.

"Does he love you?"

That I couldn't say. "It is early yet," I told her. "He is a man, he is about thirty I believe, he has seen more of life and probably loved before—it may be nothing more than friendliness with him."

"Do you think it would be a good marriage?" she asked. We had often talked of love and marriage, and Lois had helped me to form my views—hers were very clear and strong.

"Why yes—if he loves me," I said. "He has told me quite a bit about his family, good western farming people, real Americans. He is strong and well—you can read clean living in his eyes and mouth." Ford's eyes were as clear as a girl's, the whites of them were clear. Most men's eyes, when you look at them critically, are not like that. They may look at you very expressively, but when you look at them, just as features, they are not very nice.

I liked his looks, but I liked him better.

So I told her that as far as I knew it would be a good marriage—if it was one.

"How much do you love him?" she asked.

That I couldn't quite tell,—it was a good deal,—but I didn't think it would kill me to lose him.

"Do you love him enough to do something to win him—to really put yourself out somewhat for that purpose?"

"Why—yes—I think I do. If it was something I approved of. What do you mean?"

Then Lois unfolded her plan. She had been married,—unhappily married, in her youth; that was all over and done with years ago; she had told me about it long since; and she said she did not regret the pain and loss because it had given her experience. She had her maiden name again—and freedom. She was so fond of me she wanted to give me the benefit of her experience—without the pain.

"Men like music," said Lois; "they like sensible talk; they like beauty of course, and all that,—"

"Then they ought to like you!" I interrupted, and, as a matter of fact they did. I knew several who wanted to marry her, but she said "once was enough." I don't think they were "good marriages" though.

"Don't be foolish, child," said Lois, "this is serious. What they care for most after all is domesticity. Of course they'll fall in love with anything; but what they want to marry is a homemaker. Now we are living here in an idyllic sort of way, quite conducive to falling in love, but no temptation to marriage. If I were you—if I really loved this man and wished to marry him, I would make a home of this place."

"Make a home?—why it *is* a home. I never was so happy anywhere in my life. What on earth do you mean, Lois?"

"A person might be happy in a balloon, I suppose," she replied, "but it wouldn't be a home. He comes here and sits talking with us, and it's quiet and feminine and attractive—and then we hear that big gong at the Calceolaria, and off we go slopping through the wet woods—and the spell is broken. Now you can cook." I could cook. I could cook excellently. My esteemed Mama had rigorously taught me every branch of what is now called "domestic science"; and I had no objection to the work, except that it prevented my doing anything else. And one's hands are not so nice when one cooks and washes dishes,—I need nice hands for my needlework. But if it was a question of pleasing Ford Mathews—

Lois went on calmly. "Miss Caswell would put on a kitchen for us in a minute, she said she would, you know, when we took the cottage. Plenty of people keep house up here,—we can if we want to."

"But we don't want to," I said, "we never have wanted to. The very beauty of the place is that it never had any housekeeping about it. Still, as you say, it would be cosy on a wet night, we could have delicious little suppers, and have him stay—"

"He told me he had never known a home since he was eighteen," said Lois.

That was how we came to install a kitchen in the Cottagette. The men put it up in a few days, just a lean-to with a window, a sink and two doors. I did the cooking. We had nice things, there is no denying that; good fresh milk and vegetables particularly; fruit is hard to get in the country, and meat too, still we managed nicely; the less you have the more you have to manage—it takes time and brains, that's all.

Lois likes to do housework, but it spoils her hands for practicing, so she can't; and I was perfectly willing to do it—it was all in the interest of my own heart. Ford certainly enjoyed it. He dropped in often, and ate things with undeniable relish. So I was pleased, though it did interfere with my work a good deal. I always work best in the morning; but of course housework has to be done in the morning too; and it is astonishing how much work there is in the littlest kitchen. You go in for a minute, and you see this thing and that thing and the other thing to be done, and your minute is an hour before you know it.

When I was ready to sit down the freshness of the morning was gone somehow. Before, when I woke up, there was only the clean wood smell of the house, and then the blessed out-of-doors: now I always felt the call of the kitchen as soon as I woke. An oil stove will smell a little, either in or out of the house; and soap, and—well you know if you cook in a bedroom how it makes the room feel differently? Our house had been only bedroom and parlor before.

We baked too—the baker's bread was really pretty poor, and Ford did enjoy my whole wheat, and brown, and especially hot rolls and gems. It was a pleasure to feed him, but it did heat up the house, and me. I never could work much—at my work—baking days. Then, when I did get to work, the people would come with things,— milk or meat or vegetables, or children with berries; and what distressed me most was the wheelmarks on our meadow. They soon made quite a road—they had to of course, but I hated it—I lost that lovely sense of being on the last edge and looking over—we were just a bead on a string like other houses. But it was quite true that I loved this man, and would do more than this to please him. We couldn't go off so freely on excursions as we used, either; when meals are to be prepared someone has to be there, and to take in things when they come. Sometimes Lois stayed in, she always asked to, but mostly I did. I couldn't let her spoil her summer on my account. And Ford certainly liked it.

He came so often that Lois said she thought it would look better if we had an older person with us; and that her mother could come if I wanted her, and she could help with the work of course. That seemed reasonable, and she came. I wasn't very fond of Lois's mother, Mrs. Fowler, but it did seem a little conspicuous, Mr. Mathews eating with us more than he did at the Calceolaria. There were others of course, plenty of them dropping in, but I didn't encourage it much, it made so much more work. They would come in to supper, and then we would have musical evenings. They offered to help me wash dishes, some of them, but a new hand in the kitchen is not much help. I preferred to do it myself; then I knew where the dishes were.

Ford never seemed to want to wipe dishes; though I often wished he would.

So Mrs. Fowler came. She and Lois had one room, they had to,—and she really did a lot of the work, she was a very practical old lady.

Then the house began to be noisy. You hear another person in a kitchen more than you hear yourself, I think,—and the walls were only boards. She swept more than we did too. I don't think much sweeping is needed in a clean place like that; and she dusted all the time; which I know is unnecessary. I still did most of the cooking, but I could get off more to draw, out-of-doors; and to walk. Ford was in and out continually, and, it seemed to me, was really coming nearer. What was one summer of interrupted work, of noise and dirt and smell and constant meditation on what to eat next, compared to a lifetime of love? Besides—if he married me—I should have to do it always, and might as well get used to it.

Lois kept me contented, too, telling me nice things that Ford said about my cooking. "He does appreciate it so," she said.

One day he came around early and asked me to go up Hugh's Peak with him. It was a lovely climb and took all day. I demurred a little, it was Monday, Mrs. Fowler thought it was cheaper to have a woman come and wash, and we did, but it certainly made more work.

"Never mind," he said, "what's washing day or ironing day or any of that old foolishness to us? This is walking day—that's what it is." It was really, cool and sweet and fresh,—it had rained in the night,— and brilliantly clear.

"Come along!" he said. "We can see as far as Patch Mountain I'm sure. There'll never be a better day."

"Is anyone else going?" I asked.

"Not a soul. It's just us. Come."

I came gladly, only suggesting—"Wait, let me put up a lunch."

"I'll wait just long enough for you to put on knickers and a short skirt," said he. "The lunch is all in the basket on my back. I know how long it takes for you women to 'put up' sandwiches and things."

We were off in ten minutes, light-footed and happy: and the day was all that could be asked. He brought a perfect lunch, too, and had made it all himself. I confess it tasted better to me than my own cooking; but perhaps that was the climb.

When we were nearly down we stopped by a spring on a broad ledge, and supped, making tea as he liked to do out-of-doors. We saw the round sun setting at one end of a world view, and the round moon rising at the other; calmly shining each on each.

And then he asked me to be his wife.

We were very happy.

"But there's a condition!" said he all at once, sitting up straight and looking very fierce. "You mustn't cook!"

"What!" said I. "Mustn't cook?"

"No," said he, "you must give it up—for my sake."

I stared at him dumbly.

"Yes, I know all about it," he went on, "Lois told me. I've seen a good deal of Lois—since you've taken to cooking. And since I would talk about you, naturally I learned a lot. She told me how you were brought up, and how strong your domestic instincts were—but bless your artist soul, dear girl, you have some others!" Then he smiled rather queerly and murmured, "surely in vain the net is spread in the sight of any bird."

"I've watched you, dear, all summer;" he went on, "it doesn't agree with you.

"Of course the things taste good—but so do my things! I'm a good cook myself. My father was a cook, for years—at good wages. I'm used to it you see.

"One summer when I was hard up I cooked for a living—and saved money instead of starving."

"O ho!" said I, "that accounts for the tea—and the lunch!"

"And lots of other things," said he. "But you haven't done half as much of your lovely work since you started this kitchen business, and—you'll forgive me, dear—it hasn't been as good. Your work is quite too good to lose; it is a beautiful and distinctive art, and I don't want you to let it go. What would you think of me if I gave up my hard long years of writing for the easy competence of a well-paid cook!"

I was still too happy to think very clearly. I just sat and looked at him. "But you want to marry me?" I said.

"I want to marry you, Malda,—because I love you—because you are young and strong and beautiful—because you are wild and sweet and—fragrant, and—elusive, like the wild flowers you love. Because you are so truly an artist in your special way, seeing beauty and giving it to others. I love you because of all this, because you are rational and highminded and capable of friendship,—and in spite of your cooking!"

"But—how do you want to live?"

"As we did here—at first," he said. "There was peace, exquisite silence. There was beauty—nothing but beauty. There were the clean wood odors and flowers and fragrances and sweet wild wind. And there was you—your fair self, always delicately dressed, with white firm fingers sure of touch in delicate true work. I loved you then. When you took to cooking it jarred on me. I have been a cook, I tell you, and I know what it is. I hated it—to see my woodflower in a kitchen. But Lois told me about how you were brought up to it and loved it, and I said to myself, 'I love this woman; I will wait and see if I love her even as a cook.' And I do, Darling: I withdraw the condition. I will love you always, even if you insist on being my cook for life!"

"O I don't insist!" I cried. "I don't want to cook—I want to draw! But I thought—Lois said—How she has misunderstood you!"

"It is not true, always, my dear," said he, "that the way to a man's heart is through his stomach; at least it's not the only way. Lois doesn't know everything, she is young yet! And perhaps for my sake you can give it up. Can you, sweet?"

Could I? Could I? Was there ever a man like this?

AN HONEST WOMAN

"There's an honest woman if ever there was one!" said the young salesman to the old one, watching their landlady whisk inside the screen door and close it softly without letting in a single fly—those evergreen California flies not mentioned by real estate men.

"What makes you think so?" asked Mr. Burdock, commonly known as "Old Burdock," wriggling forward, with alternate jerks, the two hind legs which supported his chair, until its backward tilt was positively dangerous.

"Think!" said young Abramson with extreme decision, "I happen to know. I've put up here for three years past, twice a year; and I know a lot of people in this town—sell to 'em right along."

"Stands well in the town, does she?" inquired the other with no keen interest. He had put up at the Main House for eight years, and furthermore he knew Mrs. Main when she was a child; but he did not mention it. Mr. Burdock made no pretense of virtue, yet if he had one in especial it lay in the art of not saying things.

"I should say she does!" the plump young man replied, straightening his well-curved waistcoat. "None better. She hasn't a bill standing—settles the day they come in. Pays cash for everything she can. She must make a handsome thing of this house; but it don't go in finery—she's as plain as a hen."

"Why, I should call Mrs. Main rather a good-looking woman," Burdock gently protested.

"Oh yes, good-looking enough; but I mean her style—no show—no expense—no dress. But she keeps up the house all right—everything first class, and reasonable prices. She's got good money in the bank they tell me. And there's a daughter—away at school somewhere—won't have her brought up in a hotel. She's dead right, too."

"I dunno why a girl couldn't grow up in a hotel—with a nice mother like that," urged Mr. Burdock.

"Oh come! You know better 'n that. Get talked about in any case—probably worse. No sir! You can't be too careful about a girl, and her mother knows it."

"Glad you've got a high opinion of women. I like to see it," and Mr. Burdock tilted softly backward and forward in his chair, a balancing foot thrust forth. He wore large, square-toed, rather thin shoes with the visible outlines of feet in them.

The shoes of Mr. Abramson, on the other hand, had pronounced outlines of their own, and might have been stuffed with anything—that would go in.

"I've got a high opinion of good women," he announced with finality. "As to bad ones, the less said the better!" and he puffed his strong cigar, looking darkly experienced.

"They're doin' a good deal towards reformin' 'em, nowadays, ain't they?" ventured Mr. Burdock.

The young man laughed disagreeably. "You can't reform spilled milk," said he. "But I do like to see an honest, hard-working woman succeed."

"So do I, boy," said his companion, "so do I," and they smoked in silence.

The hotel bus drew up before the house, backed up creakingly, and one passenger descended, bearing a large, lean suitcase showing much wear. He was an elderly man, tall, well-built, but not well-carried; and wore a long, thin beard. Mr. Abramson looked him over, decided that he was neither a buyer nor a seller, and dismissed him from his mind.

Mr. Burdock looked him over and brought the front legs of his chair down with a thump.

"By Heck!" said he softly.

The newcomer went in to register. Mr. Burdock went in to buy another cigar.

Mrs. Main was at the desk alone, working at her books. Her smooth, dark hair curved away from a fine forehead, both broad and high; wide-set, steady gray eyes looked out from under level brows with a clear directness. Her mouth, at thirty-eight, was a little hard.

The tall man scarcely looked at her, as he reached for the register book; but she looked at him, and her color slowly heightened. He signed his name as one of considerable importance, "Mr. Alexander E. Main, Guthrie, Oklahoma."

"I want a sunny room," he said. "A south room, with a fire when I want it. I feel the cold in this climate very much."

"You always did," remarked Mrs. Main quietly.

Then he looked; the pen dropping from his fingers and rolling across the untouched page, making a dotted path of lessening blotches.

Mr. Burdock made himself as small as he could against the cigar stand, but she ruthlessly approached, sold him the cigar he selected, and waited calmly till he started out, the tall man still staring.

Then she turned to him.

"Here is your key," she said. "Joe, take the gentleman's grip."

The boy moved off with the worn suitcase, but the tall man leaned over the counter towards her.

Mr. Burdock was carefully closing the screen door—so carefully that he could still hear.

"Why Mary! Mary! I must see you," the man whispered.

"You may see me at any time," she answered quietly. "Here is my office."

"This evening!" he said excitedly. "I'll come down this evening when it's quiet. I have so much to tell you, Mary."

"Very well," she said. "Room 27, Joe," and turned away.

Mr. Burdock took a walk, his cigar still unlighted.

"By Heck!" said he. "By—Heck!—And she as cool as a cucumber—That confounded old skeezicks!—Hanged if I don't happen to be passin'."

—

A sturdy, long-legged little girl was Mary Cameron when he first did business with her father in a Kansas country store. Ranch born and bred, a vigorous, independent child, gravely selling knives and sewing silk, writing paper and potatoes "to help father."

Father was a freethinker—a man of keen, strong mind, scant education, and opinions which ran away with him. He trained her to think for herself, and she did; to act up to her beliefs, and she did; to worship liberty and the sacred rights of the individual, and she did.

But the store failed, as the ranch had failed before it. Perhaps "old man Cameron's" arguments were too hot for the store loafers; perhaps his free thinking scandalized them. When Burdock saw Mary again, she was working in a San Francisco restaurant. She did not remember him in the least; but he knew one of her friends there and learned of the move to California—the orange failure, the grape failure, the unexpected death of Mr. Cameron, and Mary's self-respecting efficiency since.

"She's doin' well already—got some money ahead—and she's just as straight!" said Miss Josie. "Want to meet her?"

"Oh no," said Mr. Burdock, who was of a retiring disposition. "No, she wouldn't remember me at all."

When he happened into that restaurant again a year later, Mary had gone, and her friend hinted dark things.

"She got to goin' with a married man!" she confided. "Man from Oklahoma—name o' Main. One o' these Healers—great man for talkin'. She's left here, and I don't know where she is."

Mr. Burdock was sorry, very sorry—not only because he knew Mary, but because he knew Mr. Main. First—where had he met that man first? When he was a glib young phrenologist in Cincinnati. Then he'd run against him in St. Louis—a palmist this time; and then in Topeka—"Dr. Alexander," some sort of an "opaththist." Dr. Main's system of therapy varied, it appeared, with circumstances; he treated brains or bones as it happened, and here in San Francisco had made quite a hit; had lectured, had written a book on sex.

That Mary Cameron, with her hard sense and high courage, should take up with a man like that!

But Mr. Burdock continued to travel, and some four years later, coming to a new hotel in San Diego, he had found Mary again, now Mrs. Mary Main, presiding over the affairs of the house, with a small daughter going to school sedately.

Nothing did he say, to or about her; she was closely attending to her business, and he attended to his; but the next time he was in Cincinnati he had no difficulty in hearing of Mrs. Alexander Main—and her three children—in very poor circumstances indeed.

Of Main he had heard nothing for many years—till now.

He returned to the hotel, and walked near the side window of the office. No one there yet. Selecting chewing gum for solace, as tobacco might betray him, he deliberately tucked a camp stool under the shadow of the overhanging rose bush and sat there, somewhat thornily, but well hidden.

"It's none o' my business, but I mean to get the rights o' this," said Mr. Burdock.

She came in about a quarter of ten, as neat, as plain, as quiet as ever, and sat down under the light with her sewing. Many pretty things Mrs. Main made lovingly, but never wore.

She stopped after a little, folded her strong hands in her lap, and sat looking straight before her.

"If I could only see what she's looking at, I'd get the hang of it," thought Mr. Burdock, occasionally peering.

What she was looking at was a woman's life—and she studied it calmly and with impartial justice.

A fearless, independent girl, fond of her father but recognizing his weaknesses, she had taken her life in her own hands at about the age of twenty, finding in her orphanhood mainly freedom. Her mother she hardly remembered. She was not attractive to such youths as she met in the course of business, coldly repellent to all casual advances, and determined inwardly not to marry, at least not till she had made something of herself. She had worked hard, kept her health, saved money, and read much of the "progressive litera-ture" her father loved.

Then came this man who also read—studied—thought; who felt as she felt, who shared her aspirations, who "understood her." (Quite possibly he did—he was a person of considerable experience.)

Slowly she grew to enjoy his society, to depend upon it. When he revealed himself as lonely, not over-strong, struggling with the world, she longed to help him; and when, at last, in a burst of bitter confidence, he had said he must leave her, that she had made life over for him but that he must tear himself away, that she was life and hope to him, but he was not free—she demanded the facts.

He told her a sad tale, seeming not to cast blame on any but himself; but the girl burned deep and hot with indignation at the sordid woman, older than he, who had married him in his inexperi-enced youth, drained him of all he could earn, blasted his ideals, made his life an unbearable desert waste. She had—but no, he would not blacken her who had been his wife.

"She gives me no provable cause for divorce," he told her. "She will not loosen her grip. I have left her, but she will not let me go."

"Were there any—children?" she asked after a while.

"There was one little girl—" he said with a pathetic pause. "She died—"

He did not feel it necessary to mention that there were three little boys—who had lived, after a fashion.

Then Mary Cameron made a decision which was more credit to her heart than to her head, though she would have warmly denied such a criticism.

"I see no reason why your life—your happiness—your service to the community—should all be ruined and lost because you were foolish as a boy."

"I was," he groaned. "I fell under temptation. Like any other sin-ner, I must bear my punishment. There is no escape."

"Nonsense," said Mary. "She will not let you go. You will not live with her. You cannot marry me. But I can be your wife—if you want me to."

It was nobly meant. She cheerfully risked all, gave up all, to make up to him for his "ruined life"; to give some happiness to one so long unhappy; and when he vowed that he would not take advantage of such sublime unselfishness, she said that it was not in the least unselfish—for she loved him. This was true—she was quite honest about it.

And he? It is perfectly possible that he entered into their "sacred compact" with every intention of respecting it. She made him happier than anyone else ever had, so far.

There were two happy years when Mr. and Mrs. Main—they took themselves quite seriously—lived in their little flat together and worked and studied and thought great thoughts for the advancement of humanity. Also there was a girl child born, and their contentment was complete.

But in time the income earned by Mr. Main fell away more and more; till Mrs. Main went forth again and worked in a hotel, as efficient as ever, and even more attractive.

Then he had become restless and had gone to Seattle to look for employment—a long search, with only letters to fill the void.

And then—the quiet woman's hands were clenched together till the nails were purple and white—then The Letter came.

She was sitting alone that evening, the child playing on the floor. The woman who looked after her in the daytime had gone home. The two "roomers" who nearly paid the rent were out. It was a still, soft evening.

She had not had a letter for a week—and was hungry for it. She kissed the envelope—where his hand had rested. She squeezed it tight in her hands—laid her cheek on it—pressed it to her heart.

The baby reached up and wanted to share in the game. She gave her the envelope.

He was not coming back—ever.... It was better that she should know at once.... She was a strong woman—she would not be overcome.... She was a capable woman—independent—he need not worry about her in that way.... They had been mistaken.... He had found one that was more truly his.... She had been a Great Boon to him.... Here was some money for the child.... Good-bye.

She sat there, still, very still, staring straight before her, till the child reached up with a little cry.

Then she caught that baby in her arms, and fairly crushed her with passionate caresses till the child cried in good earnest and had to be comforted. Stony-eyed, the mother soothed and rocked her till she slept, and laid her carefully in her little crib. Then she stood up and faced it.

"I suppose I am a ruined woman," she said.

She went to the glass and lit the gas on either side, facing herself with fixed gaze and adding calmly, "I don't look it!"

She did not look it. Tall, strong, nobly built, softer and richer for her years of love, her happy motherhood; the woman she saw in the glass seemed as one at the beginning of a splendid life, not at the end of a bad one.

No one could ever know all that she thought and felt that night, bracing her broad shoulders to meet this unbelievable blow.

If he had died she could have borne it better; if he had disappeared she would at least have had her memories left. But now she had not only grief but shame. She had been a fool—a plain, ordinary, old-fashioned, girl fool, just like so many others she had despised. And now?

Under the shock and torture of her shattered life, the brave, practical soul of her struggled to keep its feet, to stand erect. She was not a demonstrative woman. Possibly he had never known how much she loved him, how utterly her life had grown to lean on his.

This thought struck her suddenly and she held her head higher. "Why should he ever know?" she said to herself, and then, "At least I have the child!" Before that night was over her plans were made.

The money he had sent, which her first feeling was to tear and burn, she now put carefully aside. "He sent it for the child," she said. "She will need it." She sublet the little flat and sold the furniture to a young couple, friends of hers, who were looking for just such a quiet home. She bought a suit of mourning, not too cumbrous, and set forth with little Mollie for the South.

In that fair land to which so many invalids come too late, it is not hard to find incompetent women, widowed and penniless, struggling to make a business of the only art they know—emerging from the sheltered harbor of "keeping house" upon the troubled sea of "keeping boarders."

Accepting moderate terms because of the child, doing good work because of long experience, offering a friendly sympathy out of her own deep sorrow, Mrs. Main made herself indispensable to such a one.

When her new employer asked her about her husband, she would press her handkerchief to her eyes and say, "He has left me. I cannot bear to speak of him."

This was quite true.

In a year she had saved a little money, and had spent it for a ticket home for the bankrupt lady of the house, who gladly gave her "the goodwill of the business" for it.

Said goodwill was lodged in an angry landlord, a few discontented and largely delinquent boarders, and many unpaid tradesmen. Mrs. Main called a meeting of her creditors in the stiff boarding house parlor.

She said, "I have bought this business, such as it is, with practically my last cent. I have worked seven years in restaurants and hotels and know how to run this place better than it has been done so far. If you people will give me credit for six months, and then, if I make good, for six months more, I will assume these back debts— and pay them. Otherwise I shall have to leave here, and you will get nothing but what will come from a forced sale of this third-hand furniture. I shall work hard, for I have this fatherless child to work for." She had the fatherless child at her side—a pretty thing, about three years old.

They looked the house over, looked her over, talked a little with the boarder of longest standing, and took up her offer.

She made good in six months; at the end of the year had begun to pay debts; and now—

Mrs. Main drew a long breath and came back to the present.

Mollie, dear Mollie, was a big girl now, doing excellently well at a good school. The Main House was an established success—had been for years. She had some money laid up—for Mollie's college expenses. Her health was good, she liked her work, she was respected and esteemed in the town, a useful member of a liberal church, of the Progressive Woman's Club, of the City Improvement Association. She had won Comfort, Security, and Peace.

His step on the stairs—restrained—uncertain—eager.

Her door was open. He came in, and closed it softly behind him. She rose and opened it.

"That door stands open," she said. "You need not worry. There's no one about."

"Not many, at any rate," thought the unprincipled Burdock.

She sat down again quietly. He wanted to kiss her, to take her in his arms; but she moved back to her seat with a decided step, and motioned him to his.

"You wanted to speak to me, Mr. Main. What about?"

Then he poured forth his heart as he used to, in a flow of strong, convincing words.

He told of his wanderings, his struggles, his repeated failures; of the misery that had overwhelmed him in his last fatal mistake.

"I deserve it all," he said with the quick smile and lift of the head that once was so compelling. "I deserve everything that has come to me.... Once to have had you ... and to be so blind a fool as to let go your hand! I needed it, Mary, I needed it."

He said little of his intermediate years as to facts; much as to the waste of woe they represented.

"Now I am doing better in my business," he said. "I have an established practice in Guthrie, but my health is not good and I have been advised to come to a warmer climate at least for a while."

She said nothing but regarded him with a clear and steady eye.

He seemed an utter stranger, and an unattractive one. That fierce leap of the heart, which, in his presence, at his touch, she recalled so well—where was it now?

"Will you not speak to me, Mary?"

"I have nothing to say."

"Can you not—forgive me?"

She leaned forward, dropping her forehead in her hands. He waited breathless; he thought she was struggling with her heart.

In reality she was recalling their life together, measuring its further prospects in the light of what he had told her, and comparing it with her own life since. She raised her head and looked him squarely in the eye.

"I have nothing to forgive," she said.

"Ah, you are too generous, too noble!" he cried. "And I? The burden of my youth is lifted now. My first wife is dead—some years since—and I am free. You are my real wife, Mary, my true and loving wife. Now I can offer you the legal ceremony as well."

"I do not wish it," she answered.

"It shall be as you say," he went on. "But for the child's sake—I wish to be a father to her."

"You are her father," said she. "That cannot be helped."

"But I wish to give her my name."

"She has it. I gave it to her."

"Brave, dear woman! But now I can give it to you."

"I have it also. It has been my name ever since I—according to my conscience—married you."

"But—but—you have no *legal* right to it, Mary."

She smiled, even laughed.

"Better read a little law, Mr. Main. I have used that name for twelve years, am publicly and honorably known by it; it is mine, legally."

"But Mary, I want to help you."

"Thank you. I do not need it."

"But I want to do for the child—my child—our little one!"

"You may," said she. "I want to send her to college. You may help if you like. I should be very glad if Mollie could have some pleasant and honorable memories of her father." She rose suddenly. "You wish to marry me now, Mr. Main?"

"With all my heart I wish it, Mary. You will?—"

He stood up—he held out his arms to her.

"No," said she, "I will not. When I was twenty-four I loved you. I sympathized with you. I was willing to be your wife—truly and faithfully your wife; even though you could not legally marry me—because I loved you. Now I will not marry you because I do not love you. That is all."

He glanced about the quiet, comfortable room; he had already estimated the quiet, comfortable business; and now, from some forgotten chamber of his honey-combed heart, welled up a fierce longing for this calm, strong, tender woman whose power of love he knew so well.

"Mary! You will not turn me away! I love you—I love you as I never loved you before!"

"I'm sorry to hear it," she said. "It does not make me love you again."

His face darkened.

"Do not drive me to desperation," he cried. "Your whole life here rests on a lie, remember. I could shatter it with a word."

She smiled patiently.

"You can't shatter facts, Mr. Main. People here know that you left me years ago. They know how I have lived since. If you try to blacken my reputation here I think you will find the climate of Mexico more congenial."

On second thought, this seemed to be the opinion of Mr. Main, who presently left for that country.

It was also agreed with by Mr. Burdock, who emerged later, a little chilly and somewhat scratched, and sought his chamber.

"If that galoot says anything against her in this town, he'll find a hotter climate than Mexico—by Heck!" said Mr. Burdock to his boots as he set them down softly. And that was all he ever said about it.

MAKING A CHANGE

"Wa-a-a-a! Waa-a-a-aaa!"

Frank Gordins set down his coffee cup so hard that it spilled over into the saucer.

"Is there no way to stop that child crying?" he demanded.

"I do not know of any," said his wife, so definitely and politely that the words seemed cut off by machinery.

"*I do,*" said his mother with even more definiteness, but less politeness.

Young Mrs. Gordins looked at her mother-in-law from under her delicate level brows, and said nothing. But the weary lines about her eyes deepened; she had been kept awake nearly all night, and for many nights.

So had he. So, as a matter of fact, had his mother. She had not the care of the baby—but lay awake wishing she had.

"There's no need at all for that child's crying so, Frank. If Julia would only let me—"

"It's no use talking about it," said Julia. "If Frank is not satisfied with the child's mother he must say so—perhaps we can make a change."

This was ominously gentle. Julia's nerves were at the breaking point. Upon her tired ears, her sensitive mother's heart, the grating wail from the next room fell like a lash—burnt in like fire. Her ears were hypersensitive, always. She had been an ardent musician before her marriage, and had taught quite successfully on both piano and violin. To any mother a child's cry is painful; to a musical mother it is torment.

But if her ears were sensitive, so was her conscience. If her nerves were weak, her pride was strong. The child was her child, it was her duty to take care of it, and take care of it she would. She spent her days in unremitting devotion to its needs, and to the care of her neat flat; and her nights had long since ceased to refresh her.

Again the weary cry rose to a wail.

"It does seem to be time for a change of treatment," suggested the older woman acidly.

"Or a change of residence," offered the younger, in a deadly quiet voice.

"Well, by Jupiter! There'll be a change of some kind, and p. d. q.!" said the son and husband, rising to his feet.

His mother rose also, and left the room, holding her head high and refusing to show any effects of that last thrust.

Frank Gordins glared at his wife. His nerves were raw, too. It does not benefit anyone in health or character to be continuously deprived of sleep. Some enlightened persons use that deprivation as a form of torture.

She stirred her coffee with mechanical calm, her eyes sullenly bent on her plate.

"I will not stand having Mother spoken to like that," he stated with decision.

"I will not stand having her interfere with my methods of bringing up children."

"Your methods! Why, Julia, my mother knows more about taking care of babies than you'll ever learn! She has the real love of it—and the practical experience. Why can't you *let* her take care of the kid—and we'll all have some peace!"

She lifted her eyes and looked at him; deep inscrutable wells of angry light. He had not the faintest appreciation of her state of mind. When people say they are "nearly crazy" from weariness, they state a practical fact. The old phrase which describes reason as "tottering on her throne" is also a clear one.

Julia was more near the verge of complete disaster than the family dreamed. The conditions were so simple, so usual, so inevitable.

Here was Frank Gordins, well brought up, the only son of a very capable and idolatrously affectionate mother. He had fallen deeply and desperately in love with the exalted beauty and fine mind of the young music teacher, and his mother had approved. She too loved music and admired beauty.

Her tiny store in the savings bank did not allow of a separate home, and Julia had cordially welcomed her to share in their household.

Here was affection, propriety, and peace. Here was a noble devotion on the part of the young wife, who so worshipped her husband that she used to wish she had been the greatest musician on earth—that she might give it up for him! She had given up her music, perforce, for many months, and missed it more than she knew.

She bent her mind to the decoration and artistic management of their little apartment, finding her standards difficult to maintain by the ever-changing inefficiency of her help. The musical temperament does not always include patience; nor, necessarily, the power of management.

When the baby came, her heart overflowed with utter devotion and thankfulness; she was his wife—the mother of his child. Her happiness lifted and pushed within till she longed more than ever for her music, for the free-pouring current of expression, to give forth her love and pride and happiness. She had not the gift of words.

So now she looked at her husband, dumbly, while wild visions of separation, of secret flight—even of self-destruction—swung dizzily across her mental vision. All she said was, "All right, Frank. We'll make a change. And you shall have—some peace."

"Thank goodness for that, Jule! You do look tired, Girlie—let Mother see to His Nibs, and try to get a nap, can't you?"

"Yes," she said. "Yes . . . I think I will." Her voice had a peculiar note in it. If Frank had been an alienist, or even a general physician, he would have noticed it. But his work lay in electric coils, in dynamos and copper wiring—not in women's nerves—and he did not notice it.

He kissed her and went out, throwing back his shoulders and drawing a long breath of relief as he left the house behind him and entered his own world.

"This being married—and bringing up children—is not what it's cracked up to be." That was the feeling in the back of his mind. But it did not find full admission, much less expression.

When a friend asked him, "All well at home?" he said, "Yes, thank you—pretty fair. Kid cries a good deal—but that's natural, I suppose."

He dismissed the whole matter from his mind and bent his faculties to a man's task—how he can earn enough to support a wife, a mother, and a son.

At home his mother sat in her small room, looking out of the window at the ground-glass one just across the "well," and thinking hard.

By the disorderly little breakfast table his wife remained motionless, her chin in her hands, her big eyes staring at nothing, trying to formulate in her weary mind some reliable reason why she should not do what she was thinking of doing. But her mind was too exhausted to serve her properly.

Sleep—Sleep—Sleep—that was the one thing she wanted. Then his mother could take care of the baby all she wanted to, and Frank could have some peace.... Oh, dear! It was time for the child's bath.

She gave it to him mechanically. On the stroke of the hour, she prepared the sterilized milk and arranged the little one comfortably with his bottle. He snuggled down, enjoying it, while she stood watching him.

She emptied the tub, put the bath apron to dry, picked up all the towels and sponges and varied appurtenances of the elaborate performance of bathing the first-born, and then sat staring straight before her, more weary than ever, but growing inwardly determined.

Greta had cleared the table, with heavy heels and hands, and was now rattling dishes in the kitchen. At every slam, the young mother winced, and when the girl's high voice began a sort of doleful chant over her work, young Mrs. Gordins rose to her feet with a shiver and made her decision.

She carefully picked up the child and his bottle, and carried him to his grandmother's room.

"Would you mind looking after Albert?" she asked in a flat, quiet voice; "I think I'll try to get some sleep."

"Oh, I shall be delighted," replied her mother-in-law. She said it in a tone of cold politeness, but Julia did not notice. She laid the child on the bed and stood looking at him in the same dull way for a little while, then went out without another word.

Mrs. Gordins, senior, sat watching the baby for some long moments. "He's a perfectly lovely child!" she said softly, gloating over his rosy beauty. "There's not a *thing* the matter with him! It's just her absurd ideas. She's so irregular with him! To think of letting that child cry for an hour! He is nervous because she is. And of course she couldn't feed him till after his bath—of course not!"

She continued in these sarcastic meditations for some time, taking the empty bottle away from the small wet mouth, that sucked on for a few moments aimlessly, and then was quiet in sleep.

"I could take care of him so that he'd *never* cry!" she continued to herself, rocking slowly back and forth. "And I could take care of twenty like him—and enjoy it! I believe I'll go off somewhere and do it. Give Julia a rest. Change of residence, indeed!"

She rocked and planned, pleased to have her grandson with her, even while asleep.

Greta had gone out on some errand of her own. The rooms were very quiet. Suddenly the old lady held up her head and sniffed. She rose swiftly to her feet and sprang to the gas jet—no, it was shut off tightly. She went back to the dining-room—all right there.

"That foolish girl has left the range going and it's blown out!" she thought, and went to the kitchen. No, the little room was fresh and clean, every burner turned off.

"Funny! It must come in from the hall." She opened the door. No, the hall gave only its usual odor of diffused basement. Then the parlor—nothing there. The little alcove called by the renting agent "the music room," where Julia's closed piano and violin case stood dumb and dusty—nothing there.

"It's in her room—and she's asleep!" said Mrs. Gordins, senior; and she tried to open the door. It was locked. She knocked—there was no answer; knocked louder—shook it—rattled the knob. No answer.

Then Mrs. Gordins thought quickly. "It may be an accident, and nobody must know. Frank mustn't know. I'm glad Greta's out. I *must* get in somehow!" She looked at the transom, and the stout rod Frank had himself put up for the portieres Julia loved.

"I believe I can do it, at a pinch."

She was a remarkably active woman of her years, but no memory of earlier gymnastic feats could quite cover the exercise. She hastily brought the step-ladder. From its top she could see in, and what she saw made her determine recklessly.

Grabbing the pole with small strong hands, she thrust her light frame bravely through the opening, turning clumsily but success-fully, and dropping breathlessly and somewhat bruised to the floor, she flew to open the windows and doors.

When Julia opened her eyes she found loving arms around her, and wise, tender words to soothe and reassure.

"Don't say a thing, dearie—I understand. I *understand*, I tell you! Oh, my dear girl—my precious daughter! We haven't been half good enough to you, Frank and I! But cheer up now—I've got the *loveliest* plan to tell you about! We *are* going to make a change! Listen now!"

And while the pale young mother lay quiet, petted and waited on to her heart's content, great plans were discussed and decided on.

Frank Gordins was pleased when the baby "outgrew his crying spells." He spoke of it to his wife.

"Yes," she said sweetly. "He has better care."

"I knew you'd learn," said he, proudly.

"I have!" she agreed. "I've learned—ever so much!"

He was pleased, too, vastly pleased, to have her health improve rapidly and steadily, the delicate pink come back to her cheeks, the soft light to her eyes; and when she made music for him in the evening, soft music, with shut doors—not to waken Albert—he felt as if his days of courtship had come again.

Greta the hammer-footed had gone, and an amazing French matron who came in by the day had taken her place. He asked no questions as to this person's peculiarities, and did not know that she did the purchasing and planned the meals, meals of such new delicacy and careful variance as gave him much delight. Neither did he know that her wages were greater than her predecessor's. He turned over the same sum weekly, and did not pursue details.

He was pleased also that his mother seemed to have taken a new lease of life. She was so cheerful and brisk, so full of little jokes and stories—as he had known her in his boyhood; and above all she was so free and affectionate with Julia, that he was more than pleased.

"I tell you what it is!" he said to a bachelor friend. "You fellows don't know what you're missing!" And he brought one of them home to dinner—just to show him.

"Do you do all that on thirty-five a week?" his friend demanded.

"That's about it," he answered proudly.

"Well, your wife's a wonderful manager—that's all I can say. And you've got the best cook I ever saw, or heard of, or ate of—I suppose I might say—for five dollars."

Mr. Gordins was pleased and proud. But he was neither pleased nor proud when someone said to him, with displeasing frankness, "I shouldn't think you'd want your wife to be giving music lessons, Frank!"

He did not show surprise nor anger to his friend, but saved it for his wife. So surprised and so angry was he that he did a most unusual thing—he left his business and went home early in the afternoon. He opened the door of his flat. There was no one in it. He went through every room. No wife; no child; no mother; no servant.

The elevator boy heard him banging about, opening and shutting doors, and grinned happily. When Mr. Gordins came out, Charles volunteered some information.

"Young Mrs. Gordins is out, Sir; but old Mrs. Gordins and the baby—they're upstairs. On the roof, I think."

Mr. Gordins went to the roof. There he found his mother, a smiling, cheerful nursemaid, and fifteen happy babies.

Mrs. Gordins, senior, rose to the occasion promptly.

"Welcome to my baby-garden, Frank," she said cheerfully. "I'm so glad you could get off in time to see it."

She took his arm and led him about, proudly exhibiting her sunny roof-garden, her sand-pile, and big, shallow, zinc-lined pool; her flowers and vines, her see-saws, swings, and floor mattresses.

"You see how happy they are," she said. "Celia can manage very well for a few moments." And then she exhibited to him the whole upper flat, turned into a convenient place for many little ones to take their naps or to play in if the weather was bad.

"Where's Julia?" he demanded first.

"Julia will be in presently," she told him, "by five o'clock anyway. And the mothers come for the babies by then, too. I have them from nine or ten to five."

He was silent, both angry and hurt.

"We didn't tell you at first, my dear boy, because we knew you wouldn't like it, and we wanted to make sure it would go well. I rent the upper flat, you see—it is forty dollars a month, same as ours—and pay Celia five dollars a week, and pay Dr. Holbrook downstairs the same for looking over my little ones every day. She helped me to get them, too. The mothers pay me three dollars a week each, and don't have to keep a nursemaid. And I pay ten dollars a week board to Julia, and still have about ten of my own."

"And she gives music lessons?"

"Yes, she gives music lessons, just as she used to. She loves it, you know. You must have noticed how happy and well she is now—haven't you? And so am I. And so is Albert. You can't feel very badly about a thing that makes us all happy, can you?"

Just then Julia came in, radiant from a brisk walk, fresh and cheery, a big bunch of violets at her breast.

"Oh, Mother," she cried, "I've got tickets and we'll all go to hear Melba—if we can get Celia to come in for the evening."

She saw her husband, and a guilty flush rose to her brow as she met his reproachful eyes.

"Oh, Frank!" she begged, her arms around his neck. "Please don't mind! Please get used to it! Please be proud of us! Just think, we're all so happy, and we earn about a hundred dollars a week—all of us together. You see I have Mother's ten to add to the house money, and twenty or more of my own!"

They had a long talk together that evening, just the two of them. She told him, at last, what a danger had hung over them—how near it came.

"And Mother showed me the way out, Frank. The way to have my mind again—and not lose you! She is a different woman herself now that she has her heart and hands full of babies. Albert does enjoy it so! And *you've* enjoyed it—till you found it out!

"And dear—my own love—I don't mind it now at all! I love my home, I love my work, I love my mother, I love you. And as to children—I wish I had six!"

He looked at her flushed, eager, lovely face, and drew her close to him.

"If it makes all of you as happy as that," he said, "I guess I can stand it."

And in after years he was heard to remark, "This being married and bringing up children is as easy as can be—when you learn how!"

TURNED

In her soft-carpeted, thick-curtained, richly furnished chamber, Mrs. Marroner lay sobbing on the wide, soft bed.

She sobbed bitterly, chokingly, despairingly; her shoulders heaved and shook convulsively; her hands were tight-clenched. She had forgotten her elaborate dress, the more elaborate bed-cover; forgotten her dignity, her self-control, her pride. In her mind was an overwhelming, unbelievable horror, an immeasurable loss, a turbulent, struggling mass of emotion.

In her reserved, superior, Boston-bred life she had never dreamed that it would be possible for her to feel so many things at once, and with such trampling intensity.

She tried to cool her feelings into thoughts; to stiffen them into words; to control herself—and could not. It brought vaguely to her mind an awful moment in the breakers at York Beach, one summer in girlhood, when she had been swimming under water and could not find the top.

—

In her uncarpeted, thin-curtained, poorly furnished chamber on the top floor, Gerta Petersen lay sobbing on the narrow, hard bed.

She was of larger frame than her mistress, grandly built and strong; but all her proud young womanhood was prostrate now, convulsed with agony, dissolved in tears. She did not try to control herself. She wept for two.

—

If Mrs. Marroner suffered more from the wreck and ruin of a longer love—perhaps a deeper one; if her tastes were finer, her ideals loftier; if she bore the pangs of bitter jealousy and outraged pride, Gerta had personal shame to meet, a hopeless future, and a looming present which filled her with unreasoning terror.

She had come like a meek young goddess into that perfectly ordered house, strong, beautiful, full of goodwill and eager obedience, but ignorant and childish—a girl of eighteen.

Mr. Marroner had frankly admired her, and so had his wife. They discussed her visible perfections and as visible limitations with that perfect confidence which they had so long enjoyed. Mrs. Marroner was not a jealous woman. She had never been jealous in her life—till now.

Gerta had stayed and learned their ways. They had both been fond of her. Even the cook was fond of her. She was what is called "willing," was unusually teachable and plastic; and Mrs. Marroner, with her early habits of giving instruction, tried to educate her somewhat.

"I never saw anyone so docile," Mrs. Marroner had often commented. "It is perfection in a servant, but almost a defect in character. She is so helpless and confiding."

She was precisely that; a tall, rosy-cheeked baby; rich womanhood without, helpless infancy within. Her braided wealth of dead-gold hair, her grave blue eyes, her mighty shoulders, and long, firmly moulded limbs seemed those of a primal earth spirit; but she was only an ignorant child, with a child's weakness.

When Mr. Marroner had to go abroad for his firm, unwillingly, hating to leave his wife, he had told her he felt quite safe to leave her in Gerta's hands—she would take care of her.

"Be good to your mistress, Gerta," he told the girl that last morning at breakfast. "I leave her to you to take care of. I shall be back in a month at latest."

Then he turned, smiling, to his wife. "And you must take care of Gerta, too," he said. "I expect you'll have her ready for college when I get back."

This was seven months ago. Business had delayed him from week to week, from month to month. He wrote to his wife, long, loving, frequent letters; deeply regretting the delay, explaining how necessary, how profitable it was; congratulating her on the wide resources she had; her well-filled, well-balanced mind; her many interests.

"If I should be eliminated from your scheme of things, by any of those 'acts of God' mentioned on the tickets, I do not feel that you would be an utter wreck," he said. "That is very comforting to me. Your life is so rich and wide that no one loss, even a great one, would wholly cripple you. But nothing of the sort is likely to happen, and I shall be home again in three weeks—if this thing gets settled. And you will be looking so lovely, with that eager light in your eyes and the changing flush I know so well—and love so well! My dear wife! We shall have to have a new honeymoon—other moons come every month, why shouldn't the mellifluous kind?"

He often asked after "little Gerta," sometimes enclosed a picture postcard to her, joked with his wife about her laborious efforts to educate "the child"; was so loving and merry and wise—

All this was racing through Mrs. Marroner's mind as she lay there with the broad, hemstitched border of fine linen sheeting crushed and twisted in one hand, and the other holding a sodden handkerchief.

She had tried to teach Gerta, and had grown to love the patient, sweet-natured child, in spite of her dullness. At work with her hands, she was clever, if not quick, and could keep small accounts from week to week. But to the woman who held a Ph.D., who had been on the faculty of a college, it was like baby-tending.

Perhaps having no babies of her own made her love the big child the more, though the years between them were but fifteen.

To the girl she seemed quite old, of course; and her young heart was full of grateful affection for the patient care which made her feel so much at home in this new land.

And then she had noticed a shadow on the girl's bright face. She looked nervous, anxious, worried. When the bell rang she seemed startled, and would rush hurriedly to the door. Her peals of frank laughter no longer rose from the area gate as she stood talking with the always admiring tradesmen.

Mrs. Marroner had labored long to teach her more reserve with men, and flattered herself that her words were at last effective. She suspected the girl of homesickness, which was denied. She suspected her of illness, which was denied also. At last she suspected her of something which could not be denied.

For a long time she refused to believe it, waiting. Then she had to believe it, but schooled herself to patience and understanding. "The poor child," she said. "She is here without a mother—she is so foolish and yielding—I must not be too stern with her." And she tried to win the girl's confidence with wise, kind words.

But Gerta had literally thrown herself at her feet and begged her with streaming tears not to turn her away. She would admit nothing, explain nothing, but frantically promised to work for Mrs. Marroner as long as she lived—if only she would keep her.

Revolving the problem carefully in her mind, Mrs. Marroner thought she would keep her, at least for the present. She tried to repress her sense of ingratitude in one she had so sincerely tried to help, and the cold, contemptuous anger she had always felt for such weakness.

"The thing to do now," she said to herself, "is to see her through this safely. The child's life should not be hurt any more than is unavoidable. I will ask Dr. Bleet about it—what a comfort a woman doctor is! I'll stand by the poor, foolish thing till it's over, and then get her back to Sweden somehow with her baby. How they do come where they are not wanted—and don't come where they are wanted!" And Mrs. Marroner, sitting alone in the quiet, spacious beauty of the house, almost envied Gerta.

Then came the deluge.

She had sent the girl out for needed air toward dark. The late mail came; she took it in herself. One letter for her—her husband's letter. She knew the postmark, the stamp, the kind of typewriting. She impulsively kissed it in the dim hall. No one would suspect Mrs. Marroner of kissing her husband's letters—but she did, often.

She looked over the others. One was for Gerta, and not from Sweden. It looked precisely like her own. This struck her as a little odd, but Mr. Marroner had several times sent messages and cards to the girl. She laid the letter on the hall table and took hers to her room.

"My poor child," it began. What letter of hers had been sad enough to warrant that?

"I am deeply concerned at the news you send." What news to so concern him had she written? "You must bear it bravely, little girl. I shall be home soon, and will take care of you, of course. I hope there is no immediate anxiety—you do not say. Here is money, in case you need it. I expect to get home in a month at latest. If you have to go, be sure to leave your address at my office. Cheer up—be brave—I will take care of you."

The letter was typewritten, which was not unusual. It was unsigned, which was unusual. It enclosed an American bill—fifty dollars. It did not seem in the least like any letter she had ever had from her husband, or any letter she could imagine him writing. But a strange, cold feeling was creeping over her, like a flood rising around a house.

She utterly refused to admit the ideas which began to bob and push about outside her mind, and to force themselves in. Yet under the pressure of these repudiated thoughts she went downstairs and brought up the other letter—the letter to Gerta. She laid them side by side on a smooth dark space on the table; marched to the piano and played, with stern precision, refusing to think, till the girl came back. When she came in, Mrs. Marroner rose quietly and came to the table. "Here is a letter for you," she said.

The girl stepped forward eagerly, saw the two lying together there, hesitated, and looked at her mistress.

"Take yours, Gerta. Open it, please."

The girl turned frightened eyes upon her.

"I want you to read it, here," said Mrs. Marroner.

"Oh, ma'am—No! Please don't make me!"

"Why not?"

There seemed to be no reason at hand, and Gerta flushed more deeply and opened her letter. It was long; it was evidently puzzling to her; it began "My dear wife." She read it slowly.

"Are you sure it is your letter?" asked Mrs. Marroner. "Is not this one yours? Is not that one—mine?"

She held out the other letter to her.

"It is a mistake," Mrs. Marroner went on, with a hard quietness. She had lost her social bearings somehow; lost her usual keen sense of the proper thing to do. This was not life; this was a nightmare.

"Do you not see? Your letter was put in my envelope and my letter was put in your envelope. Now we understand it."

But poor Gerta had no antechamber to her mind; no trained forces to preserve order while agony entered. The thing swept over her, resistless, overwhelming. She cowered before the outraged wrath she expected; and from some hidden cavern that wrath arose and swept over her in pale flame.

"Go and pack your trunk," said Mrs. Marroner. "You will leave my house to-night. Here is your money."

She laid down the fifty-dollar bill. She put with it a month's wages. She had no shadow of pity for those anguished eyes, those tears which she heard drop on the floor.

"Go to your room and pack," said Mrs. Marroner. And Gerta, always obedient, went.

Then Mrs. Marroner went to hers, and spent a time she never counted, lying on her face on the bed.

But the training of the twenty-eight years which had elapsed before her marriage; the life at college, both as student and teacher; the independent growth which she had made, formed a very different background for grief from that in Gerta's mind.

After a while Mrs. Marroner arose. She administered to herself a hot bath, a cold shower, a vigorous rubbing. "Now I can think," she said.

First she regretted the sentence of instant banishment. She went upstairs to see if it had been carried out. Poor Gerta! The tempest of her agony had worked itself out at last as in a child, and left her sleeping, the pillow wet, the lips still grieving, a big sob shuddering itself off now and then.

Mrs. Marroner stood and watched her, and as she watched she considered the helpless sweetness of the face; the defenseless, unformed character; the docility and habit of obedience which made her so attractive—and so easily a victim. Also she thought of the mighty force which had swept over her; of the great process now working itself out through her; of how pitiful and futile seemed any resistance she might have made.

She softly returned to her own room, made up a little fire, and sat by it, ignoring her feelings now, as she had before ignored her thoughts.

Here were two women and a man. One woman was a wife; loving, trusting, affectionate. One was a servant; loving, trusting, affectionate—a young girl, an exile, a dependent; grateful for any kindness; untrained, uneducated, childish. She ought, of course, to have resisted temptation; but Mrs. Marroner was wise enough to know how difficult temptation is to recognize when it comes in the guise of friendship and from a source one does not suspect.

Gerta might have done better in resisting the grocer's clerk; had, indeed, with Mrs. Marroner's advice, resisted several. But where respect was due, how could she criticize? Where obedience was due, how could she refuse—with ignorance to hold her blinded—until too late?

As the older, wiser woman forced herself to understand and extenuate the girl's misdeed and foresee her ruined future, a new feeling rose in her heart, strong, clear, and overmastering; a sense of measureless condemnation for the man who had done this thing. He knew. He understood. He could fully foresee and measure the consequences of his act. He appreciated to the full the innocence, the ignorance, the grateful affection, the habitual docility, of which he deliberately took advantage.

Mrs. Marroner rose to icy peaks of intellectual apprehension, from which her hours of frantic pain seemed far indeed removed. He had done this thing under the same roof with her—his wife. He had not frankly loved the younger woman, broken with his wife, made a new marriage. That would have been heart-break pure and simple. This was something else.

That letter, that wretched, cold, carefully guarded, unsigned letter; that bill—far safer than a check—these did not speak of affection. Some men can love two women at one time. This was not love.

Mrs. Marroner's sense of pity and outrage for herself, the wife, now spread suddenly into a perception of pity and outrage for the girl. All that splendid, clean young beauty, the hope of a happy life, with marriage and motherhood; honorable independence, even— these were nothing to that man. For his own pleasure he had chosen to rob her of her life's best joys.

He would "take care of her," said the letter. How? In what capacity?

And then, sweeping over both her feelings for herself, the wife, and Gerta, his victim, came a new flood, which literally lifted her to her feet. She rose and walked, her head held high. "This is the sin of man against woman," she said. "The offense is against womanhood. Against motherhood. Against—the child."

She stopped.

The child. His child. That, too, he sacrificed and injured— doomed to degradation.

Mrs. Marroner came of stern New England stock. She was not a Calvinist, hardly even a Unitarian, but the iron of Calvinism was in her soul: of that grim faith which held that most people had to be damned "for the glory of God."

Generations of ancestors who both preached and practiced stood behind her; people whose lives had been sternly moulded to their highest moments of religious conviction. In sweeping bursts of feeling they achieved "conviction," and afterward they lived and died according to that conviction.

When Mr. Marroner reached home a few weeks later, following his letters too soon to expect an answer to either, he saw no wife upon the pier, though he had cabled, and found the house closed darkly. He let himself in with his latch-key, and stole softly upstairs, to surprise his wife.

No wife was there.

He rang the bell. No servant answered it.

He turned up light after light; searched the house from top to bottom; it was utterly empty. The kitchen wore a clean, bald, unsympathetic aspect. He left it and slowly mounted the stair, completely dazed. The whole house was clean, in perfect order, wholly vacant.

One thing he felt perfectly sure of—she knew.

Yet was he sure? He must not assume too much. She might have been ill. She might have died. He started to his feet. No, they would have cabled him. He sat down again.

For any such change, if she had wanted him to know, she would have written. Perhaps she had, and he, returning so suddenly, had missed the letter. The thought was some comfort. It must be so. He turned to the telephone, and again hesitated. If she had found out—if she had gone—utterly gone, without a word—should he announce it himself to friends and family?

He walked the floor; he searched everywhere for some letter, some word of explanation. Again and again he went to the telephone—and always stopped. He could not bear to ask: "Do you know where my wife is?"

The harmonious, beautiful rooms reminded him in a dumb, helpless way of her; like the remote smile on the face of the dead. He put out the lights; could not bear the darkness; turned them all on again.

It was a long night—

In the morning he went early to the office. In the accumulated mail was no letter from her. No one seemed to know of anything unusual. A friend asked after his wife—"Pretty glad to see you, I guess?" He answered evasively.

About eleven a man came to see him; John Hill, her lawyer. Her cousin, too. Mr. Marroner had never liked him. He liked him less now, for Mr. Hill merely handed him a letter, remarked, "I was requested to deliver this to you personally," and departed, looking like a person who is called on to kill something offensive.

"I have gone. I will care for Gerta. Good-bye. Marion."

That was all. There was no date, no address, no postmark; nothing but that.

In his anxiety and distress he had fairly forgotten Gerta and all that. Her name aroused in him a sense of rage. She had come between him and his wife. She had taken his wife from him. That was the way he felt.

At first he said nothing, did nothing; lived on alone in his house, taking meals where he chose. When people asked him about his wife he said she was traveling—for her health. He would not have it in the newspapers. Then, as time passed, as no enlightenment came to him, he resolved not to bear it any longer, and employed detectives. They blamed him for not having put them on the track earlier, but set to work, urged to the utmost secrecy.

What to him had been so blank a wall of mystery seemed not to embarrass them in the least. They made careful inquiries as to her "past," found where she had studied, where taught, and on what lines; that she had some little money of her own, that her doctor was Josephine L. Bleet, M.D., and many other bits of information.

As a result of careful and prolonged work, they finally told him that she had resumed teaching under one of her old professors; lived quietly, and apparently kept boarders; giving him town, street, and number, as if it were a matter of no difficulty whatever.

He had returned in early spring. It was autumn before he found her.

A quiet college town in the hills, a broad, shady street, a pleasant house standing in its own lawn, with trees and flowers about it. He had the address in his hand, and the number showed clear on the white gate. He walked up the straight gravel path and rang the bell. An elderly servant opened the door.

"Does Mrs. Marroner live here?"

"No, sir."

"This is number twenty-eight?"

"Yes, sir."

"Who does live here?"

"Miss Wheeling, sir."

Ah! Her maiden name. They had told him, but he had forgotten. He stepped inside. "I would like to see her," he said.

He was ushered into a still parlor, cool and sweet with the scent of flowers, the flowers she had always loved best. It almost brought tears to his eyes. All their years of happiness rose in his mind again; the exquisite beginnings; the days of eager longing before she was really his; the deep, still beauty of her love.

Surely she would forgive him—she must forgive him. He would humble himself; he would tell her of his honest remorse—his absolute determination to be a different man.

Through the wide doorway there came in to him two women. One like a tall Madonna, bearing a baby in her arms.

Marion, calm, steady, definitely impersonal; nothing but a clear pallor to hint of inner stress.

Gerta, holding the child as a bulwark, with a new intelligence in her face, and her blue, adoring eyes fixed on her friend—not upon him.

He looked from one to the other dumbly.

And the woman who had been his wife asked quietly:

"What have you to say to us?"

THE WIDOW'S MIGHT

James had come on to the funeral, but his wife had not; she could not leave the children—that is what he said. She said, privately, to him, that she would not go. She never was willing to leave New York except for Europe or for Summer vacations; and a trip to Denver in November—to attend a funeral—was not a possibility to her mind.

Ellen and Adelaide were both there: they felt it a duty—but neither of their husbands had come. Mr. Jennings could not leave his classes in Cambridge, and Mr. Oswald could not leave his business in Pittsburgh—that is what they said.

The last services were over. They had had a cold, melancholy lunch and were all to take the night train home again. Meanwhile the lawyer was coming at four to read the will.

"It is only a formality. There can't be much left," said James.

"No," agreed Adelaide, "I suppose not."

"A long illness eats up everything," said Ellen, and sighed. Her husband had come to Colorado for his lungs years before and was still delicate.

"Well," said James rather abruptly, "What are we going to do with Mother?"

"Why, of course—" Ellen began, "We *could* take her. It would depend a good deal on how much property there is—I mean, on where she'd want to go. Edward's salary is more than needed now." Ellen's mental processes seemed a little mixed.

"She can come to me if she prefers, of course," said Adelaide.

"But I don't think it would be very pleasant for her. Mother never did like Pittsburgh."

James looked from one to the other.

"Let me see—how old is Mother?"

"Oh she's all of fifty," answered Ellen, "and much broken, I think. It's been a long strain, you know." She turned plaintively to her brother. "I should think you could make her more comfortable than either of us, James—with your big house."

"I think a woman is always happier living with a son than with a daughter's husband," said Adelaide. "I've always thought so."

"That is often true," her brother admitted. "But it depends." He stopped, and the sisters exchanged glances. They knew upon what it depended.

"Perhaps if she stayed with me, you could—help some," suggested Ellen.

"Of course, of course, I could do that," he agreed with evident relief. "She might visit between you—take turns—and I could pay her board. About how much ought it to amount to? We might as well arrange everything now."

"Things cost awfully in these days," Ellen said with a criss-cross of fine wrinkles on her pale forehead. "But of course it would be only just *what* it costs. I shouldn't want to *make* anything."

"It's work and care, Ellen, and you may as well admit it. You need all your strength—with those sickly children and Edward on your hands. When she comes to me, there need be no expense, James, except for clothes. I have room enough and Mr. Oswald will never notice the difference in the house bills—but he does hate to pay out money for clothes."

"Mother must be provided for properly," her son declared. "How much ought it to cost—a year—for clothes?"

"You know what your wife's cost," suggested Adelaide, with a flicker of a smile about her lips.

"Oh, *no,*" said Ellen. "That's no criterion! Maude is in society, you see. Mother wouldn't *dream* of having so much."

James looked at her gratefully. "Board—and clothes—all told; what should you say, Ellen?"

Ellen scrabbled in her small black hand bag for a piece of paper, and found none. James handed her an envelope and a fountain pen.

"Food—just plain food materials—costs all of four dollars a week now—for one person," said she. "And heat—and light—and extra service. I should think six a week would be the *least*, James. And for clothes and carfare and small expenses—I should say— well, three hundred dollars!"

"That would make over six hundred a year," said James slowly. "How about Oswald sharing that, Adelaide?"

Adelaide flushed. "I do not think he would be willing, James. Of course, if it were absolutely necessary—"

"He has money enough," said her brother.

"Yes, but he never seems to have any outside of his business— and he has his own parents to carry now. No—I can give her a home, but that's all."

"You see, you'd have none of the care and trouble, James," said Ellen. "We—the girls—are each willing to have her with us, while perhaps Maude wouldn't care to, but if you could just pay the money—"

"Maybe there's some left, after all," suggested Adelaide. "And this place ought to sell for something."

"This place" was a piece of rolling land within ten miles of Denver. It had a bit of river bottom, and ran up towards the foothills. From the house the view ran north and south along the precipitous ranks of the "Big Rockies" to westward. To the east lay the vast stretches of sloping plain.

"There ought to be at least six or eight thousand dollars from it, I should say," he concluded.

"Speaking of clothes," Adelaide rather irrelevantly suggested, "I see Mother didn't get any new black. She's always worn it as long as I can remember."

"Mother's a long time," said Ellen. "I wonder if she wants any-thing. I'll go up and see."

"No," said Adelaide, "She said she wanted to be let alone—and rest. She said she'd be down by the time Mr. Frankland got here."

"She's bearing it pretty well," Ellen suggested, after a little silence.

"It's not like a broken heart," Adelaide explained. "Of course Father meant well—"

"He was a man who always did his duty," admitted Ellen. "But we none of us—loved him—very much."

"He is dead and buried," said James. "We can at least respect his memory."

"We've hardly seen Mother—under that black veil." Ellen went on. "It must have aged her. This long nursing."

"She had help toward the last—a man nurse," said Adelaide.

"Yes, but a long illness is an awful strain—and Mother never was good at nursing. She has surely done her duty," pursued Ellen.

"And now she's entitled to a rest," said James, rising and walking about the room. "I wonder how soon we can close up affairs here—and get rid of this place. There might be enough in it to give her almost a living—properly invested."

Ellen looked out across the dusty stretches of land.

"How I did hate to live here!" she said.

"So did I," said Adelaide.

"So did I," said James.

And they all smiled rather grimly.

"We don't any of us seem to be very—affectionate, about Mother," Adelaide presently admitted. "I don't know why it is—we never were an affectionate family, I guess."

"Nobody could be affectionate with Father," Ellen suggested timidly.

"And Mother—poor Mother! She's had an awful life."

"Mother has always done her duty," said James in a determined voice, "and so did Father, as he saw it. Now we'll do ours."

"Ah," exclaimed Ellen, jumping to her feet. "Here comes the lawyer, I'll call Mother."

She ran quickly upstairs and tapped at her mother's door.

"Mother, oh Mother," she cried. "Mr. Frankland's come."

"I know it," came back a voice from within. "Tell him to go ahead and read the will. I know what's in it. I'll be down in a few minutes."

Ellen went slowly back downstairs with the fine criss-cross of wrinkles showing on her pale forehead again, and delivered her mother's message.

The other two glanced at each other hesitatingly, but Mr. Frankland spoke up briskly.

"Quite natural, of course, under the circumstances. Sorry I couldn't get to the funeral. A case on this morning."

The will was short. The estate was left to be divided among the children in four equal parts, two to the son and one each to the daughters after the mother's legal share had been deducted, if she were still living. In such case they were furthermore directed to provide for their mother while she lived. The estate, as described, consisted of the ranch, the large, rambling house on it, with all the furniture, stock and implements, and some $5,000 in mining stocks.

"That is less than I had supposed," said James.

"This will was made ten years ago," Mr. Frankland explained. "I have done business for your father since that time. He kept his faculties to the end, and I think that you will find that the property has appreciated. Mrs. McPherson has taken excellent care of the ranch, I understand—and has had some boarders."

Both the sisters exchanged pained glances.

"There's an end to all that now," said James.

At this moment, the door opened and a tall black figure, cloaked and veiled, came into the room.

"I'm glad to hear you say that Mr. McPherson kept his faculties to the last, Mr. Frankland," said the widow. "It's true. I didn't come down to hear that old will. It's no good now."

They all turned in their chairs.

"Is there a later will, madam?" inquired the lawyer.

"Not that I know of. Mr. McPherson had no property when he died."

"No property! My dear lady—four years ago he certainly had some."

"Yes, but three years and a-half ago he gave it all to me. Here are the deeds."

There they were, in very truth—formal and correct, and quite simple and clear—for deeds. James R. McPherson, Sr., had assuredly given to his wife the whole estate.

"You remember that was the panic year," she continued. "There was pressure from some of Mr. McPherson's creditors; he thought it would be safer so."

"Why—yes," remarked Mr. Frankland. "I do remember now his advising with me about it. But I thought the step unnecessary."

James cleared his throat.

"Well, Mother, this does complicate matters a little. We were hoping that we could settle up all the business this afternoon—with Mr. Frankland's help—and take you back with us."

"We can't be spared any longer, you see, Mother," said Ellen.

"Can't you deed it back again, Mother," Adelaide suggested, "to James, or to—all of us, so we can get away?"

"Why should I?"

"Now, Mother," Ellen put in persuasively, "we know how badly you feel, and you are nervous and tired, but I told you this morning when we came, that we expected to take you back with us. You know you've been packing—"

"Yes, I've been packing," replied the voice behind the veil.

"I dare say it was safer—to have the property in your name—technically," James admitted, "but now I think it would be the simplest way for you to make it over to me in a lump, and I will see that Father's wishes are carried out to the letter."

"Your father is dead," remarked the voice.

"Yes, Mother, we know—we know how you feel," Ellen ventured.

"I am alive," said Mrs. McPherson.

"Dear Mother, it's very trying to talk business to you at such a time. We all realize it," Adelaide explained with a touch of asperity. "But we told you we couldn't stay as soon as we got here."

"And the business has to be settled," James added conclusively.

"It is settled."

"Perhaps Mr. Frankland can make it clear to you," went on James with forced patience.

"I do not doubt that your mother understands perfectly," murmured the lawyer. "I have always found her a woman of remarkable intelligence."

"Thank you, Mr. Frankland. Possibly you may be able to make my children understand that this property—such as it is—is mine now."

"Why assuredly, assuredly, Mrs. McPherson. We all see that. But we assume, as a matter of course, that you will consider Mr. McPherson's wishes in regard to the disposition of the estate."

"I have considered Mr. McPherson's wishes for thirty years," she replied. "Now, I'll consider mine. I have done my duty since the day I married him. It is eleven thousand days—to-day." The last with sudden intensity.

"But madam, your children—"

"I have no children, Mr. Frankland. I have two daughters and a son. These three grown persons here, grown up, married, having children of their own—or ought to have—were my children. I did my duty by them, and they did their duty by me—and would yet, no doubt." The tone changed suddenly. "But they don't have to. I'm tired of duty."

The little group of listeners looked up, startled.

"You don't know how things have been going on here," the voice went on. "I didn't trouble you with my affairs. But I'll tell you now. When your father saw fit to make over the property to me—to save it—and when he knew that he hadn't many years to live, I took hold of things. I had to have a nurse for your father—and a doctor coming: the house was a sort of hospital, so I made it a little more so. I had half a dozen patients and nurses here—and made money by it. I ran the garden—kept cows—raised my own chickens—worked out-doors—slept out-of-doors. I'm a stronger woman to-day than I ever was in my life!"

She stood up, tall, strong and straight, and drew a deep breath.

"Your father's property amounted to about $8,000 when he died," she continued. "That would be $4,000 to James and $2,000 to each of the girls. That I'm willing to give you now—each of you—in your own name. But if my daughters will take my advice, they'd better let me send them the yearly income—in cash—to spend as they like. It is good for a woman to have some money of her own."

"I think you are right, Mother," said Adelaide.

"Yes indeed," murmured Ellen.

"Don't you need it yourself, Mother?" asked James, with a sudden feeling of tenderness for the stiff figure in black.

"No, James, I shall keep the ranch, you see. I have good reliable help. I've made $2,000 a year—clear—off it so far, and now I've rented it for that to a doctor friend of mine—woman doctor."

"I think you have done remarkably well, Mrs. McPherson—wonderfully well," said Mr. Frankland.

"And you'll have an income of $2,000 a year," said Adelaide incredulously.

"You'll come and live with me, won't you?" ventured Ellen.

"Thank you, my dear, I will not."

"You're more than welcome in my big house," said Adelaide.

"No thank you, my dear."

"I don't doubt Maude will be glad to have you," James rather hesitatingly offered.

"I do. I doubt it very much. No thank you, my dear."

"But what *are* you going to do?"

Ellen seemed genuinely concerned.

"I'm going to do what I never did before. I'm going to *live*!"

With a firm swift step, the tall figure moved to the windows and pulled up the lowered shades. The brilliant Colorado sunshine poured into the room. She threw off the long black veil.

"That's borrowed," she said. "I didn't want to hurt your feelings at the funeral."

She unbuttoned the long black cloak and dropped it at her feet, standing there in the full sunlight, a little flushed and smiling, dressed in a well-made traveling suit of dull mixed colors.

"If you want to know my plans, I'll tell you. I've got $6,000 of my own. I earned it in three years—off my little rancho-sanitarium. One thousand I have put in the savings bank—to bring me back from anywhere on earth, and to put me in an old lady's home if it is necessary. Here is an agreement with a cremation company. They'll import me, if necessary, and have me duly—expurgated—or they don't get the money. But I've got $5,000 to play with, and I'm going to play."

Her daughters looked shocked.

"Why Mother—"

"At your age—"

James drew down his upper lip and looked like his father.

"I knew you wouldn't any of you understand," she continued more quietly. "But it doesn't matter any more. Thirty years I've given you—and your father. Now I'll have thirty years of my own."

"Are you—are you sure you're—well, Mother?" Ellen urged with real anxiety.

Her mother laughed outright.

"Well, really well, never was better, have been doing business up to to-day—good medical testimony that. No question of my sanity, my dears! I want you to grasp the fact that your mother is a Real Person with some interests of her own and half a lifetime yet. The first twenty didn't count for much—I was growing up and couldn't help myself. The last thirty have been—hard. James perhaps realizes that more than you girls, but you all know it. Now, I'm free."

"Where *do* you mean to go, Mother?" James asked.

She looked around the little circle with a serene air of decision and replied.

"To New Zealand. I've always wanted to go there," she pursued. "Now I'm going. And to Australia—and Tasmania—and Madagascar—and Terra del Fuego. I shall be gone some time."

They separated that night—three going East, one West.

IF I WERE A MAN

That was what pretty little Mollie Mathewson always said when Gerald would not do what she wanted him to—which was seldom.

That was what she said this bright morning, with a stamp of her little high-heeled slipper, just because he had made a fuss about that bill, the long one with the "account rendered," which she had forgotten to give him the first time and been afraid to the second—and now he had taken it from the postman himself.

Mollie was "true to type." She was a beautiful instance of what is reverentially called "a true woman." Little, of course—no true woman may be big. Pretty, of course—no true woman could possibly be plain. Whimsical, capricious, charming, changeable, devoted to pretty clothes and always "wearing them well," as the esoteric phrase has it. (This does not refer to the clothes—they do not wear well in the least—but to some special grace of putting them on and carrying them about, granted to but few, it appears.)

She was also a loving wife and a devoted mother; possessed of "the social gift" and the love of "society" that goes with it, and, with all these was fond and proud of her home and managed it as capably as—well, as most women do.

If ever there was a true woman it was Mollie Mathewson, yet she was wishing heart and soul she was a man.

And all of a sudden she was!

She was Gerald, walking down the path so erect and square-shouldered, in a hurry for his morning train, as usual, and, it must be confessed, in something of a temper.

Her own words were ringing in her ears—not only the "last word," but several that had gone before, and she was holding her lips tight shut, not to say something she would be sorry for. But instead of acquiescence in the position taken by that angry little figure on the veranda, what she felt was a sort of superior pride, a sympathy as with weakness, a feeling that "I must be gentle with her," in spite of the temper.

A man! Really a man; with only enough subconscious memory of herself remaining to make her recognize the differences.

At first there was a funny sense of size and weight and extra thickness, the feet and hands seemed strangely large, and her long, straight, free legs swung forward at a gait that made her feel as if on stilts.

This presently passed, and in its place, growing all day, wherever she went, came a new and delightful feeling of being *the right size*.

Everything fitted now. Her back snugly against the seat-back, her feet comfortably on the floor. Her feet? . . . His feet! She studied them carefully. Never before, since her early school days, had she felt such freedom and comfort as to feet—they were firm and solid on the ground when she walked; quick, springy, safe—as when, moved by an unrecognizable impulse, she had run after, caught, and swung aboard the car.

Another impulse fished in a convenient pocket for change—instantly, automatically, bringing forth a nickel for the conductor and a penny for the newsboy.

These pockets came as a revelation. Of course she had known they were there, had counted them, made fun of them, mended them, even envied them; but she never had dreamed of how it *felt* to have pockets.

Behind her newspaper she let her consciousness, that odd mingled consciousness, rove from pocket to pocket, realizing the armored assurance of having all those things at hand, instantly get-at-able, ready to meet emergencies. The cigar case gave her a warm feeling of comfort—it was full; the firmly held fountain-pen, safe unless she stood on her head; the keys, pencils, letters, documents, notebook, checkbook, bill folder—all at once, with a deep rushing sense of power and pride, she felt what she had never felt before in all her life—the possession of money, of her own earned money—hers to give or to withhold; not to beg for, tease for, wheedle for—hers.

That bill—why, if it had come to her—to him, that is—he would have paid it as a matter of course, and never mentioned it—to her.

Then, being he, sitting there so easily and firmly with his money in his pockets, she wakened to his life-long consciousness about money. Boyhood—its desires and dreams, ambitions. Young manhood—working tremendously for the wherewithal to make a home—for her. The present years with all their net of cares and hopes and dangers; the present moment, when he needed every cent for special plans of great importance, and this bill, long over-due and demanding payment, meant an amount of inconvenience wholly unnecessary if it had been given him when it first came; also, the man's keen dislike of that "account rendered."

"Women have no business sense!" she found herself saying, "and all that money just for hats—idiotic, useless, ugly things!"

With that she began to see the hats of the women in the car as she had never seen hats before. The men's seemed normal, dignified, becoming, with enough variety for personal taste, and with distinction in style and in age, such as she had never noticed before. But the women's—

With the eyes of a man and the brain of a man; with the memory of a whole lifetime of free action wherein the hat, close-fitting on cropped hair, had been no handicap; she now perceived the hats of women.

The massed fluffed hair was at once attractive and foolish, and on that hair, at every angle, in all colors, tipped, twisted, tortured into every crooked shape, made of any substance chance might offer, perched these formless objects. Then, on their formlessness the trimmings—these squirts of stiff feathers, these violent outstanding bows of glistening ribbon, these swaying, projecting masses of plumage which tormented the faces of bystanders.

Never in all her life had she imagined that this idolized millinery could look, to those who paid for it, like the decorations of an insane monkey.

And yet, when there came into the car a little woman, as foolish as any, but pretty and sweet-looking, up rose Gerald Mathewson and gave her his seat; and, later, when there came in a handsome red-cheeked girl, whose hat was wilder, more violent in color and eccentric in shape than any other; when she stood nearby and her soft curling plumes swept his cheek once and again, he felt a sense of sudden pleasure at the intimate tickling touch—and she, deep down within, felt such a wave of shame as might well drown a thousand hats forever.

When he took his train, his seat in the smoking car, she had a new surprise. All about him were the other men, commuters too, and many of them friends of his.

To her, they would have been distinguished as "Mary Wade's husband," "the man Belle Grant is engaged to," "that rich Mr. Shopworth," or "that pleasant Mr. Beale." And they would all have lifted their hats to her, bowed, made polite conversation if near enough—especially Mr. Beale.

Now came the feeling of open-eyed acquaintance, of knowing men—as they were. The mere amount of this knowledge was a surprise to her; the whole background of talk from boyhood up, the gossip of barber-shop and club, the conversation of morning and evening hours on trains, the knowledge of political affiliation, of business standing and prospects, of character—in a light she had never known before.

They came and talked to Gerald, one and another. He seemed quite popular. And as they talked, with this new memory and new understanding, an understanding which seemed to include all these men's minds, there poured in on the submerged consciousness beneath a new, a startling knowledge—what men really think of women.

Good, average, American men were there; married men for the most part, and happy—as happiness goes in general. In the minds of each and all there seemed to be a two-story department, quite apart from the rest of their ideas, a separate place where they kept their thoughts and feelings about women.

In the upper half were the tenderest emotions, the most exquisite ideals, the sweetest memories, all lovely sentiments as to "home" and "mother," all delicate admiring adjectives, a sort of sanctuary, where a veiled statue, blindly adored, shared place with beloved yet commonplace experiences.

In the lower half—here that buried consciousness woke to keen distress—they kept quite another assortment of ideas. Here, even in this clean-minded husband of hers, was the memory of stories told at men's dinners, of worse ones overheard in street or car, of base traditions, coarse epithets, gross experiences—known, though not shared.

And all these in the department "woman," while in the rest of the mind—here was new knowledge indeed.

The world opened before her. Not the world she had been reared in—where Home had covered all the map, almost, and the rest had been "foreign," or "unexplored country"—but the world as it was, man's world, as made, lived in, and seen, by men.

It was dizzying. To see the houses that fled so fast across the car window, in terms of builders' bills, or of some technical insight into materials and methods; to see a passing village with lamentable knowledge of who "owned it"—and of how its Boss was rapidly aspiring to State power, or of how that kind of paving was a failure; to see shops, not as mere exhibitions of desirable objects, but as business ventures, many mere sinking ships, some promising a profitable voyage—this new world bewildered her.

She—as Gerald—had already forgotten about that bill, over which she—as Mollie—was still crying at home. Gerald was "talking business" with this man, "talking politics" with that; and now sympathizing with the carefully withheld troubles of a neighbor.

Mollie had always sympathized with the neighbor's wife before.

She began to struggle violently with this large dominant masculine consciousness. She remembered with sudden clearness things she had read, lectures she had heard; and resented with increasing intensity this serene masculine preoccupation with the male point of view.

Mr. Miles, the little fussy man who lived on the other side of the street, was talking now. He had a large complacent wife; Mollie had never liked her much, but had always thought him rather nice—he was so punctilious in small courtesies.

And here he was talking to Gerald—such talk!

"Had to come in here," he said. "Gave my seat to a dame who was bound to have it. There's nothing they won't get when they make up their minds to it—eh?"

"No fear!" said the big man in the next seat. "They haven't much mind to make up, you know—and if they do, they'll change it."

"The real danger," began the Rev. Alfred Smythe, the new Episcopal clergyman, a thin, nervous, tall man, with a face several centuries behind the times, "is that they will overstep the limits of their God-appointed sphere."

"Their natural limits ought to hold 'em, I think," said cheerful Dr. Jones. "You can't get around physiology, I tell you."

"I've never seen any limits, myself, not to what they want, anyhow," said Mr. Miles. "Merely a rich husband and a fine house and no end of bonnets and dresses, and the latest thing in motors, and a few diamonds—and so on. Keeps us pretty busy."

There was a tired gray man across the aisle. He had a very nice wife, always beautifully dressed, and three unmarried daughters, also beautifully dressed—Mollie knew them. She knew he worked hard too, and she looked at him now a little anxiously.

But he smiled cheerfully.

"Do you good, Miles," he said. "What else would a man work for? A good woman is about the best thing on earth."

"And a bad one's the worst, that's sure," responded Miles.

"She's a pretty weak sister, viewed professionally," Dr. Jones averred with solemnity, and the Rev. Alfred Smythe added, "She brought evil into the world."

Gerald Mathewson sat up straight. Something was stirring in him which he did not recognize—yet could not resist.

"Seems to me we all talk like Noah," he suggested drily. "Or the ancient Hindu scriptures. Women have their limitations, but so do we, God knows. Haven't we known girls in school and college just as smart as we were?"

"They cannot play our games," coldly replied the clergyman.

Gerald measured his meager proportions with a practiced eye.

"I never was particularly good at football myself," he modestly admitted, "but I've known women who could outlast a man in all-round endurance. Besides—life isn't spent in athletics!"

This was sadly true. They all looked down the aisle where a heavy ill-dressed man with a bad complexion sat alone. He had held the top of the columns once, with headlines and photographs. Now he earned less than any of them.

"It's time we woke up," pursued Gerald, still inwardly urged to unfamiliar speech. "Women are pretty much *people*, seems to me. I know they dress like fools—but who's to blame for that? We invent all those idiotic hats of theirs, and design their crazy fashions, and, what's more, if a woman is courageous enough to wear common-sense clothes—and shoes—which of us wants to dance with her?

"Yes, we blame them for grafting on us, but are we willing to let our wives work? We are not. It hurts our pride, that's all. We are always criticizing them for making mercenary marriages, but what do we call a girl who marries a chump with no money? Just a poor fool, that's all. And they know it.

"As for Mother Eve—I wasn't there and can't deny the story, but I will say this. If she brought evil into the world, we men have had the lion's share of keeping it going ever since—how about that?"

They drew into the city, and all day long in his business, Gerald was vaguely conscious of new views, strange feelings, and the submerged Mollie learned and learned.

MR. PEEBLES' HEART

He was lying on the sofa in the homely, bare little sitting room; an uncomfortable stiff sofa, too short, too sharply upcurved at the end, but still a sofa, whereon one could, at a pinch, sleep.

Thereon Mr. Peebles slept, this hot still afternoon; slept uneasily, snoring a little, and twitching now and then, as one in some obscure distress.

Mrs. Peebles had creaked down the front stairs and gone off on some superior errands of her own; with a good palm-leaf fan for a weapon, a silk umbrella for a defense.

"Why don't you come too, Joan?" she had urged her sister, as she dressed herself for departure.

"Why should I, Emma? It's much more comfortable at home. I'll keep Arthur company when he wakes up."

"Oh, Arthur! He'll go back to the store as soon as he's had his nap. And I'm sure Mrs. Older's paper'll be real interesting. If you're going to live here, you ought to take an interest in the club, seems to me."

"I'm going to live here as a doctor—not as a lady of leisure, Em. You go on—I'm contented."

So Mrs. Emma Peebles sat in the circle of the Ellsworth Ladies' Home Club, and improved her mind, while Dr. J. R. Bascom softly descended to the sitting room in search of a book she had been reading.

There was Mr. Peebles, still uneasily asleep. She sat down quietly in a cane-seated rocker by the window and watched him awhile; first professionally, then with a deeper human interest.

Baldish, grayish, stoutish, with a face that wore a friendly smile for customers, and showed grave, set lines that deepened about the corners of his mouth when there was no one to serve; very ordinary in dress, in carriage, in appearance was Arthur Peebles at fifty. He was not "the slave of love" of the Arab tale, but the slave of duty.

If ever a man had done his duty—as he saw it—he had done his, always.

His duty—as he saw it—was carrying women. First his mother, a comfortable competent person, who had run the farm after her husband's death, and added to their income by Summer boarders until Arthur was old enough to "support her." Then she sold the old place and moved into the village to "make a home for Arthur," who incidentally provided a hired girl to perform the manual labor of that process.

He worked in the store. She sat on the piazza and chatted with her neighbors.

He took care of his mother until he was nearly thirty, when she left him finally; and then he installed another woman to make a home for him—also with the help of the hired girl. A pretty, care-less, clinging little person he married, who had long made mute appeal to his strength and carefulness, and she had continued to cling uninterruptedly to this day.

Incidentally a sister had clung until she married, another until she died; and his children—two daughters—had clung also. Both the daughters were married in due time, with sturdy young hus-bands to cling to in their turn; and now there remained only his wife to carry, a lighter load than he had ever known—at least nu-merically.

But either he was tired, very tired, or Mrs. Peebles' tendrils had grown tougher, tighter, more tenacious, with age. He did not com-plain of it. Never had it occurred to him in all these years that there was any other thing for a man to do than to carry whatsoever women came within range of lawful relationship.

Had Dr. Joan been—shall we say—carriageable—he would have cheerfully added her to the list, for he liked her extremely. She was different from any woman he had ever known, different from her sister as day from night, and, in lesser degree, from all the female inhabitants of Ellsworth.

She had left home at an early age, against her mother's will, absolutely run away; but when the whole countryside rocked with gossip and sought for the guilty man—it appeared that she had merely gone to college. She worked her way through, learning more, far more, than was taught in the curriculum; became a trained nurse, studied medicine, and had long since made good in her profession. There were even rumors that she must be "pretty well fixed" and about to "retire"; but others held that she must have failed, really, or she never would have come back home to settle.

Whatever the reason, she was there, a welcome visitor—a source of real pride to her sister, and of indefinable satisfaction to her brother-in-law. In her friendly atmosphere he felt a stirring of long unused powers; he remembered funny stories, and how to tell them; he felt a revival of interests he had thought quite outlived, early interests in the big world's movements.

"Of all unimpressive, unattractive, *good* little men—" she was thinking, as she watched, when one of his arms dropped off the slippery side of the sofa, the hand thumped on the floor, and he awoke and sat up hastily with an air of one caught off duty.

"Don't sit up as suddenly as that, Arthur, it's bad for your heart."

"Nothing the matter with my heart, is there?" he asked with his ready smile.

"I don't know—haven't examined it. Now—sit still—you know there's nobody in the store this afternoon—and if there is, Jake can attend to 'em."

"Where's Emma?"

"Oh, Emma's gone to her 'club' or something—wanted me to go, but I'd rather talk with you."

He looked pleased but incredulous, having a high opinion of that club, and a low one of himself.

"Look here," she pursued suddenly, after he had made himself comfortable with a drink from the swinging ice-pitcher, and another big cane rocker, "what would you like to do if you could?"

"Travel!" said Mr. Peebles, with equal suddenness. He saw her astonishment. "Yes, travel! I've always wanted to—since I was a kid. No use! We never could, you see. And now—even if we could— Emma hates it." He sighed resignedly.

"Do you like to keep store?" she asked sharply.

"*Like* it?" He smiled at her cheerfully, bravely, but with a queer blank hopeless background underneath. He shook his head gravely. "No, I do not, Joan. Not a little bit. But what of that?"

They were still for a little, and then she put another question. "What would you have chosen—for a profession—if you had been free to choose?"

His answer amazed her threefold; from its character, its sharp promptness, its deep feeling. It was in one word—"Music!"

"Music!" she repeated. "Music! Why I didn't know you played—or cared about it."

"When I was a youngster," he told her, his eyes looking far off through the vine-shaded window, "Father brought home a guitar— and said it was for the one that learned to play it first. He meant the girls of course. As a matter of fact I learned it first—but I didn't get it. That's all the music I ever had," he added. "And there's not much to listen to here, unless you count what's in church. I'd have a Victrola—but—" he laughed a little shamefacedly, "Emma says if I bring one into the house she'll smash it. She says they're worse than cats. Tastes differ, you know, Joan."

Again he smiled at her, a droll smile, a little pinched at the corners. "Well—I must be getting back to business."

She let him go, and turned her attention to her own business, with some seriousness.

"Emma," she proposed, a day or two later, "how would you like it if I should board here—live here, I mean, right along?"

"I should hope you would," her sister replied. "It would look nice to have you practicing in this town and not live with me—all the sister I've got."

"Do you think Arthur would like it?"

"Of course he would! Besides—even if he didn't—you're *my* sister—and this is my house. He put it in my name, long ago."

"I see," said Joan, "I see."

Then after a little—"Emma, are you contented?"

"Contented? Why, of course I am. It would be a sin not to be. The girls are well married—I'm happy about them both. This is a real comfortable house, and it runs itself—my Matilda is a jewel if ever there was one. And she don't mind company—likes to do for 'em. Yes—I've nothing to worry about."

"Your health's good—that I can see," her sister remarked, regarding with approval her clear complexion and bright eyes.

"Yes—I've nothing to complain about—that I know of," Emma admitted, but among her causes for thankfulness she did not even mention Arthur, nor seem to think of him till Dr. Joan seriously inquired her opinion as to his state of health.

"His health? Arthur's? Why he's always well. Never had a sick day in his life—except now and then he's had a kind of a breakdown," she added as an afterthought.

Dr. Joan Bascom made acquaintances in the little town, both professional and social. She entered upon her practice, taking it over from the failing hands of old Dr. Braithwaite, her first friend, and feeling very much at home in the old place. Her sister's house furnished two comfortable rooms downstairs, and a large bedroom above. "There's plenty of room now the girls are gone," they both assured her.

Then, safely ensconced and established, Dr. Joan began a secret campaign to alienate the affections of her brother-in-law. Not for herself—oh no! If ever in earlier years she had felt the need of someone to cling to, it was long, long ago. What she sought was to free him from the tentacles—without reentanglement.

She bought a noble gramophone with a set of first-class records, told her sister smilingly that she didn't have to listen, and Emma would sit sulkily in the back room on the other side of the house, while her husband and sister enjoyed the music. She grew used to it in time, she said, and drew nearer, sitting on the porch perhaps; but Arthur had his long-denied pleasure in peace.

It seemed to stir him strangely. He would rise and walk, a new fire in his eyes, a new firmness about the patient mouth, and Dr. Joan fed the fire with talk and books and pictures, with study of maps and sailing lists and accounts of economical tours.

"I don't see what you two find so interesting in all that stuff about music and those composers," Emma would say. "I never did care for foreign parts—musicians are all foreigners, anyway."

Arthur never quarrelled with her; he only grew quiet and lost that interested sparkle of the eye when she discussed the subject.

Then one day, Mrs. Peebles being once more at her club, content and yet aspiring, Dr. Joan made bold attack upon her brother-in-law's principles.

"Arthur," she said, "have you confidence in me as a physician?"

"I have," he said briskly. "Rather consult you than any doctor I ever saw."

"Will you let me prescribe for you if I tell you you need it?"

"I sure will."

"Will you take the prescription?"

"Of course I'll take it—no matter how it tastes."

"Very well. I prescribe two years in Europe."

He stared at her, startled.

"I mean it. You're in a more serious condition than you think. I want you to cut clear—and travel. For two years."

He still stared at her. "But Emma—"

"Never mind about Emma. She owns the house. She's got enough money to clothe herself—and I'm paying enough board to keep everything going. Emma don't need you."

"But the store—"

"Sell the store."

"Sell it! That's easy said. Who'll buy it?"

"I will. Yes—I mean it. You give me easy terms and I'll take the store off your hands. It ought to be worth seven or eight thousand dollars, oughtn't it—stock and all?"

He assented, dumbly.

"Well, I'll buy it. You can live abroad for two years, on a couple of thousand, or twenty-five hundred—a man of your tastes. You know those accounts we've read—it can be done easily. Then you'll have five thousand or so to come back to—and can invest it in something better than that shop. Will you do it—?"

He was full of protests, of impossibilities.

She met them firmly. "Nonsense! You can too. She doesn't need you, at all—she may later. No—the girls don't need you—and they may later. Now is your time—*now*. They say the Japanese sow their wild oats after they're fifty—suppose you do! You can't be so *very* wild on that much money, but you can spend a year in Germany—learn the language—go to the opera—take walking trips in the Tyrol—in Switzerland; see England, Scotland, Ireland, France, Belgium, Denmark—you can do a lot in two years."

He stared at her fascinated.

"Why not? Why not be your own man for once in your life—do what *you* want to—not what other people want you to?"

He murmured something as to "duty"—but she took him up sharply.

"If ever a man on earth has done his duty, Arthur Peebles, you have. You've taken care of your mother while she was perfectly able to take care of herself; of your sisters, long after they were; and of a wholly able-bodied wife. At present she does not need you the least bit in the world."

"Now that's pretty strong," he protested. "Emma'd miss me—I know she'd miss me—"

Dr. Bascom looked at him affectionately. "There couldn't a better thing happen to Emma—or to you, for that matter—than to have her miss you, real hard."

"I know she'd never consent to my going," he insisted, wistfully.

"That's the advantage of my interference," she replied serenely. "You surely have a right to choose your doctor, and your doctor is seriously concerned about your health and orders foreign travel—rest—change—and music."

"But Emma—"

"Now, Arthur Peebles, forget Emma for a while—I'll take care of her. And look here—let me tell you another thing—a change like this will do her good."

He stared at her, puzzled.

"I mean it. Having you away will give her a chance to stand up. Your letters—about those places—will interest her. She may want to go, sometime. Try it."

He wavered at this. Those who too patiently serve as props sometimes underrate the possibilities of the vine.

"Don't discuss it with her—that will make endless trouble. Fix up the papers for my taking over the store—I'll draw you a check, and you get the next boat for England, and make your plans from there. Here's a banking address that will take care of your letters and checks—"

The thing was done! Done before Emma had time to protest. Done, and she left gasping to upbraid her sister.

Joan was kind, patient, firm as adamant.

"But how it *looks,* Joan—what will people think of me! To be left deserted—like this!"

"People will think according to what we tell them and to how you behave, Emma Peebles. If you simply say that Arthur was far from well and I advised him to take a foreign trip—and if you forget yourself for once, and show a little natural feeling for him—you'll find no trouble at all."

For her own sake, the selfish woman, made more so by her husband's unselfishness, accepted the position. Yes—Arthur had gone abroad for his health—Dr. Bascom was much worried about him—chance of a complete breakdown, she said. Wasn't it pretty sudden? Yes—the doctor hurried him off. He was in England—going to take a walking trip—she did not know when he'd be back. The store? He'd sold it.

Dr. Bascom engaged a competent manager who ran that store

successfully, more so than had the unenterprising Mr. Peebles. She made it a good paying business, which he ultimately bought back and found no longer a burden.

But Emma was the principal charge. With talk, with books, with Arthur's letters followed carefully on maps, with trips to see the girls, trips in which traveling lost its terrors, with the care of the house, and the boarder or two they took "for company," she so ploughed and harrowed that long-fallow field of Emma's mind that at last it began to show signs of fruitfulness.

Arthur went away leaving a stout, dull woman who clung to him as if he was a necessary vehicle or beast of burden—and thought scarcely more of his constant service.

He returned younger, stronger, thinner, an alert vigorous man, with a mind enlarged, refreshed, and stimulated. He had found himself.

And he found her, also, most agreeably changed, having developed not merely tentacles, but feet of her own to stand on.

When next the thirst for travel seized him, she thought she'd go too, and proved unexpectedly pleasant as a companion.

But neither of them could ever wring from Dr. Bascom any definite diagnosis of Mr. Peebles' threatening disease. "A dangerous enlargement of the heart" was all she would commit herself to, and when he denied any such trouble now, she gravely wagged her head and said it had "responded to treatment."

THE UNNATURAL MOTHER

"Don't tell me!" said old Mis' Briggs, with a forbidding shake of the head. "No mother that was a mother would desert her own child for anything on earth!"

"And leaving it a care on the town, too!" put in Susannah Jacobs. "As if we hadn't enough to do to take care of our own!"

Miss Jacobs was a well-to-do old maid, owning a comfortable farm and homestead, and living alone with an impoverished cousin acting as general servant, companion, and protégée. Mis' Briggs, on the contrary, had had thirteen children, five of whom remained to bless her, so that what maternal feeling Miss Jacobs might lack, Mis' Briggs could certainly supply.

"I should think," piped little Martha Ann Simmons, the village dressmaker, "that she might a saved her young one first and then tried what she could do for the town."

Martha had been married, had lost her husband, and had one sickly boy to care for.

The youngest Briggs girl, still unmarried at thirty-six, and in her mother's eyes a most tender infant, now ventured to make a remark.

"You don't any of you seem to think what she did for all of us—if she hadn't left hers we should all have lost ours, sure."

"You ain't no call to judge, Maria 'Melia," her mother hastened to reply. "You've no children of your own, and you can't judge of a mother's duty. No mother ought to leave her child, whatever happens. The Lord gave it to her to take care of—he never gave her other people's. You needn't tell me!"

"She was an unnatural mother," repeated Miss Jacobs harshly, "as I said to begin with!"

"What is the story?" asked the City Boarder. The City Boarder was interested in stories from a business point of view, but they did not know that. "What did this woman do?" she asked.

There was no difficulty in eliciting particulars. The difficulty was rather in discriminating amidst their profusion and contradictoriness. But when the City Boarder got it clear in her mind, it was somewhat as follows:

The name of the much-condemned heroine was Esther Greenwood, and she lived and died here in Toddsville.

Toddsville was a mill village. The Todds lived on a beautiful eminence overlooking the little town, as the castles of robber barons on the Rhine used to overlook their little towns. The mills and the mill hands' houses were built close along the bed of the river. They had to be pretty close, because the valley was a narrow one, and the bordering hills were too steep for travel, but the water power was fine. Above the village was the reservoir, filling the entire valley save for a narrow road beside it, a fair blue smiling lake, edged with lilies and blue flag, rich in pickerel and perch. This lake gave them fish, it gave them ice, it gave the power that ran the mills that gave the town its bread. Blue Lake was both useful and ornamental.

In this pretty and industrious village Esther had grown up, the somewhat neglected child of a heart-broken widower. He had lost a young wife, and three fair babies before her—this one was left him, and he said he meant that she should have all the chance there was.

"That was what ailed her in the first place!" they all eagerly explained to the City Boarder. "She never knew what 'twas to have a mother, and she grew up a regular tomboy! Why, she used to roam the country for miles around, in all weather like an Injun! And her father wouldn't take no advice!"

This topic lent itself to eager discussion. The recreant father, it appeared, was a doctor, not their accepted standby, the resident physician of the neighborhood, but an alien doctor, possessed of "views."

"You never heard such things as he advocated," Miss Jacobs explained. "He wouldn't give no medicines, hardly; said 'nature' did the curing—he couldn't."

"And he couldn't either—that was clear," Mrs. Briggs agreed. "Look at his wife and children dying on his hands, as it were! 'Physician, heal thyself,' I say."

"But, Mother," Maria Amelia put in, "she was an invalid when he married her, they say; and those children died of polly—polly—what's that thing that nobody can help?"

"That may all be so," Miss Jacobs admitted, "but all the same, it's a doctor's business to give medicine. If 'nature' was all that was wanted, we needn't have any doctor at all!"

"I believe in medicine and plenty of it. I always gave my children a good clearance, spring and fall, whether anything ailed 'em or not, just to be on the safe side. And if there was anything the matter with 'em, they had plenty more. I never had anything to reproach myself with on that score," stated Mrs. Briggs, firmly. Then as a sort of concession to the family graveyard, she added piously, "The Lord giveth and the Lord taketh away."

"You should have seen the way he dressed that child!" pursued Miss Jacobs. "It was a reproach to the town. Why, you couldn't tell at a distance whether it was a boy or a girl. And barefoot! He let that child go barefoot till she was so big we was actually mortified to see her."

It appeared that a wild, healthy childhood had made Esther very different in her early womanhood from the meek, well-behaved damsels of the little place. She was well enough liked by those who knew her at all, and the children of the place adored her, but the worthy matrons shook their heads and prophesied no good of a girl who was "queer."

She was described with rich detail in reminiscence, how she wore her hair short till she was fifteen—"just shingled like a boy's—it did seem a shame that girl had no mother to look after her—and her clo'se was almost a scandal, even when she did put on shoes and stockings. Just gingham—brown gingham—and *short!*"

"I think she was a real nice girl," said Maria Amelia. "I can remember her just as well! She was so *nice* to us children. She was five or six years older than I was, and most girls that age won't have anything to do with little ones. But she was kind and pleasant. She'd take us berrying and on all sorts of walks, and teach us new games and tell us things. I don't remember anyone that ever did us the good she did!"

Maria Amelia's thin chest heaved with emotion, and there were tears in her eyes; but her mother took her up somewhat sharply.

"That sounds well I must say—right before your own mother that's toiled and slaved for you! It's all very well for a young thing that's got nothing on earth to do to make herself agreeable to young ones. That poor blinded father of hers never taught her to do the work a girl should—naturally he couldn't."

"At least he might have married again and given her another mother," said Susannah Jacobs, with decision, with so much decision, in fact, that the City Boarder studied her expression for a moment and concluded that if this recreant father had not married again it was not for lack of opportunity.

Mrs. Simmons cast an understanding glance upon Miss Jacobs, and nodded wisely.

"Yes, he ought to have done that, of course. A man's not fit to bring up children, anyhow. How can they? Mothers have the instinct—that is, all natural mothers have. But, dear me! There's some as don't seem to *be* mothers—even when they have a child!"

"You're quite right, Mis' Simmons," agreed the mother of thirteen. "It's a divine instinct, I say. I'm sorry for the child that lacks it. Now this Esther. We always knew she wasn't like other girls—she never seemed to care for dress and company and things girls naturally do, but was always philandering over the hills with a parcel of young ones. There wasn't a child in town but would run after her. She made more trouble 'n a little in families, the young ones quotin' what Aunt Esther said, and tellin' what Aunt Esther did to their own mothers, and she only a young girl. Why, she actually seemed to care more for them children than she did for beaux or anything—it wasn't natural!"

"But she did marry?" pursued the City Boarder.

"Marry! Yes, she married finally. We all thought she never would, but she did. After the things her father taught her, it did seem as if he'd ruined *all* her chances. It's simply terrible the way that girl was trained."

"Him being a doctor," put in Mrs. Simmons, "made it different, I suppose."

"Doctor or no doctor," Miss Jacobs rigidly interposed, "it was a crying shame to have a young girl so instructed."

"Maria 'Melia," said her mother, "I want you should get me my smelling salts. They're up in the spare chamber, I believe. When your Aunt Marcia was here she had one of her spells—don't you remember?—and she asked for salts. Look in the top bureau drawer—they must be there."

Maria Amelia, thirty-six but unmarried, withdrew dutifully, and the other ladies drew closer to the City Boarder.

"It's the most shocking thing I ever heard of," murmured Mrs. Briggs. "Do you know he—a father—actually taught his daughter how babies come!"

There was a breathless hush.

"He did," eagerly chimed in the little dressmaker. "All the particulars. It was perfectly awful!"

"He said," continued Mrs. Briggs, "that he expected her to be a mother and that she ought to understand what was before her!"

"He was waited on by a committee of ladies from the church, married ladies, all older than he was," explained Miss Jacobs severely. "They told him it was creating a scandal in the town—and what do you think he said?"

There was another breathless silence.

Above, the steps of Maria Amelia were heard, approaching the stairs.

"It ain't there, Ma!"

"Well, you look in the highboy and in the top drawer; they're somewhere up there," her mother replied.

Then, in a sepulchral whisper:

"He told us—yes, ma'am, I was on that committee—he told us that until young women knew what was before them as mothers, they would not do their duty in choosing a father for their children! That was his expression—'choosing a father'! A nice thing for a young girl to be thinking of—a father for her children!"

"Yes, and more than that," inserted Miss Jacobs, who, though not on the committee, seemed familiar with its workings. "He told them—" But Mrs. Briggs waved her aside and continued swiftly—

"He taught that innocent girl about—the Bad Disease! Actually!"

"He did!" said the dressmaker. "It got out, too, all over town. There wasn't a man here would have married her after that."

Miss Jacobs insisted on taking up the tale. "I understand that he said it was 'to protect her'! Protect her, indeed! Against matrimony! As if any man alive would want to marry a young girl who knew all the evil of life! I was brought up differently, I assure you!"

"Young girls should be kept innocent!" Mrs. Briggs solemnly proclaimed. "Why, when I was married I knew no more what was before me than a babe unborn, and my girls were all brought up so, too!"

Then, as Maria Amelia returned with the salts, she continued more loudly. "But she did marry after all. And a mighty queer husband she got, too. He was an artist or something, made pictures for the magazines and such as that, and they do say she met him first out in the hills. That's the first 'twas known of it here, anyhow—them two traipsing about all over; him with his painting things! They married and just settled down to live with her father, for she vowed she wouldn't leave him; and he said it didn't make no difference where he lived, he took his business with him."

"They seemed very happy together," said Maria Amelia.

"Happy! Well, they might have been, I suppose. It was a pretty

queer family, I think." And her mother shook her head in retrospec-
tion. "They got on all right for a while; but the old man died, and
those two—well, I don't call it housekeeping—the way they lived!"

"No," said Miss Jacobs. "They spent more time out-of-doors
than they did in the house. She followed him around everywhere.
And for open lovemaking—"

They all showed deep disapproval at this memory. All but the
City Boarder and Maria Amelia.

"She had one child, a girl," continued Mrs. Briggs, "and it was
just shocking to see how she neglected that child from the begin-
nin'. She never seemed to have no maternal feelin' at all!"

"But I thought you said she was very fond of children," remon-
strated the City Boarder.

"Oh, *children,* yes. She'd take up with any dirty-faced brat in
town, even them Canucks. I've seen her again and again with a
whole swarm of the mill hands' young ones round her, goin' on
some picnic or other—'open air school,' she used to call it—*such*
notions as she had. But when it come to her own child! Why—"
Here the speaker's voice sank to a horrified hush. "She never had no
baby clo'se for it! Not a single sock!"

The City Boarder was interested. "Why, what did she do with the
little thing?"

"The Lord knows!" answered old Mis' Briggs. "She never would
let us hardly see it when 'twas little. 'Shamed to, I don't doubt. But
that's strange feelin's for a mother. Why, I was so proud of my babies! And I kept 'em lookin' so pretty! I'd 'a sat up all night and
sewed and washed, but I'd 'a had my children look well!" And the
poor old eyes filled with tears as she thought of the eight little
graves in the churchyard, which she never failed to keep looking
pretty, even now. "She just let that young one roll round in the grass
like a puppy with hardly nothin' on! Why, a squaw does better. She
does keep 'em done up for a spell! That child was treated worse 'n
an Injun! We all done what we could, of course. We felt it no more
'n right. But she was real hateful about it, and we had to let her be."

"The child died?" asked the City Boarder.

"Died! Dear no! That's it you saw going by; a great strappin' girl she is, too, and promisin' to grow up well, thanks to Mrs. Stone's taking her. Mrs. Stone always thought a heap of Esther. It's a mercy to the child that she lost her mother, I do believe! How she ever survived that kind of treatment beats all! Why, that woman never seemed to have the first spark of maternal feeling to the end! She seemed just as fond of the other young ones after she had her own as she was before, and that's against nature. The way it happened was this. You see, they lived up the valley nearer to the lake than the village. He was away, and was coming home that night, it seems, driving from Drayton along the lake road. And she set out to meet him. She must 'a walked up to the dam to look for him; and we think maybe she saw the team clear across the lake. Maybe she thought he could get to the house and save little Esther in time—that's the only explanation we ever could put on it. But this is what she did; and you can judge for yourselves if any mother in her senses *could* 'a done such a thing! You see 'twas the time of that awful disaster, you've read of it, likely, that destroyed three villages. Well, she got to the dam and seen that 'twas givin' way—she was always great for knowin' all such things. And she just turned and ran. Jake Elder was up on the hill after a stray cow, and he seen her go. He was too far off to imagine what ailed her, but he said he never saw a woman run so in his life.

"And, if you'll believe it, she run right by her own house—never stopped—never looked at it. Just run for the village. Of course, she may have lost her head with the fright, but that wasn't like her. No, I think she had made up her mind to leave that innocent baby to die! She just ran down here and give warnin', and, of course, we sent word down valley on horseback, and there was no lives lost in all three villages. She started to run back as soon as we was 'roused, but 'twas too late then.

"Jake saw it all, though he was too far off to do a thing. He said he couldn't stir a foot, it was so awful. He seen the wagon drivin' along as nice as you please till it got close to the dam, and then Greenwood seemed to see the danger and shipped up like mad. He was the father, you know. But he wasn't quite in time—the dam give way and the water went over him like a tidal wave. She was almost to the gate when it struck the house and her—and we never found her body nor his for days and days. They was washed clear down river.

"Their house was strong, and it stood a little high and had some big trees between it and the lake, too. It was moved off the place and brought up against the side of the stone church down yonder, but 'twant wholly in pieces. And that child was found swimmin' round in its bed, most drowned, but not quite. The wonder is, it didn't die of a cold, but it's here yet—must have a strong constitution. Their folks never did nothing for it—so we had to keep it here."

"Well, now, Mother," said Maria Amelia Briggs. "It does seem to me that she did her duty. You know yourself that if she hadn't give warnin' all three of the villages would 'a been cleaned out—a matter of fifteen hundred people. And if she'd stopped to lug that child, she couldn't have got here in time. Don't you believe she was thinkin' of those mill-hands' children?"

"Maria 'Melia, I'm ashamed of you!" said old Mis' Briggs. "But you ain't married and ain't a mother. A mother's duty is to her own child! She neglected her own to look after other folks'—the Lord never gave her them other children to care for!"

"Yes," said Miss Jacobs, "and here's her child, a burden on the town! She was an unnatural mother!"

HERLAND

CHAPTER 1

A NOT UNNATURAL ENTERPRISE

This is written from memory, unfortunately. If I could have brought with me the material I so carefully prepared, this would be a very different story. Whole books full of notes, carefully copied records, first-hand descriptions, and the pictures—that's the worst loss. We had some bird's-eyes of the cities and parks; a lot of lovely views of streets, of buildings, outside and in, and some of those gorgeous gardens, and, most important of all, of the women themselves.

Nobody will ever believe how they looked. Descriptions aren't any good when it comes to women, and I never was good at descriptions anyhow. But it's got to be done somehow; the rest of the world needs to know about that country. . . .

It began this way. There were three of us, classmates and friends—Terry O. Nicholson (we used to call him the Old Nick, with good reason), Jeff Margrave, and I, Vandyck Jennings.

We had known each other years and years, and in spite of our differences we had a good deal in common. All of us were interested in science.

Terry was rich enough to do as he pleased. His great aim was exploration. He used to make all kinds of a row because there was nothing left to explore now, only patchwork and filling in, he said. He filled in well enough—he had a lot of talents—great on mechanics and electricity. Had all kinds of boats and motor cars, and was one of the best of our airmen.

We never could have done the thing at all without Terry.

Jeff Margrave was born to be a poet, a botanist—or both—but his folks persuaded him to be a doctor instead. He was a good one, for his age, but his real interest was in what he loved to call "the wonders of science."

As for me, Sociology's my major. You have to back that up with a lot of other sciences, of course. I'm interested in them all.

Terry was strong on facts—geography and meteorology and those; Jeff could beat him any time on biology, and I didn't care what it was they talked about, so long as it connected with human life, somehow. There are few things that don't.

We three had a chance to join a big scientific expedition. They needed a doctor, and that gave Jeff an excuse for dropping his just opening practice; they needed Terry's experience, his machine, and his money; and as for me, I got in through Terry's influence.

The expedition was up among the thousand tributaries and enormous hinterland of a great river, up where the maps had to be made, savage dialects studied, and all manner of strange flora and fauna expected.

But this story is not about that expedition. That was only the merest starter for ours.

———

My interest was first roused by talk among our guides. I'm quick at languages, know a good many, and pick them up readily. What with that and a really good interpreter we took with us, I made out quite a few legends and folk-myths of these scattered tribes.

And as we got farther and farther upstream, in a dark tangle of rivers, lakes, morasses, and dense forests, with here and there an unexpected long spur running out from the big mountains beyond, I noticed that more and more of these savages had a story about a strange and terrible "Woman Land" in the high distance.

"Up yonder," "Over there," "Way up"—was all the direction they could offer, but their legends all agreed on the main point—that there was this strange country where no men lived—only women and girl children.

None of them had ever seen it. It was dangerous, deadly, they said, for any man to go there. But there were tales of long ago, when some brave investigator had seen it—a Big Country, Big Houses, Plenty People—All Women.

Had no one else gone? Yes—a good many—but they never came back. It was no place for men—that they seemed sure of.

I told the boys about these stories, and they laughed at them. Naturally I did myself. I knew the stuff that savage dreams are made of.

But when we had reached our farthest point, just the day before we all had to turn around and start for home again, as the best of expeditions must in time, we three made a discovery.

The main encampment was on a spit of land running out into the main stream, or what we thought was the main stream. It had the same muddy color we had been seeing for weeks past, the same taste.

I happened to speak of that river to our last guide, a rather superior fellow, with quick, bright eyes.

He told me that there was another river—"over there—short river, sweet water—red and blue."

I was interested in this and anxious to see if I had understood, so I showed him a red and blue pencil I carried, and asked again.

Yes, he pointed to the river, and then to the southwestward. "River—good water—red and blue."

Terry was close by and interested in the fellow's pointing.

"What does he say, Van?"

I told him.

Terry blazed up at once.

"Ask him how far it is."

The man indicated a short journey; I judged about two hours, maybe three.

"Let's go," urged Terry. "Just us three. Maybe we can really find something. May be cinnabar in it."

"May be indigo," Jeff suggested, with his lazy smile....

It was a long two hours, nearer three. I fancy the savage could have done it alone much quicker. There was a desperate tangle of wood and water and a swampy patch we never should have found our way across alone. But there was one, and I could see Terry, with compass and notebook, marking directions and trying to place landmarks.

We came after a while to a sort of marshy lake, very big, so that the circling forest looked quite low and dim across it. Our guide told us that boats could go from there to our camp—but "long way—all day."

This water was somewhat clearer than we had left, but we could not judge well from the margin. We skirted it for another half hour or so, the ground growing firmer as we advanced, and presently turned the corner of a wooded promontory and saw a quite different country—a sudden view of mountains, steep and bare.

"One of those long easterly spurs," Terry said appraisingly. "May be hundreds of miles from the range. They crop out like that."

Suddenly we left the lake and struck directly toward the cliffs. We heard running water before we reached it, and the guide pointed proudly to his river.

It was short. We could see where it poured down a narrow vertical cataract from an opening in the face of the cliff. It was sweet water. The guide drank eagerly and so did we.

"That's snow water," Terry announced. "Must come from way back in the hills."

But as to being red and blue—it was greenish in tint. The guide seemed not at all surprised. He hunted about a little and showed us a quiet marginal pool where there were smears of red along the border; yes, and of blue.

Terry got out his magnifying glass and squatted down to investigate.

"Chemicals of some sort—I can't tell on the spot. Look to me like dye-stuffs. Let's get nearer," he urged, "up there by the fall."

We scrambled along the steep banks and got close to the pool that foamed and boiled beneath the falling water. Here we searched the border and found traces of color beyond dispute. More—Jeff suddenly held up an unlooked-for trophy.

It was only a rag, a long, ravelled fragment of cloth. But it was a well-woven fabric; with a pattern, and of a clear scarlet that the water had not faded. No savage tribe that we had heard of made such fabrics.

The guide stood serenely on the bank, well pleased with our excitement.

"One day blue—one day red—one day green," he told us, and pulled from his pouch another strip of bright-hued cloth.

"Come down," he said, pointing to the cataract. "Woman Country—up there."

Then we were interested. We had our rest and lunch right there and pumped the man for further information. He could tell us only what the others had—a land of women—no men—babies, but all girls. No place for men—dangerous. Some had gone to see—none had come back.

I could see Terry's jaw set at that. No place for men? Dangerous? He looked as if he might shin up the waterfall on the spot. But the guide would not hear of going up, even if there had been any possible method of scaling that sheer cliff, and we had to get back to our party before night.

"They might stay if we told them," I suggested.

But Terry stopped in his tracks. "Look here, fellows," he said. "This is our find. Let's not tell those cocky old professors. Let's go on home with 'em, and then come back—just us—have a little expedition of our own."

We looked at him, much impressed. There was something attractive to a bunch of unattached young men in finding an undiscovered country of a strictly Amazonian nature.

Of course we didn't believe the story—but yet!

"There is no such cloth made by any of these local tribes," I announced, examining those rags with great care. "Somewhere up yonder they spin and weave and dye—as well as we do."

"That would mean a considerable civilization, Van. There couldn't be such a place—and not known about."

"Oh, well, I don't know; what's that old republic up in the Pyrenees somewhere—Andorra? Precious few people know anything about that, and it's been minding its own business for a thousand years. Then there's Montenegro—splendid little state—you could lose a dozen Montenegroes up and down these great ranges."

We discussed it hotly, all the way back to camp. We discussed it, with care and privacy, on the voyage home. We discussed it after that, still only among ourselves, while Terry was making his arrangements.

He was hot about it. Lucky he had so much money—we might have had to beg and advertise for years to start the thing, and then it would have been a matter of public amusement—just sport for the papers.

But T. O. Nicholson could fix up his big steam yacht, load his specially made big motor-boat aboard, and tuck in a "dissembled" biplane without any more notice than a snip in the society column.

We had provisions and preventives and all manner of supplies. His previous experience stood him in good stead there. It was a very complete little outfit....

An ocean voyage is an excellent time for discussion. Now we had no eavesdroppers, we could loll and loaf in our deck-chairs and talk and talk—there was nothing else to do. Our absolute lack of facts only made the field of discussion wider.

"We'll leave papers with our consul where the yacht stays," Terry planned. "If we don't come back in—say a month—they can send a relief party after us."

"A punitive expedition," I urged. "If the ladies do eat us we must make reprisals."

"They can locate that last stopping place easy enough, and I've made a sort of chart of that lake and cliff and waterfall."

"Yes, but how will they get up?" asked Jeff.

"Same way we do, of course. If three valuable American citizens are lost up there, they will follow somehow—to say nothing of the glittering attractions of that fair land—let's call it 'Feminisia,'" he broke off.

"You're right, Terry. Once the story gets out, the river will crawl with expeditions and the airships rise like a swarm of mosquitoes."

I laughed as I thought of it. "We've made a great mistake not to let Mr. Yellow Press in on this. Save us! What headlines!"

"Not much!" said Terry grimly. "This is our party. We're going to find that place alone."

"What are you going to do with it when you do find it—if you do?" Jeff asked mildly.

Jeff was a tender soul. I think he thought that country—if there was one—was just blossoming with roses and babies and canaries and tidies—and all that sort of thing.

And Terry, in his secret heart, had visions of a sort of sublimated summer resort—just Girls and Girls and Girls—and that he was going to be—well, Terry was popular among women even when there were other men around, and it's not to be wondered at that he had pleasant dreams of what might happen. I could see it in his eyes as he lay there, looking at the long blue rollers slipping by, and fingering that impressive mustache of his.

But I thought—then—that I could form a far clearer idea of what was before us than either of them.

"You're all off, boys," I insisted. "If there is such a place—and there does seem some foundation for believing it—you'll find it's built on a sort of matriarchal principle—that's all. The men have a separate cult of their own, less socially developed than the women, and make them an annual visit—a sort of wedding call. This is a condition known to have existed—here's just a survival. They've got some peculiarly isolated valley or tableland up there, and their primeval customs have survived. That's all there is to it."

"How about the boys?" Jeff asked.

"Oh, the men take them away as soon as they are five or six, you see."

"And how about this danger theory all our guides were so sure of?"

"Danger enough, Terry, and we'll have to be mighty careful. Women of that stage of culture are quite able to defend themselves and have no welcome for unseasonable visitors."

We talked and talked....

Jeff's ideas and Terry's were so far apart that sometimes it was all I could do to keep the peace between them. Jeff idealized women in the best Southern style. He was full of chivalry and sentiment, and all that. And he was a good boy; he lived up to his ideals.

You might say Terry did, too, if you can call his views about women anything so polite as ideals. I always liked Terry. He was a man's man, very much so, generous and brave and clever; but I don't think any of us in college days was quite pleased to have him with our sisters. We weren't very stringent, heavens no! But Terry was "the limit." Later on—why, of course a man's life is his own, we held, and asked no questions.

But barring a possible exception in favor of a not impossible wife, or of his mother, or, of course, the fair relatives of his friends, Terry's idea seemed to be that pretty women were just so much game and homely ones not worth considering.

It was really unpleasant sometimes to see the notions he had.

But I got out of patience with Jeff, too. He had such rose-colored haloes on his women folks. I held a middle ground, highly scientific, of course, and used to argue learnedly about the physiological limitations of the sex.

We were not in the least "advanced" on the woman question, any of us, then.

So we joked and disputed and speculated, and after an interminable journey, got to our old camping place at last.

It was not hard to find the river, just poking along that side till we came to it, and it was navigable as far as the lake.

When we reached that and slid out on its broad glistening bosom, with that high gray promontory running out toward us, and the straight white fall clearly visible, it began to be really exciting.

There was some talk, even then, of skirting the rock wall and seeking a possible foot-way up, but the marshy jungle made that method look not only difficult but dangerous.

Terry dismissed the plan sharply.

"Nonsense, fellows! We've decided that. It might take months— we haven't the provisions. No, sir—we've got to take our chances.

If we get back safe—all right. If we don't, why, we're not the first explorers to get lost in the shuffle. There are plenty to come after us."

So we got the big biplane together and loaded it with our scientifically compressed baggage—the camera, of course; the glasses; a supply of concentrated food. Our pockets were magazines of small necessities, and we had our guns, of course—there was no knowing, what might happen.

Up and up and up we sailed, way up at first, to get "the lay of the land" and make note of it.

Out of that dark green sea of crowding forest this high-standing spur rose steeply. It ran back on either side, apparently, to the far-off white-crowned peaks in the distance, themselves probably inaccessible.

"Let's make the first trip geographical," I suggested. "Spy out the land, and drop back here for more gasoline. With your tremendous speed we can reach that range and back all right. Then we can leave a sort of map on board—for that relief expedition."

"There's sense in that," Terry agreed. "I'll put off being King of Ladyland for one more day."

So we made a long skirting voyage, turned the point of the cape which was close by, ran up one side of the triangle at our best speed, crossed over the base where it left the higher mountains, and so back to our lake by moonlight.

"That's not a bad little kingdom," we agreed when it was roughly drawn and measured. We could tell the size fairly by our speed. And from what we could see of the sides—and that icy ridge at the back end—"It's a pretty enterprising savage who would manage to get into it," Jeff said....

We had to sleep after that long sweep through the air, but we turned out early enough next day, and again we rose softly up the height till we could top the crowning trees and see the broad fair land at our pleasure.

"Semitropical. Looks like a first-rate climate. It's wonderful what a little height will do for temperature." Terry was studying the forest growth.

"Little height! Is that what you call little?" I asked. Our instruments measured it clearly. We had not realized the long gentle rise from the coast perhaps.

"Mighty lucky piece of land, I call it," Terry pursued. "Now for the folks—I've had enough scenery."

So we sailed low, crossing back and forth, quartering the country as we went, and studying it. We saw—I can't remember now how much of this we noted then and how much was supplemented by our later knowledge, but we could not help seeing this much, even on that excited day—a land in a state of perfect cultivation, where even the forests looked as if they were cared for; a land that looked like an enormous park, only it was even more evidently an enormous garden.

"I don't see any cattle," I suggested, but Terry was silent. We were approaching a village.

I confess that we paid small attention to the clean, well-built roads, to the attractive architecture, to the ordered beauty of the little town. We had our glasses out, even Terry, setting his machine for a spiral glide, clapped the binoculars to his eyes.

They heard our whirring screw. They ran out of the houses—they gathered in from the fields, swift-running light figures, crowds of them. We stared and stared until it was almost too late to catch the levers, sweep off and rise again; and then we held our peace for a long run upward.

"Gosh!" said Terry, after a while.

"Only women there—and children," Jeff urged excitedly.

"But they look—why, this is a *civilized* country!" I protested. "There must be men."

"Of course there are men," said Terry. "Come on, let's find 'em."

He refused to listen to Jeff's suggestion that we examine the country further before we risked leaving our machine.

"There's a fine landing place right there where we came over," he insisted, and it was an excellent one—a wide, flat-topped rock, overlooking the lake, and quite out of sight from the interior.

"They won't find this in a hurry," he asserted, as we scrambled with the utmost difficulty down to safer footing. "Come on, boys—there were some good lookers in that bunch."

Of course it was unwise of us.

It was quite easy to see afterward that our best plan was to have studied the country more fully before we left our swooping airship and trusted ourselves to mere foot service. But we were three young men. We had been talking about this country for over a year, hardly believing that there was such a place, and now—we were in it.

It looked safe and civilized enough, and among those upturned, crowding faces, though some were terrified enough—there was great beauty—that we all agreed.

"Come on!" cried Terry, pushing forward. "Oh, come on! Here goes for Herland!"

CHAPTER 2

RASH ADVANCES

———————

Not more than ten or fifteen miles we judged it from our landing rock to that last village. For all our eagerness we thought it wise to keep to the woods and go carefully.

Even Terry's ardor was held in check by his firm conviction that there were men to be met, and we saw to it that each of us had a good stock of cartridges.

"They may be scarce, and they may be hidden away somewhere—some kind of a matriarchate, as Van tells us; for that matter, they may live up in the mountains yonder and keep the women in this part of the country—sort of a national harem! But there are men somewhere—didn't you see the babies?"

We had all seen babies, children big and little, everywhere that we had come near enough to distinguish the people. And though by dress we could not be sure of all the grown persons, still there had not been one man that we were certain of....

All we found moving in those woods, as we started through them, were birds, some gorgeous, some musical, all so tame that it seemed almost to contradict our theory of cultivation—at least until we came upon occasional little glades, where carved stone seats and tables stood in the shade beside clear fountains, with shallow bird baths always added.

"They don't kill birds, and apparently they do kill cats," Terry declared. "*Must* be men here. Hark!"

We had heard something: something not in the least like a bird-song, and very much like a suppressed whisper of laughter—a little happy sound, instantly smothered. We stood like so many pointers, and then used our glasses, swiftly, carefully.

"It couldn't have been far off," said Terry excitedly. "How about this big tree?"

There was a very large and beautiful tree in the glade we had just entered, with thick wide-spreading branches that sloped out in lapping fans like a beech, or pine. It was trimmed underneath some twenty feet up, and stood there like a huge umbrella, with circling seats beneath.

"Look," he pursued. "There are short stumps of branches left to climb on. There's someone up that tree, I believe."

We stole near, cautiously.

"Look out for a poisoned arrow in your eye," I suggested, but Terry pressed forward, sprang up on the seat-back, and grasped the trunk. "In my heart, more likely," he answered. "Gee!—Look, boys!"

We rushed close in and looked up. There among the boughs overhead was something—more than one something—that clung motionless, close to the great trunk at first, and then, as one and all we started up the tree, separated into three swift-moving figures and fled upwards. As we climbed we could catch glimpses of them scattering above us. By the time we had reached about as far as three men together dared push, they had left the main trunk and moved outwards, each one balanced on a long branch that dipped and swayed beneath the weight.

We paused uncertain. If we pursued further, the boughs would break under the double burden. We might shake them off, perhaps, but none of us was so inclined. In the soft dappled light of these high regions, breathless with our rapid climb, we rested awhile, eagerly studying our objects of pursuit; while they in turn, with no more terror than a set of frolicsome children in a game of tag, sat as lightly as so many big bright birds on their precarious perches and frankly, curiously, stared at us.

"Girls!" whispered Jeff, under his breath, as if they might fly if he spoke aloud.

"Peaches!" added Terry, scarcely louder. "Peacherinos—Apricot-nectarines! Whew!"

They were girls, of course, no boys could ever have shown that sparkling beauty, and yet none of us was certain at first.

We saw short hair, hatless, loose, and shining; a suit of some light firm stuff, the closest of tunics and kneebreeches, met by trim gaiters; as bright and smooth as parrots and as unaware of danger, they swung there before us, wholly at ease, staring as we stared, till first one, and then all of them burst into peals of delighted laughter.

Then there was a torrent of soft talk, tossed back and forth; no savage sing-song, but clear musical fluent speech.

We met their laughter cordially, and doffed our hats to them, at which they laughed again, delightedly.

Then Terry, wholly in his element, made a polite speech, with explanatory gestures, and proceeded to introduce us, with pointing finger. "Mr. Jeff Margrave," he said clearly; Jeff bowed as gracefully as a man could in the fork of a great limb. "Mr. Vandyck Jennings"—I also tried to make an effective salute and nearly lost my balance.

Then Terry laid his hand upon his chest—a fine chest he had, too, and introduced himself: he was braced carefully for the occasion and achieved an excellent obeisance.

Again they laughed delightedly, and the one nearest me followed his tactics.

"Celis," she said distinctly, pointing to the one in blue; "Alima"—the one in rose; then, with a vivid imitation of Terry's impressive manner, she laid a firm delicate hand on her gold-green jerkin—"Ellador." This was pleasant, but we got not nearer.

"We can't sit here and learn the language," Terry protested. He beckoned to them to come nearer, most winningly—but they gaily shook their heads. He suggested, by signs, that we all go down together; but again they shook their heads, still merrily. Then Ellador clearly indicated that we should go down, pointing to each and all of us, with unmistakable firmness; and further seeming to imply by the sweep of a lithe arm that we not only go downwards, but go away altogether—at which we shook our heads in turn.

"Have to use bait," grinned Terry. "I don't know about you fellows, but I came prepared." He produced from an inner pocket a little box of purple velvet, that opened with a snap—and out of it he drew a long sparkling thing, a necklace of big varicolored stones that would have been worth a million if real ones. He held it up, swung it, glittering in the sun, offered it first to one, then to another, holding it out as far as he could reach toward the girl nearest him. He stood braced in the fork, held firmly by one hand—the other, swinging his bright temptation, reached far out along the bough, but not quite to his full stretch.

She was visibly moved, I noted, hesitated, spoke to her companions. They chattered softly together, one evidently warning her, the other encouraging. Then, softly and slowly, she drew nearer. This was Alima, a tall long-limbed lass, well-knit and evidently both strong and agile. Her eyes were splendid, wide, fearless, as free from suspicion as a child's who has never been rebuked. Her interest was more that of an intent boy playing a fascinating game than of a girl lured by an ornament.

The others moved a bit farther out, holding firmly, watching. Terry's smile was irreproachable, but I did not like the look in his eyes—it was like a creature about to spring. I could already see it happen—the dropped necklace, the sudden clutching hand—the girl's sharp cry as he seized her and drew her in. But it didn't happen. She made a timid reach with her right hand for the gay swinging thing—he held it a little nearer—then, swift as light, she seized it from him with her left, and dropped on the instant to the bough below.

He made his snatch, quite vainly, almost losing his position as his hand clutched only air; and then, with inconceivable rapidity, the three bright creatures were gone. They dropped from the ends of the big boughs to those below, fairly pouring themselves off the tree, while we climbed downward as swiftly as we could. We heard their vanishing gay laughter, we saw them fleeting away in the wide open reaches of the forest, and gave chase, but we might as well have chased wild antelopes; so we stopped at length somewhat breathless.

"No use," gasped Terry. "They got away with it. My word! The men of this country must be good sprinters!"

"Inhabitants evidently arboreal," I grimly suggested. "Civilized and still arboreal—peculiar people."

"You shouldn't have tried that way," Jeff protested. "They were perfectly friendly; now we've scared them."

But it was no use grumbling, and Terry refused to admit any mistake. "Nonsense," he said. "They expected it. Women like to be run after. Come on, let's get to that town; maybe we'll find them there. Let's see, it was in this direction and not far from the woods, as I remember."

When we reached the edge of the open country we reconnoitered with our field glasses. There it was, about four miles off, the same town, we concluded, unless, as Jeff ventured, they all had pink houses. The broad green fields and closely cultivated gardens sloped away at our feet, a long easy slant, with good roads winding pleasantly here and there, and narrower paths besides.

"Look at that!" cried Jeff suddenly. "There they go!"

Sure enough, close to the town, across a wide meadow, three bright-hued figures were running swiftly.

"How could they have got that far in this time? It can't be the same ones," I urged. But through the glasses we could identify our pretty tree-climbers quite plainly, at least by costume.

Terry watched them, we all did for that matter, till they disappeared among the houses. Then he put down his glass and turned to us, drawing a long breath. "Mother of Mike, boys—what Gorgeous Girls! To climb like that! to run like that! and afraid of nothing. This country suits me all right. Let's get ahead...."

Presently there lay before us at the foot of a long hill the town or village we were aiming for. We stopped and studied it.

Jeff drew a long breath. "I wouldn't have believed a collection of houses could look so lovely," he said.

"They've got architects and landscape gardeners in plenty, that's sure," agreed Terry....

Everything was beauty, order, perfect cleanness, and the pleasantest sense of home over it all. As we neared the center of the town the houses stood thicker, ran together as it were, grew into rambling palaces grouped among parks and open squares, something as college buildings stand in their quiet greens.

And then, turning a corner, we came into a broad paved space and saw before us a band of women standing close together in even order, evidently waiting for us.

We stopped a moment and looked back. The street behind was closed by another band, marching steadily, shoulder to shoulder. We went on—there seemed no other way to go—and presently found ourselves quite surrounded by this close-massed multitude; women, all of them, but—

They were not young. They were not old. They were not, in the girl sense, beautiful, they were not in the least ferocious; and yet, as I looked from face to face, calm, grave, wise, wholly unafraid, evidently assured and determined, I had the funniest feeling—a very early feeling—a feeling that I traced back and back in memory until I caught up with it at last. It was that sense of being hopelessly in the wrong that I had so often felt in early youth when my short legs' utmost effort failed to overcome the fact that I was late to school.

Jeff felt it too; I could see he did. We felt like small boys, very small boys, caught doing mischief in some gracious lady's house. But Terry showed no such consciousness. I saw his quick eyes darting here and there, estimating numbers, measuring distances, judging chances of escape. He examined the close ranks about us, reaching back far on every side, and murmured softly to me, "Every one of 'em over forty as I'm a sinner."

Yet they were not old women. Each was in the full bloom of rosy health, erect, serene, standing sure-footed and light as any pugilist. They had no weapons, and we had, but we had no wish to shoot.

"I'd as soon shoot my aunts," muttered Terry again. "What do they want with us anyhow? They seem to mean business." But in spite of that business-like aspect, he determined to try his favorite tactics. Terry had come armed with a theory.

He stepped forward, with his brilliant ingratiating smile, and made low obeisance to the women before him. Then he produced another tribute, a broad soft scarf of filmy texture, rich in color and pattern, a lovely thing, even to my eye, and offered it with a deep bow to the tall unsmiling woman who seemed to head the ranks before him. She took it with a gracious nod of acknowledgment, and passed it on to those behind her. He tried again, this time bringing out a circlet of rhinestones, a glittering crown that should have pleased any woman on earth.

He made a brief address, including Jeff and me as partners in his enterprise, and with another bow presented this.

Again his gift was accepted and, as before, passed out of sight.

"If they were only younger," he muttered between his teeth. "What on earth is a fellow to say to a regiment of old Colonels like this?..."

Six of them stepped forward now, one on either side of each of us, and indicated that we were to go with them. We thought it best to accede, at first anyway, and marched along, one of these close at each elbow, and the others in close masses before, behind, on both sides.

A large building opened before us, a very heavy thick-walled impressive place, big, and old-looking; of grey stone, not like the rest of the town.

"This won't do!" said Terry to us, quickly. "We mustn't let them get us in this, boys. All together, now—"

We stopped in our tracks. We began to explain, to make signs pointing away toward the big forest—indicating that we would go back to it—at once.

It makes me laugh, knowing all I do now, to think of us three boys—nothing else; three audacious impertinent boys—butting into an unknown country without any sort of a guard or defense. We seemed to think that if there were men we could fight them, and if there were only women—why, they would be no obstacles at all.

Jeff, with his gentle romantic old-fashioned notions of women as clinging vines; Terry, with his clear decided practical theories that there were two kinds of women—those he wanted and those he didn't; Desirable and Undesirable was his demarcation. The last was a large class, but negligible—he had never thought about them at all.

And now here they were, in great numbers, evidently indifferent to what he might think, evidently determined on some purpose of their own regarding him, and apparently well able to enforce their purpose.

We all thought hard just then. It had not seemed wise to object to going with them, even if we could have; our one chance was friendliness—a civilized attitude on both sides.

But once inside that building, there was no knowing what these determined ladies might do to us. Even a peaceful detention was not to our minds, and when we named it imprisonment it looked even worse.

So we made a stand, trying to make clear that we preferred the open country. One of them came forward with a sketch of our flier, asking by signs if we were the aerial visitors they had seen.

This we admitted.

They pointed to it again, and to the outlying country, in different directions—but we pretended we did not know where it was—and in truth we were not quite sure and gave a rather wild indication of its whereabouts.

Again they motioned us to advance, standing so packed about the door that there remained but the one straight path open. All around us and behind they were massed solidly—there was simply nothing to do but go forward—or fight....

"We've got to decide quick," said Terry. "I vote to go in," Jeff urged. But we were two to one against him and he loyally stood by us. We made one more effort to be let go, urgent, but not imploring. In vain.

"Now for a rush, boys!" Terry said. "And if we can't break 'em, I'll shoot in the air."

Then we found ourselves much in the position of the Suffragette trying to get to the Parliament buildings through a triple cordon of London police.

The solidity of those women was something amazing. Terry soon found that it was useless, tore himself loose for a moment, pulled his revolver, and fired upward. As they caught at it, he fired again—we heard a cry—

Instantly each of us was seized by five women, each holding arm or leg or head; we were lifted like children, straddling helpless children, and borne onward, wriggling indeed, but most ineffectually.

We were borne inside, struggling manfully, but held secure most womanfully, in spite of our best endeavors.

So carried and so held, we came into a high inner hall, grey and bare, and were brought before a majestic grey-haired woman who seemed to hold a judicial position.

There was some talk, not much, among them, and then suddenly there fell upon each of us at once a firm hand holding a wetted cloth before mouth and nose—an odor of swimming sweetness—anesthesia.

CHAPTER 3

A PECULIAR IMPRISONMENT

From a slumber as deep as death, as refreshing as that of a healthy child, I slowly awakened....

I felt as light and clean as a white feather. It took me some time to consciously locate my arms and legs, to feel the vivid sense of life radiate from the wakening center to the extremities.

A big room, high and wide, with many lofty windows whose closed blinds let through soft green-lit air; a beautiful room, in proportion, in color, in smooth simplicity; a scent of blossoming gardens outside.

I lay perfectly still, quite happy, quite conscious, and yet not actively realizing what had happened till I heard Terry.

"Gosh!" was what he said.

I turned my head. There were three beds in this chamber, and plenty of room for them.

Terry was sitting up, looking about him, alert as ever. His remarks, though not loud, roused Jeff also. We all sat up.

Terry swung his legs out of bed, stood up, stretched himself mightily. He was in a long night-robe, a sort of seamless garment, undoubtedly comfortable—we all found ourselves so covered. Shoes were beside each bed, also quite comfortable and good-looking though by no means like our own.

We looked for our clothes—they were not there, nor anything of all the varied contents of our pockets.

A door stood somewhat ajar; it opened into a most attractive bathroom, copiously provided with towels, soap, mirrors, and all such convenient comforts, with indeed our toothbrushes and combs, our notebooks, and thank goodness, our watches—but no clothes.

Then we made a search of the big room again and found a large airy closet, holding plenty of clothing, but not ours....

The garments were simple in the extreme, and absolutely comfortable, physically, though of course we all felt like supes in the theater. There was a one-piece cotton undergarment, thin and soft, that reached over the knees and shoulders, something like the one-piece pajamas some fellows wear, and a kind of half-hose, that came up to just under the knee and stayed there—had an elastic top of their own, and covered the edges of the first.

Then there was a thicker variety of union suit, a lot of them in the closet, of varying weights and somewhat sturdier material—evidently they would do at a pinch with nothing further. Then there were tunics, knee length, and some long robes. Needless to say, we took tunics.

We bathed and dressed quite cheerfully....

"Now then," Terry proclaimed, "we've had a fine long sleep—we've had a good bath—we're clothed and in our right minds, though feeling like a lot of neuters. Do you think these highly civilized ladies are going to give us any breakfast?"

"Of course they will," Jeff asserted confidently. "If they had meant to kill us, they would have done it before. I believe we are going to be treated as guests."

"Hailed as deliverers, I think," said Terry.

"Studied as curiosities," I told them. "But anyhow, we want food. So now for a sortie!"

A sortie was not so easy.

The bathroom only opened into our chamber, and that had but one outlet, a big heavy door, which was fastened.

We listened.

"There's someone outside," Jeff suggested. "Let's knock."

So we knocked, whereupon the door opened.

Outside was another large room, furnished with a great table at one end, long benches or couches against the wall, some smaller tables and chairs. All these were solid, strong, simple in structure, and comfortable in use; also, incidentally, beautiful.

This room was occupied by a number of women, eighteen to be exact, some of whom we distinctly recalled....

We had no need to make pathetic pantomime of hunger; the smaller tables were already laid with food, and we were gravely invited to be seated. The tables were set for two; each of us found ourselves placed vis-à-vis with one of our hosts, and each table had five other stalwarts nearby, unobtrusively watching. We had plenty of time to get tired of those women!

The breakfast was not profuse, but sufficient in amount and excellent in quality. We were all too good travelers to object to novelty, and this repast with its new but delicious fruit, its dish of large rich-flavored nuts, and its highly satisfactory little cakes was most agreeable. There was water to drink, and a hot beverage of a most pleasing quality, some preparation like cocoa....

It was evident that those sets of five were there to check any outbreak on our part. We had no weapons, and if we did try to do any damage, with a chair, say, why five to one was too many for us, even if they were women; that we had found out to our sorrow. It was not pleasant, having them always around, but we soon got used to it.

"It's better than being physically restrained ourselves," Jeff philosophically suggested when we were alone. "They've given us a room—with no great possibility of escape—and personal liberty— heavily chaperoned. It's better than we'd have been likely to get in a man-country."

"Man-country! Do you really believe there are no men here, you innocent? Don't you know there must be?" demanded Terry.

"Ye—es," Jeff agreed. "Of course—and yet—"

"And yet—what! Come, you obdurate sentimentalist—what are you thinking about?"

"They may have some peculiar division of labor we've never heard of," I suggested. "The men may live in separate towns, or they may have subdued them—somehow—and keep them shut up. But there must be some."

"That last suggestion of yours is a nice one, Van," Terry protested. "Same as they've got us subdued and shut up! You make me shiver."

"Well, figure it out for yourself, anyway you please. We saw plenty of kids, the first day, and we've seen those girls—"

"Real girls!" Terry agreed, in immense relief. "Glad you mentioned 'em. I declare, if I thought there was nothing in the country but those grenadiers I'd jump out the window."

"Speaking of windows," I suggested, "let's examine ours...."

We could look out east, west, and south. To the south-eastward stretched the open country, lying bright and fair in the morning light, but on either side, and evidently behind, rose great mountains.

"This thing is a regular fortress—and no women built it, I can tell you that," said Terry. We nodded agreeingly. "It's right up among the hills—they must have brought us a long way."

"And pretty fast, too," I added.

"We saw some kind of swift-moving vehicles the first day," Jeff reminded us. "If they've got motors, they *are* civilized."

"Civilized or not, we've got our work cut out for us to get away from here. I don't propose to make a rope of bedclothes and try those walls till I'm sure there is no better way."

We all concurred on this point, and returned to our discussion as to the women.

Jeff continued thoughtful. "All the same, there's something funny about it," he urged. "It isn't just that we don't see any men—but we don't see any signs of them. The—the—reaction of these women is different from any that I've ever met."

"There is something in what you say, Jeff," I agreed. "There is a different—atmosphere."

"They don't seem to notice our being men," he went on. "They treat us—well—just as they do one another. It's as if our being men was a minor incident."

I nodded. I'd noticed it myself. But Terry broke in rudely.

"Fiddlesticks!" he said. "It's because of their advanced age.

They're all grandmas, I tell you—or ought to be. Great aunts, anyhow. Those girls were girls all right, weren't they?"

"Yes—" Jeff agreed, still slowly. "But they weren't afraid—they flew up that tree and hid, like school-boys caught out of bounds—not like shy girls."

"And they ran like marathon winners—you'll admit that, Terry," he added....

Our time was quite pleasantly filled. We were free of the garden below our windows, quite long in its irregular rambling shape, bordering the cliff. The walls were perfectly smooth and high, ending in the masonry of the building; and as I studied the great stones I became convinced that the whole structure was extremely old. It was built like the pre-Incan architecture in Peru, of enormous monoliths, fitted as closely as mosaics.

"These folks have a history, that's sure," I told the others. "And *some* time they were fighters—else why a fortress?"

I said we were free of the garden, but not wholly alone in it. There was always a string of those uncomfortably strong women sitting about, always one of them watching us even if the others were reading, playing games, or busy at some kind of handiwork.

"When I see them knit," Terry said, "I can almost call them feminine."

"That doesn't prove anything," Jeff promptly replied. "Scotch shepherds knit—always knitting."

"When we get out—" Terry stretched himself and looked at the far peaks, "when we get out of this and get to where the real women are—the mothers, and the girls—"

"Well, what'll we do then?" I asked, rather gloomily. "How do you know we'll ever get out?"

This was an unpleasant idea, which we unanimously considered, returning with earnestness to our studies.

"If we are good boys and learn our lessons well," I suggested. "If we are quiet and respectful and polite and they are not afraid of us—then perhaps they will let us out. And anyway—when we do escape, it is of immense importance that we know the language."

Personally, I was tremendously interested in that language, and seeing they had books, was eager to get at them, to dig into their history, if they had one.

It was not hard to speak, smooth and pleasant to the ear, and so easy to read and write that I marvelled at it. They had an absolutely phonetic system, the whole thing was as scientific as Esperanto yet bore all the marks of an old and rich civilization.

We were free to study as much as we wished, and were not left merely to wander in the garden for recreation but introduced to a great gymnasium, partly on the roof and partly in the story below. Here we learned real respect for our tall guards. No change of costume was needed for this work, save to lay off outer clothing. The first one was as perfect a garment for exercise as need be devised, absolutely free to move in, and, I had to admit, much better looking than our usual one.

"Forty—over forty—some of 'em fifty, I bet—and look at 'em!" grumbled Terry in reluctant admiration.

There were no spectacular acrobatics, such as only the young can perform, but for all-around development they had a most excellent system. A good deal of music went with it, with posture dancing and, sometimes, gravely beautiful processional performances.

Jeff was much impressed by it. We did not know then how small a part of their physical culture methods this really was, but found it agreeable to watch, and to take part in....

They had games, too, a good many of them, but we found them rather uninteresting at first. It was like two people playing solitaire to see who would get it first; more like a race or a—a competitive examination, than a real game with some fight in it.

I philosophized a bit over this and told Terry it argued against their having any men about. "There isn't a man-size game in the lot," I said.

"But they are interesting—I like them," Jeff objected, "and I'm sure they are educational."

"I'm sick and tired of being educated," Terry protested. "Fancy going to a dame school—at our age. I want to Get Out!"

But we could not get out, and we were being educated swiftly. Our special tutors rose rapidly in our esteem. They seemed of rather finer quality than the guards, though all were on terms of easy friendliness. Mine was named Somel, Jeff's Zava, and Terry's Moadine. We tried to generalize from the names, those of the guards, and of our three girls, but got nowhere.

"They sound well enough, and they're mostly short, but there's no similarity of termination—and no two alike. However, our acquaintance is limited as yet."

There were many things we meant to ask—as soon as we could talk well enough. Better teaching I never saw. From morning to night there was Somel, always on call except between two and four; always pleasant with a steady friendly kindness that I grew to enjoy very much. Jeff said Miss Zava—he would put on a title, though they apparently had none—was a darling; that she reminded him of his Aunt Esther at home; but Terry refused to be won, and rather jeered at his own companion, when we were alone....

It was hard on Terry, so hard that he finally persuaded us to consider a plan of escape. It was difficult, it was highly dangerous, but he declared that he'd go alone if we wouldn't go with him, and of course we couldn't think of that.

It appeared he had made a pretty careful study of the environment. From our end window that faced the point of the promontory we could get a fair idea of the stretch of wall, and the drop below. Also from the roof we could make out more, and even, in one place, glimpse a sort of path below the wall....

So we waited for full moon, retired early, and spent an anxious hour or two in the unskilled manufacture of man-strong ropes.

To retire into the depths of the closet, muffle a glass in thick cloth, and break it without noise was not difficult, and broken glass will cut, though not as deftly as a pair of scissors.

The broad moonlight streamed in through four of our

windows—we had not dared leave our lights on too long—and we worked hard and fast at our task of destruction.

Hangings, rugs, robes, towels, as well as bed-furniture—even the mattress covers—we left not one stitch upon another, as Jeff put it.

Then at an end window, as less liable to observation, we fastened one end of our cable, strongly, to the firm-set hinge of the inner blind, and dropped our coiled bundle of rope softly over.

"This part's easy enough—I'll come last, so as to cut the rope," said Terry.

So I slipped down first, and stood, well braced against the wall; then Jeff on my shoulders, then Terry, who shook us a little as he sawed through the cord above his head. Then I slowly dropped to the ground, Jeff following, and at last we all three stood safe in the garden, with most of our rope with us.

"Good-bye, Grandma!" whispered Terry, under his breath, and we crept softly toward the wall, taking advantage of the shadow of every bush and tree. He had been foresighted enough to mark the very spot, only a scratch of stone on stone, but we could see to read in that light. For anchorage there was a tough, fair-sized shrub close to the wall.

"Now I'll climb up on you two again and go over first," said Terry. "That'll hold the rope firm till you both get up on top. Then I'll go down to the end. If I can get off safely, you can see me and follow—or, say, I'll twitch it three times. If I find there's absolutely no footing—why I'll climb up again, that's all. I don't think they'll kill us."

From the top he reconnoitered carefully, waved his hand, and whispered, "o.k.," then slipped over. Jeff climbed up and I followed, and we rather shivered to see how far down that swaying, wavering figure dropped, hand under hand, till it disappeared in a mass of foliage far below.

Then there were three quick pulls, and Jeff and I, not without a joyous sense of recovered freedom, successfully followed our leader.

CHAPTER 4

OUR VENTURE

_____

We were standing on a narrow, irregular, all too slanting little ledge, and should doubtless have ignominiously slipped off and broken our rash necks but for the vine. This was a thick-leaved, wide-spreading thing, a little like Amphelopsis....

Terry slid down first—said he'd show us how a Christian meets his death. Luck was with us. We had put on the thickest of those intermediate suits, leaving our tunics behind, and made this scramble quite successfully, though I got a pretty heavy fall just at the end, and was only kept on the second ledge by main force. The next stage was down a sort of "chimney"—a long irregular fissure; and so with scratches many and painful and bruises not a few, we finally reached the stream.

It was darker there, but we felt it highly necessary to put as much distance as possible behind us; so we waded, jumped, and clambered down that rocky river-bed, in the flickering black and white moonlight and leaf shadow, till growing daylight forced a halt.

We found a friendly nut-tree, those large, satisfying, soft-shelled nuts we already knew so well, and filled our pockets....

It was not a very comfortable place, not at all easy to get at, just a sort of crevice high up along the steep bank, but it was well veiled with foliage and dry. After our exhausting three- or four-hours scramble and the good breakfast food, we all lay down along the crack—heads and tails, as it were—and slept till the afternoon sun almost toasted our faces....

It was no use to leave there by daylight. We could not see much of the country, but enough to know that we were now at the beginning of the cultivated area, and no doubt there would be an alarm sent out far and wide....

We soon dozed off again.

The long rest and penetrating dry heat were good for us, and that night we covered a considerable distance, keeping always in the rough forested belt of land which we knew bordered the whole country. Sometimes we were near the outer edge, and caught sudden glimpses of the tremendous depths beyond....

What we could see inland was peaceable enough, but only moonlit glimpses; by daylight we lay very close. As Terry said, we did not wish to kill the old ladies—even if we could; and short of that they were perfectly competent to pick us up bodily and carry us back, if discovered. There was nothing for it but to lie low, and sneak out unseen if we could do it....

...Careful we were, feeling pretty sure that if we did not make good this time we were not likely to have another opportunity; and at last we reached a point from which we could see, far below, the broad stretch of that still lake from which we had made our ascent.

"That looks pretty good to me!" said Terry, gazing down at it. "Now, if we can't find the 'plane, we know where to aim if we have to drop over this wall some other way."

The wall at that point was singularly uninviting. It rose so straight that we had to put our heads over to see the base, and the country below seemed to be a far-off marshy tangle of rank vegetation. We did not have to risk our necks to that extent, however, for at last, stealing along among the rocks and trees like so many creeping savages, we came to that flat space where we had landed; and there, in unbelievable good fortune, we found our machine.

"Covered, too, by jingo! Would you think they had that much sense?" cried Terry.

"If they had that much, they're likely to have more," I warned him, softly. "Bet you the thing's watched."

We reconnoitered as widely as we could in the failing

moonlight—moons are of a painfully unreliable nature; but the growing dawn showed us the familiar shape, shrouded in some heavy cloth like canvas and no slightest sign of any watchman near. We decided to make a quick dash as soon as the light was strong enough for accurate work.

"I don't care if the old thing'll go or not," Terry declared. "We can run her to the edge, get aboard, and just plane down—plop!—beside our boat there. Look there—see the boat!"

Sure enough—there was our motor, lying like a gray cocoon on the flat pale sheet of water.

Quietly but swiftly we rushed forward and began to tug at the fastenings of that cover.

"Confound the thing!" Terry cried in desperate impatience. "They've got it sewed up in a bag! And we've not a knife among us!"

Then, as we tugged and pulled at that tough cloth we heard a sound that made Terry lift his head like a war horse—the sound of an unmistakable giggle, yes—three giggles.

There they were—Celis, Alima, Ellador—looking just as they had when we first saw them, standing a little way off from us, as interested, as mischievous as three school-boys.

"Hold on, Terry—hold on!" I warned. "That's too easy—look out for a trap."

"Let us appeal to their kind hearts," Jeff urged. "I think they will help us. Perhaps they've got knives."

"It's no use rushing them, anyhow." I was absolutely holding on to Terry. "We know they can out-run and out-climb us."

He reluctantly admitted this; and after a brief parley among ourselves, we all advanced slowly toward them, holding out our hands in token of friendliness.

They stood their ground till we had come fairly near, and then indicated that we should stop. To make sure, we advanced a step or two and they promptly and swiftly withdrew. So we stopped at the distance specified. Then we used their language, as far as we were able, to explain our plight, telling how we were imprisoned, how we had escaped—a good deal of pantomime here and vivid interest on their part—how we had traveled by night and hidden by day, living on nuts—and here Terry pretended great hunger.

I know he could not have been hungry; we had found plenty to eat and had not been sparing in helping ourselves. But they seemed somewhat impressed; and after a murmured consultation they produced from their pockets certain little packages, and with the utmost ease and accuracy tossed them into our hands.

Jeff was most appreciative of this; and Terry made extravagant gestures of admiration, which seemed to set them off, boy-fashion, to show their skill. While we ate the excellent biscuits they had thrown us, and while Ellador kept a watchful eye on our movements, Celis ran off to some distance, and set up a sort of "duck-on-a-rock" arrangement, a big yellow nut on top of three balanced sticks; Alima, meanwhile, gathering stones.

They urged us to throw at it, and we did, but the thing was a long way off, and it was only after a number of failures, at which those elvish damsels laughed delightedly, that Jeff succeeded in bringing the whole structure to the ground. It took me still longer, and Terry, to his intense annoyance, came third.

Then Celis set up the little tripod again, and looked back at us, knocking it down, pointing at it, and shaking her short curls severely. "No," she said. "Bad—wrong!" We were quite able to follow her.

Then she set it up once more, put the fat nut on top, and returned to the others; and there those aggravating girls sat and took turns throwing little stones at that thing, while one stayed by as a setter-up; and they just popped that nut off, two times out of three, without upsetting the sticks. Pleased as Punch they were, too, and we pretended to be, but weren't.

We got very friendly over this game, but I told Terry we'd be sorry if we didn't get off while we could, and then we begged for knives. It was easy to show what we wanted to do, and they each proudly produced a sort of strong clasp-knife from their pockets.

"Yes," we said eagerly, "that's it! Please——" We had learned quite a bit of their language, you see. And we just begged for those knives, but they would not give them to us. If we came a step too near they backed off, standing light and eager for flight.

"It's no sort of use," I said. "Come on—let's get a sharp stone or something—we must get this thing off."

So we hunted about and found what edged fragments we could, and hacked away, but it was like trying to cut sailcloth with a clam-shell.

Terry hacked and dug, but said to us under his breath, "Boys—we're in pretty good condition—let's make a life and death dash and get hold of those girls—we've got to."

They had drawn rather nearer, to watch our efforts, and we did take them rather by surprise; also, as Terry said, our recent training had strengthened us in wind and limb, and for a few desperate moments those girls were scared and we almost triumphant.

But just as we stretched out our hands, the distance between us widened; they had got their pace apparently, and then, though we ran at our utmost speed, and much farther than I thought wise, they kept just out of reach all the time.

We stopped breathless, at last, at my repeated admonitions.

"This is stark foolishness," I urged. "They are doing it on purpose—come back or you'll be sorry."

We went back, much slower than we came, and in truth we were sorry.

As we reached our swaddled machine, and sought again to tear loose its covering, there rose up from all around the sturdy forms, the quiet determined faces we knew so well.

"Oh Lord!" groaned Terry. "The Colonels! It's all up—they're forty to one."

It was no use to fight. These women evidently relied on num-bers, not so much as a drilled force but as a multitude actuated by a common impulse. They showed no sign of fear, and since we had no weapons whatever and there were at least a hundred of them, stand-ing ten deep about us, we gave in as gracefully as we might.

Of course we looked for punishment—a closer imprisonment, solitary confinement maybe—but nothing of the kind happened.

They treated us as truants only, and as if they quite understood our truancy.

Back we went; not under an anesthetic this time but skimming along in electric motors enough like ours to be quite recognizable, each of us in a separate vehicle with one able-bodied lady on either side and three facing him....

Well—before nightfall we were all safely back in our big room. The damage we had done was quite ignored; the beds as smooth and comfortable as before, new clothing and towels supplied. The only thing those women did was to illuminate the gardens at night, and to set an extra watch. But they called us to account next day. Our three tutors, who had not joined in the recapturing expedition, had been quite busy in preparing for us, and now made explanation.

They knew well we would make for our machine, and also that there was no other way of getting down—alive. So our flight had troubled no one; all they did was to call the inhabitants to keep an eye on our movements all along the edge of the forest between the two points. It appeared that many of those nights we had been seen, by careful ladies sitting snugly in big trees by the riverbed, or up among the rocks.

Terry looked immensely disgusted, but it struck me as extremely funny. Here we had been risking our lives, hiding and prowling like outlaws, living on nuts and fruit, getting wet and cold at night, and dry and hot by day, and all the while these estimable women had just been waiting for us to come out.

Now they began to explain, carefully using such words as we could understand. It appeared that we were considered as guests of the country—sort of public wards. Our first violence had made it necessary to keep us safeguarded for a while, but as soon as we learned the language—and would agree to do no harm—they would show us all about the land.

Jeff was eager to reassure them. Of course he did not tell on Terry, but he made it clear that he was ashamed of himself, and that he would now conform. As to the language—we all fell upon it with redoubled energy. They brought us books, in greater numbers, and I began to study them seriously.

"Pretty punk literature," Terry burst forth one day, when we were in the privacy of our own room. "Of course one expects to begin on child-stories, but I would like something more interesting now."

"Can't expect stirring romance and wild adventure without men, can you?" I asked. Nothing irritated Terry more than to have us assume that there were no men; but there were no signs of them in the books they gave us, or the pictures.

"Shut up!" he growled. "What infernal nonsense you talk! I'm going to ask 'em outright—we know enough now."

In truth we had been using our best efforts to master the language, and were able to read fluently and to discuss what we read with considerable ease.

That afternoon we were all sitting together on the roof—we three and the tutors gathered about a table, no guards about. We had been made to understand some time earlier that if we would agree to do no violence they would withdraw their constant attendance, and we promised most willingly.

So there we sat, at ease; all in similar dress; our hair, by now, as long as theirs, only our beards to distinguish us. We did not want those beards, but had so far been unable to induce them to give us any cutting instruments.

"Ladies," Terry began, out of a clear sky, as it were, "are there no men in this country?"

"Men?" Somel answered. "Like you?"

"Yes, men," Terry indicated his beard, and threw back his broad shoulders. "Men, real men."

"No," she answered quietly. "There are no men in this country. There has not been a man among us for two thousand years."

Her look was clear and truthful and she did not advance this astonishing statement as if it was astonishing, but quite as a matter of fact.

"But—the people—the children," he protested, not believing her in the least, but not wishing to say so.

"Oh yes," she smiled. "I do not wonder you are puzzled. We are mothers—all of us—but there are no fathers. We thought you would ask about that long ago—why have you not?" Her look was as frankly kind as always, her tone quite simple.

Terry explained that we had not felt sufficiently used to the language, making rather a mess of it, I thought, but Jeff was franker.

"Will you excuse us all," he said, "if we admit that we find it hard to believe? There is no such—possibility—in the rest of the world."

"Have you no kind of life where it is possible?" asked Zava.

"Why, yes—some low forms, of course."

"How low—or how high, rather?"

"Well—there are some rather high forms of insect life in which it occurs. Parthenogenesis, we call it—that means virgin birth."

She could not follow him.

"*Birth*, we know, of course; but what is *virgin?*"

Terry looked uncomfortable, but Jeff met the question quite calmly. "Among mating animals, the term *virgin* is applied to the female who has not mated," he answered.

"Oh, I see. And does it apply to the male also? Or is there a different term for him?"

He passed this over rather hurriedly, saying that the same term would apply, but was seldom used.

"No?" she said. "But one cannot mate without the other surely. Is not each then—virgin—before mating? And, tell me, have you any forms of life in which there is birth from a father only?"

"I know of none," he answered, and I inquired seriously.

"You ask us to believe that for two thousand years there have been only women here, and only girl babies born?"

"Exactly," answered Somel, nodding gravely. "Of course we know that among other animals it is not so, that there are fathers as well as mothers; and we see that you are fathers, that you come from a people who are of both kinds. We have been waiting, you see, for you to be able to speak freely with us, and teach us about your country and the rest of the world. You know so much, you see, and we know only our own land...."

"We want you to teach us all you can," Somel went on, her firm shapely hands clasped on the table before her, her clear quiet eyes meeting ours frankly. "And we want to teach you what we have that is novel and useful. You can well imagine that it is a wonderful event to us, to have men among us—after two thousand years. And we want to know about your women."

What she said about our importance gave instant pleasure to Terry. I could see by the way he lifted his head that it pleased him. But when she spoke of our women—someway I had a queer little indescribable feeling, not like any feeling I ever had before when "women" were mentioned.

"Will you tell us how it came about?" Jeff pursued. "You said 'for two thousand years'—did you have men here before that?"

"Yes," answered Zava.

They were all quiet for a little.

"You should have our full history to read—do not be alarmed—it has been made clear and short. It took us a long time to learn how to write history. Oh, how I should love to read yours!"

She turned with flashing eager eyes, looking from one to the other of us.

"It would be so wonderful—would it not? To compare the history of two thousand years, to see what the differences are—between us, who are only mothers, and you, who are mothers and fathers, too. Of course we see, with our birds, that the father is as useful as the mother, almost; but among insects we find him of less importance, sometimes very little. Is it not so with you?"

"Oh, yes, birds and bugs," Terry said, "but not among animals—have you *no* animals?"

"We have cats," she said. "The father is not very useful."

"Have you no cattle—sheep—horses?" I drew some rough outlines of these beasts and showed them to her.

"We had, in the very old days, these," said Somel, and sketched with swift sure touches a sort of sheep or llama, "and these"—dogs, of two or three kinds, "and that"—pointing to my absurd but recognizable horse.

"What became of them?" asked Jeff.

"We do not want them anymore. They took up too much room—we need all our land to feed our people. It is such a little country, you know."

"Whatever do you do without milk?" Terry demanded incredulously.

"*Milk?* We have milk in abundance—our own."

"But—but—I mean for cooking—for grown people," Terry blundered, while they looked amazed and a shade displeased.

Jeff came to the rescue. "We keep cattle for their milk, as well as for their meat," he explained. "Cow's milk is a staple article of diet—there is a great milk industry—to collect and distribute it."

Still they looked puzzled. I pointed to my outline of a cow. "The farmer milks the cow," I said, and sketched a milk pail, the stool, and in pantomime showed the man milking. "Then it is carried to the city and distributed by milkmen—everybody has it at the door in the morning."

"Has the cow no child?" asked Somel earnestly.

"Oh, yes, of course, a calf, that is."

"Is there milk for the calf and you, too?"

It took some time to make clear to those three sweet-faced women the process which robs the cow of her calf, and the calf of its true food; and the talk led us into a further discussion of the meat business. They heard it out, looking very white, and presently begged to be excused.

CHAPTER 5

A UNIQUE HISTORY

It is no use for me to try to piece out this account with adventures. If the people who read it are not interested in these amazing women and their history, they will not be interested at all....

And I'll summarize here a bit as to our opportunities for learning it. I will not try to repeat the careful, detailed account I lost; I'll just say that we were kept in that fortress a good six months all told, and after that, three in a pleasant enough city where—to Terry's infinite disgust—there were only "Colonels" and little children—no young women whatever. Then we were under surveillance for three more—always with a tutor or a guard or both. But those months were pleasant because we were really getting acquainted with the girls. That was a chapter!—or will be—I will try to do justice to it.

We learned their language pretty thoroughly—had to; and they learned ours much more quickly and used it to hasten our own studies.

Jeff, who was never without reading matter of some sort, had two little books with him, a novel and a little anthology of verse; and I had one of those pocket encyclopedias—a fat little thing, bursting with facts. These were used in our education—and theirs. Then as soon as we were up to it, they furnished us with plenty of their own books, and I went in for the history part—I wanted to understand the genesis of this miracle of theirs.

And this is what happened, according to their records:

As to geography—at about the time of the Christian era this land had a free passage to the sea. I'm not saying where, for good reasons. But there was a fairly easy pass through that wall of mountains behind us, and there is no doubt in my mind that these people were of Aryan stock, and were once in contact with the best civilization of the old world. They were "white," but somewhat darker than our northern races because of their constant exposure to sun and air.

The country was far larger then, including much land beyond the pass, and a strip of coast. They had ships, commerce, an army, a king—for at that time they were what they so calmly called us—a bi-sexual race.

What happened to them first was merely a succession of historic misfortunes such as have befallen other nations often enough. They were decimated by war, driven up from their coastline till finally the reduced population, with many of the men killed in battle, occupied this hinterland, and defended it for years, in the mountain passes. Where it was open to any possible attack from below they strengthened the natural defenses so that it became unscalably secure, as we found it.

They were a polygamous people, and a slave-holding people, like all of their time; and during the generation or two of this struggle to defend their mountain home they built the fortresses, such as the one we were held in, and other of their oldest buildings, some still in use. Nothing but earthquakes could destroy such architecture—huge solid blocks, holding by their own weight. They must have had efficient workmen and enough of them in those days.

They made a brave fight for their existence, but no nation can stand up against what the steamship companies call "an act of God." While the whole fighting force was doing its best to defend their mountain pathway, there occurred a volcanic outburst, with some local tremors, and the result was the complete filling up of the pass—their only outlet. Instead of a passage, a new ridge, sheer and high, stood between them and the sea; they were walled in, and beneath that wall lay their whole little army. Very few men were left alive, save the slaves; and these now seized their opportunity, rose in revolt, killed their remaining masters even to the youngest boy, killed the old women too, and the mothers, intending to take possession of the country with the remaining young women and girls.

But this succession of misfortunes was too much for those infuriated virgins. There were many of them, and but few of these would-be masters, so the young women, instead of submitting, rose in sheer desperation and slew their brutal conquerors.

This sounds like Titus Andronicus, I know, but that is their account. I suppose they were about crazy—can you blame them?

There was literally no one left on this beautiful high garden land but a bunch of hysterical girls and some older slave women.

That was about two thousand years ago.

At first there was a period of sheer despair. The mountains towered between them and their old enemies, but also between them and escape. There was no way up or down or out—they simply had to stay there. Some were for suicide, but not the majority. They must have been a plucky lot, as a whole, and they decided to live—as long as they did live. Of course they had hope, as youth must, that something would happen to change their fate.

So they set to work, to bury the dead, to plow and sow, to care for one another. . . .

Well—that original bunch of girls set to work to clean up the place and make their living as best they could. Some of the remaining slave women rendered invaluable service, teaching such trades as they knew. They had such records as were then kept, all the tools and implements of the time, and a most fertile land to work in.

There were a handful of the younger matrons who had escaped slaughter, and a few babies were born after the cataclysm—but only two boys, and they both died.

For five or ten years they worked together, growing stronger and wiser and more and more mutually attached, and then the miracle happened—one of these young women bore a child. Of course they all thought there must be a man somewhere, but none was found. Then they decided it must be a direct gift from the gods, and placed the proud mother in the Temple of Maaia—their Goddess of Motherhood—under strict watch. And there, as years passed, this wonder-woman bore child after child, five of them—all girls.

I did my best, keenly interested as I have always been in sociology and social psychology, to reconstruct in my mind the real position of these ancient women. There were some five or six hundred of them, and they were harem-bred; yet for the few preceding generations they had been reared in the atmosphere of such heroic struggle that the stock must have been toughened somewhat. Left alone in that terrific orphanhood, they had clung together, supporting one another and their little sisters, and developing unknown powers in the stress of new necessity. To this pain-hardened and work-strengthened group, who had lost not only the love and care of parents, but the hope of ever having children of their own, there now dawned the new hope.

Here at last was Motherhood, and though it was not for all of them personally, it might—if the power was inherited—found here a new race.

It may be imagined how those five Daughters of Maaia, Children of the Temple, Mothers of the Future—they had all the titles that love and hope and reverence could give—were reared. The whole little nation of women surrounded them with loving service, and waited, between a boundless hope and an as boundless despair, to see if they, too, would be Mothers.

And they were! As fast as they reached the age of twenty-five they began bearing. Each of them, like her mother, bore five daughters. Presently there were twenty-five New Women, Mothers in their own right, and the whole spirit of the country changed from mourning and mere courageous resignation to proud joy. The older women, those who remembered men, died off; the youngest of all the first lot of course died too, after a while, and by that time there were left one hundred and fifty-five parthenogenetic women, founding a new race.

They inherited all that the devoted care of that declining band of original ones could leave them. Their little country was quite safe. Their farms and gardens were all in full production. Such industries as they had were in careful order. The records of their past were all preserved, and for years the older women had spent their time in the best teaching they were capable of, that they might leave to the little group of sisters and mothers all they possessed of skill and knowledge.

There you have the start of Herland! One family, all descended from one mother! She lived to a hundred years old; lived to see her hundred and twenty-five great-granddaughters born; lived as Queen-Priestess-Mother of them all; and died with a nobler pride and a fuller joy than perhaps any human soul has ever known—she alone had founded a new race!...

Terry, incredulous, even contemptuous, when we were alone, refused to believe the story. "A lot of traditions as old as Herodotus—and about as trustworthy!" he said. "It's likely women—just a pack of women—would have hung together like that! We all know women can't organize—that they scrap like anything—are frightfully jealous."

"But these New Ladies didn't have anyone to be jealous of, remember," drawled Jeff.

"That's a likely story," Terry sneered.

"Why don't you invent a likelier one?" I asked him. "Here *are* the women—nothing but women, and you yourself admit there's no trace of a man in the country." This was after we had been about a good deal.

"I'll admit that," he growled. "And it's a big miss, too. There's not only no fun without 'em—no real sport—no competition; but these women aren't *womanly*. You know they aren't."

That kind of talk always set Jeff going; and I gradually grew to side with him. "Then you don't call a breed of women whose one concern is motherhood—womanly?" he asked.

"Indeed I don't," snapped Terry. "What does a man care for motherhood—when he hasn't a ghost of a chance at fatherhood? And besides—what's the good of talking sentiment when we are just men together? What a man wants of women is a good deal more than all this 'motherhood'!"

We were as patient as possible with Terry. He had lived about nine months among the "Colonels" when he made that outburst; and with no chance at any more strenuous excitement than our gymnastics gave us—save for our escape fiasco. I don't suppose Terry had ever lived so long with neither Love, Combat, nor Danger to employ his superabundant energies, and he was irritable. Neither Jeff nor I found it so wearing. I was so much interested intellectually that our confinement did not wear on me; and as for Jeff, bless his heart!—he enjoyed the society of that tutor of his almost as much as if she had been a girl—I don't know but more.

As to Terry's criticism, it was true. These women, whose essential distinction of motherhood was the dominant note of their whole culture, were strikingly deficient in what we call "femininity." This led me very promptly to the conviction that those "feminine charms" we are so fond of are not feminine at all, but mere reflected masculinity—developed to please us because they had to please us, and in no way essential to the real fulfillment of their great process. But Terry came to no such conclusion.

"Just you wait till I get out!" he muttered.

Then we both cautioned him. "Look here, Terry, my boy! You be careful! They've been mighty good to us—but do you remember the anesthesia? If you do any mischief in this virgin land, beware of the vengeance of the Maiden Aunts! Come, be a man! It won't be forever...."

As I learned more and more to appreciate what these women had accomplished, the less proud I was of what we, with all our manhood, had done.

You see, they had had no wars. They had had no kings, and no priests, and no aristocracies. They were sisters, and as they grew, they grew together—not by competition, but by united action.

We tried to put in a good word for competition, and they were keenly interested. Indeed, we soon found from their earnest questions of us that they were prepared to believe our world must be better than theirs. They were not sure; they wanted to know; but there was no such arrogance about them as might have been expected.

We rather spread ourselves, telling of the advantages of competition: how it developed fine qualities; that without it there would be "no stimulus to industry." Terry was very strong on that point.

"No stimulus to industry," they repeated, with that puzzled look we had learned to know so well. "*Stimulus? To Industry?* But don't you *like* to work?"

"No man would work unless he had to," Terry declared.

"Oh, no *man!* You mean that is one of your sex distinctions?"

"No, indeed!" he said hastily. "No one, I mean, man or woman, would work without incentive. Competition is the—the motor power, you see."

"It is not with us," they explained gently, "so it is hard for us to understand. Do you mean, for instance, that with you no mother would work for her children without the stimulus of competition?"

No, he admitted that he did not mean that. Mothers, he supposed, would of course work for their children in the home; but the world's work was different—that had to be done by men, and required the competitive element.

All our teachers were eagerly interested.

"We want so much to know—you have the whole world to tell us of, and we have only our little land! And there are two of you—the two sexes—to love and help one another. It must be a rich and wonderful world. Tell us—what is the work of the world, that men do—which we have not here?"

"Oh, everything," Terry said grandly. "The men do everything, with us." He squared his broad shoulders and lifted his chest. "We do not allow our women to work. Women are loved—idolized—honored—kept in the home to care for the children."

"What is 'the home'?" asked Somel a little wistfully.

But Zava begged: "Tell me first, do *no* women work, really?"

"Why, yes," Terry admitted. "Some have to, of the poorer sort."

"About how many—in your country?"

"About seven or eight million," said Jeff, as mischievous as ever.

CHAPTER 6

COMPARISONS ARE ODIOUS

———

I had always been proud of my country, of course. Everyone is. Compared with the other lands and other races I knew, the United States of America had always seemed to me, speaking modestly, as good as the best of them.

But just as a clear-eyed, intelligent, perfectly honest, and well-meaning child will frequently jar one's self-esteem by innocent questions, so did these women, without the slightest appearance of malice or satire, continually bring up points of discussion which we spent our best efforts in evading.

Now that we were fairly proficient in their language, had read a lot about their history, and had given them the general outlines of ours, they were able to press their questions closer.

So when Jeff admitted the number of "women wage earners" we had, they instantly asked for the total population, for the proportion of adult women, and found that there were but twenty million or so at the outside.

"Then at least a third of your women are—what is it you call them—wage earners? And they are all *poor*. What is *poor*, exactly?"

"Ours is the best country in the world as to poverty," Terry told them. "We do not have the wretched paupers and beggars of the older countries, I assure you. Why, European visitors tell us we don't know what poverty is."

"Neither do we," answered Zava. "Won't you tell us?"

Terry put it up to me, saying I was the sociologist, and I explained that the laws of nature require a struggle for existence, and that in the struggle the fittest survive, and the unfit perish. In our economic struggle, I continued, there was always plenty of opportunity for the fittest to reach the top, which they did, in great numbers, particularly in our country; that where there was severe economic pressure the lowest classes of course felt it the worst, and that among the poorest of all, the women were driven into the labor market by necessity.

They listened closely, with the usual note-taking.

"About one-third, then, belong to the poorest class," observed Moadine gravely. "And two-thirds are the ones who are—how was it you so beautifully put it?—'loved, honored, kept in the home to care for the children.' This inferior one-third have no children, I suppose?"

Jeff—he was getting as bad as they were—solemnly replied that, on the contrary, the poorer they were, the more children they had. That too, he explained, was a law of nature: "Reproduction is in inverse proportion to individuation."

"These 'laws of nature,'" Zava gently asked, "are they all the laws you have?"

"I should say not!" protested Terry. "We have systems of law that go back thousands and thousands of years—just as you do, no doubt," he finished politely.

"Oh no," Moadine told him. "We have no laws over a hundred years old, and most of them are under twenty. In a few weeks more," she continued, "we are going to have the pleasure of showing you over our little land and explaining everything you care to know about. We want you to see our people."

"And I assure you," Somel added, "that our people want to see you."

Terry brightened up immensely at this news, and reconciled himself to the renewed demands upon our capacity as teachers. It was lucky that we knew so little, really, and had no books to refer to, else, I fancy we might all be there yet, teaching those eager-minded women about the rest of the world....

With what we told them, from what sketches and models we

were able to prepare, they constructed a sort of working outline to fill in as they learned more.

A big globe was made, and our uncertain maps, helped out by those in that precious year-book thing I had, were tentatively indicated upon it.

They sat in eager groups, masses of them who came for the purpose, and listened while Jeff roughly ran over the geologic history of the earth, and showed them their own land in relation to the others. Out of that same pocket reference book of mine came facts and figures which were seized upon and placed in right relation with unerring acumen.

Even Terry grew interested in this work. "If we can keep this up, they'll be having us lecture to all the girls' schools and colleges—how about that?" he suggested to us. "Don't know as I'd object to being an Authority to such audiences."

They did, in fact, urge us to give public lectures later, but not to the hearers or with the purpose we expected.

What they were doing with us was like—like—well, say like Napoleon extracting military information from a few illiterate peasants. They knew just what to ask, and just what use to make of it; they had mechanical appliances for disseminating information almost equal to ours at home; and by the time we were led forth to lecture, our audiences had thoroughly mastered a well-arranged digest of all we had previously given to our teachers, and were prepared with such notes and questions as might have intimidated a university professor.

They were not audiences of girls, either. It was some time before we were allowed to meet the young women.

—

"Do you mind telling what you intend to do with us?" Terry burst forth one day, facing the calm and friendly Moadine with that funny half-blustering air of his. At first he used to storm and flourish quite a good deal, but nothing seemed to amuse them more; they would gather around and watch him as if it was an exhibition, politely, but with evident interest. So he learned to check himself, and was almost reasonable in his bearing—but not quite.

She announced smoothly and evenly: "Not in the least. I thought it was quite plain. We are trying to learn of you all we can, and to teach you what you are willing to learn of our country."

"Is that all?" he insisted.

She smiled a quiet enigmatic smile. "That depends."

"Depends on what?"

"Mainly on yourselves," she replied.

"Why do you keep us shut up so closely?"

"Because we do not feel quite safe in allowing you at large where there are so many young women."

Terry was really pleased at that. He had thought as much, inwardly; but he pushed the question. "Why should you be afraid? We are gentlemen."

She smiled that little smile again, and asked: "Are 'gentlemen' always safe?"

"You surely do not think that any of us," he said it with a good deal of emphasis on the "us," "would hurt your young girls?"

"Oh no," she said quickly, in real surprise. "The danger is quite the other way. They might hurt you. If, by any accident, you did harm any one of us, you would have to face a million mothers."

He looked so amazed and outraged that Jeff and I laughed outright, but she went on gently.

"I do not think you quite understand yet. You are but men, three men, in a country where the whole population are mothers—or are going to be. Motherhood means to us something which I cannot yet discover in any of the countries of which you tell us. You have spoken"—she turned to Jeff, "of Human Brotherhood as a great idea among you, but even that I judge is far from a practical expression?"

Jeff nodded rather sadly. "Very far—" he said.

"Here we have Human Motherhood—in full working use," she went on. "Nothing else except the literal sisterhood of our origin, and the far higher and deeper union of our social growth.

"The children in this country are the one center and focus of all our thoughts. Every step of our advance is always considered in its effect on them—on the race. You see, we are *Mothers*," she repeated, as if in that she had said it all.

"I don't see how that fact—which is shared by all women—constitutes any risk to us," Terry persisted. "You mean they would defend their children from attack. Of course. Any mothers would. But we are not Savages, my dear Lady; we are not going to hurt any mother's child."

They looked at one another and shook their heads a little, but Zava turned to Jeff and urged him to make us see—said he seemed to understand more fully than we did. And he tried.

I can see it now, or at least much more of it, but it has taken me a long time, and a good deal of honest intellectual effort.

What they call Motherhood was like this:

They began with a really high degree of social development, something like that of Ancient Egypt or Greece. Then they suffered the loss of everything masculine, and supposed at first that all human power and safety had gone too. Then they developed this virgin birth capacity. Then, since the prosperity of their children depended on it, the fullest and subtlest coordination began to be practiced....

They developed all this close inter-service in the interests of their children. To do the best work they had to specialize, of course; the children needed spinners and weavers, farmers and gardeners, carpenters and masons, as well as mothers.

Then came the filling up of the place. When a population multiplies by five every thirty years it soon reaches the limits of a country, especially a small one like this. They very soon eliminated all the grazing cattle—sheep were the last to go, I believe. Also, they worked out a system of intensive agriculture surpassing anything I ever heard of, with the very forests all reset with fruit- or nut-bearing trees.

Do what they would, however, there soon came a time when they were confronted with the problem of "the pressure of population"

in an acute form. There was really crowding, and with it, unavoid-
ably, a decline in standards.

And how did those women meet it?

Not by a "struggle for existence" which would result in an everlasting writhing mass of underbred people trying to get ahead of
one another—some few on top, temporarily, many constantly
crushed out underneath, a hopeless substratum of paupers and de-
generates, and no serenity or peace for anyone—no possibility for
really noble qualities among the people at large.

Neither did they start off on predatory excursions to get more
land from somebody else, or to get more food from somebody else,
to maintain their struggling mass.

Not at all. They sat down in council together and thought it out.
Very clear, strong thinkers they were. They said: "With our best
endeavors this country will support about so many people, with the
standard of peace, comfort, health, beauty, and progress we demand. Very well. That is all the people we will make."

———

[...]

There followed a period of "negative Eugenics" which must have
been an appalling sacrifice. We are commonly willing to "lay down
our lives" for our country, but they had to forego motherhood for
their country—and it was precisely the hardest thing for them
to do.

When I got this far in my reading I went to Somel for more light.
We were as friendly by that time as I had ever been in my life with
any woman. A mighty comfortable soul she was, giving one the nice
smooth mother-feeling a man likes in a woman, and yet giving also
the clear intelligence and dependableness I used to assume to be
masculine qualities. We had talked volumes already.

"See here," said I. "Here was this dreadful period when they got
far too thick, and decided to limit the population. We have a lot of
talk about that among us, but your position is so different that I'd
like to know a little more about it.

"I understand that you make Motherhood the highest Social

Service—a Sacrament, really; that it is only undertaken once, by the majority of the population; that those held unfit are not allowed even that; and that to be encouraged to bear more than one child is the very highest reward and honor in the power of the State."

(She interpolated here that the nearest approach to an aristocracy they had was to come of a line of "Over Mothers"—those who had been so honored.)

"But what I do not understand, naturally, is how you prevent it. I gathered that each woman had five. You have no tyrannical husbands to hold in check—and you surely do not destroy the unborn—"

The look of ghastly horror she gave me I shall never forget. She started from her chair, pale, her eyes blazing.

"Destroy the unborn—!" she said in a hard whisper. "Do men do that in your country?"

"Men!" I began to answer, rather hotly, and then saw the gulf before me. None of us wanted these women to think that *our* women, of whom we boasted so proudly, were in any way inferior to them. I am ashamed to say that I equivocated. I told her about Malthus and his fears. I told her of certain criminal types of women—perverts, or crazy, who had been known to commit infanticide. I told her, truly enough, that there was much in our land which was open to criticism, but that I hated to dwell on our defects until they understood us and our conditions better.

And, making a wide detour, I scrambled back to my question of how they limited the population....

"We were living on rations before we worked it out," she said. "But we did work it out. You see, before a child comes to one of us there is a period of utter exaltation—the whole being is uplifted and filled with a concentrated desire for that child. We learned to look forward to that period with the greatest caution. Often our young women, those to whom motherhood had not yet come, would voluntarily defer it. When that deep inner demand for a child began to be felt she would deliberately engage in the most active work, physical and mental; and even more important, would solace her longing by the direct care and service of the babies we already had."

She paused. Her wise sweet face grew deeply, reverently tender.

"We soon grew to see that mother-love has more than one channel of expression. I think the reason our children are so—so fully loved, by all of us, is that we never—any of us—have enough of our own."

This seemed to me infinitely pathetic, and I said so. "We have much that is bitter and hard in our life at home," I told her, "but this seems to me piteous beyond words—a whole nation of starving mothers!"

But she smiled her deep contented smile, and said I quite misunderstood.

"We each go without a certain range of personal joy," she said, "but remember—we each have a million children to love and serve—*our* children."

It was beyond me. To hear a lot of women talk about "our children"! But I suppose that is the way the ants and bees would talk—do talk, maybe.

That was what they did, anyhow.

When a woman chose to be a mother, she allowed the child-longing to grow within her till it worked its natural miracle. When she did not so choose she put the whole thing out of her mind, and fed her heart with the other babies.

Let me see—with us, children—minors, that is—constitute about three-fifths of the population; with them only about one-third, or less. And precious—! No sole heir to an empire's throne, no solitary millionaire baby, no only child of middle-aged parents, could compare as an idol with these Herland Children....

CHAPTER 7

OUR GROWING MODESTY

[...]

Our first step of comparative freedom was a personally conducted tour of the country. No pentagonal bodyguard now! Only our special tutors, and we got on famously with them. Jeff said he loved Zava like an aunt—"only jollier than any aunt I ever saw"; Somel and I were as chummy as could be—the best of friends; but it was funny to watch Terry and Moadine. She was patient with him, and courteous, but it was like the patience and courtesy of some great man, say a skilled, experienced diplomat, with a schoolgirl. Her grave acquiescence with his most preposterous expression of feeling; her genial laughter, not only with, but, I often felt, at him—though impeccably polite; her innocent questions, which almost invariably led him to say more than he intended—Jeff and I found it all amusing to watch.

He never seemed to recognize that quiet background of superiority. When she dropped an argument he always thought he had silenced her; when she laughed he thought it tribute to his wit.

I hated to admit to myself how much Terry had sunk in my esteem. Jeff felt it too, I am sure; but neither of us admitted it to the other. At home we had measured him with other men, and, though we knew his failings, he was by no means an unusual type. We knew his virtues too, and they had always seemed more prominent than the faults. Measured among women—our women at home, I mean—he had always stood high. He was visibly popular. Even where his habits were known, there was no discrimination against him; in some cases his reputation for what was felicitously termed "gaiety" seemed a special charm.

But here, against the calm wisdom and quiet restrained humor of these women, with only that blessed Jeff and my inconspicuous self to compare with, Terry did stand out rather strong.

As "a man among men," he didn't; as a man among—I shall have to say, "females," he didn't; his intense masculinity seemed only fit complement to their intense femininity. But here he was all out of drawing.

Moadine was a big woman, with a balanced strength that seldom showed. Her eye was as quietly watchful as a fencer's. She maintained a pleasant relation with her charge, but I doubt if many, even in that country, could have done as well.

He called her "Maud," amongst ourselves, and said she was "a good old soul, but a little slow"; wherein he was quite wrong. Needless to say, he called Jeff's teacher "Java," and sometimes "Mocha," or plain "Coffee"; when specially mischievous, "Chicory," and even "Postum." But Somel rather escaped this form of humor, save for a rather forced "Some 'ell."

"Don't you people have but one name?" he asked one day, after we had been introduced to a whole group of them, all with pleasant, few-syllabled strange names, like the ones we knew.

"Oh yes," Moadine told him. "A good many of us have another, as we get on in life—a descriptive one. That is the name we earn. Sometimes even that is changed, or added to, in an unusually rich life. Such as our present Land-Mother—what you call president or king, I believe. She was called Mera, even as a child; that means 'thinker.' Later there was added Du—Du-mera—the wise thinker, and now we all know her as O-du-mera—great and wise thinker. You shall meet her."

"No surnames at all then?" pursued Terry, with his somewhat patronizing air. "No family name?"

"Why no," she said. "Why should we? We are all descended from a common source—all one 'family' in reality. You see, our comparatively brief and limited history gives us that advantage at least."

"But does not each mother want her own child to bear her name?" I asked.

"No—why should she? The child has its own."

"Why for—for identification—so people will know whose child she is."

"We keep the most careful records," said Somel. "Each one of us has our exact line of descent all the way back to our dear First Mother. There are many reasons for doing that. But as to everyone knowing which child belongs to which mother—why should she?"

Here, as in so many other instances, we were led to feel the difference between the purely maternal and the paternal attitude of mind. The element of personal pride seemed strangely lacking.

"How about your other works?" asked Jeff. "Don't you sign your names to them—books and statues and so on?"

"Yes, surely, we are all glad and proud to. Not only books and statues, but all kinds of work. You will find little names on the houses, on the furniture, on the dishes sometimes. Because otherwise one is likely to forget, and we want to know to whom to be grateful."

"You speak as if it were done for the convenience of the consumer—not the pride of the producer," I suggested.

"It's both," said Somel. "We have pride enough in our work."

"Then why not in your children?" urged Jeff.

"But we have! We're magnificently proud of them," she insisted.

"Then why not sign 'em?" said Terry triumphantly.

Moadine turned to him with her slightly quizzical smile. "Because the finished product is not a private one. When they are babies, we do speak of them, at times, as 'Essa's Lato,' or 'Novine's Amel'; but that is merely descriptive and conversational. In the records, of course, the child stands in her own line of mothers; but in dealing with it personally it is Lato, or Amel, without dragging in its ancestors."

"But have you names enough to give a new one to each child?"

"Assuredly we have, for each living generation."

Then they asked about our methods, and found first that "we" did so and so, and then that other nations did differently. Upon which they wanted to know which method has been proved best—and we had to admit that so far as we knew there had been no attempt at comparison, each people pursuing its own custom in the fond conviction of superiority, and either despising or quite ignoring the others.

With these women the most salient quality in all their institutions was reasonableness. When I dug into the records to follow out any line of development, that was the most astonishing thing—the conscious effort to make it better. . . .

This was nowhere better shown than in that matter of food supply, which I will now attempt to describe.

Having improved their agriculture to the highest point, and carefully estimated the number of persons who could comfortably live on their square miles; having then limited their population to that number, one would think that was all there was to be done. But they had not thought so. To them the country was a unit—it was Theirs. They themselves were a unit, a conscious group; they thought in terms of the community. As such, their time-sense was not limited to the hopes and ambitions of an individual life. Therefore, they habitually considered and carried out plans for improvement which might cover centuries.

I had never seen, had scarcely imagined, human beings undertaking such a work as the deliberate replanting of an entire forest area with different kinds of trees. Yet this seemed to them the simplest common sense, like a man's plowing up an inferior lawn and reseeding it. Now every tree bore fruit—edible fruit, that is. In the case of one tree, in which they took especial pride, it had originally no fruit at all—that is, none humanly edible—yet was so beautiful that they wished to keep it. For nine hundred years they had experimented, and now showed us this particularly lovely graceful tree, with a profuse crop of nutritious seeds.

That trees were the best food plants, they had early decided, requiring far less labor in tilling the soil, and bearing a larger amount of food for the same ground space; also doing much to preserve and enrich the soil....

What impressed me particularly was their scheme of fertilization. Here was this little shut-in piece of land where one would have thought an ordinary people would have been starved out long ago or reduced to an annual struggle for life. These careful culturists had worked out a perfect scheme of refeeding the soil with all that came out of it. All the scraps and leavings of their food, plant waste from lumber work or textile industry, all the solid matter from the sewage, properly treated and combined—everything which came from the earth went back to it.

The practical result was like that in any healthy forest; an increasingly valuable soil was being built, instead of the progressive impoverishment so often seen in the rest of the world.

When this first burst upon us we made such approving comments that they were surprised that such obvious common sense should be praised; asked what our methods were; and we had some difficulty in—well, in diverting them, by referring to the extent of our own land, and the—admitted—carelessness with which we had skimmed the cream of it.

At least we thought we had diverted them. Later I found that besides keeping a careful and accurate account of all we told them, they had a sort of skeleton chart, on which the things we said and the things we palpably avoided saying were all set down and studied. It really was child's play for those profound educators to work out a painfully accurate estimate of our conditions—in some lines. When a given line of observation seemed to lead to some very dreadful inference, they always gave us the benefit of the doubt, leaving it open to further knowledge. Some of the things we had grown to accept as perfectly natural, or as belonging to our human limitations, they literally could not have believed; and, as I have said, we had all of us joined in a tacit endeavor to conceal much of the social status at home.

"Confound their grandmotherly minds!" Terry said. "Of course they can't understand a Man's World! They aren't human—they're just a pack of Fe-Fe-Females!" This was after he had to admit their parthenogenesis.

"I wish our grandfatherly minds had managed as well," said Jeff. "Do you really think it's to our credit that we have muddled along with all our poverty and disease and the like? They have peace and plenty, wealth and beauty, goodness and intellect. Pretty good people, I think!"

"You'll find they have their faults too," Terry insisted; and partly in self-defense, we all three began to look for those faults of theirs. We had been very strong on this subject before we got there—in those baseless speculations of ours.

"Suppose there are," Jeff would put it, over and over. "What'll they be like?"

And we had been cocksure as to the inevitable limitations, the faults and vices, of a lot of women. We had expected them to be given over to what we called "feminine vanity"—"frills and furbelows," and we found they had evolved a costume more perfect than the Chinese dress, richly beautiful when so desired, always useful, of unfailing dignity and good taste.

We had expected a dull submissive monotony, and found a daring social inventiveness far beyond our own, and a mechanical and scientific development fully equal to ours.

We had expected pettiness, and found a social consciousness besides which our nations looked like quarreling children—feebleminded ones at that.

We had expected jealousy, and found a broad sisterly affection, a fair-minded intelligence, to which we could produce no parallel.

We had expected hysteria, and found a standard of health and vigor, a calmness of temper, to which the habit of profanity, for instance, was impossible to explain—we tried it.

All these things even Terry had to admit, but he still insisted that we should find out the other side pretty soon.

"It stands to reason, doesn't it?" he argued. "The whole thing's deuced unnatural—I'd say impossible if we weren't in it. And an unnatural condition's sure to have unnatural results. You'll find some awful characteristics—see if you don't! For instance—we don't know yet what they do with their criminals—their defectives—their aged. You notice we haven't seen any! There's got to be something!"

I was inclined to believe that there had to be something, so I took the bull by the horns—the cow, I should say!—and asked Somel.

"I want to find some flaw in all this perfection," I told her flatly. "It simply isn't possible that three million people have no faults. We are trying our best to understand and learn—would you mind helping us by saying what, to your minds, are the worst qualities of this unique civilization of yours?"

We were sitting together in a shaded arbor, in one of those eating-gardens of theirs. The delicious food had been eaten, a plate of fruit still before us. We could look out on one side over a stretch of open country, quietly rich and lovely; on the other, the garden, with tables here and there, far apart enough for privacy. Let me say right here that with all their careful "balance of population" there was no crowding in this country. There was room, space, a sunny breezy freedom everywhere.

Somel set her chin upon her hand, her elbow on the low wall beside her, and looked off over the fair land.

"Of course we have faults—all of us," she said. "In one way you might say that we have more than we used to—that is, our standard of perfection seems to get farther and farther away. But we are not discouraged, because our records do show gain—considerable gain.

"When we began—even with the start of one particularly noble mother—we inherited the characteristics of a long race-record behind her. And they cropped out from time to time—alarmingly. But it is—yes, quite six hundred years since we have had what you call a 'criminal.'

"We have, of course, made it our first business to train out, to breed out, when possible, the lowest types."

"Breed out?" I asked. "How could you—with parthenogenesis?"

"If the girl showing the bad qualities had still the power to appreciate social duty, we appealed to her, by that, to renounce motherhood. Some of the few worst types were, fortunately, unable to reproduce. But if the fault was in a disproportionate egotism—then the girl was sure she had the right to have children, even that hers would be better than others."

"I can see that," I said. "And then she would be likely to rear them in the same spirit."

"That we never allowed," answered Somel quietly.

"Allowed?" I queried. "Allowed a mother to rear her own children?"

"Certainly not," said Somel, "unless she was fit for that supreme task."

This was rather a blow to my previous convictions.

"But I thought motherhood was for each of you—"

"Motherhood—yes, that is, maternity, to bear a child. But education is our highest art, only allowed to our highest artists."

"Education?" I was puzzled again. "I don't mean education. I mean by motherhood not only child-bearing, but the care of babies."

"The care of babies involves education and is entrusted only to the most fit," she repeated.

"Then you separate mother and child!" I cried in cold horror, something of Terry's feeling creeping over me, that there must be something wrong among these many virtues.

"Not usually," she patiently explained. "You see, almost every woman values her maternity above everything else. Each girl holds it close and dear, an exquisite joy, a crowning honor, the most intimate, most personal, most precious thing. That is, the child-rearing has come to be with us a culture so profoundly studied, practiced with such subtlety and skill, that the more we love our children the less we are willing to trust that process to unskilled hands—even our own."

"But a mother's love—" I ventured.

She studied my face, trying to work out a means of clear explanation.

"You told us about your dentists," she said, at length, "those quaintly specialized persons who spend their lives filling little holes in other persons' teeth—even in children's teeth sometimes."

"Yes?" I said, not getting her drift.

"Does mother-love urge mothers—with you—to fill their own children's teeth? Or to wish to?"

"Why no—of course not," I protested. "But that is a highly specialized craft. Surely the care of babies is open to any woman—any mother!"

"We do not think so," she gently replied. "Those of us who are the most highly competent fulfill that office; and a majority of our girls eagerly try for it—I assure you we have the very best."

"But the poor mother—bereaved of her baby—"

"Oh no!" she earnestly assured me. "Not in the least bereaved. It is her baby still—it is with her—she has not lost it. But she is not the only one to care for it. There are others whom she knows to be wiser. She knows it because she has studied as they did, practiced as they did, and honors their real superiority. For the child's sake, she is glad to have for it this highest care."

I was unconvinced. Besides, this was only hearsay; I had yet to see the motherhood of Herland.

CHAPTER 8

THE GIRLS OF HERLAND

At last Terry's ambition was realized. We were invited, always courteously and with free choice on our part, to address general audiences and classes of girls. . . .

Girls—hundreds of them—eager, bright-eyed, attentive young faces; crowding questions, and, I regret to say, an increasing inability on our part to answer them effectively.

Our special guides, who were on the platform with us, and sometimes aided in clarifying a question or, oftener, an answer, noticed this effect, and closed the formal lecture part of the evening rather shortly.

"Our young women will be glad to meet you," Somel suggested, "to talk with you more personally, if you are willing?"

Willing! We were impatient and said as much, at which I saw a flickering little smile cross Moadine's face. Even then, with all those eager young things waiting to talk to us, a sudden question crossed my mind: "What was their point of view? What did they think of us?" We learned that later.

Terry plunged in among those young creatures with a sort of rapture, somewhat as a glad swimmer takes to the sea. Jeff, with a rapt look on his high-bred face, approached as to a sacrament. But I was a little chilled by that last thought of mine, and kept my eyes open. I found time to watch Jeff, even while I was surrounded by an eager group of questioners—as we all were—and saw how his worshipping eyes, his grave courtesy, pleased and drew some of them;

while others, rather stronger spirits they looked to be, drew away from his group to Terry's or mine.

I watched Terry with special interest, knowing how he had longed for this time, and how irresistible he had always been at home. And I could see, just in snatches, of course, how his suave and masterful approach seemed to irritate them; his too-intimate glances were vaguely resented, his compliments puzzled and annoyed. Sometimes a girl would flush, not with drooped eyelids and inviting timidity, but with anger and a quick lift of the head. Girl after girl turned on her heel and left him, till he had but a small ring of questioners, and they, visibly, were the least "girlish" of the lot.

I saw him looking pleased at first, as if he thought he was making a strong impression; but, finally, casting a look at Jeff, or me, he seemed less pleased—and less.

As for me, I was most agreeably surprised. At home I never was "popular." I had my girl friends, good ones, but they were friends—nothing else. Also they were of somewhat the same clan, not popular in the sense of swarming admirers. But here, to my astonishment, I found my crowd was the largest.

I have to generalize, of course, rather telescoping many impressions; but the first evening was a good sample of the impression we made. Jeff had a following, if I may call it that, of the more sentimental—though that's not the word I want. The less practical, perhaps; the girls who were artists of some sort, ethicists, teachers—that kind.

Terry was reduced to a rather combative group: keen, logical, inquiring minds, not over sensitive, the very kind he liked least; while, as for me—I became quite cocky over my general popularity.

Terry was furious about it. We could hardly blame him.

"Girls!" he burst forth, when that evening was over and we were by ourselves once more. "Call those *girls*!"

"Most delightful girls, I call them," said Jeff, his blue eyes dreamily contented.

"What do *you* call them?" I mildly inquired.

"Boys! Nothing but boys, most of 'em. A standoffish, disagreeable lot at that. Critical, impertinent youngsters. No girls at all."

He was angry and severe, not a little jealous, too, I think. Afterward, when he found out just what it was they did not like, he changed his manner somewhat and got on better. He had to. For, in spite of his criticism, they were girls, and, furthermore, all the girls there were! Always excepting our three!—with whom we presently renewed our acquaintance.

When it came to courtship, which it soon did, I can of course best describe my own—and am least inclined to. But of Jeff I heard somewhat; he was inclined to dwell reverently and admiringly, at some length, on the exalted sentiment and measureless perfection of his Celis; and Terry—Terry made so many false starts and met so many rebuffs, that by the time he really settled down to win Alima, he was considerably wiser. At that, it was not smooth sailing. They broke and quarreled, over and over; he would rush off to console himself with some other fair one—the other fair one would have none of him—and he would drift back to Alima, becoming more and more devoted each time.

She never gave an inch. A big, handsome creature, rather exceptionally strong even in that race of strong women, with a proud head and sweeping level brows that lined across above her dark eager eyes like the wide wings of a soaring hawk.

I was good friends with all three of them but best of all with Ellador, long before that feeling changed, for both of us.

From her, and from Somel, who talked very freely with me, I learned at last something of the viewpoint of Herland toward its visitors.

Here they were, isolated, happy, contented, when the booming buzz of our biplane tore the air above them.

Everybody heard it—saw it—for miles and miles, word flashed all over the country, and a council was held in every town and village.

And this was their rapid determination:

"From another country. Probably men. Evidently highly civilized. Doubtless possessed of much valuable knowledge. May be dangerous. Catch them if possible; tame and train them if necessary. This may be a chance to re-establish a bi-sexual state for our people."

They were not afraid of us—three million highly intelligent women—or two million, counting only grown-ups—were not likely to be afraid of three young men. We thought of them as "Women," and therefore timid; but it was two thousand years since they had had anything to be afraid of, and certainly more than one thousand since they had outgrown the feeling.

We thought—at least Terry did—that we could have our pick of them. They thought—very cautiously and farsightedly—of picking us, if it seemed wise....

They were interested, profoundly interested, but it was not the kind of interest we were looking for.

To get an idea of their attitude you have to hold in mind their extremely high sense of solidarity. They were not each choosing a lover; they hadn't the faintest idea of love—sex-love, that is. These girls—to each of whom motherhood was a lodestar, and that motherhood exalted above a mere personal function, looked forward to as the highest social service, as the sacrament of a lifetime—were now confronted with an opportunity to make the great step of changing their whole status, of reverting to their earlier bi-sexual order of nature....

As for Ellador: Suppose you come to a strange land and find it pleasant enough—just a little more than ordinarily pleasant—and then you find rich farmland, and then gardens, gorgeous gardens, and then palaces full of rare and curious treasures—incalculable, inexhaustible, and then—mountains—like the Himalayas, and then the sea.

I liked her that day she balanced on the branch before me and named the trio. I thought of her most. Afterward I turned to her like a friend when we met for the third time, and continued the acquaintance. While Jeff's ultra-devotion rather puzzled Celis, really put off their day of happiness, while Terry and Alima quarreled and parted, re-met and re-parted, Ellador and I grew to be close friends....

As I've said, I had never cared very much for women, nor they for me—not Terry-fashion. But this one—

At first I never even thought of her "in that way," as the girls have it. I had not come to the country with any Turkish-harem intentions, and I was no woman-worshipper like Jeff. I just liked that girl "as a friend," as we say. That friendship grew like a tree. She was *such* a good sport! We did all kinds of things together. She taught me games and I taught her games, and we raced and rowed and had all manner of fun, as well as higher comradeship....

A still day—on the edge of the world, their world. The two of us, gazing out over the far dim forestland below, talking of heaven and earth and human life, and of my land and other lands and what they needed and what I hoped to do for them—

"If you will help me," I said.

She turned to me, with that high, sweet look of hers, and then, as her eyes rested in mine and her hands too—then suddenly there blazed out between us a farther glory, instant, overwhelming— quite beyond any words of mine to tell.

Celis was a blue-and-gold-and-rose person; Alima, black-and-white-and-red, a blazing beauty. Ellador was brown: hair dark and soft, like a seal coat; clear brown skin with a healthy red in it; brown eyes—all the way from topaz to black velvet they seemed to range— splendid girls, all of them.

They had seen us first of all, far down in the lake below, and flashed the tidings across the land even before our first exploring flight. They had watched our landing, flitted through the forest with us, hidden in that tree and—I shrewdly suspect—giggled on purpose.

They had kept watch over our hooded machine, taking turns at it; and when our escape was announced, had followed alongside for a day or two, and been there at the last, as described. They felt a special claim on us—called us "their men"—and when we were at liberty to study the land and people, and be studied by them, their claim was recognized by the wise leaders.

But I felt, we all did, that we should have chosen them among millions, unerringly.

And yet, "the path of true love never did run smooth"; this period of courtship was full of the most unsuspected pitfalls....

Ellador and I talked it all out together, so that we had an easier experience of it when the real miracle time came. Also, between us, we made things clearer to Jeff and Celis. But Terry would not listen to reason.

He was madly in love with Alima. He wanted to take her by storm, and nearly lost her forever....

But I think Alima retained some faint vestige of long-descended feeling which made Terry more possible to her than to others; and that she had made up her mind to the experiment and hated to renounce it.

However it came about, we all three at length achieved full understanding, and solemnly faced what was to them a step of measureless importance, a grave question as well as a great happiness; to us a strange, new joy....

CHAPTER 9

OUR RELATIONS AND THEIRS

[...]

To these women we came, filled with the ideas, convictions, traditions, of our culture, and undertook to rouse in them the emotions which—to us—seemed proper.

However much, or little, of true sex-feeling there was between us, it phrased itself in their minds in terms of friendship, the one purely personal love they knew, and of ultimate parentage. Visibly we were not mothers, nor children, nor compatriots; so, if they loved us, we must be friends.

That we should pair off together in our courting days was natural to them; that we three should remain much together, as they did themselves, was also natural. We had as yet no work, so we hung about them in their forest tasks; that was natural, too.

But when we began to talk about each couple having "homes" of our own, they could not understand it.

"Our work takes us all around the country," explained Celis. "We cannot live in one place all the time."

"We are together now," urged Alima, looking proudly at Terry's stalwart nearness. (This was one of the times when they were "on," though presently "off" again.)

"It's not the same thing at all," he insisted. "A man wants a home of his own, with his wife and family in it."

"Staying in it? All the time?" asked Ellador. "Not imprisoned, surely!"

"Of course not! Living there—naturally," he answered.

"What does she do there—all the time?" Alima demanded. "What is her work?"

Then Terry patiently explained again that our women did not work—with reservations.

"But what do they do—if they have no work?" she persisted.

"They take care of the home—and the children."

"At the same time?" asked Ellador.

"Why yes. The children play about, and the mother has charge of it all. There are servants, of course."

It seemed so obvious, so natural to Terry, that he always grew impatient; but the girls were honestly anxious to understand.

"How many children do your women have?" Alima had her notebook out now, and a rather firm set of lip. Terry began to dodge.

"There is no set number, my dear," he explained. "Some have more, some have less."

"Some have none at all," I put in mischievously.

They pounced on this admission and soon wrung from us the general fact that those women who had the most children had the least servants, and those who had the most servants had the least children.

"There!" triumphed Alima. "One or two or no children, and three or four servants. Now what do those women *do?*"

We explained as best we might. We talked of "social duties," disingenuously banking on their not interpreting the words as we did; we talked of hospitality, entertainment, and various "interests." All the time we knew that to these large-minded women whose whole mental outlook was so collective, the limitations of a wholly personal life were inconceivable.

"We cannot really understand it," Ellador concluded. "We are only half a people. We have our woman-ways and they have their man-ways and their both-ways. We have worked out a system of living which is, of course, limited. They must have a broader, richer, better one. I should like to see it."

"You shall, dearest," I whispered.

—

"There's nothing to smoke," complained Terry. He was in the midst of a prolonged quarrel with Alima, and needed a sedative. "There's nothing to drink. These blessed women have no pleasant vices. I wish we could get out of here!"

This wish was vain. We were always under a certain degree of watchfulness. When Terry burst forth to tramp the streets at night he always found a "Colonel" here or there; and when, on an occasion of fierce though temporary despair, he had plunged to the cliff edge with some vague view to escape, he found several of them close by. We were free—but there was a string to it.

"They've no unpleasant ones, either," Jeff reminded him.

"Wish they had!" Terry persisted. "They've neither the vices of men, nor the virtues of women—they're neuters!"

"You know better than that. Don't talk nonsense," said I, severely.

I was thinking of Ellador's eyes when they gave me a certain look, a look she did not at all realize.

Jeff was equally incensed. "I don't know what 'virtues of women' you miss. Seems to me they have all of them."

"They've no modesty," snapped Terry. "No patience, no submissiveness, none of that natural yielding which is woman's greatest charm."

I shook my head pityingly. "Go and apologize and make friends again, Terry. You've got a grouch, that's all. These women have the virtue of humanity, with less of its faults than any folks I ever saw. As for patience—they'd have pitched us over the cliffs the first day we lit among 'em, if they hadn't that."

"There are no—distractions," he grumbled. "Nowhere a man can go and cut loose a bit. It's an everlasting parlor and nursery."

"And workshop," I added. "And school, and office, and laboratory, and studio, and theater, and—home."

"Home!" he sneered. "There isn't a home in the whole pitiful place."

"There isn't anything else, and you know it," Jeff retorted hotly. "I never saw, I never dreamed of, such universal peace and good will and mutual affection."

"Oh, well, of course, if you like a perpetual Sunday school, it's all very well. But I like Something Doing. Here it's all done."

There was something to this criticism. The years of pioneering lay far behind them. Theirs was a civilization in which the initial difficulties had long since been overcome. The untroubled peace, the unmeasured plenty, the steady health, the large good will and smooth management which ordered everything, left nothing to overcome. It was like a pleasant family in an old established, perfectly run country place.

I liked it because of my eager and continued interest in the sociological achievements involved. Jeff liked it as he would have liked such a family and such a place anywhere.

Terry did not like it because he found nothing to oppose, to struggle with, to conquer.

"Life is a struggle, has to be," he insisted. "If there is no struggle, there is no life—that's all."

"You're talking nonsense—masculine nonsense," the peaceful Jeff replied. He was certainly a warm defender of Herland. "Ants don't raise their myriads by a struggle, do they? Or the bees?"

"Oh, if you go back to insects—and want to live in an anthill!— I tell you the higher grades of life are reached only through struggle—combat. There's no Drama here. Look at their plays! They make me sick."

He rather had us there. The drama of the country was—to our taste—rather flat. You see, they lacked the sex motive and, with it, jealousy. They had no interplay of warring nations, no aristocracy and its ambitions, no wealth and poverty opposition.

I see I have said little about the economics of the place; it should have come before, but I'll go on about the drama now.

They had their own kind. There was a most impressive array of pageantry, of processions, a sort of grand ritual, with their arts and their religion broadly blended. The very babies joined in it. To see one of their great annual festivals, with the massed and marching stateliness of those great mothers; the young women brave and noble, beautiful and strong; and then the children, taking part as naturally as ours would frolic round a Christmas tree—it was over-powering in the impression of joyous, triumphant life.

They had begun at a period when the drama, the dance, music, religion, and education were all very close together; and instead of developing them in detached lines, they had kept the connection. Let me try again to give, if I can, a faint sense of the difference in the life view—the background and basis on which their culture rested....

We have two life cycles: the man's and the woman's. To the man there is growth, struggle, conquest, the establishment of his family, and as much further success in gain or ambition as he can achieve.

To the woman, growth, the securing of a husband, the subordinate activities of family life, and afterward such "social" or charitable interests as her position allows.

Here was but one cycle, and that a large one.

The child entered upon a broad open field of life, in which motherhood was the one great personal contribution to the national life, and all the rest the individual share in their common activities. Every girl I talked to, at any age above babyhood, had her cheerful determination as to what she was going to be when she grew up.

What Terry meant by saying they had no "modesty" was that this great life-view had no shady places; they had a high sense of personal decorum, but no shame—no knowledge of anything to be ashamed of.

Even their shortcomings and misdeeds in childhood never were presented to them as sins; merely as errors and misplays—as in a game. Some of them, who were palpably less agreeable than others or who had a real weakness or fault, were treated with cheerful allowance, as a friendly group at whist would treat a poor player.

Their religion, you see, was maternal; and their ethics, based on the full perception of evolution, showed the principle of growth and the beauty of wise culture. They had no theory of the essential opposition of good and evil; life to them was Growth; their pleasure was in growing, and their duty also....

It was the eager happiness of the children and young people

which first made me see the folly of that common notion of ours—that if life was smooth and happy, people would not enjoy it. As I studied these youngsters, vigorous, joyous, eager little creatures, and their voracious appetite for life, it shook my previous ideas so thoroughly that they have never been re-established. The steady level of good health gave them all that natural stimulus we used to call "animal spirits"—an odd contradiction in terms. They found themselves in an immediate environment which was agreeable and interesting, and before them stretched the years of learning and discovery, the fascinating, endless process of education.

As I looked into these methods and compared them with our own, my strange uncomfortable sense of race-humility grew apace.

Ellador could not understand my astonishment. She explained things kindly and sweetly, but with some amazement that they needed explaining, and with sudden questions as to how we did it that left me meeker than ever.

I betook myself to Somel one day, carefully not taking Ellador. I did not mind seeming foolish to Somel—she was used to it.

"I want a chapter of explanation," I told her. "You know my stupidities by heart, and I do not want to show them to Ellador—she thinks me so wise!"

She smiled delightedly. "It is beautiful to see," she told me, "this new wonderful love between you. The whole country is interested, you know—how can we help it!"

I had not thought of that. We say: "All the world loves a lover," but to have a couple of million people watching one's courtship—and that a difficult one—was rather embarrassing.

"Tell me about your theory of education," I said. "Make it short and easy. And, to show you what puzzles me, I'll tell you that in our theory great stress is laid on the forced exertion of the child's mind; we think it is good for him to overcome obstacles."

"Of course it is," she unexpectedly agreed. "All our children do that—they love to."

That puzzled me again. If they loved to do it, how could it be educational?

"Our theory is this," she went on carefully. "Here is a young human being. The mind is as natural a thing as the body, a thing that grows, a thing to use and to enjoy. We seek to nourish, to stimulate, to exercise the mind of a child as we do the body. There are the two main divisions in education—you have those of course?—the things it is necessary to know, and things it is necessary to do."

"To do? Mental exercises, you mean?"

"Yes. Our general plan is this: in the matter of feeding the mind, of furnishing information, we use our best powers to meet the natural appetite of a healthy young brain; not to overfeed it, to provide such amount and variety of impressions as seem most welcome to each child. That is the easiest part. The other division is in arranging a properly graduated series of exercises which will best develop each mind; the common faculties we all have, and most carefully, the especial faculties some of us have. You do this also, do you not?"

"In a way," I said rather lamely. "We have not so subtle and highly developed a system as you, not approaching it; but tell me more. As to the information—how do you manage? It appears that all of you know pretty much everything—is that right?"

This she laughingly disclaimed. "By no means. We are, as you soon found out, extremely limited in knowledge. I wish you could realize what a ferment the country is in over the new things you have told us; the passionate eagerness among thousands of us to go to your country and learn—learn—learn! But what we do know is readily divisible into common knowledge and special knowledge. The common knowledge we have long since learned to feed into the minds of our little ones with no waste of time or strength; the special knowledge is open to all, as they desire it. Some of us specialize in one line only. But most take up several—some for their regular work, some to grow with."

"To grow with?"

"Yes. When one settles too close in one kind of work there is a tendency to atrophy in the disused portions of the brain. We like to keep on learning, always."

"What do you study?"

"As much as we know of the different sciences. We have, within our limits, a good deal of knowledge of anatomy, physiology, nutrition—all that pertains to a full and beautiful personal life. We have our botany and chemistry, and so on—very rudimentary, but interesting; our own history, with its accumulating psychology."

"You put psychology with history—not with personal life?"

"Of course. It is ours; it is among and between us, and it changes with the succeeding and improving generations. We are at work, slowly and carefully, developing our whole people along these lines. It is glorious work—splendid! To see the thousands of babies improving, showing stronger clearer minds, sweeter dispositions, higher capacities—don't you find it so in your country?"

This I evaded flatly. I remembered the cheerless claim that the human mind was no better than in its earliest period of savagery, only better informed—a statement I had never believed.

"We try most earnestly for two powers," Somel continued. "The two that seem to us basically necessary for all noble life: a clear, far-reaching judgment, and a strong, well-used will. We spend our best efforts, all through childhood and youth, in developing these faculties, individual judgment and will."

"As part of your system of education, you mean?"

"Exactly. As the most valuable part. With the babies, as you may have noticed, we first provide an environment which feeds the mind without tiring it; all manner of simple and interesting things to do, as soon as they are old enough to do them; physical properties, of course, come first. But as early as possible, going very carefully, not to tax the mind, we provide choices, simple choices, with very obvious causes and consequences. You've noticed the games?"

I had. The children seemed always playing something; or else, sometimes, engaged in peaceful researches of their own. I had wondered at first when they went to school, but soon found that they never did—to their knowledge. It was all education but no schooling.

"We have been working for some sixteen hundred years, devising better and better games for children," continued Somel.

I sat aghast. "Devising games?" I protested. "Making up new ones, you mean?"

"Exactly," she answered. "Don't you?"

Then I remembered the kindergarten, and the "material" devised by Signora Montessori, and guardedly replied: "To some extent." But most of our games, I told her, were very old—came down from child to child, along the ages, from the remote past.

"And what is their effect?" she asked. "Do they develop the faculties you wish to encourage?"

Again I remembered the claims made by the advocates of "sports," and again replied guardedly that that was, in part, the theory.

"But do the children *like* it?" I asked. "Having things made up and set before them that way? Don't they want the old games?"

"You can see the children," she answered. "Are yours more contented—more interested—happier?"

Then I thought, as in truth I never had thought before, of the dull, bored children I had seen, whining: "What can I do now?"; of the little groups and gangs hanging about; of the value of some one strong spirit who possessed initiative and would "start something"; of the children's parties and the onerous duties of the older people set to "amuse the children"; also of that troubled ocean of misdirected activity we call "mischief," the foolish, destructive, sometimes evil things done by unoccupied children.

"No," said I grimly. "I don't think they are."

The Herland child was born not only into a world carefully prepared, full of the most fascinating materials and opportunities to learn, but into the society of plentiful numbers of teachers, teachers born and trained, whose business it was to accompany the children along that, to us, impossible thing—the royal road to learning. . . .

CHAPTER 10

THEIR RELIGIONS AND OUR MARRIAGES

It took me a long time, as a man, a foreigner, and a species of Christian—I was that as much as anything—to get any clear understanding of the religion of Herland.

Its deification of motherhood was obvious enough; but there was far more to it than that; or, at least, than my first interpretation of that.

I think it was only as I grew to love Ellador more than I believed anyone could love anybody, as I grew faintly to appreciate her inner attitude and state of mind, that I began to get some glimpses of this faith of theirs.

When I asked her about it, she tried at first to tell me, and then, seeing me flounder, asked for more information about ours. She soon found that we had many, that they varied widely, but had some points in common. A clear methodical luminous mind had my Ellador, not only reasonable, but swiftly perceptive.

She made a sort of chart, superimposing the different religions as I described them, with a pin run through them all, as it were; their common basis being a Dominant Power or Powers, and some Special Behavior, mostly taboos, to please or placate. There were some common features in certain groups of religions, but the one always present was this Power, and the things which must be done or not done because of it. It was not hard to trace our human imagery of the Divine Force up through successive stages of bloodthirsty, sensual, proud, and cruel gods of early times to the conception of a Common Father with its corollary of a Common Brotherhood.

This pleased her very much, and when I expatiated on the Omniscience, Omnipotence, Omnipresence, and so on, of our God, and of the loving kindness taught by his Son, she was much impressed.

The story of the Virgin birth naturally did not astonish her, but she was greatly puzzled by the Sacrifice, and still more by the Devil, and the theory of Damnation.

When in an inadvertent moment I said that certain sects had believed in infant damnation—and explained it—she sat very still indeed.

"They believed that God was Love—and Wisdom—and Power?"

"Yes—all of that."

Her eyes grew large, her face ghastly pale.

"And yet that such a God could put little new babies to burn—for eternity?" She fell into a sudden shuddering and left me, running swiftly to the nearest Temple.

Every smallest village had its Temple, and in those gracious retreats sat wise and noble women, quietly busy at some work of their own until they were wanted, always ready to give comfort, light, or help, to any applicant.

Ellador told me afterward how easily this grief of hers was assuaged and seemed ashamed of not having helped herself out of it.

"You see, we are not accustomed to horrible ideas," she said, coming back to me rather apologetically. "We haven't any. And when we get a thing like that into our minds, it's like—oh, like red pepper in your eyes. So I just ran to her, blinded and almost screaming, and she took it out so quickly—so easily!"

"How?" I asked, very curious.

"'Why, you blessed child,' she said, 'you've got the wrong idea altogether. You do not have to think that there ever was such a God—for there wasn't. Or such a happening—for there wasn't. Nor even that this hideous false idea was believed by anybody. But only this—that people who are utterly ignorant will believe anything—which you certainly knew before.'"

"Anyhow," pursued Ellador, "she turned pale for a minute when I first said it."

This was a lesson to me. No wonder this whole nation of women was peaceful and sweet in expression—they had no horrible ideas.

"Surely you had some when you began," I suggested.

"Oh, yes, no doubt. But as soon as our religion grew to any height at all we left them out of course."

From this, as from many other things, I grew to see what I finally put in words.

"Have you no respect for the past? For what was thought and believed by your foremothers?"

"Why, no," she said. "Why should we? They are all gone. They knew less than we do. If we are not beyond them, we are unworthy of them—and unworthy of the children who must go beyond us."

This set me thinking in good earnest. I had always imagined—simply from hearing it said, I suppose—that women were by nature conservative. Yet these women, quite unassisted by any masculine spirit of enterprise, had ignored their past and built daringly for the future.

Ellador watched me think. She seemed to know pretty much what was going on in my mind.

"It's because we began in a new way, I suppose. All our folks were swept away at once, and then, after that time of despair, came those wonder children—the first. And then the whole breathless hope of us was for *their* children—if they should have them. And they did! Then there was the period of pride and triumph till we grew too numerous; and after that, when it all came down to one child apiece, we began to really work—to make better ones."

"But how does this account for such a radical difference in your religion?" I persisted.

She said she couldn't talk about the difference very intelligently, not being familiar with other religions, but that theirs seemed simple enough. Their great Mother Spirit was to them what their own motherhood was—only magnified beyond human limits. That meant that they felt beneath and behind them an upholding, unfailing, serviceable love—perhaps it was really the accumulated mother-love of the race they felt—but it was a Power.

"Just what is your theory of worship?" I asked her.

"Worship? What is that?"

I found it singularly difficult to explain. This Divine Love which they felt so strongly did not seem to ask anything of them—"any more than our mothers do," she said.

"But surely your mothers expect honor, reverence, obedience, from you. You have to do things for your mothers, surely?"

"Oh, no," she insisted, smiling, shaking her soft brown hair. "We do things *from* our mothers—not *for* them. We don't have to do things *for* them—they don't need it, you know. But we have to live on—splendidly—because of them; and that's the way we feel about God."

I meditated again. I thought of that "God of Battles" of ours, that Jealous God, that "Vengeance-is-mine God." I thought of our world-nightmare—Hell.

"You have no theory of eternal punishment then, I take it?"

Ellador laughed. Her eyes were as bright as stars, and there were tears in them, too. She was so sorry for me.

"How could we?" she asked, fairly enough. "We have no punishments in life, you see, so we don't imagine them after death."

"Have you *no* punishments? Neither for children nor criminals—such mild criminals as you have?" I urged.

"Do you punish a person for a broken leg or a fever? We have preventive measures, and cures; sometimes we have to 'send the patient to bed,' as it were; but that's not a punishment—it's only part of the treatment," she explained.

Then studying my point of view more closely, she added: "You see, we recognize, in our human motherhood, a great tender limitless uplifting force—patience and wisdom and all subtlety of delicate method. We credit God—our idea of God—with all that and more. Our mothers are not angry with us—why should God be?"

"Does God mean a person to you?"

This she thought over a little. "Why—in trying to get close to it in our minds we personify the idea, naturally; but we certainly do not assume a Big Woman somewhere, who is God. What we call

God is a Pervading Power, you know, an Indwelling Spirit, something inside of us that we want more of. Is your God a Big Man?" she asked innocently.

"Why—yes, to most of us, I think. Of course we call it an Indwelling Spirit just as you do, but we insist that it is Him, a Person, and a Man—with whiskers."

"Whiskers? Oh yes—because you have them! Or do you wear them because He does?"

"On the contrary, we shave them off—because it seems cleaner and more comfortable."

"Does He wear clothes—in your idea, I mean?"

I was thinking over the pictures of God I had seen—rash advances of the devout mind of man, representing his Omnipotent Deity as an old man in a flowing robe, flowing hair, flowing beard, and in the light of her perfectly frank and innocent questions this concept seemed rather unsatisfying.

I explained that the God of the Christian world was really the ancient Hebrew God, and that we had simply taken over the patriarchal idea—that ancient one which quite inevitably clothed its thought of God with the attributes of the patriarchal ruler, the Grandfather.

"I see," she said eagerly, after I had explained the genesis and development of our religious ideals. "They lived in separate groups, with a male head, and he was probably a little—domineering?"

"No doubt of that," I agreed.

"And we live together without any 'head,' in that sense—just our chosen leaders—that *does* make a difference."

"Your difference is deeper than that," I assured her. "It is in your common motherhood. Your children grow up in a world where everybody loves them. They find life made rich and happy for them by the diffused love and wisdom of all mothers. So it is easy for you to think of God in the terms of a similar diffused and competent love. I think you are far nearer right than we are...."

They developed their central theory of a Loving Power, and assumed that its relation to them was motherly—that it desired their welfare and especially their development. Their relation to it, similarly, was filial, a loving appreciation and a glad fulfillment of its high purposes. Then, being nothing if not practical, they set their keen and active minds to discover the kind of conduct expected of them. This worked out in a most admirable system of ethics. The principle of Love was universally recognized—and used.

Patience, gentleness, courtesy, all that we call "good breeding," was part of their code of conduct. But where they went far beyond us was in the special application of religious feeling to every field of life. They had no ritual, no little set of performances called "divine service," save those glorious pageants I have spoken of, and those were as much educational as religious, and as much social as either. But they had a clear established connection between everything they did—and God. Their cleanliness, their health, their exquisite order, the rich peaceful beauty of the whole land, the happiness of the children, and above all the constant progress they made—all this was their religion.

They applied their minds to the thought of God, and worked out the theory that such an inner power demanded outward expression. They lived as if God was real and at work within them.

As for those little temples everywhere—some of the women were more skilled, more temperamentally inclined, in this direction, than others. These, whatever their work might be, gave certain hours to the Temple Service, which meant being there with all their love and wisdom and trained thought, to smooth out rough places for anyone who needed it. Sometimes it was a real grief, very rarely a quarrel, most often a perplexity; even in Herland the human soul had its hours of darkness. But all through the country their best and wisest were ready to give help.

If the difficulty was unusually profound, the applicant was directed to someone more specially experienced in that line of thought.

Here was a religion which gave to the searching mind a rational basis in life, the concept of an immense Loving Power working steadily out through them, toward good. It gave to the "soul" that sense of contact with the inmost force, of perception of the utter-most purpose, which we always crave. It gave to the "heart" the blessed feeling of being loved, loved and *understood*. It gave clear, simple, rational directions as to how we should live—and why. And for ritual it gave first those triumphant group demonstrations, when with a union of all the arts, the revivifying combination of great multitudes moved rhythmically with march and dance, song and music, among their own noblest products and the open beauty of their groves and hills. Second, it gave these numerous little centers of wisdom where the least wise could go to the most wise and be helped.

"It is beautiful!" I cried enthusiastically. "It is the most practical, comforting, progressive religion I ever heard of. You *do* love one another—you *do* bear one another's burdens—you *do* realize that a little child is a type of the kingdom of heaven. You are more Christian than any people I ever saw. But—how about Death? And the Life Everlasting? What does your religion teach about Eternity?"

"Nothing," said Ellador. "What is Eternity?"

What indeed? I tried, for the first time in my life, to get a real hold on the idea.

"It is—never stopping."

"Never stopping?" She looked puzzled.

"Yes, life, going on forever."

"Oh—we see that, of course. Life does go on forever, all about us."

"But eternal life goes on *without dying*."

"The same person?"

"Yes, the same person, unending, immortal." I was pleased to think that I had something to teach from our religion, which theirs had never promulgated.

"Here?" asked Ellador. "Never to die—here?" I could see her practical mind heaping up the people, and hurriedly reassured her.

"Oh no, indeed, not here—hereafter. We must die here, of course, but then we 'enter into eternal life.' The soul lives forever."

"How do you know?" she inquired.

"I won't attempt to prove it to you," I hastily continued. "Let us assume it to be so. How does this idea strike you?"

Again she smiled at me, that adorable, dimpling, tender, mischievous, motherly smile of hers. "Shall I be quite, quite honest?"

"You couldn't be anything else," I said, half gladly and half a little sorry. The transparent honesty of these women was a never-ending astonishment to me.

"It seems to me a singularly foolish idea," she said calmly. "And if true, most disagreeable."

Now I had always accepted the doctrine of personal immortality as a thing established. The efforts of inquiring Spiritualists, always seeking to woo their beloved ghosts back again, never seemed to me necessary. I don't say I had ever seriously and courageously discussed the subject with myself even; I had simply assumed it to be a fact. And here was the girl I loved, this creature whose character constantly revealed new heights and ranges far beyond my own, this superwoman of a superland, saying she thought immortality foolish! She meant it, too.

"What do you *want* it for?" she asked.

"How can you *not* want it!" I protested. "Do you want to go out like a candle? Don't you want to go on and on—growing and—and—being happy, forever?"

"Why, no," she said. "I don't in the least. I want my child—and my child's child—to go on—and they will. Why should *I* want to?"

"But it means Heaven!" I insisted. "Peace and Beauty and Comfort and Love—with God." I had never been so eloquent on the subject of religion. She could be horrified at Damnation, and question the justice of Salvation, but Immortality—that was surely a noble faith.

"Why, Van," she said, holding out her hands to me. "Why Van—darling! How splendid of you to feel it so keenly. That's what we all want, of course—Peace and Beauty, and Comfort and Love—with God! And Progress too, remember; Growth, always and always. That is what our religion teaches us to want and to work for, and we do!"

"But that is *here*," I said, "only for this life on earth."

"Well? And do not you in your country, with your beautiful religion of love and service have it here, too—for this life—on earth?"

—

None of us were willing to tell the women of Herland about the evils of our own beloved land. It was all very well for us to assume them to be necessary and essential, and to criticize—strictly among ourselves—their all-too-perfect civilization, but when it came to telling them about the failures and wastes of our own, we never could bring ourselves to do it.

Moreover, we sought to avoid too much discussion, and to press the subject of our approaching marriages.

Jeff was the determined one on this score.

"Of course they haven't any marriage ceremony or service, but we can make it a sort of Quaker wedding, and have it in the Temple—it is the least we can do for them."

It was. There was so little, after all, that we could do for them. Here we were, penniless guests and strangers, with no chance even to use our strength and courage—nothing to defend them from or protect them against.

"We can at least give them our names," Jeff insisted.

They were very sweet about it, quite willing to do whatever we asked, to please us. As to the names, Alima, frank soul that she was, asked what good it would do.

Terry, always irritating her, said it was a sign of possession. "You are going to be Mrs. Nicholson," he said, "Mrs. T. O. Nicholson. That shows everyone that you are my wife."

"What is a 'wife' exactly?" she demanded, a dangerous gleam in her eye.

"A wife is the woman who belongs to a man," he began.

But Jeff took it up eagerly: "And a husband is the man who belongs to a woman. It is because we are monogamous, you know. And marriage is the ceremony, civil and religious, that joins the two together—'until death do us part,'" he finished, looking at Celis with unutterable devotion.

"What makes us all feel foolish," I told the girls, "is that here we have nothing to give you—except, of course, our names."

"Do your women have no names before they are married?" Celis suddenly demanded.

"Why, yes," Jeff explained. "They have their maiden names— their father's names, that is."

"And what becomes of them?" asked Alima.

"They change them for their husbands', my dear," Terry answered her.

"Change them? Do the husbands then take the wives' 'maiden names'?"

"Oh, no," he laughed. "The man keeps his own and gives it to her, too."

"Then she just loses hers and takes a new one—how unpleasant! We won't do that!" Alima said decidedly.

Terry was good-humored about it. "I don't care what you do or don't do so long as we have that wedding pretty soon," he said, reaching a strong brown hand after Alima's, quite as brown and nearly as strong.

"As to giving us things—of course we can see that you'd like to, but we are glad you can't," Celis continued. "You see, we love you just for yourselves—we wouldn't want you to—to pay anything. Isn't it enough to know that you are loved personally—and just as men?"

Enough or not, that was the way we were married. We had a great triple wedding in the biggest Temple of all, and it looked as if most of the nation were present. It was very solemn and very beautiful. Someone had written a new song for the occasion, nobly beautiful, about the New Hope for their people—the New Tie with other lands—Brotherhood as well as Sisterhood, and, with evident awe, Fatherhood....

CHAPTER 11

OUR DIFFICULTIES

We say, "Marriage is a lottery"; also "Marriages are made in Heaven"—but this is not so widely accepted as the other.

We have a well-founded theory that it is best to marry "in one's class," and certain well-grounded suspicions of international marriages, which seem to persist in the interests of social progress, rather than in those of the contracting parties.

But no combination of alien races, of color, caste, or creed, was ever so basically difficult to establish as that between us, three modern American men, and these three women of Herland.

It is all very well to say that we should have been frank about it beforehand. We had been frank. We had discussed—at least Ellador and I had—the conditions of The Great Adventure, and thought the path was clear before us. But there are some things one takes for granted, supposes are mutually understood, and to which both parties may repeatedly refer without ever meaning the same thing.

The differences in the education of the average man and woman are great enough, but the trouble they make is not mostly for the man; he generally carries out his own views of the case. The woman may have imagined the conditions of married life to be different; but what she imagined, was ignorant of, or might have preferred, did not seriously matter.

I can see clearly and speak calmly about this now, writing after a lapse of years, years full of growth and education, but at the time it was rather hard sledding for all of us—especially for Terry. Poor Terry! You see, in any other imaginable marriage among the peoples of the earth, whether the woman were black, red, yellow, brown, or white; whether she were ignorant or educated, submissive or rebellious, she would have behind her the marriage tradition of our general history. This tradition relates the woman to the man. He goes on with his business, and she adapts herself to him and to it. Even in citizenship, by some strange hocus-pocus, that fact of birth and geography was waved aside, and the woman automatically acquired the nationality of her husband.

Well—here were we, three aliens in this land of women. It was small in area, and the external differences were not so great as to astound us. We did not yet appreciate the differences between the race-mind of this people and ours.

In the first place, they were a "pure stock" of two thousand uninterrupted years. Where we have some long connected lines of thought and feeling, together with a wide range of differences, often irreconcilable, these people were smoothly and firmly agreed on most of the basic principles of their life; and not only agreed in principle, but accustomed for these sixty-odd generations to act on those principles.

This is one thing which we did not understand—had made no allowance for. When in our pre-marital discussions one of those dear girls had said: "We understand it thus and thus," or "We hold such and such to be true," we men, in our own deep-seated convictions of the power of love, and our easy views about beliefs and principles, fondly imagined that we could convince them otherwise. What we imagined, before marriage, did not matter any more than what an average innocent young girl imagines. We found the facts to be different....

———

[...]

These people had, it now became clear to us, the highest, keenest, most delicate sense of personal privacy, but not the faintest idea of that *"solitude à deux"* we are so fond of. They had, every one of them, the "two rooms and a bath" theory realized. From earliest childhood each had a separate bedroom with toilet conveniences, and one of the marks of coming of age was the addition of an outer room in which to receive friends.

Long since we had been given our own two rooms apiece, and as being of a different sex and race, these were in a separate house. It seemed to be recognized that we should breathe easier if able to free our minds in real seclusion.

For food we either went to any convenient eating-house, ordered a meal brought in, or took it with us to the woods, always and equally good. All this we had become used to and enjoyed—in our courting days.

After marriage there arose in us a somewhat unexpected urge of feeling that called for a separate house; but this feeling found no response in the hearts of those fair ladies.

"We *are* alone, dear," Ellador explained to me with gentle patience. "We are alone in these great forests; we may go and eat in any little summer-house—just we two, or have a separate table anywhere—or even have a separate meal in our own rooms. How could we be aloner?"

This was all very true. We had our pleasant mutual solitude about our work, and our pleasant evening talks in their apartments or ours; we had, as it were, all the pleasures of courtship carried right on; but we had no sense of—perhaps it may be called possession.

"Might as well not be married at all," growled Terry. "They only got up that ceremony to please us—please Jeff, mostly. They've no real idea of being married."

I tried my best to get Ellador's point of view, and naturally I tried to give her mine. Of course, what we, as men, wanted to make them see was that there were other, and as we proudly said "higher," uses in this relation than what Terry called "mere parentage." In the highest terms I knew I tried to explain this to Ellador.

"Anything higher than for mutual love to hope to give life, as we did?" she said. "How is it higher?"

"It develops love," I explained. "All the power of beautiful permanent mated love comes through this higher development."

"Are you sure?" she asked gently. "How do you know that it was so developed? There are some birds who love each other so that they mope and pine if separated, and never pair again if one dies, but they never mate except in the mating season. Among your people do you find high and lasting affection appearing in proportion to this indulgence?"

It is a very awkward thing, sometimes, to have a logical mind.

Of course I knew about those monogamous birds and beasts too, that mate for life and show every sign of mutual affection, without ever having stretched the sex relationship beyond its original range. But what of it?

"Those are lower forms of life!" I protested. "They have no capacity for faithful and affectionate, and apparently happy—but oh, my dear! my dear!—what can they know of such a love as draws us together? Why, to touch you—to be near you—to come closer and closer—to lose myself in you—surely you feel it too, do you not?"

I came nearer. I seized her hands.

Her eyes were on mine, tender, radiant, but steady and strong. There was something so powerful, so large and change-less, in those eyes that I could not sweep her off her feet by my own emotion as I had unconsciously assumed would be the case.

It made me feel as, one might imagine, a man might feel who loved a goddess—not a Venus, though! She did not resent my attitude, did not repel it, did not in the least fear it, evidently. There was not a shade of that timid withdrawal or pretty resistance which are so—provocative.

"You see, dearest," she said, "you have to be patient with us. We are not like the women of your country. We are Mothers, and we are People, but we have not specialized in this line."

"We" and "we" and "we"—it was so hard to get her to be personal. And, as I thought that, I suddenly remembered how we were always criticizing *our* women for *being* so personal.

Then I did my earnest best to picture to her the sweet intense joy of married lovers, and the result in higher stimulus to all creative work.

"Do you mean," she asked quite calmly, as if I was not holding her cool firm hands in my hot and rather quivering ones, "that with you, when people marry, they go right on doing this in season and out of season, with no thought of children at all?"

"They do," I said, with some bitterness. "They are not mere parents. They are men and women, and they love each other."

"How long?" asked Ellador, rather unexpectedly.

"How long?" I repeated, a little dashed. "Why as long as they live."

"There is something very beautiful in the idea," she admitted, still as if she were discussing life on Mars. "This climactic expression, which, in all the other life-forms, has but the one purpose, has with you become specialized to higher, purer, nobler uses. It has—I judge from what you tell me—the most ennobling effect on character. People marry, not only for parentage, but for this exquisite interchange—and, as a result, you have a world full of continuous lovers, ardent, happy, mutually devoted, always living on that high tide of supreme emotion which we had supposed to belong only to one season and one use. And you say it has other results, stimulating all high creative work. That must mean floods, oceans of such work, blossoming from this intense happiness of every married pair! It is a beautiful idea!"

She was silent, thinking.

So was I.

She slipped one hand free, and was stroking my hair with it in a gentle motherly way. I bowed my hot head on her shoulder and felt a dim sense of peace, a restfulness which was very pleasant.

"You must take me there someday, darling," she was saying. "It is not only that I love you so much, I want to see your country—your people—your mother—" she paused reverently. "Oh, how I shall love your mother!"

I had not been in love many times—my experience did not compare with Terry's. But such as I had was so different from this that I was perplexed, and full of mixed feelings: partly a growing sense of common ground between us, a pleasant rested calm feeling, which

I had imagined could only be attained in one way; and partly a bewildered resentment because what I found was not what I had
looked for.

It was their confounded psychology! Here they were with this
profound highly developed system of education so bred into them
that even if they were not teachers by profession they all had a general proficiency in it—it was second nature to them.

And no child, stormily demanding a cookie "between meals,"
was ever more subtly diverted into an interest in house-building
than was I when I found an apparently imperative demand had disappeared without my noticing it.

And all the time those tender mother eyes, those keen scientific
eyes, noting every condition and circumstance, and learning how to
"take time by the forelock" and avoid discussion before occasion
arose.

I was amazed at the results. I found that much, very much, of
what I had honestly supposed to be a physiological necessity was a
psychological necessity—or so believed. I found, after my ideas of
what was essential had changed, that my feelings changed also. And
more than all, I found this—a factor of enormous weight—these
women were not provocative. That made an immense difference....

So we grew together in friendship and happiness, Ellador and I,
and so did Jeff and Celis.

When it comes to Terry's part of it, and Alima's, I'm sorry—and
I'm ashamed. Of course I blame her somewhat. She wasn't as fine a
psychologist as Ellador, and what's more, I think she had a far-
descended atavistic trace of more marked femaleness, never apparent till Terry called it out. But when all that is said, it doesn't excuse
him. I hadn't realized to the full Terry's character—I couldn't,
being a man.

The position was the same as with us, of course, only with these
distinctions: Alima, a shade more alluring, and several shades less able
as a practical psychologist; Terry, a hundredfold more demanding—
and proportionately less reasonable.

Things grew strained very soon between them. I fancy at first, when they were together, in her great hope of parentage and his keen joy of conquest—that Terry was inconsiderate. In fact, I know it, from things he said.

"You needn't talk to me," he snapped at Jeff one day, just before our weddings. "There never was a woman yet that did not enjoy being *mastered*. All your pretty talk doesn't amount to a hill o' beans—I *know*." And Terry would hum:

> *"I've taken my fun where I found it.*
> *I've rogued and I've ranged in my time, and*
> *The things that I learned from the yellow and black,*
> *They 'ave helped me a 'eap with the white."*

Jeff turned sharply and left him at the time. I was a bit disquieted myself.

Poor old Terry! The things he'd learned didn't help him a heap in Herland. His idea was To Take—he thought that was the way. He thought, he honestly believed, that women like it. Not the women of Herland! Not Alima!

I can see her now—one day in the very first week of their marriage, setting forth to her day's work with long determined strides and hard-set mouth, and sticking close to Ellador. She didn't wish to be alone with Terry—you could see that.

But the more she kept away from him, the more he wanted her—naturally.

He made a tremendous row about their separate establishments, tried to keep her in his rooms, tried to stay in hers. But there she drew the line sharply.

He came away one night, and stamped up and down the moonlit road, swearing under his breath. I was taking a walk that night too, but I wasn't in his state of mind. To hear him rage you'd not have believed that he loved Alima at all—you'd have thought that she was some quarry he was pursuing, something to catch and conquer.

I think that, owing to all those differences I spoke of, they soon lost the common ground they had at first, and were unable to meet sanely and dispassionately. I fancy too—this is pure conjecture—that he had succeeded in driving Alima beyond her best judgment, her real conscience, and that after that her own sense of shame, the reaction of the thing, made her bitter perhaps.

They quarreled, really quarreled, and after making it up once or twice, they seemed to come to a real break—she would not be alone with him at all. And perhaps she was a bit nervous, I don't know, but she got Moadine to come and stay next door to her. Also, she had a sturdy assistant detailed to accompany her in her work.

Terry had his own ideas, as I've tried to show. I daresay he thought he had a right to do as he did. Perhaps he even convinced himself that it would be better for her. Anyhow, he hid himself in her bedroom one night...

The women of Herland have no fear of men. Why should they have? They are not timid in any sense. They are not weak; and they all have strong trained athletic bodies. Othello could not have extinguished Alima with a pillow, as if she were a mouse.

Terry put in practice his pet conviction that a woman loves to be mastered, and by sheer brute force, in all the pride and passion of his intense masculinity, he tried to master this woman.

It did not work. I got a pretty clear account of it later from Ellador, but what we heard at the time was the noise of a tremendous struggle, and Alima calling to Moadine. Moadine was close by and came at once; one or two more strong grave women followed.

Terry dashed about like a madman; he would cheerfully have killed them—he told me that, himself—but he couldn't. When he swung a chair over his head one sprang in the air and caught it, two threw themselves bodily upon him and forced him to the floor; it was only the work of a few moments to have him tied hand and foot, and then, in sheer pity for his futile rage, to anesthetize him.

———

Alima was in a cold fury. She wanted him killed—actually.

There was a trial before the local Over Mother, and this woman, who did not enjoy being mastered, stated her case.

In a court in our country he would have been held quite "within his rights," of course. But this was not our country; it was theirs. They seemed to measure the enormity of the offense by its effect upon a possible fatherhood, and he scorned even to reply to this way of putting it.

He did let himself go once, and explained in definite terms that they were incapable of understanding a man's needs, a man's desires, a man's point of view. He called them neuters, epicenes, bloodless, sexless creatures. He said they could of course kill him—as so many insects could—but that he despised them nonetheless.

And all those stern grave mothers did not seem to mind his despising them, not in the least.

It was a long trial, and many interesting points were brought out as to their views of our habits, and after a while Terry had his sentence. He waited, grim and defiant. The sentence was: "You must go home!"

CHAPTER 12

EXPELLED

We had all meant to go home again. Indeed we had *not* meant—not by any means—to stay as long as we had. But when it came to being turned out, dismissed, sent away for bad conduct, we none of us really liked it.

Terry said he did. He professed great scorn of the penalty and the trial, as well as all the other characteristics of "this miserable half-country." But he knew, and we knew, that in any "whole" country we should never have been as forgivingly treated as we had been here.

"If the people had come after us according to the directions we left, there'd have been quite a different story!" said Terry. We found out later why no reserve party had arrived. All our careful directions had been destroyed in a fire. We might have all died there and no one at home have ever known our whereabouts.

Terry was under guard now, all the time, known as unsafe, convicted of what was to them an unpardonable sin.

He laughed at their chill horror. "Parcel of old maids!" he called them. "They're all old maids—children or not. They don't know the first thing about Sex."

When Terry said *Sex,* sex with a very large *S,* he meant the male sex, naturally; its special values, its profound conviction of being "the life force," its cheerful ignoring of the true life process, and its interpretation of the other sex solely from its own point of view.

I had learned to see these things very differently since living with Ellador; and as for Jeff, he was so thoroughly Herlandized that he wasn't fair to Terry, who fretted sharply in his new restraint.

Moadine, grave and strong, as sadly patient as a mother with a degenerate child, kept steady watch on him, with enough other women close at hand to prevent an outbreak. He had no weapons, and well knew that all his strength was of small avail against those grim, quiet women.

We were allowed to visit him freely, but he had only his room, and a small high-walled garden to walk in, while the preparations for our departure were under way.

Three of us were to go: Terry, because he must; I, because two were safer for our flyer, and the long boat trip to the coast; Ellador, because she would not let me go without her.

If Jeff had elected to return, Celis would have gone too—they were the most absorbed of lovers; but Jeff had no desire that way.

"Why should I want to go back to all our noise and dirt, our vice and crime, our disease and degeneracy?" he demanded of me privately. We never spoke like that before the women. "I wouldn't take Celis there for anything on earth!" he protested. "She'd die! She'd die of horror and shame to see our slums and hospitals. How can you risk it with Ellador? You'd better break it to her gently before she really makes up her mind."

Jeff was right. I ought to have told her more fully than I did, of all the things we had to be ashamed of. But it is very hard to bridge the gulf of as deep a difference as existed between our life and theirs. I tried to.

"Look here, my dear," I said to her. "If you are really going to my country with me, you've got to be prepared for a good many shocks. It's not as beautiful as this—the cities, I mean, the civilized parts—of course the wild country is."

"I shall enjoy it all," she said, her eyes starry with hope. "I understand it's not like ours. I can see how monotonous our quiet life must seem to you, how much more stirring yours must be. It must be like the biological change you told me about when the second sex was introduced—a far greater movement, constant change, with new possibilities of growth."

I had told her of the later biological theories of sex, and she was deeply convinced of the superior advantages of having two, the superiority of a world with men in it.

"We have done what we could alone; perhaps we have some things better in a quiet way, but you have the whole world—all the people of the different nations—all the long rich history behind you—all the wonderful new knowledge. Oh, I just can't wait to see it."

What could I do? I told her in so many words that we had our unsolved problems, that we had dishonesty and corruption, vice and crime, disease and insanity, prisons and hospitals; and it made no more impression on her than it would to tell a South Sea Islander about the temperature of the Arctic Circle. She could intellectually see that it was bad to have those things; but she could not *feel* it....

Well—we had to get the flyer in order, and be sure there was enough fuel left, though Terry said we could glide all right, down to that lake, once we got started. We'd have gone gladly in a week's time, of course, but there was a great to-do all over the country about Ellador's leaving them. She had interviews with some of the leading ethicists—wise women with still eyes, and with the best of the teachers. There was a stir, a thrill, a deep excitement everywhere.

Our teaching about the rest of the world had given them all a sense of isolation, of remoteness, of being a little outlying sample of a country, overlooked and forgotten among the family of nations. We had called it "the family of nations," and they liked the phrase immensely.

They were deeply aroused on the subject of evolution; indeed, the whole field of natural science drew them irresistibly. Any number of them would have risked everything to go to the strange unknown lands and study; but we could take only one, and it had to be Ellador, naturally.

We planned greatly about coming back, about establishing a connecting route by water; about penetrating those vast forests and civilizing—or exterminating—the dangerous savages. That is, we

224 · CHARLOTTE PERKINS GILMAN

men talked of that last—not with the women. They had a definite aversion to killing things.

But meanwhile there was high council being held among the wisest of them all. The students and thinkers who had been gathering facts from us all this time, collating and relating them, and making inferences, laid the result of their labors before the council.

Little had we thought that our careful efforts at concealment had been so easily seen through, with never a word to show us that they saw. They had followed up words of ours on the science of optics, asked innocent questions about glasses and the like, and were aware of the defective eyesight so common among us.

With the lightest touch, different women asking different questions at different times, and putting all our answers together like a picture puzzle, they had figured out a sort of skeleton chart as to the prevalence of disease among us. Even more subtly with no show of horror or condemnation, they had gathered something— far from the truth, but something pretty clear—about poverty, vice, and crime. They even had a goodly number of our dangers all itemized, from asking us about insurance and innocent things like that.

They were well posted as to the different races, beginning with their poison-arrow natives down below and widening out to the broad racial divisions we had told them about. Never a shocked expression of the face or exclamation of revolt had warned us; they had been extracting the evidence without our knowing it all this time, and now were studying with the most devout earnestness the matter they had prepared.

The result was rather distressing to us. They first explained the matter fully to Ellador, as she was the one who purposed visiting the Rest of the World. To Celis they said nothing. She must not be in any way distressed, while the whole nation waited on her Great Work.

Finally Jeff and I were called in. Somel and Zava were there, and Ellador, with many others that we knew.

They had a great globe, quite fairly mapped out from the small section maps in that compendium of ours. They had the different

peoples of the earth roughly outlined, and their status in civilization indicated. They had charts and figures and estimates, based on
the facts in that traitorous little book and what they had learned
from us.

Somel explained: "We find that in all your historic period, so
much longer than ours, that with all the interplay of services, the
exchange of inventions and discoveries, and the wonderful progress
we so admire, that in this widespread Other World of yours, there is
still much disease, often contagious."

We admitted this at once.

"Also there is still, in varying degree, ignorance, with prejudice
and unbridled emotion."

This too was admitted.

"We find also that in spite of the advance of democracy and the
increase of wealth, that there is still unrest and sometimes combat."

Yes, yes, we admitted it all. We were used to these things and saw
no reason for so much seriousness.

"All things considered," they said, and they did not say a hundredth part of the things they were considering, "we are unwilling
to expose our country to free communication with the rest of the
world—as yet. If Ellador comes back, and we approve her report, it
may be done later—but not yet.

"So we have this to ask of you gentlemen (they knew that word
was held a title of honor with us), that you promise not in any way
to betray the location of this country until permission—after Ellador's return."

Jeff was perfectly satisfied. He thought they were quite right. He
always did. I never saw an alien become naturalized more quickly
than that man in Herland.

I studied it awhile, thinking of the time they'd have if some of
our contagions got loose there, and concluded they were right. So I
agreed.

Terry was the obstacle. "Indeed I won't!" he protested. "The first
thing I'll do is to get an expedition fixed up to force an entrance into
Ma-land."

"Then," they said quite calmly, "he must remain an absolute prisoner, always."

"Anesthesia would be kinder," urged Moadine.

"And safer," added Zava.

"He will promise, I think," said Ellador.

And he did. With which agreement we at last left Herland.

SELECTIONS FROM
WOMEN AND ECONOMICS

A STUDY OF THE ECONOMIC RELATION
BETWEEN MEN AND WOMEN

Since we have learned to study the development of human life as we study the evolution of species throughout the animal kingdom, some peculiar phenomena which have puzzled the philosopher and moralist for so long, begin to show themselves in a new light. We begin to see that, so far from being inscrutable problems, requiring another life to explain, these sorrows and perplexities of our lives are but the natural results of natural causes, and that, as soon as we ascertain the causes, we can do much to remove them.

In spite of the power of the individual will to struggle against conditions, to resist them for a while, and sometimes to overcome them, it remains true that the human creature is affected by his environment, as is every other living thing. The power of the individual will to resist natural law is well proven by the life and death of the ascetic. In any one of those suicidal martyrs may be seen the will, misdirected by the ill-informed intelligence, forcing the body to defy every natural impulse,—even to the door of death, and through it.

But, while these exceptions show what the human will can do, the general course of life shows the inexorable effect of conditions upon humanity. Of these conditions we share with other living things the environment of the material universe. We are affected by climate and locality, by physical, chemical, electrical forces, as are all animals and plants. With the animals, we farther share the effect of our own activity, the reactionary force of exercise. What we do, as well as what is done to us, makes us what we are. But, beyond these forces, we come under the effect of a third set of conditions peculiar to our human status; namely, social conditions. In the organic interchanges which constitute social life, we are affected by each other to a degree beyond what is found even among the most gregarious of animals. This third factor, the social environment, is of enormous force as a modifier of human life. Throughout all these environing conditions, those which affect us through our economic necessities are most marked in their influence.

Without touching yet upon the influence of the social factors, treating the human being merely as an individual animal, we see that he is modified most by his economic conditions, as is every other animal. Differ as they may in color and size, in strength and speed, in minor adaptation to minor conditions, all animals that live on grass have distinctive traits in common, and all animals that eat flesh have distinctive traits in common,—so distinctive and so common that it is by teeth, by nutritive apparatus in general, that they are classified, rather than by means of defence or locomotion. The food supply of the animal is the largest passive factor in his development; the processes by which he obtains his food supply, the largest active factor in his development. It is these activities, the incessant repetition of the exertions by which he is fed, which most modify his structure and develope his functions. The sheep, the cow, the deer, differ in their adaptation to the weather, their locomotive ability, their means of defence; but they agree in main characteristics, because of their common method of nutrition.

The human animal is no exception to this rule. Climate affects him, weather affects him, enemies affect him; but most of all he is affected, like every other living creature, by what he does for his living. Under all the influence of his later and wider life, all the reactive effect of social institutions, the individual is still inexorably modified by his means of livelihood: "the hand of the dyer is subdued to what he works in." As one clear, world-known instance of the effect of economic conditions upon the human creature, note the marked race-modification of the Hebrew people under the enforced restrictions of the last two thousand years. Here is a people rising to national prominence, first as a pastoral, and then as an agricultural nation; only partially commercial through race affinity with the Phœnicians, the pioneer traders of the world. Under the social power of a united Christendom—united at least in this most unchristian deed—the Jew was forced to get his livelihood by commercial methods solely. Many effects can be traced in him to the fierce pressure of the social conditions to which he was subjected: the intense family devotion of a people who had no country, no king, no room for joy and pride except the family; the reduced size and tremendous vitality and endurance of the pitilessly selected survivors of the Ghetto; the repeated bursts of erratic genius from the human spirit so inhumanly restrained. But more patent still is the effect of the economic conditions,—the artificial development of a race of traders and dealers in money, from the lowest pawnbroker to the house of Rothschild; a special kind of people, bred of the economic environment in which they were compelled to live.

One rough but familiar instance of the same effect, from the same cause, we can all see in the marked distinction between the pastoral, the agricultural, and the manufacturing classes in any nation, though their other conditions be the same. On the clear line of argument that functions and organs are developed by use, that what we use most is developed most, and that the daily processes of supplying economic needs are the processes that we most use, it follows that, when we find special economic conditions affecting any special class of people, we may look for special results, and find them.

In view of these facts, attention is now called to a certain marked and peculiar economic condition affecting the human race, and unparalleled in the organic world. We are the only animal species in which the female depends on the male for food, the only animal species in which the sex-relation is also an economic relation. With us an entire sex lives in a relation of economic dependence upon the other sex, and the economic relation is combined with the sex-relation. The economic status of the human female is relative to the sex-relation.

It is commonly assumed that this condition also obtains among other animals, but such is not the case. There are many birds among which, during the nesting season, the male helps the female feed the young, and partially feeds her; and, with certain of the higher carnivora, the male helps the female feed the young, and partially feeds her. In no case does she depend on him absolutely, even during this season, save in that of the hornbill, where the female, sitting on her nest in a hollow tree, is walled in with clay by the male, so that only her beak projects; and then he feeds her while the eggs are developing. But even the female hornbill does not expect to be fed at any other time. The female bee and ant are economically dependent, but not on the male. The workers are females, too, specialized to economic functions solely. And with the carnivora, if the young are to lose one parent, it might far better be the father: the mother is quite competent to take care of them herself. With many species, as in the case of the common cat, she not only feeds herself and her young, but has to defend the young against the male as well. In no case is the female throughout her life supported by the male.

In the human species the condition is permanent and general, though there are exceptions, and though the present century is witnessing the beginnings of a great change in this respect. We have not been accustomed to face this fact beyond our loose generalization that it was "natural," and that other animals did so, too.

To many this view will not seem clear at first; and the case of working peasant women or females of savage tribes, and the general household industry of women, will be instanced against it. Some careful and honest discrimination is needed to make plain to ourselves the essential facts of the relation, even in these cases. The horse, in his free natural condition, is economically independent. He gets his living by his own exertions, irrespective of any other creature. The horse, in his present condition of slavery, is economically dependent. He gets his living at the hands of his master; and his exertions, though strenuous, bear no direct relation to his living. In fact, the horses who are the best fed and cared for and the horses who are the hardest worked are quite different animals. The horse works, it is true; but what he gets to eat depends on the power and will of his master. His living comes through another. He is economically dependent. So with the hard-worked savage or peasant women. Their labor is the property of another: they work under another will; and what they receive depends not on their labor, but on the power and will of another. They are economically dependent. This is true of the human female both individually and collectively.

In studying the economic position of the sexes collectively, the difference is most marked. As a social animal, the economic status of man rests on the combined and exchanged services of vast numbers of progressively specialized individuals. The economic progress of the race, its maintenance at any period, its continued advance, involve the collective activities of all the trades, crafts, arts, manufactures, inventions, discoveries, and all the civil and military institutions that go to maintain them. The economic status of any race at any time, with its involved effect on all the constituent individuals, depends on their world-wide labors and their free exchange. Economic progress, however, is almost exclusively masculine. Such economic processes as women have been allowed to exercise are of the earliest and most primitive kind. Were men to perform no economic services save such as are still performed by women, our racial status in economics would be reduced to most painful limitations.

To take from any community its male workers would paralyze it economically to a far greater degree than to remove its female workers. The labor now performed by the women could be performed by the men, requiring only the setting back of many advanced workers into earlier forms of industry; but the labor now performed by the men could not be performed by the women without generations of effort and adaptation. Men can cook, clean, and sew as well as women; but the making and managing of the great engines of modern industry, the threading of earth and sea in our vast systems of transportation, the handling of our elaborate machinery of trade, commerce, government,—these things could not be done so well by women in their present degree of economic development.

This is not owing to lack of the essential human faculties necessary to such achievements, nor to any inherent disability of sex, but to the present condition of woman, forbidding the development of this degree of economic ability. The male human being is thousands of years in advance of the female in economic status. Speaking collectively, men produce and distribute wealth; and women receive it at their hands. As men hunt, fish, keep cattle, or raise corn, so do women eat game, fish, beef, or corn. As men go down to the sea in ships, and bring coffee and spices and silks and gems from far away, so do women partake of the coffee and spices and silks and gems the men bring.

The economic status of the human race in any nation, at any time, is governed mainly by the activities of the male: the female obtains her share in the racial advance only through him.

Studied individually, the facts are even more plainly visible, more open and familiar. From the day laborer to the millionnaire, the wife's worn dress or flashing jewels, her low roof or her lordly one, her weary feet or her rich equipage,—these speak of the economic ability of the husband. The comfort, the luxury, the necessities of life itself, which the woman receives, are obtained by the husband, and given her by him. And, when the woman, left alone with no man to "support" her, tries to meet her own economic necessities, the difficulties which confront her prove conclusively what the general economic status of the woman is. None can deny these patent facts,—that the economic status of women generally depends upon that of men generally, and that the economic status of women individually depends upon that of men individually, those men to whom they are related. But we are instantly confronted by the commonly received opinion that, although it must be admitted that men make and distribute the wealth of the world, yet women earn their share of it as wives. This assumes either that the husband is in the position of employer and the wife as employee, or that marriage is a "partnership," and the wife an equal factor with the husband in producing wealth.

Economic independence is a relative condition at best. In the broadest sense, all living things are economically dependent upon others,—the animals upon the vegetables, and man upon both. In a narrower sense, all social life is economically interdependent, man producing collectively what he could by no possibility produce separately. But, in the closest interpretation, individual economic independence among human beings means that the individual pays for what he gets, works for what he gets, gives to the other an equivalent for what the other gives him. I depend on the shoemaker for shoes, and the tailor for coats; but, if I give the shoemaker and the tailor enough of my own labor as a house-builder to pay for the shoes and coats they give me, I retain my personal independence. I have not taken of their product, and given nothing of mine. As long as what I get is obtained by what I give, I am economically independent.

Women consume economic goods. What economic product do they give in exchange for what they consume? The claim that marriage is a partnership, in which the two persons married produce wealth which neither of them, separately, could produce, will not bear examination. A man happy and comfortable can produce more than one unhappy and uncomfortable, but this is as true of a father or son as of a husband. To take from a man any of the conditions which make him happy and strong is to cripple his industry, generally speaking. But those relatives who make him happy are not therefore his business partners, and entitled to share his income.

Grateful return for happiness conferred is not the method of exchange in a partnership. The comfort a man takes with his wife is not in the nature of a business partnership, nor are her frugality and industry. A housekeeper, in her place, might be as frugal, as industrious, but would not therefore be a partner. Man and wife are partners truly in their mutual obligation to their children,—their common love, duty, and service. But a manufacturer who marries, or a doctor, or a lawyer, does not take a partner in his business, when he takes a partner in parenthood, unless his wife is also a manufacturer, a doctor, or a lawyer. In his business, she cannot even advise wisely without training and experience. To love her husband, the composer, does not enable her to compose; and the loss of a man's wife, though it may break his heart, does not cripple his business, unless his mind is affected by grief. She is in no sense a business partner, unless she contributes capital or experience or labor, as a man would in like relation. Most men would hesitate very seriously before entering a business partnership with any woman, wife or not.

If the wife is not, then, truly a business partner, in what way does she earn from her husband the food, clothing, and shelter she receives at his hands? By house service, it will be instantly replied. This is the general misty idea upon the subject,—that women earn all they get, and more, by house service. Here we come to a very practical and definite economic ground. Although not producers of wealth, women serve in the final processes of preparation and distribution. Their labor in the household has a genuine economic value.

For a certain percentage of persons to serve other persons, in order that the ones so served may produce more, is a contribution not to be overlooked. The labor of women in the house, certainly, enables men to produce more wealth than they otherwise could; and in this way women are economic factors in society. But so are horses. The labor of horses enables men to produce more wealth than they otherwise could. The horse is an economic factor in society. But the horse is not economically independent, nor is the woman. If a man plus a valet can perform more useful service than he could minus a valet, then the valet is performing useful service. But, if the valet is the property of the man, is obliged to perform this service, and is not paid for it, he is not economically independent.

The labor which the wife performs in the household is given as part of her functional duty, not as employment. The wife of the poor man, who works hard in a small house, doing all the work for the family, or the wife of the rich man, who wisely and gracefully manages a large house and administers its functions, each is entitled to fair pay for services rendered.

To take this ground and hold it honestly, wives, as earners through domestic service, are entitled to the wages of cooks, house-maids, nursemaids, seamstresses, or housekeepers, and to no more. This would of course reduce the spending money of the wives of the rich, and put it out of the power of the poor man to "support" a wife at all, unless, indeed, the poor man faced the situation fully, paid his wife her wages as house servant, and then she and he combined their funds in the support of their children. He would be keeping a servant: she would be helping keep the family. But no-where on earth would there be "a rich woman" by these means. Even the highest class of private housekeeper, useful as her services are, does not accumulate a fortune. She does not buy diamonds and sables and keep a carriage. Things like these are not earned by house service.

But the salient fact in this discussion is that, whatever the economic value of the domestic industry of women is, they do not get it. The women who do the most work get the least money, and the women who have the most money do the least work. Their labor is neither given nor taken as a factor in economic exchange. It is held to be their duty as women to do this work; and their economic status bears no relation to their domestic labors, unless an inverse one. Moreover, if they were thus fairly paid,—given what they earned, and no more,—all women working in this way would be reduced to the economic status of the house servant. Few women—or men either—care to face this condition. The ground that women earn their living by domestic labor is instantly forsaken, and we are told that they obtain their livelihood as mothers. This is a peculiar position. We speak of it commonly enough, and often with deep feeling, but without due analysis.

In treating of an economic exchange, asking what return in goods or labor women make for the goods and labor given them,—either to the race collectively or to their husbands individually,—what payment women make for their clothes and shoes and furniture and food and shelter, we are told that the duties and services of the mother entitle her to support.

If this is so, if motherhood is an exchangeable commodity given by women in payment for clothes and food, then we must of course find some relation between the quantity or quality of the motherhood and the quantity and quality of the pay. This being true, then the women who are not mothers have no economic status at all; and the economic status of those who are must be shown to be relative to their motherhood. This is obviously absurd. The childless wife has as much money as the mother of many,—more; for the children of the latter consume what would otherwise be hers; and the inefficient mother is no less provided for than the efficient one. Visibly, and upon the face of it, women are not maintained in economic prosperity proportioned to their motherhood. Motherhood bears no relation to their economic status. Among primitive races, it is true,—in the patriarchal period, for instance,—there was some truth in this position. Women being of no value whatever save as bearers of children, their favor and indulgence did bear direct relation to maternity; and they had reason to exult on more grounds than one when they could boast a son. To-day, however, the maintenance of the woman is not conditioned upon this. A man is not allowed to discard his wife because she is barren. The claim of motherhood as a factor in economic exchange is false to-day. But suppose it were true. Are we willing to hold this ground, even in theory? Are we willing to consider motherhood as a business, a form of commercial exchange? Are the cares and duties of the mother, her travail and her love, commodities to be exchanged for bread?

It is revolting so to consider them; and, if we dare face our own thoughts, and force them to their logical conclusion, we shall see that nothing could be more repugnant to human feeling, or more socially and individually injurious, than to make motherhood a trade. Driven off these alleged grounds of women's economic independence; shown that women, as a class, neither produce nor distribute wealth; that women, as individuals, labor mainly as house servants, are not paid as such, and would not be satisfied with such an economic status if they were so paid; that wives are not business partners or co-producers of wealth with their husbands, unless they actually practise the same profession; that they are not salaried as mothers, and that it would be unspeakably degrading if they were,—what remains to those who deny that women are supported by men? This (and a most amusing position it is),—that the function of maternity unfits a woman for economic production, and, therefore, it is right that she should be supported by her husband.

The ground is taken that the human female is not economically independent, that she is fed by the male of her species. In denial of this, it is first alleged that she is economically independent,—that she does support herself by her own industry in the house. It being shown that there is no relation between the economic status of woman and the labor she performs in the home, it is then alleged that not as house servant, but as mother, does woman earn her living. It being shown that the economic status of woman bears no relation to her motherhood, either in quantity or quality, it is then alleged that motherhood renders a woman unfit for economic production, and that, therefore, it is right that she be supported by her husband. Before going farther, let us seize upon this admission,—that she *is* supported by her husband.

Without going into either the ethics or the necessities of the case, we have reached so much common ground: the female of genus homo is supported by the male. Whereas, in other species of animals, male and female alike graze and browse, hunt and kill, climb, swim, dig, run, and fly for their livings, in our species the female does not seek her own living in the specific activities of our race, but is fed by the male.

Now as to the alleged necessity. Because of her maternal duties, the human female is said to be unable to get her own living. As the maternal duties of other females do not unfit them for getting their own living and also the livings of their young, it would seem that the human maternal duties require the segregation of the entire energies of the mother to the service of the child during her entire adult life, or so large a proportion of them that not enough remains to devote to the individual interests of the mother.

Such a condition, did it exist, would of course excuse and justify the pitiful dependence of the human female, and her support by the male. As the queen bee, modified entirely to maternity, is supported, not by the male, to be sure, but by her co-workers, the "old maids," the barren working bees, who labor so patiently and lovingly in their branch of the maternal duties of the hive, so would the human female, modified entirely to maternity, become unfit for any other exertion, and a helpless dependant.

Is this the condition of human motherhood? Does the human mother, by her motherhood, thereby lose control of brain and body, lose power and skill and desire for any other work? Do we see before us the human race, with all its females segregated entirely to the uses of motherhood, consecrated, set apart, specially developed, spending every power of their nature on the service of their children?

We do not. We see the human mother worked far harder than a mare, laboring her life long in the service, not of her children only, but of men; husbands, brothers, fathers, whatever male relatives she has; for mother and sister also; for the church a little, if she is allowed; for society, if she is able; for charity and education and reform,—working in many ways that are not the ways of motherhood.

It is not motherhood that keeps the housewife on her feet from dawn till dark; it is house service, not child service. Women work longer and harder than most men, and not solely in maternal duties. The savage mother carries the burdens, and does all menial service for the tribe. The peasant mother toils in the fields, and the workingman's wife in the home. Many mothers, even now, are wage-earners for the family, as well as bearers and rearers of it. And the women who are not so occupied, the women who belong to rich men,—here perhaps is the exhaustive devotion to maternity which is supposed to justify an admitted economic dependence. But we do not find it even among these. Women of ease and wealth provide for their children better care than the poor woman can; but they do not spend more time upon it themselves, nor more care and effort. They have other occupation.

In spite of her supposed segregation to maternal duties, the human female, the world over, works at extra-maternal duties for hours enough to provide her with an independent living, and then is denied independence on the ground that motherhood prevents her working!

If this ground were tenable, we should find a world full of women who never lifted a finger save in the service of their children, and of men who did *all* the work besides, and waited on the women whom motherhood prevented from waiting on themselves. The ground is not tenable. A human female, healthy, sound, has twenty-five years of life before she is a mother, and should have twenty-five years more after the period of such maternal service as is expected of her has been given. The duties of grandmotherhood are surely not alleged as preventing economic independence.

The working power of the mother has always been a prominent factor in human life. She is the worker *par excellence*, but her work is not such as to affect her economic status. Her living, all that she gets,—food, clothing, ornaments, amusements, luxuries,—these bear no relation to her power to produce wealth, to her services in the house, or to her motherhood. These things bear relation only to the man she marries, the man she depends on,—to how much he has and how much he is willing to give her. The women whose splendid extravagance dazzles the world, whose economic goods are the greatest, are often neither houseworkers nor mothers, but simply the women who hold most power over the men who have the most money. The female of genus homo is economically dependent on the male. He is her food supply.

In its psychic manifestation this intense sex-distinction is equally apparent. The primal instinct of sex-attraction has developed under social forces into a conscious passion of enormous power, a deep and lifelong devotion, overwhelming in its force. This is excessive in both sexes, but more so in women than in men,—not so commonly in its simple physical form, but in the unreasoning intensity of emotion that refuses all guidance, and drives those possessed by it to risk every other good for this one end. It is not at first sight easy, and it may seem an irreverent and thankless task, to discriminate here between what is good in the "master passion" and what is evil, and especially to claim for one sex more of this feeling than for the other; but such discrimination can be made.

It is good for the individual and for the race to have developed such a degree of passionate and permanent love as shall best promote the happiness of individuals and the reproduction of species. It is not good for the race or for the individual that this feeling should have become so intense as to override all other human faculties, to make a mock of the accumulated wisdom of the ages, the stored power of the will; to drive the individual—against his own plain conviction—into a union sure to result in evil, or to hold the individual helpless in such an evil union, when made.

Such is the condition of humanity, involving most evil results to its offspring and to its own happiness. And, while in men the immediate dominating force of the passion may be more conspicuous, it is in women that it holds more universal sway. For the man has other powers and faculties in full use, whereby to break loose from the force of this; and the woman, specially modified to sex and denied racial activity, pours her whole life into her love, and, if injured here, she is injured irretrievably. With him it is frequently light and transient, and, when most intense, often most transient. With her it is a deep, all-absorbing force, under the action of which she will renounce all that life offers, take any risk, face any hardships, bear any pain. It is maintained in her in the face of a lifetime of neglect and abuse. The common instance of the police court trials—the woman cruelly abused who will not testify against her husband— shows this. This devotion, carried to such a degree as to lead to the mismating of individuals with its personal and social injury, is an excessive sex-distinction.

But it is in our common social relations that the predominance of sex-distinction in women is made most manifest. The fact that, speaking broadly, women have, from the very beginning, been spoken of expressively enough as "the sex," demonstrates clearly that this is the main impression which they have made upon observers and recorders. Here one need attempt no farther proof than to turn the mind of the reader to an unbroken record of facts and feelings perfectly patent to every one, but not hitherto looked at as other than perfectly natural and right. So utterly has the status of woman been accepted as a sexual one that it has remained for the woman's movement of the nineteenth century to devote much contention to the claim that women are persons! That women are persons as well as females,—an unheard of proposition!

In a "Handbook of Proverbs of All Nations," a collection comprising many thousands, these facts are to be observed: first, that the proverbs concerning women are an insignificant minority compared to those concerning men; second, that the proverbs concerning women almost invariably apply to them in general,—to the sex. Those concerning men qualify, limit, describe, specialize. It is "a lazy man," "a violent man," "a man in his cups." Qualities and actions are predicated of man individually, and not as a sex, unless he is flatly contrasted with woman, as in "A man of straw is worth a woman of gold," "Men are deeds, women are words," or "Man, woman, and the devil are the three degrees of comparison." But of woman it is always and only "a woman," meaning simply a female, and recognizing no personal distinction: "As much pity to see a woman weep as to see a goose go barefoot." "He that hath an eel by the tail and a woman by her word hath a slippery handle." "A woman, a spaniel, and a walnut-tree,—the more you beat 'em, the better they be." Occasionally a distinction is made between "a fair woman" and "a black woman"; and Solomon's "virtuous woman," who commanded such a high price, is familiar to us all. But in common thought it is simply "a woman" always. The boast of the profligate that he knows "the sex," so recently expressed by a new poet,—"The things you will learn from the Yellow and Brown, they'll 'elp you an' 'eap with the White"; the complaint of the angry rejected that "all women are just alike!"—the consensus of public opinion of all time goes to show that the characteristics common to the sex have predominated over the characteristics distinctive of the individual,—a marked excess in sex-distinction.

From the time our children are born, we use every means known to accentuate sex-distinction in both boy and girl; and the reason that the boy is not so hopelessly marked by it as the girl is that he has the whole field of human expression open to him besides. In our steady insistence on proclaiming sex-distinction we have grown to consider most human attributes as masculine attributes, for the simple reason that they were allowed to men and forbidden to women.

A clear and definite understanding of the difference between race-attributes and sex-attributes should be established. Life consists of action. The action of a living thing is along two main lines,—self-preservation and race-preservation. The processes that keep the individual alive, from the involuntary action of his internal organs to the voluntary action of his external organs,—every act, from breathing to hunting his food, which contributes to the maintenance of the individual life,—these are the processes of self-preservation. Whatever activities tend to keep the race alive, to reproduce the individual, from the involuntary action of the internal organs to the voluntary action of the external organs; every act from the development of germ-cells to the taking care of children, which contributes to the maintenance of the racial life,—these are the processes of race-preservation. In race-preservation, male and female have distinctive organs, distinctive functions, distinctive lines of action. In self-preservation, male and female have the same organs, the same functions, the same lines of action. In the human species our processes of race-preservation have reached a certain degree of elaboration; but our processes of self-preservation have gone farther, much farther.

All the varied activities of economic production and distribution, all our arts and industries, crafts and trades, all our growth in science, discovery, government, religion,—these are along the line of self-preservation: these are, or should be, common to both sexes. To teach, to rule, to make, to decorate, to distribute,—these are not sex-functions: they are race-functions. Yet so inordinate is the sex-distinction of the human race that the whole field of human progress has been considered a masculine prerogative. What could more absolutely prove the excessive sex-distinction of the human race? That this difference should surge over all its natural boundaries and blazon itself across every act of life, so that every step of the human creature is marked "male" or "female,"—surely, this is enough to show our over-sexed condition.

Little by little, very slowly, and with most unjust and cruel opposition, at cost of all life holds most dear, it is being gradually established by many martyrdoms that human work is woman's as well as man's. Harriet Martineau must conceal her writing under her sewing when callers came, because "to sew" was a feminine verb, and "to write" a masculine one. Mary Somerville must struggle to hide her work from even relatives, because mathematics was a "masculine" pursuit. Sex has been made to dominate the whole human world,—all the main avenues of life marked "male," and the female left to be a female, and nothing else.

But while with the male the things he fondly imagined to be

"masculine" were merely human, and very good for him, with the female the few things marked "feminine" were feminine, indeed; and her ceaseless reiterance of one short song, however sweet, has given it a conspicuous monotony. In garments whose main purpose is unmistakably to announce her sex; with a tendency to ornament which marks exuberance of sex-energy, with a body so modified to sex as to be grievously deprived of its natural activities; with a manner and behavior wholly attuned to sex-advantage, and frequently most disadvantageous to any human gain; with a field of action most rigidly confined to sex-relations; with her overcharged sensibility, her prominent modesty, her "eternal femininity,"—the female of genus homo is undeniably over-sexed.

This excessive distinction shows itself again in a marked precocity of development. Our little children, our very babies, show signs of it when the young of other creatures are serenely asexual in general appearance and habit. We eagerly note this precocity. We are proud of it. We carefully encourage it by precept and example, taking pains to develope the sex-instinct in little children, and think no harm. One of the first things we force upon the child's dawning consciousness is the fact that he is a boy or that she is a girl, and that, therefore, each must regard everything from a different point of view. They must be dressed differently, not on account of their personal needs, which are exactly similar at this period, but so that neither they, nor any one beholding them, may for a moment forget the distinction of sex.

Our peculiar inversion of the usual habit of species, in which the male carries ornament and the female is dark and plain, is not so much a proof of excess indeed, as a proof of the peculiar reversal of our position in the matter of sex-selection. With the other species the males compete in ornament, and the females select. With us the females compete in ornament, and the males select. If this theory of sex-ornament is disregarded, and we prefer rather to see in masculine decoration merely a form of exuberant sex-energy, expending itself in non-productive excess, then, indeed, the fact that with us the females manifest such a display of gorgeous adornment is another sign of excessive sex-distinction. In either case the forcing upon girl-children of an elaborate ornamentation which interferes with their physical activity and unconscious freedom, and fosters a premature sex-consciousness, is as clear and menacing a proof of our condition as could be mentioned. That the girl-child should be so dressed as to require a difference in care and behavior, resting wholly on the fact that she is a girl,—a fact not otherwise present to her thought at that age,—is a precocious insistence upon sex-distinction, most unwholesome in its results. Boys and girls are expected, also, to behave differently to each other, and to people in general,—a behavior to be briefly described in two words. To the boy we say, "Do"; to the girl, "Don't." The little boy must "take care" of the little girl, even if she is larger than he is. "Why?" he asks. Because he is a boy. Because of sex. Surely, if she is the stronger, she ought to take care of him, especially as the protective instinct is purely feminine in a normal race. It is not long before the boy learns his lesson. He is a boy, going to be a man; and that means all. "I thank the Lord that I was not born a woman," runs the Hebrew prayer. She is a girl, "only a girl," "nothing but a girl," and going to be a woman,—only a woman. Boys are encouraged from the beginning to show the feelings supposed to be proper to their sex. When our infant son bangs about, roars, and smashes things, we say proudly that he is "a regular boy!" When our infant daughter coquettes with visitors, or wails in maternal agony because her brother has broken her doll, whose sawdust remains she nurses with piteous care, we say proudly that "she is a perfect little mother already!" What business has a little girl with the instincts of maternity? No more than the little boy should have with the instincts of paternity. They are sex-instincts, and should not appear till the period of adolescence. The most normal girl is the "tom-boy,"—whose numbers increase among us in these wiser days,—a healthy young creature, who is human through and through, not feminine till it is time to be. The most normal boy has calmness and gentleness as well as vigor

_____

There seems to have come a time when it occurred to the dawning intelligence of this amiable savage that it was cheaper and easier to fight a little female, and have it done with, than to fight a big male every time. So he instituted the custom of enslaving the female; and she, losing freedom, could no longer get her own food nor that of her young. The mother ape, with her maternal function well fulfilled, flees leaping through the forest,—plucks her fruit and nuts, keeps up with the movement of the tribe, her young one on her back or held in one strong arm. But the mother woman, enslaved, could not do this. Then man, the father, found that slavery had its obligations: he must care for what he forbade to care for itself, else it died on his hands. So he slowly and reluctantly shouldered the duties of his new position. He began to feed her, and not only that, but to express in his own person the thwarted uses of maternity: he had to feed the children, too. It seems a simple arrangement. When we have thought of it at all, we have thought of it with admiration. The naturalist defends it on the ground of advantage to the species through the freeing of the mother from all other cares and confining her unreservedly to the duties of maternity. The poet and novelist, the painter and sculptor, the priest and teacher, have all extolled this lovely relation. It remains for the sociologist, from a biological point of view, to note its effects on the constitution of the human race, both in the individual and in society.

When man began to feed and defend woman, she ceased proportionately to feed and defend herself. When he stood between her

and her physical environment, she ceased proportionately to feel
the influence of that environment and respond to it. When he became her immediate and all-important environment, she began
proportionately to respond to this new influence, and to be modified accordingly. In a free state, speed was of as great advantage to
the female as to the male, both in enabling her to catch prey and in
preventing her from being caught by enemies; but, in her new condition, speed was a disadvantage. She was not allowed to do the
catching, and it profited her to be caught by her new master. Free
creatures, getting their own food and maintaining their own lives,
develope an active capacity for attaining their ends. Parasitic creatures, whose living is obtained by the exertions of others, develope
powers of absorption and of tenacity,—the powers by which they
profit most. The human female was cut off from the direct action of
natural selection, that mighty force which heretofore had acted on
male and female alike with inexorable and beneficial effect, developing strength, developing skill, developing endurance, developing
courage,—in a word, developing species. She now met the influence of natural selection acting indirectly through the male, and
developing, of course, the faculties required to secure and obtain a
hold on him. Needless to state that these faculties were those of
sex-attraction, the one power that has made him cheerfully maintain, in what luxury he could, the being in whom he delighted. For
many, many centuries she had no other hold, no other assurance of
being fed. The young girl had a prospective value, and was maintained for what should follow; but the old woman, in more primitive
times, had but a poor hold on life. She who could best please her
lord was the favorite slave or favorite wife, and she obtained the
best economic conditions.

With the growth of civilization, we have gradually crystallized
into law the visible necessity for feeding the helpless female; and
even old women are maintained by their male relatives with a comfortable assurance. But to this day—save, indeed, for the increasing
army of women wage-earners, who are changing the face of the
world by their steady advance toward economic independence—

the personal profit of women bears but too close a relation to their power to win and hold the other sex. From the odalisque with the most bracelets to the débutante with the most bouquets, the relation still holds good,—woman's economic profit comes through the power of sex-attraction.

When we confront this fact boldly and plainly in the open market of vice, we are sick with horror. When we see the same economic relation made permanent, established by law, sanctioned and sanctified by religion, covered with flowers and incense and all accumulated sentiment, we think it innocent, lovely, and right. The transient trade we think evil. The bargain for life we think good. But the biological effect remains the same. In both cases the female gets her food from the male by virtue of her sex-relationship to him. In both cases, perhaps even more in marriage because of its perfect acceptance of the situation, the female of genus homo, still living under natural law, is inexorably modified to sex in an increasing degree.

Followed in specific detail, the action of the changed environment upon women has been in given instances as follows: In the matter of mere passive surroundings she has been immediately restricted in her range. This one factor has an immense effect on man and animal alike. An absolutely uniform environment, one shape, one size, one color, one sound, would render life, if any life could be, one helpless, changeless thing. As the environment increases and varies, the development of the creature must increase and vary with it; for he acquires knowledge and power, as the material for knowledge and the need for power appear. In migratory species the female is free to acquire the same knowledge as the male by the same means, the same development by the same experiences. The human female has been restricted in range from the earliest beginning. Even among savages, she has a much more restricted knowledge of the land she lives in. She moves with the camp, of course, and follows her primitive industries in its vicinity; but the war-path and the hunt are the man's. He has a far larger habitat. The life of the female savage is freedom itself, however, compared with the increasing constriction of custom closing in upon the woman, as civilization advanced, like the iron torture chamber of romance. Its culmination is expressed in the proverb: "A woman should leave her home but three times,—when she is christened, when she is married, and when she is buried." Or this: "The woman, the cat, and the chimney should never leave the house." The absolutely stationary female and the wide-ranging male are distinctly human institutions, after we leave behind us such low forms of life as the gypsy moth, whose female seldom moves more than a few feet from the pupa moth. She has aborted wings, and cannot fly. She waits humbly for the winged male, lays her myriad eggs, and dies,—a fine instance of modification to sex.

To reduce so largely the mere area of environment is a great check to race-development; but it is not to be compared in its effects with the reduction in voluntary activity to which the human female has been subjected. Her restricted impression, her confinement to the four walls of the home, have done great execution, of course, in limiting her ideas, her information, her thought-processes, and power of judgment; and in giving a disproportionate prominence and intensity to the few things she knows about; but this is innocent in action compared with her restricted expression, the denial of freedom to act. A living organism is modified far less through the action of external circumstances upon it and its reaction thereto, than through the effect of its own exertions. Skin may be thickened gradually by exposure to the weather; but it is thickened far more quickly by being rubbed against something, as the handle of an oar or of a broom. To be surrounded by beautiful things has much influence upon the human creature: to make beautiful things has more. To live among beautiful surroundings and make ugly things is more directly lowering than to live among ugly surroundings and make beautiful things. What we do modifies us more than what is done to us. The freedom of expression has been more restricted in women than the freedom of impression, if that be possible. Something of the world she lived in she has seen from her barred windows. Some air has come through the purdah's folds, some knowledge has filtered to her eager ears from the talk of men. Desdemona learned somewhat of Othello. Had she known more, she might have lived longer. But in the ever-growing human impulse to create, the power and will to make, to do, to express one's new spirit in new forms,—here she has been utterly debarred. She might work as she had worked from the beginning,—at the primitive labors of the household; but in the inevitable expansion of even those industries to professional levels we have striven to hold her back. To work with her own hands, for nothing, in direct body-service to her own family,—this has been permitted,—yes, compelled. But to be and do anything further from this she has been forbidden. Her labor has not only been limited in kind, but in degree. Whatever she has been allowed to do must be done in private and alone, the first-hand industries of savage times.

Our growth in industry has been not only in kind, but in class. The baker is not in the same industrial grade with the house-cook, though both make bread. To specialize any form of labor is a step up: to organize it is another step. Specialization and organization are the basis of human progress, the organic methods of social life. They have been forbidden to women almost absolutely. The greatest and most beneficent change of this century is the progress of women in these two lines of advance. The effect of this check in industrial development, accompanied as it was by the constant inheritance of increased racial power, has been to intensify the sensations and emotions of women, and to develope great activity in the lines allowed. The nervous energy that up to present memory has impelled women to labor incessantly at something, be it the veriest folly of fancy work, is one mark of this effect.

In religious development the same dead-line has held back the growth of women through all the races and ages. In dim early times she was sharer in the mysteries and rites; but, as religion developed, her place receded, until Paul commanded her to be silent in the churches. And she has been silent until to-day. Even now, with all the ground gained, we have but the beginnings—the slowly forced and disapproved beginnings—of religious equality for the sexes. In some nations, religion is held to be a masculine attribute exclusively, it being even questioned whether women have souls. An early Christian council settled that important question by vote, fortunately deciding that they had. In a church whose main strength has always been derived from the adherence of women, it would have been an uncomfortable reflection not to have allowed them souls. Ancient family worship ran in the male line. It was the son who kept the sacred grandfathers in due respect, and poured libations to their shades. When the woman married, she changed her ancestors, and had to worship her husband's progenitors instead of her own. This is why the Hindu and the Chinaman and many others of like stamp must have a son to keep them in countenance,— a deep-seated sex-prejudice, coming to slow extinction as women rise in economic importance.

It is painfully interesting to trace the gradual cumulative effect of these conditions upon women: first, the action of large natural laws, acting on her as they would act on any other animal; then the evolution of social customs and laws (with her position as the active cause), following the direction of mere physical forces, and adding heavily to them; then, with increasing civilization, the unbroken accumulation of precedent, burnt into each generation by the growing force of education, made lovely by art, holy by religion, desirable by habit; and, steadily acting from beneath, the unswerving pressure of economic necessity upon which the whole structure rested. These are strong modifying conditions, indeed.

The process would have been even more effective and far less painful but for one important circumstance. Heredity has no Salic law. Each girl-child inherits from her father a certain increasing percentage of human development, human power, human tendency; and each boy as well inherits from his mother the increasing percentage of sex-development, sex-power, sex-tendency. The action of heredity has been to equalize what every tendency of environment and education made to differ. This has saved us from such a female as the gypsy moth. It has held up the woman, and held down the man. It has set iron bounds to our absurd effort to make a race with one sex a million years behind the other. But it has added terribly to the pain and difficulty of human life,—a difficulty and a pain that should have taught us long since that we were living on wrong lines. Each woman born, re-humanized by the current of race activity carried on by her father and re-womanized by her traditional position, has had to live over again in her own person the same process of restriction, repression, denial; the smothering "no" which crushed down all her human desires to create, to discover, to learn, to express, to advance. Each woman has had, on the other hand, the same single avenue of expression and attainment; the same one way in which alone she might do what she could, get what she might. All other doors were shut, and this one always open; and the whole pressure of advancing humanity was upon her. No wonder that young Daniel in the apocryphal tale proclaimed: "The king is strong! Wine is strong! But women are stronger!"

To the young man confronting life the world lies wide. Such powers as he has he may use, must use. If he chooses wrong at first, he may choose again, and yet again. Not effective or successful in one channel, he may do better in another. The growing, varied needs of all mankind call on him for the varied service in which he finds his growth. What he wants to be, he may strive to be. What he wants to get, he may strive to get. Wealth, power, social distinction, fame,—what he wants he can try for.

To the young woman confronting life there is the same world beyond, there are the same human energies and human desires and ambition within. But all that she may wish to have, all that she may wish to do, must come through a single channel and a single choice. Wealth, power, social distinction, fame,—not only these, but home and happiness, reputation, ease and pleasure, her bread and butter,—all must come to her through a small gold ring. This is a heavy pressure. It has accumulated behind her through heredity, and continued about her through environment. It has been subtly trained into her through education, till she herself has come to think it a right condition, and pours its influence upon her daughter with increasing impetus. Is it any wonder that women are over-sexed? But for the constant inheritance from the more human male, we should have been queen bees, indeed, long before this. But the daughter of the soldier and the sailor, of the artist, the inventor, the great merchant, has inherited in body and brain her share of his development in each generation, and so stayed somewhat human for all her femininity.

All morbid conditions tend to extinction. One check has always existed to our inordinate sex-development,—nature's ready relief, death. Carried to its furthest excess, the individual has died, the family has become extinct, the nation itself has perished, like Sodom and Gomorrah. Where one function is carried to unnatural excess, others are weakened, and the organism perishes. We are familiar with this in individual cases,—at least, the physician is. We can see it somewhat in the history of nations. From younger races, nearer savagery, nearer the healthful equality of pre-human creatures, has come each new start in history. Persia was older than Greece, and its highly differentiated sexuality had produced the inevitable result of enfeebling the racial qualities. The Greek commander stripped the rich robes and jewels from his Persian captives, and showed their unmanly feebleness to his men. "You have such bodies as these to fight for such plunder as this," he said. In the country, among peasant classes, there is much less sex-distinction than in cities, where wealth enables the women to live in absolute idleness; and even the men manifest the same characteristics. It is from the country and the lower classes that the fresh blood pours into the cities, to be weakened in its turn by the influence of this unnatural distinction until there is none left to replenish the nation.

The inevitable trend of human life is toward higher civilization; but, while that civilization is confined to one sex, it inevitably exaggerates sex-distinction, until the increasing evil of this condition is stronger than all the good of the civilization attained, and the nation falls. Civilization, be it understood, does not consist in the acquisition of luxuries. Social development is an organic development. A civilized State is one in which the citizens live in organic industrial relation. The more full, free, subtle, and easy that relation; the more perfect the differentiation of labor and exchange of product, with their correlative institutions,—the more perfect is that civilization. To eat, drink, sleep, and keep warm,—these are common to all animals, whether the animal couches in a bed of leaves or one of eiderdown, sleeps in the sun to avoid the wind or builds a furnace-heated house, lies in wait for game or orders a dinner at a hotel. These are but individual animal processes. Whether one lays an egg or a million eggs, whether one bears a cub, a kitten, or a baby, whether one broods its chickens, guards its litter, or tends a nursery full of children, these are but individual animal processes. But to serve each other more and more widely; to live only by such service; to develope special functions, so that we depend for our living on society's return for services that can be of no direct use to ourselves,—this is civilization, our human glory and race-distinction.

All this human progress has been accomplished by men. Women have been left behind, outside, below, having no social relation whatever, merely the sex-relation, whereby they lived. Let us bear in mind that all the tender ties of family are ties of blood, of sex-relationship. A friend, a comrade, a partner,—this is a human relative. Father, mother, son, daughter, sister, brother, husband, wife,—these are sex-relatives. Blood is thicker than water, we say. True. But ties of blood are not those that ring the world with the succeeding waves of progressive religion, art, science, commerce, education, all that makes us human. Man is the human creature. Woman has been checked, starved, aborted in human growth; and the swelling forces of race-development have been driven back in each generation to work in her through sex-functions alone.

This is the way in which the sexuo-economic relation has operated in our species, checking race-development in half of us, and stimulating sex-development in both.

The facts stated in the foregoing chapters are familiar and undeniable, the argument seems clear; yet the mind reacts violently from the conclusions it is forced to admit, and tries to find relief in the commonplace conditions of every-day life. From this looming phantom of the over-sexed female of genus homo we fly back in satisfaction to familiar acquaintances and relatives,—to Mrs. John Smith and Miss Imogene Jones, to mothers and sisters and daughters and sweethearts and wives. We feel that such a dreadful state of things cannot be true, or we should surely have noticed it. We may even perform that acrobatic feat so easy to most minds,—admit that the statement may be theoretically true, but practically false!

Two simple laws of brain action are responsible for the difficulty of convincing the human race of any large general truths concerning itself. One is common to all brains, to all nerve sensations indeed, and is cheerfully admitted to have nothing to do with the sexuo-economic relation. It is this simple fact, in popular phrase,—that what we are used to we do not notice. This rests on the law of adaptation, the steady, ceaseless pressure that tends to fit the organism to the environment. A nerve touched for the first time with a certain impression feels this first impression far more than the hundredth or thousandth, though the thousandth be far more violent than the first. If an impression be constant and regular, we become utterly insensitive to it, and only respond under some special condition, as the ticking of a clock, the noise of running water or waves on the beach, even the clatter of railroad trains, grows imverceptible to those who hear it constantly. It is perfectly possible for an individual to become accustomed to the most disadvantageous conditions, and fail to notice them.

It is equally possible for a race, a nation, a class, to become accustomed to most disadvantageous conditions, and fail to notice them. Take, as an individual instance, the wearing of corsets by women. Put a corset, even a loose one, on a vigorous man or woman who never wore one, and there is intense discomfort, and a vivid consciousness thereof. The healthy muscles of the trunk resent the pressure, the action of the whole body is checked in the middle, the stomach is choked, the process of digestion interfered with; and the victim says, "How can you bear such a thing?"

But the person habitually wearing a corset does not feel these evils. They exist, assuredly, the facts are there, the body is not deceived; but the nerves have become accustomed to these disagreeable sensations, and no longer respond to them. The person "does not feel it." In fact, the wearer becomes so used to the sensations that, when they are removed,—with the corset,—there is a distinct sense of loss and discomfort. The heavy folds of the cravat, stock, and neckcloth of earlier men's fashions, the heavy horse-hair peruke, the stiff high collar of to-day, the kind of shoes we wear,—these are perfectly familiar instances of the force of habit in the individual.

This is equally true of racial habits. That a king should rule because he was born, passed unquestioned for thousands of years. That the eldest son should inherit the titles and estates was a similar phenomenon as little questioned. That a debtor should be imprisoned, and so entirely prevented from paying his debts, was common law. So glaring an evil as chattel slavery was an unchallenged social institution from earliest history to our own day among the most civilized nations of the earth. Christ himself let it pass unnoticed. The hideous injustice of Christianity to the Jew attracted no attention through many centuries. That the serf went with the soil, and was owned by the lord thereof, was one of the foundations of society in the Middle Ages.

Social conditions, like individual conditions, become familiar by use, and cease to be observed. This is the reason why it is so much easier to criticise the customs of other persons or other nations than our own. It is also the reason why we so naturally deny and resent the charges of the critic. It is not necessarily because of any injustice on the one side or dishonesty on the other, but because of a simple and useful law of nature. The Englishman coming to America is much struck by America's political corruption; and, in the earnest desire to serve his brother, he tells us all about it. That which he has at home he does not observe, because he is used to it. The American in England finds also something to object to, and omits to balance his criticism by memories of home.

When a condition exists among us which began in those unrecorded ages back of tradition even, which obtains in varying degree among every people on earth, and which begins to act upon the individual at birth, it would be a miracle past all belief if people should notice it. The sexuo-economic relation is such a condition. It began in primeval savagery. It exists in all nations. Each boy and girl is born into it, trained into it, and has to live in it. The world's progress in matters like these is attained by a slow and painful process, but one which works to good ends.

In the course of social evolution there are developed individuals so constituted as not to fit existing conditions, but to be organically adapted to more advanced conditions. These advanced individuals respond in sharp and painful consciousness to existing conditions, and cry out against them according to their lights. The history of religion, of political and social reform, is full of familiar instances of this. The heretic, the reformer, the agitator, these feel what their compeers do not, see what they do not, and, naturally, say what they do not. The mass of the people are invariably displeased by the outcry of these uneasy spirits. In simple primitive periods they were promptly put to death. Progress was slow and difficult in those days. But this severe process of elimination developed the kind of progressive person known as a martyr; and this remarkable sociological law was manifested: that the strength of a current of social force is increased by the sacrifice of individuals who are willing to die in the effort to promote it. "The blood of the martyrs is the seed of the church." This is so commonly known to-day, though not formulated, that power hesitates to persecute, lest it intensify the undesirable heresy. A policy of "free speech" is found to let pass most of the uneasy pushes and spurts of these stirring forces, and lead to more orderly action. Our great anti-slavery agitation, the heroic efforts of the "women's rights" supporters, are fresh and recent proofs of these plain facts: that the mass of the people do not notice existing conditions, and that they are not pleased with those who do. This is one strong reason why the sexuo-economic relation passes unobserved among us, and why any statement of it will be so offensive to many.

The other law of brain action which tends to prevent our perception of general truth is this: it is easier to personalize than to generalize. This is due primarily to the laws of mental development, but it is greatly added to by the very relation under discussion. As a common law of mental action, the power to observe and retain an individual impression marks a lower degree of development than the power to classify and collate impressions and make generalizations therefrom. There are savages who can say "hot fire," "hot stone," "hot water," but cannot say "heat," cannot think it. Similarly, they can say "good man," "good knife," "good meat"; but they cannot say "goodness," they cannot think it. They have observed specific instances, but are unable to collate them, to generalize therefrom. So, in our common life, individual instances of injustice or cruelty are observed long before the popular mind is able to see that it is a condition which causes these things, and that the condition must be altered before the effects can be removed. A bad priest, a bad king, a bad master, were long observed and pointedly objected to before it began to be held that the condition of monarchy or the condition of slavery must needs bear fruit, and that, if we did not like the fruit, we might better change the tree. Any slaveholder would admit that there were instances of cruelty, laziness, pride, among masters, and of deceit, laziness, dishonesty, among slaves.

262 · CHARLOTTE PERKINS GILMAN

What the slaveholder did not see was that, given the relation of chattel slavery, it inevitably tended to produce these evils, and did produce them, in spite of all the efforts of the individual to the contrary. To see the individual instance is easy. To see the general cause is harder, requires a further brain development. We, as a race, have long since reached the degree of general intelligence which ought to enable us to judge more largely and wisely of social questions; but here the deteriorating effect of the sexuo-economic relation is shown.

The sex relation is intensely personal. All the functions and relations ensuing are intensely personal. The spirit of "me and my wife, my son John and his wife, us four, and no more," is the natural spirit of this phase of life. By confining half the world to this one set of functions, we have confined it absolutely to the personal. And man that is born of woman is reared by her in this same atmosphere of concentrated personality, and afterward spends a large part of his life in it. This condition tends to magnify the personal and minimize the general in our minds, with results that are familiar to us all. The difficulty of enforcing sanitary laws, where personal convenience must be sacrificed to general safety, the size of the personal grievance as against the general, the need of "having it brought home to us," which hinders every step of public advancement, and our eager response when it is "brought home to us,"—these are truisms. So far as a comparison can be made, women are in this sense more personal than men, more personally sensitive, less willing to "stand in line" and "take turns," less able to see why a general restriction is just when it touches them or their children. This is natural enough, inevitable enough, and only mentioned here as partially explaining why people do not see the general facts as to our oversexed condition. Yet they are patent everywhere, not only patent, but painful. Being used to them, we do not notice them, or, forced to notice them, we attribute the pain we feel to the evil behavior of some individual, and never think of it as being the result of a condition common to us all.

If we have among us such a condition as has been stated,—a state of morbid and excessive sex-development,—it must, of course, show itself in daily life in a thousand ways. The non-observer, not having seen any such manifestation, concludes that there is none, and so denies the alleged condition,—says it sounds all right, but he does not see any proof of it! Having clearly in mind that, if such proof exists, such commensurate evil in common life as would naturally result from an abnormal sex-distinction, these evils must be so common and habitual as to pass unobserved; and, farther, that, when forced upon our notice, we only see them as matters of personal behavior,—let us, in spite of these hindrances, see if the visible results among us are not such as must follow such a cause, and let us seek them merely in the phenomena of every-day life as we know it, not in the deeper sexual or social results.

A concrete instance, familiar as the day, and unbelievable in its ill effects, is the attitude of the mother toward her children in regard to the sex-relation. With very few exceptions, the mother gives her daughter no warning or prevision of what life holds for her, and so lets innocence and ignorance go on perpetuating sickness and sin and pain through ceaseless generations. A normal motherhood wisely and effectively guards its young from evil. An abnormal motherhood, over-anxious and under-wise, hovers the child to its harm, and turns it out defenceless to the worst of evils. This is known to millions and millions personally. Only very lately have we thought to consider it generally. And not yet do we see that it is not the fault of the individual mother, but of her economic status. Because of our abnormal sex-development, the whole field has become something of an offence,—a thing to be hidden and ignored, passed over without remark or explanation. Hence this amazing paradox of mothers ashamed of motherhood, unable to explain it, and—measure this well—lying to their children about the primal truths of life,—mothers lying to their own children about motherhood!

The pressure under which this is done is an economic one. The girl must marry: else how live? The prospective husband prefers the girl to know nothing. He is the market, the demand. She is the supply. And with the best intentions the mother serves her child's economic advantage by preparing her for the market. This is an excellent instance. It is common. It is most evil. It is plainly traceable to our sexuo-economic relation.

Another instance of so grossly unjust, so palpable, so general an evil that it has occasionally aroused some protest even from our dull consciousness is this: the enforced attitude of the woman toward marriage. To the young girl, as has been previously stated, marriage is the one road to fortune, to life. She is born highly specialized as a female: she is carefully educated and trained to realize in all ways her sex-limitations and her sex-advantages. What she has to gain even as a child is largely gained by feminine tricks and charms. Her reading, both in history and fiction, treats of the same position for women; and romance and poetry give it absolute predominance. Pictorial art, music, the drama, society, everything, tells her that she is *she*, and that all depends on whom she marries. Where young boys plan for what they will achieve and attain, young girls plan for whom they will achieve and attain. Little Ellie and her swan's nest among the reeds is a familiar illustration. It is the lover on the red roan steed she planned for. It is Lancelot riding through the sheaves that called the Lady from her loom at Shalott: "he" is the coming world.

With such a prospect as this before her; with an organization specially developed to this end; with an education adding every weight of precept and example, of wisdom and virtue, to the natural instincts; with a social environment the whole machinery of which is planned to give the girl a chance to see and to be seen, to provide her with "opportunities"; and with all the pressure of personal advantage and self-interest added to the sex-instinct,—what one would logically expect is a society full of desperate and eager husband-hunters, regarded with popular approval.

Not at all! Marriage is the woman's proper sphere, her divinely ordered place, her natural end. It is what she is born for, what she is trained for, what she is exhibited for. It is, moreover, her means of honorable livelihood and advancement. *But*—she must not even look as if she wanted it! She must not turn her hand over to get it. She must sit passive as the seasons go by, and her "chances" lessen with each year. Think of the strain on a highly sensitive nervous organism to have so much hang on one thing, to see the possibility of attaining it grow less and less yearly, and to be forbidden to take any step toward securing it! This she must bear with dignity and grace to the end.

To what end? To the end that, if she does not succeed in being chosen, she becomes a thing of mild popular contempt, a human being with no further place in life save as an attachée, a dependant upon more fortunate relatives, an old maid. The open derision and scorn with which unmarried women used to be treated is lessening each year in proportion to their advance in economic independence. But it is not very long since the popular proverb, "Old maids lead apes in hell," was in common use; since unwelcome lovers urged their suit with the awful argument that they might be the last askers; since the hapless lady in the wood prayed for a husband, and, when the owl answered, "Who? who?" cried, "Anybody, good Lord!" There is still a pleasant ditty afloat as to the "Three Old Maids of Lynn," who did not marry when they could, and could not when they would.

The cruel and absurd injustice of blaming the girl for not getting what she is allowed no effort to obtain seems unaccountable; but it becomes clear when viewed in connection with the sexuo-economic relation. Although marriage is a means of livelihood, it is not honest employment where one can offer one's labor without shame, but a relation where the support is given outright, and enforced by law in return for the functional service of the woman, the "duties of wife and mother." Therefore no honorable woman can ask for it. It is not only that the natural feminine instinct is to retire, as that of the male is to advance, but that, because marriage means support, a woman must not ask a man to support her. It is economic beggary as well as a false attitude from a sex point of view.

Observe the ingenious cruelty of the arrangement. It is just as humanly natural for a woman as for a man to want wealth. But, when her wealth is made to come through the same channels as her love, she is forbidden to ask for it by her own sex-nature and by business honor. Hence the millions of mismade marriages with "anybody, good Lord!" Hence the million broken hearts which must let all life pass, unable to make any attempt to stop it. Hence the many "maiden aunts," elderly sisters and daughters, unattached women everywhere, who are a burden on their male relatives and society at large. This is changing for the better, to be sure, but changing only through the advance of economic independence for women. A "bachelor maid" is a very different thing from "an old maid."

This, then, is the reason for the Andromeda position of the possibly-to-be-married young woman, and for the ridicule and reproach meted out to her. Since women are viewed wholly as creatures of sex even by one another, and since everything is done to add to their young powers of sex-attraction; since they are marriageable solely on this ground, unless, indeed, "a fortune" has been added to their charms,—failure to marry is held a clear proof of failure to attract, a lack of sex-value. And, since they have no other value, save in a low order of domestic service, they are quite naturally despised. What else is the creature good for, failing in the functions for which it was created? The scorn of male and female alike falls on this sexless thing: she is a human failure.

It is not strange, therefore, though just as pitiful,—this long chapter of patient, voiceless, dreary misery in the lives of women; and it is not strange, either, to see the marked and steady change in opinion that follows the development of other faculties in woman besides those of sex. Now that she is a person as well as a female, filling economic relation to society, she is welcomed and accepted as a human creature, and need not marry the wrong man for her bread and butter. So sharp is the reaction from this unlovely yoke that there is a limited field of life to-day wherein women choose not to marry, preferring what they call "their independence,"—a new-born, hard-won, dear-bought independence. That any living woman should prefer it to home and husband, to love and motherhood, throws a fierce light on what women must have suffered for lack of freedom before.

This tendency need not be feared, however. It is merely a reaction, and a most natural one. It will pass as naturally, as more and more women become independent, when marriage is not the price of liberty. The fear exhibited that women generally, once fully independent, will not marry, is proof of how well it has been known that only dependence forced them to marriage as it was. There will be needed neither bribe nor punishment to force women to true marriage with independence.

Along this line it is most interesting to mark the constant struggle between natural instinct and natural law, and social habit and social law, through all our upward course. Beginning with the natural functions and instincts of sex, holding her great position as selecter of the best among competing males, woman's beautiful work is to improve the race by right marriage. The feeling by which this is accomplished, growing finer as we become more civilized, developes into that wide, deep, true, and lasting love which is the highest good to individual human beings. Following its current, we have always reverenced and admired "true love"; and our romances, from the earliest times, abound in praise of the princess who marries the page or prisoner, venerating the selective power in woman, choosing "the right man" for his own sake. Directly against this runs the counter-current, resulting in the marriage of convenience, a thing which the true inner heart of the world has always hated. Young Lochinvar is not an eternal hero for nothing. The personified type of a great social truth is sure of a long life. The poor young hero, handsome, brave, good, but beset with difficulties, stands ever against the wealth and power of the bad man. The woman is pulled hither and thither between them, and the poor hero wins in the end. That he is heaped with honor and riches, after all, merely signifies our recognition that he is the higher good. This is better than a sun-myth. It is a race-myth, and true as truth.

So we have it among us in life to-day, endlessly elaborated and weakened by profuse detail, as is the nature of that life, but there yet. The girl who marries the rich old man or the titled profligate is condemned by the popular voice; and the girl who marries the poor young man, and helps him live his best, is still approved by the same great arbiter. And yet why should we blame the woman for pursuing her vocation? Since marriage is her only way to get money, why should she not try to get money in that way? Why cast the weight of all self-interest on the "practical" plane so solidly against the sex-interest of the individual and of the race? The mercenary marriage is a perfectly natural consequence of the economic dependence of women.

On the other hand, note the effect of this dependence upon men. As the excessive sex-distinction and economic dependence of women increase, so do the risk and difficulty of marriage increase, so is marriage deferred and avoided, to the direct injury of both sexes and society at large. In simpler relations, in the country, wherever women have a personal value in economic relation as well as a feminine value in sex-relation, an early marriage is an advantage. The young farmer gets a profitable servant when he marries. The young business man gets nothing of the kind,—a pretty girl, a charming girl, ready for "wifehood and motherhood"—so far as her health holds out,—but having no economic value whatever. She is merely a consumer, and he must wait till he can "afford to marry." These are instances frequent everywhere, and familiar to us all, of the palpable effects in common life of our sexuo-economic relation.

If there is one unmixed evil in human life, it is that known to us in all ages, and popularly called "the social evil," consisting of promiscuous and temporary sex-relations. The inherent wrong in these relations is sociological before it is legal or moral. The recognition by the moral sense of a given thing as wrong requires that it be wrong, to begin with. A thing is not wrong merely because it is called so. The wrongness of this form of sex-relation in an advanced social state rests solidly on natural laws. In the evolution of better and better means of reproducing the species, a longer period of infancy was developed. This longer period of infancy required longer care, and it was accordingly developed that the best care during

this time was given by both parents. This induced a more permanent mating. And the more permanent mating, bound together by
the common interests and duties, developed higher psychic attributes in the parents by use, in the children by heredity. That is why
society is right in demanding of its constituent individuals the virtue of chastity, the sanctity of marriage. Society is perfectly right,
because social evolution is as natural a process as individual evolution; and the permanent parent is proven an advantageous social
factor. But social evolution, deep, unconscious, slow, is one thing;
and self-conscious, loud-voiced society is another.

The deepest forces of nature have tended to evolve pure, lasting, monogamous marriage in the human race. But our peculiar arrangement of feeding one sex by the other has tended to produce
a very different thing, and has produced it. In no other animal species is the female economically dependent on the male. In no other
animal species is the sex-relation for sale. A coincidence. Where,
on the one hand, every condition of life tends to develope sex in
women, to crush out the power and the desire for economic production and exchange, and to develope also the age-long habit of seeking all earthly good at a man's hands and of making but one return;
where, on the other hand, man inherits the excess in sex-energy,
and is never blamed for exercising it, and where he developes also
the age-long habit of taking what he wants from women, for whose
helpless acquiescence he makes an economic return,—what should
naturally follow? Precisely what has followed. We live in a world
of law, and humanity is no exception to it. We have produced a
certain percentage of females with inordinate sex-tendencies and
inordinate greed for material gain. We have produced a certain
percentage of males with inordinate sex-tendencies and a cheerful
willingness to pay for their gratification. And, as the percentage of
such men is greater than the percentage of such women, we have
worked out most evil methods of supplying the demand. But always
in the healthy social heart we have known that it was wrong, a racial wrong, productive of all evil. Being a man's world, it was quite
inevitable that he should blame woman for their mutual misdoing.

There is reason in it, too. Bad as he is, he is only seeking gratification natural in kind, though abnormal in degree. She is not only in some cases doing this, but in most cases showing the falseness of the deed by doing it for hire,—physical falsehood,—a sin against nature.

It is a true instinct that revolts against obtaining bread by use of the sex-functions. Why, then, are we so content to do this in marriage? Legally and religiously, we say that it is right; but in its reactionary effect on the parties concerned and on society at large it is wrong. The physical and psychical effects are evil, though modified by our belief that it is right. The physical and psychical effects of prostitution were still evil when the young girls of Babylon earned their dowries thereby in the temple of Bela, and thought it right. What we think and feel alters the moral quality of an act in our consciousness as we do it, but does not alter its subsequent effect. We justify and approve the economic dependence of women upon the sex-relation in marriage. We condemn it unsparingly out of marriage. We follow it with our blame and scorn up to the very doors of marriage,—the mercenary bride,—but think no harm of the mercenary wife, filching her husband's pockets in the night. Love sanctifies it, we say: love must go with it.

Love never yet went with self-interest. The deepest antagonism lies between them: they are diametrically opposed forces. In the beautiful progress of evolution we find constant opposition between the instincts and processes of self-preservation and the instinct and processes of race-preservation. From those early forms where birth brought death, as in the flowering aloe, the ephemeral may-fly, up to the highest glory of self-effacing love; these two forces work in opposition. We have tied them together. We have made the woman, the mother,—the very source of sacrifice through love,—get gain through love,—a hideous paradox. No wonder that our daily lives are full of the flagrant evils produced by this unnatural state. No wonder that men turn with loathing from the kind of women they have made.

But other things are not equal. Half the human race is denied free productive expression, is forced to confine its productive human energies to the same channels as its reproductive sex-energies. Its creative skill is confined to the level of immediate personal bodily service, to the making of clothes and preparing of food for individuals. No social service is possible. While its power of production is checked, its power of consumption is inordinately increased by the showering upon it of the "unearned increment" of masculine gifts. For the woman there is, first, no free production allowed; and, second, no relation maintained between what she does produce and what she consumes. She is forbidden to make, but encouraged to take. Her industry is not the natural output of creative energy, not the work she does because she has the inner power and strength to do it; nor is her industry even the measure of her gain. She has, of course, the natural desire to consume; and to that is set no bar save the capacity or the will of her husband.

Thus we have painfully and laboriously evolved and carefully maintain among us an enormous class of non-productive consumers,—a class which is half the world, and mother of the other half. We have built into the constitution of the human race the habit and desire of taking, as divorced from its natural precursor and concomitant of making. We have made for ourselves this endless array of "horse-leech's daughters, crying, Give! give!" To consume food, to consume clothes, to consume houses and furniture and decorations and ornaments and amusements, to take and take and take forever,—from one man if they are virtuous, from many if they are vicious, but always to take and never to think of giving anything in return except their womanhood,—this is the enforced condition of the mothers of the race. What wonder that their sons go into business "for what there is in it"! What wonder that the world is full of the desire to get as much as possible and to give as little as possible! What wonder, either, that the glory and sweetness of love are but a name among us, with here and there a strange and beautiful exception, of which our admiration proves the rarity!

Between the brutal ferocity of excessive male energy struggling in the market-place as in a battlefield and the unnatural greed generated by the perverted condition of female energy, it is not remarkable that the industrial evolution of humanity has shown peculiar symptoms. One of the minor effects of this last condition—this limiting of female industry to close personal necessities, and this tendency of her over-developed sex-nature to overestimate the so-called "duties of her position"—has been to produce an elaborate devotion to individuals and their personal needs,—not to the understanding and developing of their higher natures, but to the intensification of their bodily tastes and pleasure. The wife and mother, pouring the rising tide of racial power into the same old channels that were allowed her primitive ancestors, constantly ministers to the physical needs of her family with a ceaseless and concentrated intensity. They like it, of course. But it maintains in the individuals of the race an exaggerated sense of the importance of food and clothes and ornaments to themselves, without at all including a knowledge of their right use and value to us all. It developes personal selfishness.

Again, the consuming female, debarred from any free production, unable to estimate the labor involved in the making of what she so lightly destroys, and her consumption limited mainly to those things which minister to physical pleasure, creates a market for sensuous decoration and personal ornament, for all that is luxurious and enervating, and for a false and capricious variety in such supplies, which operates as a most deadly check to true industry and true art. As the priestess of the temple of consumption, as the limitless demander of things to use up, her economic influence is reactionary and injurious. Much, very much, of the current of useless production in which our economic energies run waste—man's strength poured out like water on the sand—depends on the creation and careful maintenance of this false market, this sink into which human labor vanishes with no return. Woman, in her false economic position, reacts injuriously upon industry, upon art, upon science, discovery, and progress. The sexuo-economic relation in its effect on the constitution of the individual keeps alive in us the in-

The more absolutely woman is segregated to sex-functions only, cut off from all economic use and made wholly dependent on the sex-relation as means of livelihood, the more pathological does her motherhood become. The over-development of sex caused by her economic dependence on the male reacts unfavorably upon her essential duties. She is too female for perfect motherhood! Her excessive specialization in the secondary sexual characteristics is a detrimental element in heredity. Small, weak, soft, ill-proportioned women do not tend to produce large, strong, sturdy, well-made men or women. When Frederic the Great wanted grenadiers of great size, he married big men to big women,—not to little ones. The female segregated to the uses of sex alone naturally deteriorates in racial development, and naturally transmits that deterioration to her offspring. The human mother, in the processes of reproduction, shows no gain in efficiency over the lower animals, but rather a loss, and so far presents no evidence to prove that her specialization to sex is of any advantage to her young. The mother of a dead baby or the baby of a dead mother; the sick baby, the crooked baby, the idiot baby; the exhausted, nervous, prematurely aged mother,—these are not uncommon among us; and they do not show much progress in our motherhood.

Since we cannot justify the human method of maternity in the physical processes of reproduction, can we prove its advantages in the other branch, education? Though the mother be sickly and the child the same, will not her loving care more than make up for it?

Will not the tender devotion of the mother, and her unflagging attendance upon the child, render human motherhood sufficiently successful in comparison with that of other species to justify our peculiar method? We must now show that our motherhood, in its usually accepted sense, the "care" of the child (more accurately described as education), is of a superior nature.

Here, again, we lack the benefit of comparison. No other animal species is required to care for its young so long, to teach it so much. So far as they have it to do, they do it well. The hen with her brood is an accepted model of motherhood in this respect. She not only lays eggs and hatches them, but educates and protects her young so far as it is necessary. But beyond such simple uses as this we have no standard of comparison for educative motherhood. We can only study it among ourselves, comparing the child left motherless with the child mothered, the child with a mother and nothing else with the child whose mother is helped by servants and teachers, the child with what we recognize as a superior mother to the child with an inferior mother. This last distinction, a comparison between mothers, is of great value. We have tacitly formulated a certain vague standard of human motherhood, and loosely apply it, especially in the epithets "natural" and "unnatural" mother.

But these terms again show how prone we still are to consider the whole field of maternal action as one of instinct rather than of reason, as a function rather than a service. We do have a standard, however, loose and vague as it is; and even by that standard it is painful to see how many human mothers fail. Ask yourselves honestly how many of the mothers whose action toward their children confronts you in street and shop and car and boat, in hotel and boarding-house and neighboring yard,—how many call forth favorable comment compared with those you judge unfavorably? Consider not the rosy ideal of motherhood you have in your mind, but the coarse, hard facts of motherhood as you see them, and hear them, in daily life.

Motherhood in its fulfilment of educational duty can be measured only by its effects. If we take for a standard the noble men and women whose fine physique and character we so fondly attribute to "a devoted mother," what are we to say of the motherhood which has filled the world with the ignoble men and women, of depraved physique and character? If the good mother makes the good man, how about the bad ones? When we see great men and women, we give credit to their mothers. When we see inferior men and women,—and that is a common circumstance,—no one presumes to question the motherhood which has produced them. When it comes to congenital criminality, we are beginning to murmur something about "heredity"; and, to meet gross national ignorance, we do demand a better system of education. But no one presumes to suggest that the mothering of mankind could be improved upon; and yet there is where the responsibility really lies. If our human method of reproduction is defective, let the mother answer. She is the main factor in reproduction. If our human method of education is defective, let the mother answer. She is the main factor in education.

To this it is bitterly objected that such a claim omits the father and his responsibility. When the mother of the world is in her right place and doing her full duty, she will have no ground of complaint against the father. In the first place, she will make better men. In the second, she will hold herself socially responsible for the choice of a right father for her children. In the third place, as an economic free agent, she will do half duty in providing for the child. Men who are not equal to good fatherhood under such conditions will have no chance to become fathers, and will die with general pity instead of living with general condemnation. In his position, doing all the world's work, all the father's, and half the mother's, man has made better shift to achieve the impossible than woman has in hers. She has been supposed to have no work or care on earth save as mother. She has really had the work of the mother and that of the world's house service besides. But she has surely had as much time and strength to give to motherhood as man to fatherhood; and not until she can show that the children of the world are as well mothered as they are well fed can she cast on him the blame for our general deficiency.

There is no personal blame to be laid on either party. The sexuo-economic relation has its inevitable ill-effects on both motherhood and fatherhood. But it is to the mother that the appeal must be made to change this injurious relation. Having the deeper sense of duty to the young, the larger love, she must come to feel how her false position hurts her motherhood, and for her children's sake break away from it. Of man and his fatherhood she can make what she will.

The duty of the mother is first to produce children as good as or better than herself; to hand down the constitution and character of those behind her the better for her stewardship; to build up and improve the human race through her enormous power as mother; to make better people. This being done, it is then the duty of the mother, the human mother, so to educate her children as to complete what bearing and nursing have only begun. She carries the child nine months in her body, two years in her arms, and as long as she lives in her heart and mind. The education of the young is a tremendous factor in human reproduction. A right motherhood should be able to fulfil this great function perfectly. It should understand with an ever-growing power the best methods of developing, strengthening, and directing the child's faculties of body and mind, so that each generation, reaching maturity, would start clear of the last, and show a finer, fuller growth, both physically and mentally, than the preceding. That humanity does slowly improve is not here denied; but, granting our gradual improvement, is it all that we could make? And is the gain due to a commensurate improvement in motherhood?

To both we must say no. When we see how some families improve, while others deteriorate, and how uncertain and irregular is such improvement as appears, we know that we could make better progress if all children had the same rich endowment and wise care that some receive. And, when we see how much of our improvement is due to gains made in hygienic knowledge, in public provision for education and sanitary regulation, none of which has been accomplished by mothers, we are forced to see that whatever advance the race has made is not exclusively attributable to mother-hood. The human mother does less for her young, both absolutely and proportionately, than any kind of mother on earth. She does not obtain food for them, nor covering, nor shelter, nor protection, nor defence. She does not educate them beyond the personal habits required in the family circle and in her limited range of social life. The necessary knowledge of the world, so indispensable to every human being, she cannot give, because she does not possess it. All this provision and education are given by other hands and brains than hers. Neither does the amount of physical care and labor be-stowed on the child by its mother warrant her claims to superiority in motherhood: this is but a part of our idealism of the subject.

The poor man's wife has far too much of other work to do to spend all her time in waiting on her children. The rich man's wife could do it, but does not, partly because she hires some one to do it for her, and partly because she, too, has other duties to occupy her time. Only in isolated cases do we find a mother deputing all other service to others, and concentrating her energies on feeding, cloth-ing, washing, dressing, and, as far as may be, educating her own child. When such cases are found, it remains to be shown that the child so reared is proportionately benefited by this unremitting de-votion of its mother. On the contrary, the best service and education a child can receive involve the accumulated knowledge and ex-changed activities of thousands upon thousands besides his mother,—the fathers of the race.

There does not appear, in the care and education of the child as given by the mother, any special superiority in human maternity. Measuring woman first in direct comparison of her reproductive processes with those of other animals, she does not fulfil this func-tion so easily or so well as they. Measuring her educative processes by inter-personal comparison, the few admittedly able mothers with the many painfully unable ones, she seems more lacking, if possible, than in the other branch. The gain in human education thus far has not been acquired or distributed through the mother, but through men and single women; and there is nothing in the achievements of human motherhood to prove that it is for the advantage of the race to have women give all their time to it. Giving all their time to it does not improve it either in quantity or quality. The woman who works is usually a better reproducer than the woman who does not. And the woman who does not work is not proportionately a better educator.

An extra-terrestrial sociologist, studying human life and hearing for the first time of our so-called "maternal sacrifice" as a means of benefiting the species, might be touched and impressed by the idea. "How beautiful!" he would say. "How exquisitely pathetic and tender! One-half of humanity surrendering all other human interests and activities to concentrate its time, strength, and devotion upon the functions of maternity! To bear and rear the majestic race to which they can never fully belong! To live vicariously forever, through their sons, the daughters being only another vicarious link! What a supreme and magnificent martyrdom!" And he would direct his researches toward discovering what system was used to develope and perfect this sublime consecration of half the race to the perpetuation of the other half. He would view with intense and pathetic interest the endless procession of girls, born human as their brothers were, but marked down at once as "female—abortive type—only use to produce males." He would expect to see this "sex sacrificed to reproductive necessities," yet gifted with human consciousness and intelligence, rise grandly to the occasion, and strive to fit itself in every way for its high office. He would expect to find society commiserating the sacrifice, and honoring above all the glorious creature whose life was to be sunk utterly in the lives of others, and using every force properly to rear and fully to fit these functionaries for their noble office. Alas for the extra-terrestrial sociologist and his natural expectations! After exhaustive study, finding nothing of these things, he would return to Mars or Saturn or wherever he came from, marvelling within himself at the vastness of the human paradox.

If the position of woman is to be justified by the doctrine of maternal sacrifice, surely society, or the individual, or both, would make some preparation for it. No such preparation is made. Society recognizes no such function. Premiums have been sometimes paid for large numbers of children, but they were paid to the fathers of them. The elaborate social machinery which constitutes our universal marriage market has no department to assist or advance motherhood. On the contrary, it is directly inimical to it, so that in our society life motherhood means direct loss, and is avoided by the social devotee. And the individual? Surely here right provision will be made. Young women, glorying in their prospective duties, their sacred and inalienable office, their great sex-martyrdom to race-advantage, will be found solemnly preparing for this work. What do we find? We find our young women reared in an attitude which is absolutely unconscious of and often injurious to their coming motherhood,—an irresponsible, indifferent, ignorant class of beings, so far as motherhood is concerned. They are fitted to attract the other sex for economic uses or, at most, for mutual gratification, but not for motherhood. They are reared in unbroken ignorance of their supposed principal duties, knowing nothing of these duties till they enter upon them.

This is as though all men were to be soldiers with the fate of nations in their hands; and no man told or taught a word of war or military service until he entered the battle-field!

The education of young women has no department of maternity. It is considered indelicate to give this consecrated functionary any previous knowledge of her sacred duties. This most important and wonderful of human functions is left from age to age in the hands of absolutely untaught women. It is tacitly supposed to be fulfilled by the mysterious working of what we call "the divine instinct of maternity." Maternal instinct is a very respectable and useful instinct common to most animals. It is "divine" and "holy" only as all the laws of nature are divine and holy; and it is such only when it works to the right fulfilment of its use. If the race-preservative processes are to be held more sacred than the self-preservative processes, we must admit all the functions and faculties of reproduction to the same degree of reverence,—the passion of the male for the female as well as the passion of the mother for her young. And if, still further, we are to honor the race-preservative processes most in their highest and latest development, which is the only comparison to be made on a natural basis, we should place the great, disinterested, social function of education far above the second-selfishness of individual maternal functions. Maternal instinct, merely as an instinct, is unworthy of our superstitious reverence. It should be measured only as a means to an end, and valued in proportion to its efficacy.

Among animals, which have but a low degree of intelligence, instinct is at its height, and works well. Among savages, still incapable of much intellectual development, instinct holds large place. The mother beast can and does take all the care of her young by instinct; the mother savage, nearly all, supplemented by the tribal traditions, the educative influences of association, and some direct instruction. As humanity advances, growing more complex and varied, and as human intelligence advances to keep pace with new functions and new needs, instinct decreases in value. The human creature prospers and progresses not by virtue of his animal instinct, but by the wisdom and force of a cultivated intelligence and will, with which to guide his action and to control and modify the very instincts which used to govern him.

The human female, denied the enlarged activities which have developed intelligence in man, denied the education of the will which only comes by freedom and power, has maintained the rudimentary forces of instinct to the present day. With her extreme modification to sex, this faculty of instinct runs mainly along sex-lines, and finds fullest vent in the processes of maternity, where it has held unbroken sway. So the children of humanity are born into the arms of an endless succession of untrained mothers, who bring to the care and teaching of their children neither education for that wonderful work nor experience therein: they bring merely the intense accumulated force of a brute instinct,—the blind devoted passion of the mother for the child. Maternal love is an enormous force, but force needs direction. Simply to love the child does not serve him unless specific acts of service express this love. What these acts of service are and how they are performed make or mar his life forever.

Observe the futility of unaided maternal love and instinct in the simple act of feeding the child. Belonging to order mammalia, the human mother has an instinctive desire to suckle her young. (Some ultra-civilized have lost even that.) But this instinct has not taught her such habits of life as insure her ability to fulfil this natural function. Failing in the natural method, of what further use is instinct in the nourishment of the child? Can maternal instinct discriminate between Marrow's Food and Bridge's Food, Hayrick's Food and Pestle's Food, Pennywhistle's Sterilized Milk, and all the other infants' foods which are prepared and put upon the market by—men! These are not prepared by instinct, maternal or paternal, but by chemical analysis and physiological study; and their effect is observed and the diet varied by physicians, who do not do their work by instinct, either.

If the bottle-baby survive the loss of mother's milk, when he comes to the table, does maternal instinct suffice then to administer a proper diet for young children? Let the doctor and the undertaker answer. The wide and varied field of masculine activity in the interests of little children, from the peculiar human phenomenon of masculine assistance in parturition (there is one animal, the obstetric frog, where it also appears) to the manufacture of articles for feeding, clothing, protecting, amusing, and educating the baby, goes to show the utter inadequacy of maternal instinct in the human female. Another thing it shows also,—the criminal failure of that human female to supply by intelligent effort what instinct can no longer accomplish. For a reasoning, conscious being deliberately to undertake the responsibility of maintaining human life without making due preparation for the task is more than carelessness.

Before a man enters a trade, art, or profession, he studies it. He qualifies himself for the duties he is to undertake. He would be held a presuming imposter if he engaged in work he was not fitted to do, and his failure would mark him instantly with ridicule and reproach. In the more important professions, especially in those dealing with what we call "matters of life and death," the shipmaster or pilot, doctor or druggist, is required not only to study his business, but to pass an examination under those who have already become past masters, and obtain a certificate or a diploma or some credential to show that he is fit to be intrusted with the direct responsibility for human life.

Women enter a position which gives into their hands direct responsibility for the life or death of the whole human race with neither study nor experience, with no shadow of preparation or guarantee of capability. So far as they give it a thought, they fondly imagine that this mysterious "maternal instinct" will see them through. Instruction, if needed, they will pick up when the time comes: experience they will acquire as the children appear. "I guess I know how to bring up children!" cried the resentful old lady who was being advised: "I've buried seven!" The record of untrained instinct as a maternal faculty in the human race is to be read on the rows and rows of little gravestones which crowd our cemeteries. The experience gained by practising on the child is frequently buried with it.

No, the maternal sacrifice theory will not bear examination. As a sex specialized to reproduction, giving up all personal activity, all honest independence, all useful and progressive economic service for her glorious consecration to the uses of maternity, the human female has little to show in the way of results which can justify her position. Neither the enormous percentage of children lost by death nor the low average health of those who survive, neither physical nor mental progress, give any proof of race advantage from the maternal sacrifice.

Marriage and "the family" are two institutions, not one, as is commonly supposed. We confuse the natural result of marriage in children, common to all forms of sex-union, with the family,—a purely social phenomenon. Marriage is a form of sex-union recognized and sanctioned by society. It is a relation between two or more persons, according to the custom of the country, and involves mutual obligations. Although made by us an economic relation, it is not essentially so, and will exist in much higher fulfilment after the economic phase is outgrown.

The family is a social group, an entity, a little state. It holds an important place in the evolution of society quite aside from its connection with marriage. There was a time when the family was the highest form of social relation,—indeed, the only form of social relation,—when to the minds of pastoral, patriarchal tribes there was no conception so large as "my country," no State, no nation. There was only a great land spotted with families, each family its own little world, of which Grandpa was priest and king. The family was a social unit. Its interests were common to its members, and inimical to those of other families. It moved over the earth, following its food supply, and fighting occasionally with stranger families for the grass or water on which it depended. Indissoluble common interests are what make organic union, and those interests long rested on blood relationship.

While the human individual was best fed and guarded by the family, and so required the prompt, correlative action of all the members of that family, naturally the family must have a head; and that form of government known as the patriarchal was produced. The natural family relation, as seen in parents and young of other species, or in ourselves in later forms, involves no such governmental development: that is a feature of the family as a social entity alone.

One of the essentials of the patriarchal family life was polygamy, and not only polygamy, but open concubinage, and a woman slavery which was almost the same thing. The highest period of the family as a social institution was a very low period for marriage as a social institution,—a period, in fact, when marriage was but partially evolved from the early promiscuity of the primitive savage. The family seems indeed to be a gradually disappearing survival of the still looser unit of the horde, which again is more closely allied to the band or pack of gregarious carnivora than to an organic social relation. A loose, promiscuous group of animals is not a tribe; and the most primitive savage groups seem to have been no more than this.

The tribe in its true form follows the family,—is a natural extension of it, and derives its essential ties from the same relationship. These social forms, too, are closely related to economic conditions. The horde was the hunting unit; the family, and later the tribe, the pastoral unit. Agriculture and its resultant, commerce and manufacture, gradually weaken these crude blood ties, and establish the social relationship which constitutes the State. Before the pastoral era the family held no important position, and since that era it has gradually declined. With social progress we find human relations resting less and less on a personal and sex basis, and more and more on general economic independence. As individuals have become more highly specialized, they have made possible a higher form of marriage.

The family is a decreasing survival of the earliest grouping known to man. Marriage is an increasing development of high social life, not fully evolved. So far from being identical with the family, it improves and strengthens in inverse ratio to the family, as is easily seen by the broad contrast between the marriage relations of Jacob and the unquenchable demand for lifelong single mating that grows in our hearts to-day. There was no conception of marriage as a personal union for life of two well-matched individuals during the patriarchal era. Wives were valued merely for child-bearing. The family needed numbers of its own blood, especially males; and the manchild was the price of favor to women then. It was but a few degrees beyond the horde, not yet become a tribe in the full sense. Its bonds of union were of the loosest,—merely common paternity, with a miscellaneous maternity of inimical interests. Such a basis forever forbade any high individualization, and high individualization with its demands for a higher marriage forbids any numerical importance to the family. Marriage has risen and developed in social importance as the family has sunk and decreased.

It is most interesting to note that, under the comparatively similar conditions of the settlement of Utah, the numerical strength and easily handled common interests of many people under one head, which distinguish the polygamous family, were found useful factors in that great pioneering enterprise. In the further development of society a relation of individuals more fluent, subtle, and extensive was needed. The family as a social unit makes a ponderous body of somewhat irreconcilable constituents, requiring a sort of military rule to make it work at all; and it is only useful while the ends to be attained are of a simple nature, and allow of the slowest accomplishment. It is easy to see the family extending to the tribe by its own physical increase; and, similarly, the father hardening into the chief, under the necessities of larger growth. Then, as the steadily enlarging forces of national unity make the chief an outgrown name and the tribe an outgrown form, the family dwindles to a monogamic basis, as the higher needs of the sex-relation become differentiated from the more primitive economic necessities of the family.

And now, further, when our still developing social needs call for an ever-increasing delicacy and freedom in the inter-service and common service of individuals, we find that even what economic unity remains to the family is being rapidly eliminated. As the economic relation becomes rudimentary and disappears, the sex-relation asserts itself more purely; and the demand in the world today for a higher and nobler sex-union is as sharply defined as the growing objection to the existing economic union. Strange as it may seem to us, so long accustomed to confound the two, it is precisely the outgrown relics of a previously valuable family relation which so painfully retard the higher development of the monogamic marriage relation.

Each generation of young men and women comes to the formation of sex-union with higher and higher demands for a true marriage, with ever-growing needs for companionship. Each generation of men and women need and ask more of each other. A woman is no longer content and grateful to have "a kind husband": a man is no longer content with a patient Griselda; and, as all men and women, in marrying, revert to the economic status of the earlier family, they come under conditions which steadily tend to lower the standard of their mutual love, and make of the average marriage only a sort of compromise, borne with varying ease or difficulty according to the good breeding and loving-kindness of the parties concerned. This is not necessarily, to their conscious knowledge, an "unhappy marriage." It is as happy as those they see about them, as happy perhaps as we resignedly expect "on earth"; and in heaven we do not expect marriages. But it is not what they looked forward to when they were young.

When two young people love each other, in the long hours which are never long enough for them to be together in, do they dwell in ecstatic forecast on the duties of housekeeping? They do not. They dwell on the pleasure of having a home, in which they can be "at last alone"; on the opportunity of enjoying each other's society; and, always, on what they will *do* together. To act with those we love,—to walk together, work together, read together, paint, write, sing, anything you please, so that it be together,—that is what love looks forward to.

Human love, as it rises to an ever higher grade, looks more and more for such companionship. But the economic status of marriage rudely breaks in upon love's young dream. On the economic side, apart from all the sweetness and truth of the sex-relation, the woman in marrying becomes the house-servant, or at least the housekeeper, of the man. Of the world we may say that the intimate personal necessities of the human animal are ministered to by woman. Married lovers do not work together. They may, if they have time, rest together: they may, if they can, play together; but they do not make beds and sweep and cook together, and they do not go down town to the office together. They are economically on entirely different social planes, and these constitute a bar to any higher, truer union than such as we see about us. Marriage is not perfect unless it is between class equals. There is no equality in class between those who do their share in the world's work in the largest, newest, highest ways and those who do theirs in the smallest, oldest, lowest ways.

Granting squarely that it is the business of women to make the home life of the world true, healthful, and beautiful, the economically dependent woman does not do this, and never can. The economically independent woman can and will. As the family is by no means identical with marriage, so is the home by no means identical with either.

A home is a permanent dwelling-place, whether for one, two, forty, or a thousand, for a pair, a flock, or a swarm. The hive is the home of the bees as literally and absolutely as the nest is the home of mating birds in their season. Home and the love of it may dwindle to the one chamber of the bachelor or spread to the span of a continent, when the returning traveller sees land and calls it "home." There is no sweeter word, there is no dearer fact, no feeling closer to the human heart than this.

On close analysis, what are the bases of our feelings in this connection? and what are their supporting facts? Far down below humanity, where "the foxes have holes, and the birds of the air have nests," there begins the deep home feeling. Maternal instinct seeks a place to shelter the defenceless young, while the mother goes abroad to search for food. The first sharp impressions of infancy are associated with the sheltering walls of home, be it the swinging cradle in the branches, the soft dark hollow in the trunk of a tree, or the cave with its hidden lair. A place to be safe in; a place to be warm and dry in; a place to eat in peace and sleep in quiet; a place whose close, familiar limits rest the nerves from the continuous hail of impressions in the changing world outside; the same place over and over,—the restful repetition, rousing no keen response, but healing and soothing each weary sense,—that "feels like home." All this from our first consciousness. All this for millions and millions of years. No wonder we love it.

Then comes the gradual addition of tenderer associations, family ties of the earliest. Then, still primitive, but not yet outgrown, the grouping religious sentiment of early ancestor-worship, adding sanctity to safety, and driving deep our sentiment for home. It was the place in which to pray, to keep alight the sacred fire, and pour libations to departed grandfathers. Following this, the slow-dying era of paternal government gave a new sense of honor to the place of comfort and the place of prayer. It became the seat of government also,—the palace and the throne. Upon this deep foundation we have built a towering superstructure of habit, custom, law; and in it dwell together every deepest, oldest, closest, and tenderest emotion of the human individual. No wonder we are blind and deaf to any suggested improvement in our lordly pleasure-house.

But look farther. Without contradicting any word of the above, it is equally true that the highest emotions of humanity arise and live outside the home and apart from it. While religion stayed at home, in dogma and ceremony, in spirit and expression, it was a low and narrow religion. It could never rise till it found a new spirit and a new expression in human life outside the home, until it found a common place of worship, a ceremonial and a morality on a human basis, not a family basis. Science, art, government, education, industry,—the home is the cradle of them all, and their grave, if they stay in it. Only as we live, think, feel, and work outside the home, do we become humanly developed, civilized, socialized.

The exquisite development of modern home life is made possible only as an accompaniment and result of modern social life. If the reverse were true, as is popularly supposed, all nations that have homes would continue to evolve a noble civilization. But they do not. On the contrary, those nations in which home and family worship most prevail, as in China, present a melancholy proof of the result of the domestic virtues without the social. A noble home life is the product of a noble social life. The home does not produce the virtues needed in society. But society does produce the virtues needed in such homes as we desire to-day. The members of the freest, most highly civilized and individualized nations, make the most delightful members of the home and family. The members of the closest and most highly venerated homes do not necessarily make the most delightful members of society.

In social evolution as in all evolution the tendency is from "indefinite, incoherent homogeneity to definite, coherent heterogeneity"; and the home, in its rigid maintenance of a permanent homogeneity, constitutes a definite limit to social progress. What we need is not less home, but more; not a lessening of the love of human beings for a home, but its extension through new and more effective expression. And, above all, we need the complete disentanglement in our thoughts of the varied and often radically opposed interests and industries so long supposed to be component parts of the home and family.

The change in the economic position of woman from dependence to independence must bring with it a rearrangement of these home interests and industries, to our great gain.

CHAPTER XII

As self-conscious creatures, to whom is always open the easy error of mistaking feeling for fact, to whose consciousness indeed the feeling is the fact,—a further process of reasoning being required to infer the fact from the feeling,—we are not greatly to be blamed for laying such stress on sentiment and emotion. We may perhaps admit, in the light of cold reasoning, that the home is not the best place in which to do so much work in, nor the wife and mother the best person to do it. But this intellectual conviction by no means alters our feeling on the subject. Feeling, deep, long established, and over-stimulated, lies thick over the whole field of home life. Not what we think about it (for we never have thought about it very much), but what we feel about it, constitutes the sum of our opinion. Many of our feelings are true, right, legitimate. Some are fatuous absurdities, mere dangling relics of outgrown tradition, slowly moulting from us as we grow.

Consider, for instance, that long-standing popular myth known as "the privacy of the home." There is something repugnant in the idea of food cooked outside the home, even though served within it; still more in the going out of the family to eat, and more yet in the going out of separate individuals to eat. The limitless personal taste developed by "home cooking" fears that it will lose its own particular shade of brown on the bacon, its own hottest of hot cakes, its own corner biscuit.

This objection must be honestly faced, and admitted in some degree. A *menu*, however liberally planned by professional cooks, would not allow so much play for personal idiosyncrasy as do those prepared by the numerous individual cooks now serving us. There would be a far larger range of choice in materials, but not so much in methods of preparation and service. The difference would be like that between every man's making his own coat or having his women servants make it for him, on the one hand, and his selecting one from many ready made or ordering it of his tailor, on the other.

In the regular professional service of food there would be a good general standard, and the work of specialists for special occasions. We have long seen this process going on in the steady increase of professionally prepared food, from the cheap eating-house to the fashionable caterer, from the common "cracker" to the delicate "wafer." "Home cooking," robbed of its professional adjuncts, would fall a long way. We do not realize how far we have already progressed in this line, nor how fast we are going.

One of the most important effects of a steady general standard of good food will be the elevation of the popular taste. We should acquire a cultivated appreciation of what *is* good food, far removed from the erratic and whimsical self-indulgence of the private table. Our only standard of taste in cooking is personal appetite and caprice. That we "like" a dish is enough to warrant full approval. But liking is only adaptation. Nature is forever seeking to modify the organism to the environment; and, when it becomes so modified, so adapted, the organism "likes" the environment. In the earlier form, "it likes me," this derivation is plainer.

Each nation, each locality, each family, each individual, "likes," in large measure, those things to which it has been accustomed. What else it might have liked, if it had had it, can never be known; but the slow penetration of new tastes and habits, the reluctant adoption of the potato, the tomato, maize, and other new vegetables by old countries, show that it is quite possible to change a liking.

In the narrow range of family capacity to supply and of family ability to prepare our food, and in our exaggerated intensity of personal preference, we have grown very rigid in our little field of choice. We insist on the superiority of our own methods, and despise the methods of our neighbors, with a sublime ignorance of any higher standard of criticism than our own uneducated tastes. When we become accustomed from childhood to scientifically and artistically prepared foods, we shall grow to know what is good and to enjoy it, as we learn to know good music by hearing it.

As we learn to appreciate a wider and higher range of cooking, we shall also learn to care for simplicity in this art. Neither is attainable under our present system by the average person. As cooking becomes dissociated from the home, we shall gradually cease to attach emotions to it; and we shall learn to judge it impersonally upon a scientific and artistic basis. This will not, of course, prevent some persons' having peculiar tastes; but these will know that they are peculiar, and so will their neighbors. It will not prevent, either, the woman who has a dilettante fondness for some branch of cookery, wherewith she loves to delight herself and her friends, from keeping a small cooking plant within reach, as she might a sewing-machine or a turning-lathe.

In regard to the eating of food we are still more opposed by the "privacy of the home" idea, and a marked—indeed, a pained—disinclination to dissociate that function from family life. To eat together does, of course, form a temporary bond. To establish a medium of communication between dissimilar persons, some common ground must be found,—some rite, some game, some entertainment,—something that they can *do* together. And, if the persons desiring to associate have no other common ground than this physical function,—which is so common, indeed, that it includes not only all humanity, but all the animal kingdom,—then by all means let them seek that. On occasions of general social rejoicing to celebrate some event of universal importance, the feast will always be a natural and satisfying institution.

To the primitive husband with fighting for his industry, the primitive wife with domestic service for hers, the primitive children with no relation to their parents but the physical,—to such a common table was the only common tie; and the simplicity of their food furnished a medium that hurt no one. But in the higher individualization of modern life the process of eating is by no means the only common interest among members of a family, and by no means the best. The sweetest, tenderest, holiest memories of family life are not connected with the table, though many jovial and pleasant ones may be so associated. And on many an occasion of deep feeling, whether of joy or of pain, the ruthless averaging of the whole group three times a day at table becomes an unbearable strain. If good food suited to a wide range of needs were always attainable, a family could go and feast together when it chose or simply eat together when it chose; and each individual could go alone when he chose. This is not to be forced or hurried; but, with a steady supply of food, easy of access to all, the stomach need no longer be compelled to serve as a family tie.

We have so far held that the lower animals ate alone in their brutality, and that man has made eating a social function, and so elevated it. The elevation is the difficult part to prove, when we look at humanity's gross habits, morbid tastes, and deadly diseases, its artifice, and its unutterable depravity of gluttony and intemperance. The animals may be lower than we in their simple habit of eating what is good for them when they are hungry, but it serves their purpose well.

One result of our making eating a social function is that, the more elaborately we socialize it, the more we require at our feasts the service of a number of strangers absolutely shut out from social intercourse,—functionaries who do not eat with us, who do not talk with us, who must not by the twinkling of an eyelash show any interest in this performance, save to minister to the grosser needs of the occasion on a strictly commercial basis. Such extraneous presence must and does keep the conversation at one level. In the family without a servant both mother and father are too hard worked to make the meal a social success; and, as soon as servants are introduced, a limit is set to the range of conversation. The effect of our social eating, either in families or in larger groups, is not wholly good. It is well open to question whether we cannot, in this particular, improve our system of living.

When the cooking of the world is open to full development by those whose natural talent and patient study lead them to learn how better and better to meet the needs of the body of delicate and delicious combinations of the elements of nutrition, we shall begin to understand what food means to us, and how to build up the human body in sweet health and full vigor. A world of pure, strong, beautiful men and women, knowing what they ought to eat and drink, and taking it when they need it, will be capable of much higher and subtler forms of association than this much-prized common table furnishes. The contented grossness of to-day, the persistent self-indulgence of otherwise intelligent adults, the fatness and leanness and feebleness, the whole train of food-made disorders, together with all drug habits,—these morbid phenomena are largely traceable to the abnormal attention given to both eating and cooking, which must accompany them as family functions. When we detach them from this false position by untangling the knot of our sexuo-economic relation, we shall give natural forces a chance to work their own pure way in us, and make us better.

Our domestic privacy is held to be further threatened by the invasion of professional cleaners. We should see that a kitchenless home will require far less cleaning than is now needed, and that the daily ordering of one's own room could be easily accomplished by the individual, when desired. Many would so desire, keeping their own rooms, their personal inner chambers, inviolate from other presence than that of their nearest and dearest. Such an ideal of privacy may seem ridiculous to those who accept contentedly the gross publicity of our present method. Of all popular paradoxes, none is more nakedly absurd than to hear us prate of privacy in a place where we cheerfully admit to our table-talk and to our door service—yes, and to the making of our beds and to the handling of our clothing—a complete stranger, a stranger not only by reason of new acquaintance and of the false view inevitable to new eyes let in upon our secrets, but a stranger by birth, almost always an alien in race, and, more hopeless still, a stranger by breeding, one who can never truly understand.

This stranger all of us who can afford it summon to our homes,—one or more at once, and many in succession. If, like barbaric kings of old or bloody pirates of the main, we cut their tongues out that they might not tell, it would still remain an irreconcilable intrusion. But, as it is, with eyes to see, ears to hear, and tongues to speak, with no other interests to occupy their minds, and with the retaliatory fling that follows the enforced silence of those who must not "answer back,"—with this observing and repeating army lodged in the very bosom of the family, may we not smile a little bitterly at our fond ideal of "the privacy of the home"? The swift progress of professional sweepers, dusters, and scrubbers, through rooms where they were wanted, and when they were wanted, would be at least no more injurious to privacy than the present method. Indeed, the exclusion of the domestic servant, and the entrance of woman on a plane of interest at once more social and more personal, would bring into the world a new conception of the sacredness of privacy, a feeling for the rights of the individual as yet unknown.

Closely connected with the question of cleaning is that of household decoration and furnishing. The economically dependent woman, spending the accumulating energies of the race in her small cage, has thrown out a tangled mass of expression, as a large plant throws out roots in a small pot. She has crowded her limited habitat with unlimited things,—things useful and unuseful, ornamental and unornamental, comfortable and uncomfortable; and the labor of her life is to wait upon these things, and keep them clean.

The free woman, having room for full individual expression in her economic activities and in her social relation, will not be forced so to pour out her soul in tidies and photograph holders. The home will be her place of rest, not of uneasy activity; and she will learn to love simplicity at last. This will mean better sanitary conditions in the home, more beauty and less work. And the trend of the new conditions, enhancing the value of real privacy and developing the sense of beauty, will be toward a delicate loveliness in the interiors of our houses, which the owners can keep in order without undue exertion.

Besides these comparatively external conditions, there are psychic effects produced upon the family by the sexuo-economic relation not altogether favorable to our best growth. One is the levelling effect of the group upon its members, under pressure of this relation. Such privacy as we do have in our homes is family privacy, an aggregate privacy; and this does not insure—indeed, it prevents—individual privacy. This is another of the lingering rudiments of methods of living belonging to ages long since outgrown, and maintained among us by the careful preservation of primitive customs in the unchanged position of women. In very early times a crude and undifferentiated people could flock in family groups in one small tent without serious inconvenience or injury. The effects of such grouping on modern people is known in the tenement districts of large cities, where families live in single rooms; and these effects are of a distinctly degrading nature.

The progressive individuation of human beings requires a personal home, one room at least for each person. This need forces some recognition for itself in family life, and is met so far as private purses in private houses can meet it; but for the vast majority of the population no such provision is possible. To women, especially, a private room is the luxury of the rich alone. Even where a partial provision for personal needs is made under pressure of social development, the other pressure of undeveloped family life is constantly against it. The home is the one place on earth where no one of the component individuals can have any privacy. A family is a crude aggregate of persons of different ages, sizes, sexes, and temperaments, held together by sex-ties and economic necessity; and the affection which should exist between the members of a family is not increased in the least by the economic pressure, rather it is lessened. Such affection as is maintained by economic forces is not the kind which humanity most needs.

At present any tendency to withdraw and live one's own life on any plane of separate interest or industry is naturally resented, or at least regretted, by the other members of the family. This affects women more than men, because men live very little in the family and very much in the world. The man has his individual life, his personal expression and its rights, his office, studio, shop: the women and children live in the home—because they must. For a woman to wish to spend much time elsewhere is considered wrong, and the children have no choice. The historic tendency of women to "gad abroad," of children to run away, to be forever teasing for permission to go and play somewhere else; the ceaseless, futile, well-meant efforts to "keep the boys at home,"—these facts, together with the definite absence of the man of the home for so much of the time, constitute a curious commentary upon our patient belief that we live at home, and like it. Yet the home ties bind us with a gentle dragging hold that few can resist. Those who do resist, and who insist upon living their individual lives, find that this costs them loneliness and privation; and they lose so much in daily comfort and affection that others are deterred from following them.

There is no reason why this painful choice should be forced upon us, no reason why the home life of the human race should not be such as to allow—yes, to promote—the highest development of personality. We need the society of those dear to us, their love and their companionship. These will endure. But the common cook-shops of our industrially undeveloped homes, and all the allied evils, are not essential, and need not endure.

To our general thought the home just as it stands is held to be what is best for us. We imagine that it is at home that we learn the higher traits, the nobler emotions,—that the home teaches us how to live. The truth beneath this popular concept is this: the love of the mother for the child is at the base of all our higher love for one another. Indeed, even behind that lies the generous giving impulse of sex-love, the out-going force of sex-energy. The family relations ensuing do underlie our higher, wider social relations. The "home comforts" are essential to the preservation of individual life. And the bearing and forbearing of home life, with the dominant, cease-less influence of conservative femininity, is a most useful check to the irregular flying impulses of masculine energy. While the world lasts, we shall need not only the individual home, but the family home, the common sheath for the budded leaflets of each new branch, held close to the parent stem before they finally diverge.

Granting all this, there remains the steadily increasing ill effect, not of home life *per se,* but of the kind of home life based on the sexuo-economic relation. A home in which the rightly dominant feminine force is held at a primitive plane of development, and denied free participation in the swift, wide, upward movement of the world, reacts upon those who hold it down by holding them down in turn. A home in which the inordinate love of receiving things, so long bred into one sex, and the fierce hunger for procuring things, so carefully trained into the other, continually act upon the child, keeps ever before his eyes the fact that life consists in getting dinner and in getting the money to pay for it, getting the food from the market, working forever and ever to cook and serve it. These are the prominent facts of the home as we have made it. The kind of care in which our lives are spent, the things that wear and worry us, are things that should have been outgrown long, long ago if the human race had advanced evenly. Man has advanced, but woman has been kept behind. By inheritance she advances, by experience she is retarded, being always forced back to the economic grade of many thousand years ago.

If a modern man, with all his intellect and energy and resource, were forced to spend all his days hunting with a bow and arrow, fishing with a bone-pointed spear, waiting hungrily on his traps and snares in hope of prey, he could not bring to his children or to his wife the uplifting influences of the true manhood of our time. Even if he started with a college education, even if he had large books to read (when he had time to read them) and improving conversation, still the economic efforts of his life, the steady daily pressure of what he had to do for his living, would check the growth of higher powers. If all men had to be hunters from day to day, the world would be savage still. While all women have to be house servants from day to day, we are still a servile world.

A home life with a dependent mother, a servant-wife, is not an ennobling influence. We all feel this at times. The man, spreading and growing with the world's great growth, comes home, and settles into the tiny talk and fret, or the alluring animal comfort of the place, with a distinct sense of coming down. It is pleasant, it is gratifying to every sense, it is kept warm and soft and pretty to suit the needs of the feebler and smaller creature who is forced to stay in it. It is even considered a virtue for the man to stay in it and to prize it, to value his slippers and his newspaper, his hearth fire and his supper table, his spring bed, and his clean clothes above any other interests.

The harm does not lie in loving home and in staying there as one can, but in the kind of a home and in the kind of womanhood that it fosters, in the grade of industrial development on which it rests. And here, without prophesying, it is easy to look along the line of present progress, and see whither our home life tends. From the cave and tent and hovel up to a graded, differentiated home, with as much room for the individual as the family can afford; from the surly dominance of the absolute patriarch, with his silent servile women and chattel children, to the comparative freedom, equality, and finely diversified lives of a well-bred family of to-day; from the bottom grade of industry in the savage camp, where all things are cooked together by the same person in the same pot,—without neatness, without delicacy, without specialization,—to the million widely separated hands that serve the home to-day in a thousand wide-spread industries,—the man and the mill have achieved it all; the woman has but gone shopping outside, and stayed at the base of the pyramid within.

And, more important and suggestive yet, mark this: whereas, in historic beginnings, nothing but the home of the family existed; slowly, as we have grown, has developed the home of the individual. The first wider movement of social life meant a freer flux of population,—trade, commerce, exchange, communication. Along river courses and sea margins, from canoe to steamship, along paths and roads as they made them, from "shank's mare to the iron horse," faster and freer, wider and oftener, the individual human beings have flowed and mingled in the life that is humanity. At first the traveller's only help was hospitality,—the right of the stranger; but his increasing functional use brought with it, of necessity, the organic structure which made it easy, the transitory individual home. From the most primitive caravansary up to the square miles of floor-space in our grand hotels, the public house has met the needs of social evolution as no private house could have done.

To man, so far the only fully human being of his age, the bachelor apartment of some sort has been a temporary home for that part of his life wherein he had escaped from one family and not yet entered another. To woman this possibility is opening to-day. More and more we see women presuming to live and have a home, even though they have not a family. The family home itself is more and more yielding to the influence of progress. Once it was stationary and permanent, occupied from generation to generation. Now we move, even in families,—move with reluctance and painful objection and with bitter sacrifice of household gods; but move we must under the increasing irritation of irreconcilable conditions. And so has sprung up and grown to vast proportions that startling portent of our times, the "family hotel."

Consider it. Here is the inn, once a mere makeshift stopping-place for weary travellers. Yet even so the weary traveller long since noted the difference between his individual freedom there and his home restrictions, and cheerfully remarked, "I take mine ease in mine inn." Here is this temporary stopping-place for single men become a permanent dwelling-place for families! Not from financial necessity. These are inhabited by people who could well afford to "Keep house." But they do not want to keep house. They are tired of keeping house. It is so difficult to keep house, the servant problem is so trying. The health of their wives is not equal to keeping house. These are the things they say.

But under these vague perceptions and expressions is heaving and stirring a slow, uprising social tide. The primitive home, based on the economic dependence of woman, with its unorganized industries, its servile labors, its smothering drag on individual development, is becoming increasingly unsuitable to the men and women of to-day. Of course, they hark back to it, of necessity, so long as marriage and childbearing are supposed to require it, so long as our fondest sentiments and our earliest memories so closely cling to it. But in its practical results, as shown by the ever-rising draught upon the man's purse and the woman's strength, it is fast wearing out.

We have watched the approach of this condition, and have laid it to every cause but the real one. We have blamed men for not staying at home as they once did. We have blamed women for not being as good housekeepers as they once were. We have blamed the children for their discontent, the servants for their inefficiency, the very brick and mortar for their poor construction. But we have never thought to blame the institution itself, and see whether it could not be improved upon.

On wide Western prairies, or anywhere in lonely farm houses, the women of to-day, confined absolutely to this strangling cradle of the race, go mad by scores and hundreds. Our asylums show a greater proportion of insane women among farmers' wives than in any other class. In the cities, where there is less "home life," people seem to stand it better. There are more distractions, the men say, and seek them. There is more excitement, amusement, variety, the women say, and seek them. What is really felt is the larger social interests and the pressure of forces newer than those of the home circle.

Many fear this movement, and vainly strive to check it. There is no cause for alarm. We are not going to lose our homes nor our families, nor any of the sweetness and happiness that go with them. But we are going to lose our kitchens, as we have lost our laundries and bakeries. The cook-stove will follow the loom and wheel, the wool-carder and shears. We shall have homes that are places to live in and love in, to rest in and play in, to be alone in and to be together in; and they will not be confused and declassed by admixture with any industry whatever.

In homes like these the family life will have all its finer, truer spirit well maintained; and the cares and labors that now mar its beauty will have passed out into fields of higher fulfilment. The

In reconstructing in our minds the position of woman under conditions of economic independence, it is most difficult to think of her as a mother.

We are so unbrokenly accustomed to the old methods of motherhood, so convinced that all its processes are inter-relative and indispensable, and that to alter one of them is to endanger the whole relation, that we cannot conceive of any desirable change.

When definite plans for such change are suggested,—ways in which babies might be better cared for than at present,—we either deny the advantages of the change proposed or insist that these advantages can be reached under our present system. Just as in cooking we seek to train the private cook and to exalt and purify the private taste, so in baby-culture we seek to train the individual mother, and to call for better conditions in the private home; in both cases ignoring the relation between our general system and its particular phenomena. Though it may be shown, with clearness, that in physical conditions the private house, as a place in which to raise children, may be improved upon, yet all the more stoutly do we protest that the mental life, the emotional life, of the home is the best possible environment for the young.

There was a time in human history when this was true. While progress derived its main impetus from the sex-passion, and the highest emotions were those that held us together in the family relation, such education and such surroundings as fostered and intensified these emotions were naturally the best. But in the stage into which we are now growing, when the family relation is only a part of life, and our highest duties lie between individuals in social relation, the child has new needs.

This does not mean, as the scared rush of the unreasoning mind to an immediate opposite would suggest, a disruption of the family circle or the destruction of the home. It does not mean the separation of mother and child,—that instant dread of the crude instinct of animal maternity. But it does mean a change of basis in the family relation by the removal of its previous economic foundation, and a change of method in our child-culture. We are no more bound to maintain forever our early methods in baby-raising than we are bound to maintain them in the education of older children, or in floriculture. All human life is in its very nature open to improvement, and motherhood is not excepted. The relation between men and women, between husband and wife, between parent and child, changes inevitably with social advance; but we are loath to admit it. We think a change here must be wrong, because we are so convinced that the present condition is right.

On examination, however, we find that the existing relation between parents and children in the home is by no means what we unquestioningly assume. We all hold certain ideals of home life, of family life. When we see around us, or read of, scores and hundreds of cases of family unhappiness and open revolt, we lay it to the individual misbehavior of the parties concerned, and go on implicitly believing in the intrinsic perfection of the institution. When, on the other hand, we find people living together in this relation, in peace and love and courtesy, we do not conversely attribute this to individual superiority and virtue; but we point to it as instancing the innate beauty of the relation.

To the careful sociological observer what really appears is this: when individual and racial progress was best served by the close associations of family life, people were very largely developed in capacity for family affection. They were insensitive to the essential limitations and incessant friction of the relation. They assented to the absolute authority of the head of the family and to the minor despotism of lower functionaries, manifesting none of those sharply defined individual characteristics which are so inimical to the family relation.

But we have reached a stage where individual and racial progress is best served by the higher specialization of individuals and by a far wider sense of love and duty. This change renders the psychic condition of home life increasingly disadvantageous. We constantly hear of the inferior manners of the children of to-day, of the restlessness of the young, of the flat treason of deserting parents. It is visibly not so easy to live at home as it used to be. Our children are not more perversely constituted than the children of earlier ages, but the conditions in which they are reared are not suited to develope the qualities now needed in human beings.

This increasing friction between members of families should not be viewed with condemnation from a moral point of view, but studied with scientific interest. If our families are so relatively uncomfortable under present conditions, are there not conditions wherein the same families could be far more comfortable? No: we are afraid not. We think it is right to have things as they are, wrong to wish to change them. We think that virtue lies largely in being uncomfortable, and that there is special virtue in the existing family relation.

Virtue is a relative term. Human virtues change from age to age with the change in conditions. Consider the great virtue of loyalty,— our highest name for duty. This is a quality that became valuable in human life the moment we began to do things which were not instantly and visibly profitable to ourselves. The permanent application of the individual to a task not directly attractive was an indispensable social quality, and therefore a virtue. Steadfastness, faithfulness, loyalty, duty, that conscious, voluntary attitude of the individual which holds him to a previously assumed relation, even to his extreme personal injury,—to death itself,—from this results the cohesion of the social body: it is a first principle of social existence.

To the personal conscience a social necessity must express itself in a recognized and accepted pressure,—a force to which we bow, a duty, a virtue. So the virtue of loyalty came into early and lasting esteem, whether in the form of loyalty to one's own spoken word or vow—"He that sweareth to his hurt, and doeth it"—to a friend or group of friends in temporary union for some common purpose, or to a larger and more permanent relation. The highest form is, of course, loyalty to the largest common interest; and here we can plainly trace the growth of this quality.

First, we see it in the vague, nebulous, coherence of the horde of savages, then in the tense devotion of families,—that absolute duty to the highest known social group. It was in this period that obedience to parents was writ so large in our scale of virtues. The family feud, the *vendetta* of the Corsicans, is an over-development of this force of family devotion. Next came loyalty to the chief, passing even that due the father. And with the king—that dramatic personification of a nation, "Lo! royal England comes!"—loyalty became a very passion. It took precedence of every virtue, with good reason; for it was not, as was supposed, the person of the king which was so revered: it was the embodied nation, the far-reaching, collective interests of every citizen, the common good, which called for the willing sacrifice of every individual. We still exhibit all these phases of loyalty, in differently diminishing degrees; but we show, also, a larger form of this great virtue peculiar to our age.

The lines of social relation to-day are mainly industrial. Our individual lives, our social peace and progress, depend more upon our economic relations than upon any other. For a long time society was organized only on a sex-basis, a religious basis, or a military basis, each of such organizations being comparatively transient; and its component individuals labored alone on an economic basis of helpless individualism.

Duty is a social sense, and developes only with social organization. As our civil organization has become national, we have developed the sense of duty to the State. As our industrial organization has grown to the world-encircling intricacies of to-day, as we have come to hold our place on earth by reason of our vast and elaborate economic relation with its throbbing and sensitive machinery of communication and universal interservice, the unerring response of the soul to social needs has given us a new kind of loyalty,—loyalty to our work. The engineer who sticks to his engine till he dies, that his trainload of passengers may live; the cashier who submits to torture rather than disclose the secret of the safe,—these are loyal exactly as was the servitor of feudal times, who followed his master to the death, or the subject who gave up all for his king. Professional honor, duty to one's employers, duty to the work itself, at any cost,—this is loyalty, faithfulness, the power to stay put in a relation necessary to the social good, though it may be directly against personal interest.

It is in the training of children for this stage of human life that the private home has ceased to be sufficient, or the isolated, primitive, dependent woman capable. Not that the mother does not have an intense and overpowering sense of loyalty and of duty; but it is duty to individuals, just as it was in the year one. What she is unable to follow, in her enforced industrial restriction, is the higher specialization of labor, and the honorable devotion of human lives to the development of their work. She is most slavishly bound to her daily duty, it is true; but it does not occur to her as a duty to raise the grade of her own labor for the sake of humanity, nor as a sin so to keep back the progress of the world by her contented immobility.

She cannot teach what she does not know. She cannot in any sincerity uphold as a duty what she does not practise. The child learns more of the virtues needed in modern life—of fairness, of justice, of comradeship, of collective interest and action—in a common school than can be taught in the most perfect family circle. We may preach to our children as we will of the great duty of loving and serving one's neighbor; but what the baby is born into, what the child grows up to see and feel, is the concentration of one entire life—his mother's—upon the personal aggrandizement of one family, and the human service of another entire life—his father's—so warped and strained by the necessity of "supporting his family" that treason to society is the common price of comfort in the home. For a man to do any base, false work for which he is hired, work that injures producer and consumer alike; to prostitute what power and talent he possesses to whatever purchaser may use them,—this is justified among men by what they call duty to the family, and is unblamed by the moral sense of dependent women.

And this is the atmosphere in which the wholly home-bred, mother-taught child grows up. Why should not food and clothes and the comforts of his own people stand first in his young mind? Does he not see his mother, the all-loved, all-perfect one, peacefully spending her days in the arrangement of these things which his father's ceaseless labor has procured? Why should he not grow up to care for his own, to the neglect and willing injury of all the rest, when his earliest, deepest impressions are formed under such exclusive devotion?

It is not the home as a place of family life and love that injures the child, but as the centre of a tangled heap of industries, low in their ungraded condition, and lower still because they are wholly personal. Work the object of which is merely to serve one's self is the lowest. Work the object of which is merely to serve one's family is the next lowest. Work the object of which is to serve more and more people, in widening range, till it approximates the divine spirit that cares for all the world, is social service in the fullest sense, and the highest form of service that we can reach.

It is this personality in home industry that keeps it hopelessly down. The short range between effort and attainment, the constant attention given to personal needs, is bad for the man, worse for the woman, and worst for the child. It belittles his impressions of life at the start. It accustoms him to magnify the personal duties and minify the social ones, and it greatly retards his adjustment to larger life. This servant-motherhood, with all its unavoidable limitation and ill results, is the concomitant of the economic dependence of woman upon man, the direct and inevitable effect of the sexuo-economic relation.

The child is affected by it during his most impressionable years, and feels the effect throughout life. The woman is permanently retarded by it; the man, less so, because of his normal social activities, wherein he is under more developing influence. But he is injured in great degree, and our whole civilization is checked and perverted.

We suffer also, our lives long, from an intense self-consciousness, from a sensitiveness beyond all need; we demand measureless personal attention and devotion, because we have been born and reared in a very hotbed of these qualities. A baby who spent certain hours of every day among other babies, being cared for because he was a baby, and not because he was "my baby," would grow to have a very different opinion of himself from that which is forced upon each new soul that comes among us by the ceaseless adoration of his own immediate family. What he needs to learn at once and for all, to learn softly and easily, but inexorably, is that he is one of many. We all dimly recognize this in our praise of large families, and in our saying that "an only child is apt to be selfish." So is an only family. The earlier and more easily a child can learn that human life means many people, and their behavior to one another, the happier and stronger and more useful his life will be.

This could be taught him with no difficulty whatever, under certain conditions, just as he is taught his present sensitiveness and egotism by the present conditions. It is not only temperature and diet and rest and exercise which affect the baby. "He does love to be noticed," we say. "He is never so happy as when he has a dozen worshippers around him." But what is the young soul learning all the while? What does he gather, as he sees, and hears and slowly absorbs impressions? With the inflexible inferences of a clear, young brain, unsupplied with any counter-evidence until later in life, he learns that women are meant to wait on people, to get dinner, and sweep and pick up things; that men are made to bring home things, and are to be begged of according to circumstances; that babies are the object of concentrated admiration; that their hair, hands, feet, are specially attractive; that they are the heated focus of attention, to be passed from hand to hand, swung and danced and amused most violently, and also be laid aside and have nothing done to them, with no regard to their preference in either case.

And then, in the midst of all this tingling self-consciousness and desire for loving praise, he learns that he is "naughty"! The grief, the shame, the anger at injustice, the hopeless bewilderment, the morbid sensitiveness of conscience or the stolid dulling of it, the gradual retirement of the baffled brain from all these premature sensations to a contentment with mere personal gratification and a growing ingenuity in obtaining it,—all these experiences are the common lot of the child among us, our common lot when we were children. Of course, we don't remember. Of course, we loved our mother, and thought her perfect. Comparisons among mothers are difficult for a baby. Of course, we loved our homes, and never dreamed of any other way of being "brought up." And, of course, when we have children of our own, we bring them up in the same way. What other way is there? What is there to be said on the subject? Children always were brought up at home. Isn't that enough?

And yet, insidiously, slowly, irresistibly, while we flatter ourselves that things remain the same, they are changing under our very eyes from year to year, from day to day. Education, hiding itself behind a wall of books, but consisting more and more fully in the grouping of children and in the training of faculties never mentioned in the curriculum,—education, which is our human motherhood, has crept nearer and nearer to its true place, its best work,—the care and training of the little child. Some women there are, and some men, whose highest service to humanity is the care of children. Such should not concentrate their powers upon their own children alone,—a most questionable advantage,—but should be so placed that their talent and skill, their knowledge and experience, would benefit the largest number of children. Many women there are, and many men, who, though able to bring forth fine children, are unable to educate them properly. Simply to bear children is a personal matter,—an animal function. Education is collective, human, a social function.

As we now arrange life, our children must take their chances while babies, and live or die, improve or deteriorate, according to the mother to whom they chance to be born. An inefficient mother does not prevent a child from having a good school education or a good college education; but the education of babyhood, the most important of all, is wholly in her hands. It is futile to say that mothers should be taught how to fulfil their duties. You cannot teach every mother to be a good school educator or a good college educator. Why should you expect every mother to be a good nursery educator? Whatever our expectations, she is not; and our mistrained babies, such of them as survive the maternal handling, grow to be such people as we see about us.

The growth and change in home and family life goes steadily on under and over and through our prejudices and convictions; and the education of the child has changed and become a social function, while we still imagine the mother to be doing it all.

In its earliest and most rudimentary manifestations, education was but part of the individual maternal function of the female animal. But no sooner did the human mind begin to show capacity for giving and receiving its impressions through language (thus attaining the power of acquiring information through sources other than its own experience) than the individual mother ceased to be the sole educator. The young savage receives not only guidance from his anxious mother, but from the chiefs and elders of his tribe. For a long time the aged were considered the only suitable teachers, because the major part of knowledge was still derived from personal experience; and, of course, the older the person, the greater his experience, other things being equal, and they were rather equal then. This primitive notion still holds among us. People still assume superior wisdom because of superior age, putting mere number of experiences against a more essential and better arranged variety, and quite forgetting that the needed wisdom of to-day is not the accumulation of facts, but the power to think about them to some purpose.

With our increased power to preserve and transmit individual experience through literature, and to disseminate such information through systematic education, we see younger and younger people, more rich in, say, chemical or electrical experience than "the oldest inhabitant" could have been in earlier times. Therefore, the teacher of to-day is not the graybeard and beldame, but the man and woman most newly filled with the gathered experience of the world. As this change from age to youth has taken place in the teacher, it has also shown itself in the taught. Grown men frequented the academic groves of Greece. Youths filled the universities of the Middle Ages. Boys and, later, girls were given the increasing school advantages of progressive centuries.

To-day the beautiful development of the kindergarten has brought education to the nursery door. Even our purblind motherhood is beginning to open that door; and we have at last entered upon the study of babyhood, its needs and powers, and are seeing that education begins with life itself. It is no new and daring heresy to suggest that babies need better education than the individual mother now gives them. It is simply a little further extension of the steadily expanding system of human education which is coming upon us, as civilization grows. And it no more infringes upon the mother's rights, the mother's duties, the mother's pleasures, than does the college or the school.

We think no harm of motherhood because our darlings go out each day to spend long hours in school. The mother is not held neglectful, nor the child bereft. It is not called a "separation of mother and child." There would be no further harm or risk or loss in a babyhood passed among such changed surroundings and skilled service as should meet its needs more perfectly than it is possible for the mother to meet them alone at home.

Better surroundings and care for babies, better education, do not mean, as some mothers may imagine, that the tiny monthling is to be taught to read, or even that it is to be exposed to cabalistical arrangements of color and form and sound which shall mysteriously force the young intelligence to flower. It would mean, mainly, a far quieter and more peaceful life than is possible for the heavily loved and violently cared for baby in the busy household; and the impressions which it did meet would be planned and maintained with an intelligent appreciation of its mental powers. The mother would not be excluded, but supplemented, as she is now, by the teacher and the school.

Try and imagine for yourself, if you like, a new kind of coming alive,—the mother breast and mother arms there, of course, fulfilling the service which no other, however tender, could supervene; but there would be other service also. The long, bright hours of the still widening days would find one in sunny, soft-colored rooms, or among the grass and flowers, or by the warm sand and waters. There would be about one more of one's self, others of the same size and age, in restful, helpful companionship. A year means an enormous difference in the ages of babies. Think what a passion little children have for playmates of exactly their own age, because in them alone is perfect equality; and then think that the home-kept baby never has such companionship, unless, indeed, there are twins!

In this larger grouping, in full companionship, the child would unconsciously absorb the knowledge that "we" were humanity, that "we" were creatures to be so fed, so watched, so laid to sleep, so kissed and cuddled and set free to roll and play. The mother-hours would be sweetest of all, perhaps. Here would be something wholly one's own, and the better appreciated for the contrast. But the long, steady days would bring their peaceful lessons of equality and common interest instead of the feverish personality of the isolated one-baby household, or the innumerable tyrannies and exactions, the forced submissions and exclusions, of the nursery full of brothers and sisters of widely differing ages and powers. Mothers accustomed to consider many babies besides their own would begin, on the one hand, to learn something of mere general babyness, and so understand that stage of life far better, and, on the other, to outgrow the pathetic idolatry of the fabled crow,—to recognize a difference in babies, and so to learn a new ideal in their great work of motherhood.

This alone is reason good for a wider maternity. As long as each mother dotes and gloats upon her own children, knowing no others, so long this animal passion overestimates or underestimates real human qualities in the child. So long as this endures, we must grow up with the false, unbalanced opinion of ourselves forced upon us in our infancy. We may think too well of ourselves or we may think too ill of ourselves; but we think always too much of ourselves, because of this untrained and unmodified concentration of maternal feeling. Our whole attitude toward the child is too intensely personal. Through all our aching later life we labor to outgrow the false perspective taught by primitive motherhood.

A baby, brought up with other babies, would never have that labor or that pain. However much his mother might love him, and he might enjoy her love, he would still find that for most of the time he was treated precisely like other people of the same age. Such a change would not involve any greater loss to home and family life than does the school or kindergarten. It would not rob the baby of his mother nor the mother of her baby. And such a change would give the mother certain free hours as a human being, as a member of a civilized community, as an economic producer, as a growing, self-realizing individual. This freedom, growth, and power will make her a wiser, stronger, and nobler mother.

After all is said of loving gratitude to our unfailing mother-nurse, we must have a most exalted sense of our own personal importance so to canonize the service of ourselves. The mother as a social servant instead of a home servant will not lack in true mother duty. She will love her child as well, perhaps better, when she is not in hourly contact with it, when she goes from its life to her own life, and back from her own life to its life, with ever new delight and power. She can keep the deep, thrilling joy of motherhood far fresher in her heart, far more vivid and open in voice and eyes and tender hands, when the hours of individual work give her mind another channel for her own part of the day. From her work, loved and honored though it is, she will return to the home life, the child life, with an eager, ceaseless pleasure, cleansed of all the fret and friction and weariness that so mar it now.

The child, also, will feel this beneficent effect. It is a mistake to suppose that the baby, more than the older child, needs the direct care and presence of the mother. Careful experiment has shown that a new-born baby does not know its own mother, and that a new-made mother does not know her own baby. They have been changed without the faintest recognition on either side.

The services of a foster-mother, a nurse, a grandma, are often liked by a baby as well as, and perhaps better than, those of its own mother. The mere bodily care of a young infant is as well given by one wise, loving hand as another. It is that trained hand that the baby needs, not mere blood-relationship. While the mother keeps her beautiful prerogative of nursing, she need never fear that any other will be dearer to the little heart than she who is the blessed provider of his highest known good. A healthy, happy, rightly occupied motherhood should be able to keep up this function longer than is now customary,—to the child's great gain. Aside from this special relationship, however, the baby would grow easily into the sense of other and wider relationship.

In the freedom and peace of his baby bedroom and baby parlor, in his easy association with others of his own age, he would absorb a sense of right human relation with his mother's milk, as it were,— a sense of others' rights and of his own. Instead of finding life a place in which all the fun was in being carried round and "done to" by others, and a place also in which these others were a tyranny and a weariness unutterable; he would find life a place in which to spread out, unhindered, getting acquainted with his own unfolding powers of body and mind in an atmosphere of physical warmth and ease and of quiet peace of mind.

Direct, concentrated, unvarying personal love is too hot an atmosphere for a young soul. Variations of loneliness, anger, and injustice, are not changes to be desired. A steady, diffused love, lighted with wisdom, based always on justice, and varied with rapturous draughts of our own mother's depth of devotion, would make us into a new people in a few generations. The bent and reach of our whole lives are largely modified by the surroundings of infancy; and those surroundings are capable of betterment, though not to be attained by the individual mother in the individual home.

There are three reasons why the individual mother can never be fit to take all the care of her children. The first two are so commonly true as to have much weight, the last so absolutely and finally true as to be sufficient in itself alone.

First, not every woman is born with the special qualities and powers needed to take right care of children: she has not the talent for it. Second, not every woman can have the instruction and training needed to fit her for the right care of children: she has not the education for it. Third, while each woman takes all the care of her own children herself, no woman can ever have the requisite experience for it. That is the final bar. That is what keeps back our human motherhood. No mother knows more than her mother knew: no mother has ever learned her business; and our children pass under the well-meaning experiments of an endless succession of amateurs.

We try to get "an experienced nurse." We insist on "an experienced physician." But our idea of an experienced mother is simply one who has borne many children, as if parturition was an educative process!

To experience the pangs of child-birth, or the further pangs of a baby's funeral, adds nothing whatever to the mother's knowledge of the proper care, clothing, feeding, and teaching of the child. The educative department of maternity is not a personal function: it is in its very nature a social function; and we fail grievously in its fulfilment.

The economically independent mother, widened and freed, strengthened and developed, by her social service, will do better service as mother than it has been possible to her before. No one thing could do more to advance the interests of humanity than the wiser care and wider love of organized human motherhood around our babies. This nobler mother, bearing nobler children, and rearing them in nobler ways, would go far toward making possible the world which we want to see. And this change is coming upon us overpoweringly in spite of our foolish fears.

What the human race requires is permanent provision for the needs of individuals, disconnected from the sex-relation. Our assumption that only married people and their immediate relatives have any right to live in comfort and health is erroneous. Every human being needs a home,—bachelor, husband, or widower, girl, wife, or widow, young or old. They need it from the cradle to the grave, and without regard to sex-connections. We should so build and arrange for the shelter and comfort of humanity as not to interfere with marriage, and yet not to make that comfort dependent upon marriage. With the industries of home life managed professionally, with rooms and suites of rooms and houses obtainable by any person or persons desiring them, we could live singly without losing home comfort and general companionship, we could meet bereavement without being robbed of the common conveniences of living as well as of the heart's love, and we could marry in ease and freedom without involving any change in the economic base of either party concerned.

Married people will always prefer a home together, and can have it; but groups of women or groups of men can also have a home together if they like, or contiguous rooms. And individuals even could have a house to themselves, without having, also, the business of a home upon their shoulders.

Take the kitchens out of the houses, and you leave rooms which are open to any form of arrangement and extension; and the occupancy of them does not mean "housekeeping." In such living, personal character and taste would flower as never before; the home of each individual would be at last a true personal expression; and the union of individuals in marriage would not compel the jumbling together of all the external machinery of their lives,—a process in which much of the delicacy and freshness of love, to say nothing of the power of mutual rest and refreshment, is constantly lost. The sense of lifelong freedom and self-respect and of the peace and permanence of one's own home will do much to purify and uplift the personal relations of life, and more to strengthen and extend the social relations. The individual will learn to feel himself an integral part of the social structure, in close, direct, permanent connection with the needs and uses of society.

This is especially needed for women, who are generally considered, and who consider themselves, mere fractions of families, and incapable of any wholesome life of their own. The knowledge that peace and comfort may be theirs for life, even if they do not marry,—and may be still theirs for life, even if they do,—will develope a serenity and strength in women most beneficial to them and to the world. It is a glaring proof of the insufficient and irritating character of our existing form of marriage that women must be forced to it by the need of food and clothes, and men by the need of cooks and housekeepers. We are absurdly afraid that, if men or women can meet these needs of life by other means, they will cheerfully renounce the marriage relation. And yet we sing adoringly of the power of love!

In reality, we may hope that the most valuable effect of this change in the basis of living will be the cleansing of love and marriage from this base admixture of pecuniary interest and creature comfort, and that men and women, eternally drawn together by the deepest force in nature, will be able at last to meet on a plane of pure and perfect love. We shame our own ideals, our deepest instincts, our highest knowledge, by this gross assumption that the noblest race on earth will not mate, or, at least, not mate monogamously, unless bought and bribed through the common animal necessities of food and shelter, and chained by law and custom.

The depth and purity and permanence of the marriage relation rest on the necessity for the prolonged care of children by both parents,—a law of racial development which we can never escape. When parents are less occupied in getting food and cooking it, in getting furniture and dusting it, they may find time to give new thought and new effort to the care of their children. The necessities of the child are far deeper than for bread and bed: those are his mere racial needs, held in common with all his kind. What he needs far more and receives far less is the companionship, the association, the personal touch, of his father and mother. When the common labors of life are removed from the home, we shall have the time, and perhaps the inclination, to make the personal acquaintance of our children. They will seem to us not so much creatures to be waited on as people to be understood. As the civil and military protection of society has long since superseded the tooth-and-claw defence of the fierce parent, without in the least endangering the truth and intensity of the family relation, so the economic provision of society will in time supersede the bringing home of prey by the parent, without evil effects to the love or prosperity of the family. These primitive needs and primitive methods of meeting them are unquestionably at the base of the family relation; but we have long passed them by, and the ties between parent and child are not weakened, but strengthened, by the change.

The more we grow away from these basic conditions, the more fully we realize the deeper and higher forms of relation which are the strength and the delight of human life. Full and permanent provision for individual life and comfort will not cut off the forces that draw men and women together or hold children to their parents; but it will purify and intensify these relations to a degree which we can somewhat foretell by observing the effect of such changes as are already accomplished in this direction. And, in freeing the individual, old and young, from enforced association on family lines, and allowing this emergence into free association on social lines, we shall healthfully assist the development of true social intercourse.

The present economic basis of family life holds our friendly and familiar intercourse in narrow grooves. Such visiting and mingling as is possible to us is between families rather than between individuals; and the growing specialization of individuals renders it increasingly unlikely that all the members of a given family shall please a given visitor or he please them. This, on our present basis, either checks the intercourse or painfully strains the family relation. The change of economic relation in families from a sex-basis to a social basis will make possible wide individual intercourse without this accompanying strain on the family ties.

This outgoing impulse among members of families, their growing desire for general and personal social intercourse, has been considered as a mere thirst for amusement, and deprecated by the moralist. He has so far maintained that the highest form of association was association with one's own family, and that a desire for a wider and more fluent relationship was distinctly unworthy. "He is a good family man," we say admiringly of him who asks only for his newspaper and slippers in the evening; and for the woman who dares admit that she wishes further society than that of her husband we have but one name. With the children, too, our constant effort is to "keep the boys at home," to "make home attractive," so that our ancient ideal, the patriarchal ideal, of a world of families and nothing else, may be maintained.

But this is a world of persons as well as of families. We are persons as soon as we are born, though born into families. We are persons when we step out of families, and persons still, even when we step into new families of our own. As persons, we need more and more, in each generation, to associate with other persons. It is most interesting to watch this need making itself felt, and getting itself supplied, by fair means or foul, through all these stupid centuries. In our besotted exaggeration of the sex-relation, we have crudely supposed that a wish for wider human relationship was a wish for wider sex-relationship, and was therefore to be discouraged, as in Spain it was held unwise to teach women to write, lest they become better able to communicate with their lovers, and so shake the foundations of society.

But, when our sex-relation is made pure and orderly by the economic independence of women, when sex-attraction is no longer a consuming fever, forever convulsing the social surface, under all its bars and chains, we shall not be content to sit down forever with half a dozen blood relations for our whole social arena. We shall need each other more, not less, and shall recognize that social need of one another as the highest faculty of this the highest race on earth.

The force which draws friends together is a higher one than that which draws the sexes together,—higher in the sense of belonging to a later race-development. "Passing the love of women" is no unmeaning phrase. Children need one another: young people need one another. Middle-aged people need one another: old people need one another. We all need one another, much and often. Just as every human creature needs a place to be alone in, a sacred, private "home" of his own, so all human creatures need a place to be together in, from the two who can show each other their souls uninterruptedly, to the largest throng that can throb and stir in unison.

Humanity means being together, and our unutterably outgrown way of living keeps us apart. How many people, if they dare face the fact, have often hopelessly longed for some better way of seeing their friends, their own true friends, relatives by soul, if not by body!

Acting always under the heated misconceptions of our over-sexed minds, we have pictured mankind as a race of beasts whose only desire to be together was based on one great, overworked passion, and who were only kept from universal orgies of promiscuity by being confined in homes. This is not true. It is not true even now in our over-sexed condition. It will be still less true when we are released from the artificial pressure of the sexuo-economic relation and grow natural again.

Men, women, and children need freedom to mingle on a human basis; and that means to mingle in their daily lives and occupations, not to go laboriously to see each other, with no common purpose. We all know the pleasant acquaintance and deep friendship that springs up when people are thrown together naturally, at school, at college, on shipboard, in the cars, in a camping trip, in business. The social need of one another rests at bottom on a common, functional development; and the common, functional service is its natural opportunity.

The reason why friendship means more to men than to women, and why they associate so much more easily and freely, is that they are further developed in race-functions, and that they *work together*. In the natural association of common effort and common relaxation is the true opening for human companionship. Just to put a number of human beings in the same room, to relate their bodies as to cubic space, does not relate their souls. Our present methods of association, especially for women, are most unsatisfactory. They arise, and go to "call" on one another. They solemnly "return" these calls. They prepare much food, and invite many people to come and eat it; or some dance, music, or entertainment is made the temporary ground of union. But these people do not really meet one another. They pass whole lifetimes in going through the steps of these elaborate games, and never become acquainted. There is a constant thirst among us for fuller and truer social intercourse; but our social machinery provides no means for quenching it.

Men have satisfied this desire in large measure; but between women, or between men and women, it is yet far from accomplishment. Men meet one another freely in their work, while women work alone. But the difference is sharpest in their play. "Girls don't have any fun!" say boys, scornfully; and they don't have very much. What they do have must come, like their bread and butter, on lines of sex. Some man must give them what amusement they have, as he must give them everything else. Men have filled the world with games and sports, from the noble contests of the Olympic plain to the brain and body training sports of to-day, good, bad, and indifferent. Through all the ages the men have played; and the women have looked on, when they were asked. Even the amusing occupation of seeing other people do things was denied them, unless they were invited by the real participants. The "queen of the ball-room" is but a wall-flower, unless she is asked to dance by the real king.

Even to-day, when athletics are fast opening to women, when tennis and golf and all the rest are possible to them, the two sexes are far from even in chances to play. To want a good time is not the same thing as to want the society of the other sex, and to make a girl's desire for a good time hang so largely on her power of sex-attraction is another of the grievous strains we put upon that faculty. That people want to see each other is construed by us to mean that "he" wants to see "her," and "she" wants to see "him." The fun and pleasure of the world are so interwound with the sex-dependence of women upon men that women are forced to court "attentions," when not really desirous of anything but amusement; and, as we force the association of the sexes on this plane, so we restrict it on a more wholesome one.

Even our little children in their play are carefully trained to accentuate sex; and a line of conduct for boys, differing from that for girls, is constantly insisted upon long before either would think of a necessity for such difference. Girls and boys, as they associate, are so commented on and teased as to destroy all wholesome friendliness, and induce a premature sex-consciousness. Young men and women are allowed to associate more or less freely, but always on a strictly sex-basis, friendship between man and woman being a common laughing-stock. Every healthy boy and girl resent this, and try to hold free, natural relation; but such social pressure is hard to resist. She may have as many "beaux" as she can compass, he may "pay attention" to as many girls as he pleases; but that is their only way to meet.

The general discontinuance of all friendly visiting, upon the engagement of either party, proves the nature of the bond. Having chosen the girl he is to marry, why care to call upon any others? having chosen the man she is to marry, why receive attention from any others? these "calls" and "attentions" being all in the nature of tentative preliminaries to possible matrimony. And, after marriage, the wife is never supposed to wish to see any other man than her husband, or the husband any other woman than his wife. In some countries, we vary this arrangement by increasing the social freedom of married people; but the custom is accompanied by a commensurate lack of freedom before marriage, which causes questionable results, both in married life and in social life. In the higher classes of society there is always more freedom of social intercourse between the sexes after marriage; but, speaking generally of America, there is very little natural and serious acquaintance between men and women after the period of pre-matrimonial visiting.

Even the friendship which may have existed between husband and wife before marriage is often destroyed by that relation and its economic complications. They have not time to talk about things as they used: they are too near together, and too deeply involved in the industrial and financial concern of their new business. This works steadily against the development of higher and purer relations between men and women, and tends to keep them forever to the one primitive bond of sex-union.

A young man goes to a city to live and work. He needs the society of women as well as of men. Formerly he had his mother, his sisters, and his sisters' friends, his schoolmates. Now he must face our constrained social conditions. He may visit two kinds of women,—those whom we call "good," and those whom we call "bad." (This classification rests on but one moral quality, and that a sexual one.) He naturally prefers the good. The good are divided, again, into two kinds,—married and single. If he visit a married woman frequently, it is remarked upon: it becomes unpleasant, he does not do it. If he visit an unmarried woman frequently, it is also remarked upon; and he is considered to have "intentions." His best alternative is to visit a number of unmarried women, and distribute his attentions so cautiously that no one can claim them as personal.

Here he enters on the first phase of our sexuo-economic relation: he cannot even visit girls freely without paying for it. Simply to see the girl by calling on her in the family circle is hardly what either wants of the other. One does not meet half a dozen people of various ages and of both sexes as one meets a friend alone. To seek to see her alone is an "attention." To "take her out" costs money, and he cheerfully pays it. But he cannot do this too often, or he will become involved in what is naturally considered a "serious" affair; and every step of the acquaintance is watched and commented upon from a sexual point of view.

There is no natural, simple medium of social intercourse between men and women. The young man can but learn that his popularity depends largely on his pocket-book. The money that he might be saving for marriage is wasted on these miscellaneous preliminaries. As he sees what women like and how much it costs to please them, his hope of marriage recedes farther and farther. The period during which he must live as an individual grows longer; and he becomes accustomed to superficial acquaintance with many women, on the shallowest side of life, with no opportunity for genuine association and true friendship. What wonder that the other kind of woman, who also costs money, it is true, but who does not involve permanent obligation, has come to be so steady a factor in our social life? The sexuo-economic relation promotes vice in more ways than one.

The economic independence of woman will change all these conditions as naturally and inevitably as her dependence has introduced them. In her specialization in industry, she will develope more personality and less sexuality; and this will lower the pressure on this one relation in both women and men. And, in our social intercourse, the new character and new method of living will allow of broad and beautiful developments in human association. As the private home becomes a private home indeed, and no longer the woman's social and industrial horizon; as the workshops of the world—woman's sphere as well as man's—become homelike and beautiful under her influence; and as men and women move freely together in the exercise of common racial functions,—we shall have new channels for the flow of human life.

We shall not move from the isolated home to the sordid shop and back again, in a world torn and dissevered by the selfish production of one sex and the selfish consumption of the other; but we shall live in a world of men and women humanly related, as well as sexually related, working together, as they were meant to do, for the common good of all. The home will be no longer an economic entity, with its cumbrous industrial machinery huddled vulgarly behind it, but a peaceful and permanent expression of personal life as withdrawn from social contact; and that social contact will be provided for by the many common meeting-places necessitated by the organization of domestic industries.

The assembling-room is as deep a need of human life as the retiring-room,—not some ball-room or theatre, to which one must be invited of set purpose, but great common libraries and parlors, baths and gymnasia, work-rooms and play-rooms, to which both sexes have the same access for the same needs, and where they may mingle freely in common human expression. The kind of buildings essential to the carrying out of the organization of home industry will provide such places. There will be the separate rooms for individuals and the separate houses for families; but there will be, also, the common rooms for all. These must include a place for the children, planned and built for the happy occupancy of many children for many years,—a home such as no children have ever had. This, as well as rooms everywhere for young people and old people, in which they can be together as naturally as they can be alone, without effort, question, or remark.

Such an environment would allow of free association among us, on lines of common interest; and, in its natural, easy flow, we should develop far higher qualities than are brought out by the uneasy struggles of our present "society" to see each other without wanting to. It would make an enormous difference to woman's power of choosing the right man. Cut off from the purchasing power which is now his easiest way to compass his desires, freely seen and known in his daily work and amusements, a woman could know and judge a man as she is wholly unable to do now. Her personality developed by a free and useful life, clear-headed and open-eyed,—a woman still, but a personality as well as a woman,—the girl trained to economic independence, and associating freely with young men in their common work and play, would learn a new estimate of what constitutes noble manhood.

The young man, no longer able to cover all his shortcomings with a dress-coat, and to obtain absolution for every offence by the simple penance of paying for it, unable really to do much that was wrong for lack of the old opportunity and the old incentive, constantly helped and inspired by the friendly presence of honest and earnest womanhood, would have all the force of natural law to lift him up instead of pulling him heavily downward, as it does now.

With the pressure of our over-developed sex-instinct lifted off the world, born clean and strong, of noble-hearted, noble-minded, noble-bodied mothers, trained in the large wisdom of the new motherhood, and living freely in daily association with the best womanhood, a new kind of man can and will grow on earth. What this will mean to the race in power and peace and happiness no eye can foresee. But this much we can see:—that our once useful sexuo-economic relation is being outgrown, that it now produces many evil phenomena, and that its displacement by the economic freedom of woman will of itself set free new forces, to develope in us, by their natural working, the very virtues for which we have striven and agonized so long.

This change is not a thing to prophesy and plead for. It is a change already instituted, and gaining ground among us these many years with marvellous rapidity. Neither men nor women wish the change. Neither men nor women have sought it. But the same great force of social evolution which brought us into the old relation—to our great sorrow and pain—is bringing us out, with equal difficulty and distress. The time has come when it is better for the world that women be economically independent, and therefore they are becoming so.

It is worth while for us to consider the case fully and fairly, that we may see what it is that is happening to us, and welcome with open arms the happiest change in human condition that ever came into the world. To free an entire half of humanity from an artificial position; to release vast natural forces from a strained and clumsy combination, and set them free to work smoothly and easily as they were intended to work; to introduce conditions that will change

A NOTE ON THE TEXT

The source of the text of "The Yellow Wall-paper" included in this volume is from the first published version of the story, which appeared in *The New England Magazine* in January 1892. The story was written in 1890.

The presentation of the word *wall-paper* is inconsistent in the one surviving fair copy manuscript and in the *New England Magazine* version. According to Julie Dock in her critical edition of the story (*Charlotte Perkins Gilman's "The Yellow Wall-paper" and the History of Its Publication and Reception* [University Park, Pa.: Pennsylvania State Press, 1998]), in the manuscript, the word is hyphenated in the title and six other places (two of which are end-of-line breaks), and is presented as two words in five other places; in *The New England Magazine*, it is hyphenated in the title and seven other places, and presented as one word five times.

Dock explains that it was only with the publication of the story in book form, in the 1899 Small, Maynard edition, that the spelling was standardized. In the version that appeared in William Dean Howells's 1920 compilation, *The Great Modern American Stories*, it is presented as two words, while in the 1927 Oxford University Press edition and the version that appeared in *The Golden Book Magazine* in 1933, it is hyphenated throughout. More recent editions have opted for *wallpaper*, the current accepted spelling. However, a couple have preserved the inconsistencies of the 1892 publication. In the 1973 Feminist Press edition, the editor wanted to present the story "exactly as it appeared in its first published form" (cited in

Dock), and the editor of the 1995 Oxford University Press edition retained the eight hyphenated instances on the grounds that the hyphenation graphically reinforces the two elements of wallpaper that make it symbolic of the narrator's experience: it is both a wall or barrier and it is paper; just as there is a pattern printed on wall-paper, she can project her feelings on paper.

Dock argues convincingly that the inconsistencies have "little to do with the author or any intentions she may have had." While Gilman variously uses "wall-paper" and "wall paper" in the manuscript, in her diary and logs during this time, Dock explains, "she usually treats the term as one word, 'wallpaper,' and she continues this usage in later discussions of the story: her typescript note, her discussion in *The Forerunner*, and her autobiography all use 'wallpaper.'" Following Dock in her critical edition of the story, where she opts for the majority usage in the 1892 version, this edition uses "wall-paper" throughout. In the critical pieces included in this edition, however, including a passage from Gilman's autobiography, the author's usage is preserved.

"Grotesques" on page 10, line 20, is "grotesque" in the 1892 version but "grotesques" in the manuscript and the 1899 Small, Maynard edition; thus "grotesques" is adopted in this edition.

The rest of the stories in this volume, and the excerpts from *Women and Economics* and the abridged version of *Herland*, are, with the exception of "The Unnatural Mother," from their original sources and appear here as published. *Herland* and most of the short stories were first published in Gilman's magazine, *The Forerunner*. The exceptions are "The Unnatural Mother," which was first published in *Impress* in 1895 as "An Unnatural Mother" and reprinted in *The Forerunner* in 1914 (the source for this volume), and "If I Were a Man," first published in *Physical Culture* in 1914. *Women and Economics* was first published by Small, Maynard in 1898. Gilman was notoriously sloppy in matters of punctuation and spelling, and the texts have been silently emended where her sloppiness has led to grammatical infelicities. Obvious typographical errors have also been corrected. Several other, more substantive corrections have also been made, and are noted here: in "The Widow's Might," two instances of "Pittsburg" have been corrected to "Pittsburgh"; "hundred" on page 94, line 16, has been changed to "thousand"; and "two" on page 94, line 20, has been changed to "three."

After "The Yellow Wall-paper," the stories are arranged chronologically by year of publication.

ABOUT THE AUTHOR

CHARLOTTE PERKINS GILMAN was born in Hartford, Connecticut, on July 3, 1860. As a child she was influenced by the progressive ideas and attitudes of her reform-minded great-aunts: Harriet Beecher Stowe, the abolitionist and author of *Uncle Tom's Cabin* (1852); Catharine Beecher, an educator and advocate of new domestic roles for women; and Isabella Beecher Hooker, an ardent suffragist.

Despite strong misgivings about the institution of marriage, Charlotte Perkins wed painter Charles Walter Stetson in 1884. One year later she sank into a deep depression following the birth of her only child, Katharine. A controversial rest-cure treatment in a Philadelphia sanitarium ultimately prompted Charlotte Perkins Stetson to write "The Yellow Wall-paper" (1892). Likewise, the scandal surrounding her divorce in 1894, in which she relinquished custody of her daughter, inspired the short story "The Unnatural Mother" (1895). Yet her marriage in 1900 to first cousin George Houghton Gilman, an erudite lawyer who encouraged her feminist endeavors, lasted until his death in 1934.

Gilman was diagnosed with inoperable breast cancer early in 1932. Convinced that her usefulness had ended and long an advocate of euthanasia, Charlotte Perkins Gilman committed suicide in Pasadena, California, on August 17, 1935.

THE MODERN LIBRARY
TORCHBEARERS

A new series featuring women who wrote on their own terms,
with boldness, creativity, and a spirit of resistance.

The Custom of the Country by Edith Wharton
Lady Audley's Secret by Mary Elizabeth Braddon
Love, Anger, Madness by Marie Vieux-Chauvet
Nada by Carmen Laforet
Persuasion by Jane Austen
The Return of the Soldier by Rebecca West
The Transformation of Philip Jettan by Georgette Heyer
There Is Confusion by Jessie Redmon Fauset
Villette by Charlotte Brontë

MODERNLIBRARY.COM